Grecian Vendetta

Desert Sailors Series Book 3

by

K.J. Frolander

Grecian Vendetta
by K.J. Frolander
© November 2016, second printing 2021

Cover art designed by Janis Teller. Contact at
Chelsea2583@hotmail.com

ISBN: 978-0-9977245-1-6

Dedication

With many thanks to Mrs. Zefo's 2016-2017 Creative Writing class for the fun day of learning together how to critique in love and make each of us better in our craft.

So the phone no longer 'jingles,' it 'shrieks'!

Thanks, Mrs. Zefo, CF, OL, CL, KB, KR, LS, MRW, AV, CP and KM for welcoming me to your class and offering such kind and insightful feedback. All the best as each of you fulfill your writing dreams!

Chapter One

"These 15-hour shifts have to let up soon." Judah Wakefield hung her khaki naval uniform in the closet and rubbed knuckles into her burning eyelids. She leaned her head against the closet doorframe and emptied her lungs of the day's weight. Staring at a computer all day to identify terrorists, make connections within cells, and call in SEAL teams to deal with uncooperative men wore on a person's outlook. Pushing aside two silky nightgowns, Judah reached for a ragged, gray T-shirt with *MARINES* emblazoned across the chest.

Her apartment phone had not rung with a personal call in ten days. "But, at least I'm at home." Her lips flattened into a frown as she stared at the silent handset on her bedside table. The clock read 10:33. He never called this late.

Night nine of tossing worry.

She blew out her breath in a huff. He must have drawn the assignment to mop up the Central American drug-funneling cell she uncovered week before last. She reached over and snapped off the bedroom light.

"It's his job to go." Judah tried to persuade herself not to worry. She flopped back on her thick mattress; her damp hair slapped her shoulder. "This is his eighth unannounced mission in less than a year. Will I ever convince myself that he is fine? God, please take care of David for me."

At 11:47, the red digits morphed into strange shapes as she lifted open one eyelid in the slightest crack, laying as still as possible trying to force her body to drift into oblivion. She slid her eye closed again. Don't think. Don't move. Relax into the soft mattress, she coaxed herself.

The phone shrieked.

She bolted upright and stiff in one motion; her eyes moved over the outline of her new cherrywood dresser to the vigilant chair striped with moonlight through the blinds, back to the phone. The backlit caller ID showed a Coronado, California number.

Ring two. It was not David Rivers' number.

Her stomach tightened and she touched her neck. A shiver crept up her spine. Her pulse raced in her throat. *Is Rivers calling to say hello, or is his commanding officer calling to say he is dead*? Ring three.

Her fingers trembled as she gripped the gray handset and brought it to her ear. "Rivers?" Her voice caught with tension.

"Is this Lieutenant Commander Rivers?" a tenor voice enunciated.

"Rivers? What? Who is this?" Was her SEAL joking with her? Confusion stirred into a fluttering panic.

"This is Petty Officer First Class Ingles. I need to speak with Lieutenant Commander David Rivers. Ma'am?"

"What?" She spoke the only word that tumbled through her normally articulate mind.

"David Rivers left this as his call back number. May I speak with him?"

"I don't understand." She rubbed her forehead.

"Look, you don't have to understand. Just put Rivers on the phone. I need to speak with him."

"*You* look." Judah snapped at the curt enlisted man. "I know what a call back number is. I am a lieutenant commander with Naval Intelligence. But I have not talked to Commander Rivers since last Saturday."

"The twenty-first, ma'am?" His tone changed appropriately to one she was more accustomed to hearing with her rank.

She stretched to the right for the bedside lamp switch. "The fourteenth. Why would he leave my number? He is on a mission with the Teams." Light pierced her eyes and she winced.

"No, ma'am. He's been on a 30-day leave that began on Friday, September thirteenth. We need him back on base for a training drill. You saw him when?"

So, Team Seven was assigned to Europe not Central America. She frowned and traced the three-inch white scar down her right cheek.

Six hours earlier, she had made final confirmation on a cell of 23 terrorists working out of Chechnya. She knew the Special Forces would be sweeping up the area before the shipment of weapons left the compound for more dangerous hands. She planned to watch the video feed in real time when the operation went down. "He didn't come here."

"He showed me his ticket for D.C., ma'am. Please, put him on the phone, I got a lot more calls to make."

"He came to Washington and did not stop to see me?" The words were out of her mouth before she could stop them. Her chest tightened. "Did he think I wouldn't found out? I'm sorry," Judah scraped her lower teeth across her upper lip. "You don't know anything more than I do." She pivoted the phone receiver even with her eyes to exhale hard.

"I guess he's not there. If you talk to him, ask him to report in. I will give him until twelve hundred hours tomorrow before I report."

"Generous of you," she whispered, rolling her eyes before replacing the receiver. "Lieutenant Commander Rivers, you are in big trouble, mister. And now, not just with me." Wakefield kicked back the jumbled covers. There was no use trying to go to sleep now. "Why would he take all of his leave time at once?" Barefoot, she meandered into the kitchen for hot tea. "I thought he was saving it to come see me."

Opening the oak cabinet next to the sink, the dark feeling came over her again. She shuddered and tugged her Marine Corps t-shirt down to cover more of her thighs. "Why do I think you are up to no good?"

She abandoned her cup of steeping tea on the counter and retrieved her Nokia from her Navy-issue blue purse in the top drawer of the front door credenza. She pressed autodial 8. Her call went through on the second ring.

"Dietz, here."

She identified herself to the director of counterintelligence of the CIA, not liking the shaky sound that had entered her honey alto voice. "Listen, do you have Rivers on some op that he has not told me about?" She raked back her still-damp blond hair with unsteady fingers.

"Wakefield. Have you looked at the clock?"

"Far too often in the last two hours. Sorry." She was unrepentant. "Is Rivers working for you?"

"No. I haven't seen him since your bronze star ceremony for saving the president. When was that, March?" The director was sounding more alert now. "Is he missing?"

"I'm not sure. He took all his leave time two weeks ago. No one has talked to him since."

"Maybe he freaked and had to get away. Weren't you guys getting close to the big event?"

"Getting married? No. We talk about it," she fudged a bit, "but don't have any plans or a ring." She shook her head. His explanation did not make any sense. "You wouldn't lie to me, would you, Dietz?"

"Do you even have to ask?"

"You're CIA. You people lie more often than you speak the truth."

"Well, you're half-CIA, and you do okay." The director chuckled, apparently not taking offence at her tone or words. Still, he had not answered the question plainly.

Trying a different tactic, Judah smiled into the phone. "Assuming I find Rivers, and I'm not in jail for murdering him, are you ready to go to church with me on Sunday, yet?"

"Wow. Where did that come from?" She could hear the tension creep into his voice as if a vine had wrapped itself around his vocal chords and was choking the breath out of him.

"I've been working up to it. You're not scared are you?" A hint of challenge seemed to work well in other arenas with this man; why not try it on the Christianity issue? She shrugged and switched her small Nokia to her left ear.

He was quiet and she wondered if she had pushed too hard. Wakefield never made a secret of God's relevance to life. Every time she left on a mission of treachery, she had to reassure Dietz of God's every-ready provision. She thought they had been making progress.

"A little. I like my Sunday morning sleep-ins."

"You have not slept-in a day in your life." Judah chuckled deep in her chest.

"But what if I wanted to? I am not sure I want to serve a God who demands attention every Sunday morning."

"He doesn't demand anything."

"I am just not ready, yet. But you can keep praying for me."

"Sounds fair. Just don't wait too long." Wakefield's words were slow. This was the first time they had talked about personal things when she wasn't rushing to catch a plane. In the lapse, she could hear traffic outside her window moving steadily around the insomniac city. "If you hear anything from Rivers, you'll let me know?" She stared at her reflection in the empty television screen.

"Yes, Judah, but don't sit up worrying. Get some sleep."

A snort left her throat. "Easier said than done."

CIA Headquarters, Langley, VA
Wednesday, September 25, 2002
6:10 AM

"Director Dietz. Director?" The door to his office burst open with no semblance of order. "You've got to see this!"

"Agent Woodstock to see you, Director," the intercom announced.

"No kidding, Ms. Cravits." Dietz growled at his secretary in the outer office.

"Don't take out your bad mood on me, sir," came the harsh reply, "if you can't control your agents."

Dietz stared at the black intercom box on his desk. When had she gotten so mouthy? He could not recall a single time that his secretary of six years had ever talked back to him. She was a mature woman in her late forties. Her beauty was creased by 18 years of CIA secrecy. He slapped the leather-bound book in his hand into the bottom drawer of his old-world style desk.

"She always talk to you like that?" Woodstock, the CIA's top profiler, who had just turned 30, gestured at the squawk box with his ever-present 20-ounce bottle of Mountain Dew.

"No. Just since—what do you want, Woodstock?" Dietz studied the man of Native Indian ancestry with an intent eye. He hated to be interrupted.

The tan-skinned man with a flat nose and thick body bursting out of his black suit tossed three photos onto his desk. The slicks slid against each other spreading like a Chinese fan. "What am I looking at?"

A line of small bright green dots strung from a larger rectangular one on the first infrared photo.

"We have movement. They are unloading the weapons."

Dietz looked up sharply. Sometimes getting information from these young agents was like trying to eat an apple without breaking the peel. "What country are we looking at?" He was currently dealing with France, Iraq, North Korea, Syria, Libya and China, Brazil and Panama,

Chechnya and Paraguay. It seemed like there was one more, but he couldn't remember it in the moment.

"This is the weapons compound in Chechnya where SEAL Team Seven was just detailed."

"You're the wrong person to be telling me this information. You aren't in operations. What's your role?" Dietz shifted in his chair and he took up the next picture.

"We found Barhai. I used that facial recognition software in beta testing. This is his current façade." Woodstock pointed with his green Mountain Dew bottle cap. "And his role is consistent with the computer findings. He drove up, went in, and two hours later the trucks pulled out."

Dietz studied the photograph while he worked his jaw in circles. According to inside sources, Amir Barhai was the last person to brief the terrorists who operated on September 11th. He was a low-level planner for bin Laden's al Qaeda, but the highest coordinator who was *named* in the CIA computer system. "Why is Amir Barhai in Chechnya?"

"Take a look at the third photo, Director."

Dietz caught his breath. The body of his mole inside the Chechen warehouse lay with a slit throat at the feet of Barhai. A second woman, a Caucasian, with her mouth open in a silent scream and her eyes closed in terror strained against the Arab with her neck in the crook of his bare arm.

"Who is this woman?"

"She's not in any of the data banks."

"Check her against the FBI's missing persons list. Who sent the photos to us if Mickie is dead?" Dietz knew he only had one person inside.

"Barhai did. As an attachment to the e-mail that said, 'Wanna play?' Sir, this was not an email intercept. Barhai sent it directly to my home email address. My wife saw it first. She was not happy."

"He does look quite confident in this picture." Dietz tapped a pen against his desk as he studied the Arab's hard eyes, deciding to ignore the break in protocol over the wife checking an agent's email, even a personal account. It was going to be a rough game, and Dietz didn't want Woodstock distracted with an inquiry. "Wonder how he got your e-mail address." Dietz murmured.

Arafeh Filasek's Villa, Poros, Greece
Wednesday 25 September 2002
5:18 PM GMT+1

Filasek leaned into the iron and stucco balcony of his white villa carved into a cliff 15 meters above silken-blue Aegean waters, and he stroked his coal-black beard with his first finger and thumb on either side of his chin. It was short and neatly trimmed, like his figure. He admired his sleek new cigarette boat bobbing next to the teak pier across from his two-seater Cessna on floats.

He allowed his usually sour mouth to extend upward in the semblance of a smile. "The boat is probably faster than the plane, now."

He removed his phone from his cream-colored suitcoat pocket and dialed.

"Jake Lambert here." A man in California picked up after the first ring. As well he should have; it was his direct, private line.

"Lambert, how did yesterday's meeting with Marin County go? I told you to call no matter the time."

"Yes, well, the meeting adjourned at 11PM, my time. It's only been eight hours, half of which I slept on the couch in this office. It's only 7 o'clock, man."

He did sound a bit over extended. "The verdict?"

"It's not a court case, but we won the contract."

Filasek closed his eyes. *Finally, something is right.* "When do they issue the permits?"

"We can begin closing no more than two lanes in either direction in two weeks." The 44-year-old construction company manager sounded giddy at the prospect.

Filasek walked to the farthest end of his balcony to admire the port side of his boat. "That will give us time to have signs printed with our name. Have the printer add 'we love SF' with a heart instead of the word 'love,' and a line drawing of the Golden Gate at the bottom. I want them everywhere. Every vehicle, the bridge entrance and exit, coming and going, and as many barrels and cones as you can keep the signs attached to. I want the people of San Francisco to love us."

"That- that will add thousands to our overhead," Lambert protested.

Lambert, while he was excellent at the construction side of business, had no head for the spin of business contracting. But that was why Filasek had hired him two years out of prison. He was a hard worker and a knowledgeable manager who would not question Sunshine Construction's parentage. "I already figured it into our bid."

"You do realize that there is absolutely no way we can get this job completed by the time we specified in the bid and in the contract I signed." The tiredness had crept back into Jack Lambert's voice.

"You just work as fast as you can. I will be sending some men to help. Leave the worrying up to me, hmm?" Filasek punched a button to break their connection.

He flopped into a cypress deck chair positioned to view his new possession. Two-and-a-half months to go. He laced his small fingers over his flat belly as he reclined. "Ah," he breathed in the briny air. "I would move to Indonesia where there are plenty of good Muslims and hardly any of these braying Catholics, but I love this sea. The waters of the best beaches in Bali cannot compare." He sucked in another lungful of the moist seaside air. "America will be stung more deeply in November than they were last September." He touched the short hair below his lower lip. "Allah will be pleased. And so will I. Bin Laden will no longer ignore me."

He tramped inside to grab the boat key. He could not wait for morning to take her out for another spin. *Just one lap around the island*, he promised himself, knowing even as he spoke, one would become a minimum of two.

Traipsing down the hewn rock stairs to the beach below his house, Filasek murmured, "I could almost say thank you to the fool who blew up my catamaran."

Chapter Two

Office of Naval Intelligence
Suitland, Maryland
Wednesday 25 September 2002
0950 hours EDT

Lieutenant Commander Judah Wakefield ambled back to her office with another cup of breakroom coffee. A two-day old banana muffin from her desk became an early lunch. She had been at work for four hours already. She was too tired to get anything done and too keyed up to get any rest.

"What I need," she whispered in the painted concrete-block office, "is access to the FBI's data base. I wouldn't keep hitting all these firewalls." It was not a problem, per se. Wakefield kept an updated program that would find a way in, it was just time consuming.

She filed her paper backlog while she waited for the program to get her inside. She twisted in her chair to look at the screen. A black line shortened and lengthened across her screen as the program worked.

"Where are you Rivers?" She rolled her eyes at the pitiful sound of her voice echoing in the closed office space and turned back to the task at hand. Judah Wakefield hated weakness; she despised it when she found it in herself.

At the stop of the computer's mechanical gurgling, Wakefield turned from her filing drawer. "All right, I'm in." She tucked her lips between her teeth as she left the drawer open and slid into her chair, swiveling toward the monitor.

"Let's see what you've been up to, o friend of mine." She spoke to herself, a habit she had acquired from too many years of singleness.

She did a quick search with the FAA that recorded data on every airline's passenger manifests. "So you *did* come through D.C. without seeing me." She frowned and cocked her jaw to the right. She hopped over to Delta's network. Her knee jogged up and down as she scrolled through the screen in her search.

Rivers had purchased his passage Friday night at 2208 hours with his visa. She flipped back in her personal cell call log to be sure, and yes, there it was. Rivers had talked to her on Saturday afternoon at 1604 Eastern time, noon for him, for 62 minutes, then he caught the flight just over 2 hours later. He had never mentioned a thing about his plans. According to Delta, his boarding pass had been scanned at the gate, one checked bag, and his flight arrived in D.C. just before midnight. Then he disappeared. His flight did not connect to any other destination, and was one way.

"What are you hiding?" she asked while she scanned Rivers' timeline again. Whatever he was hiding, it would come down to whomever was better at their job. As a Navy SEAL, it was his occupation to hide his movements. Her career as a Naval Intelligence profiler was to identify people who did not want to be found and figure out their psychological motivations.

She clicked into checked baggage details. Sixty-seven pounds. "Jeez! I'd have taken two bags," Wakefield smirked at the screen, "but that's just me."

She typed in the information to run a search of all his credit cards. A money trail was the easiest way to track a body.

Nothing. No other tickets were listed, no meals, no pit stops. Not even a cash withdrawal. The Delta ticket was the last entry. "Hold it." She tapped the screen in front of her, then wiped off her fingerprints with a Beanie Baby bear that sat on top of her boxy monitor. "Rivers did not pay $1796 for a one-way ticket to Dulles Airport. I'll have to start searching for another departure, just a different day. It was only a layover here."

She maneuvered the screens until she had them side by side so she could work both at once. A David Rivers with no rank was listed with Lufthansa on a flight between Dulles and Rome, Italy on Sunday at 1102 hours. "I didn't know Lufthansa made flights that did not include Germany on the itinerary," Judah mumbled sipping her coffee. It was too cool and she plunked it back down on her desk. Tan liquid sloshed onto the bare surface.

"Rome?" She shook her head. "What is in Rome?" Vatican City and gelato were the only things that came to mind. The R faded in and out as she stared at the screen wishing it would speak to her. She remembered an afternoon in March at the end of his first visit when she put him on a plane going west for some meeting or another. They arrived early because she was driving, and they decided to sample every flavor of gelato in Dulles Airport's Italian eatery. It hadn't been as good as the street vendor she had met near the Spanish Steps in Rome, but the raspberry cream cheese gelato ran a close second.

A knock on her door dragged her out of her revelry. "Enter," she called out. She looked at her desk before the door had a chance to open. Judah frowned. Trying to appear busy with paperwork on a cleared desk with a coffee splash was futile. She folded her fingers together and looked up expectantly.

Chief Mason Black, a reservist called up from Virginia two weeks earlier, opened the door. He was fitting in well in place of the two petty officers and the office manager who had been transferred to cover personnel who were deploying to the Pacific Fleet. Five more of the meager office administration staff were slated to be deployed in the next month. Three of the twelve officers in her Intelligence division were already aboard carriers or destroyers in the Arabian Sea or the Gulf of Oman.

"Ma'am?" The enlisted reservist smiled confidently. His uniform hugged his body in perfect order, crisp and clean. His three ribbons kept watch in a tight row above his heart. "Lieutenant Sampson asked to see you. He says he's sorry to send for you, but he found a development in the Norfolk case."

"No problem. Thank you, Chief. After Sampson's motorcycle accident I suppose I'm glad to make a trip to his office instead of Arlington."

Black gave her an appreciative chuckle. They were roughly the same age, and Wakefield found the tall, dark-featured man interesting. "Have I ever told you that you remind me of a friend I have worked with on occasion?"

Black shook his head and raised a thick eyebrow as she locked down the computer screen and gathered the small file on Petty Officer Tanner, Norfolk Naval Base, from her lap drawer. She threw a wrinkled napkin over the puddle of cold coffee on her desktop. "His name is David Rivers. He's a SEAL trainer out at Coronado."

"Thank you for the compliment, ma'am." His grin showed bleached-white teeth in his toothpaste-ad smile.

"Dismissed," she gave him leave before she ran over him on her way out of the office. Wakefield pulled the door closed behind her, taking a look at the faded WWII Navy woman poster and a few black and white photos taken at different Temporary Away Duty (TAD) stations on her walls. "I need to redecorate." She added it to her mental to-do list. She locked the office, not because of any top secret files she was supposed to be working on, but out of habit.

"Lieutenant Sampson," she rapped on his open doorframe, "What do we have on Petty Officer Tanner?"

"Thanks for coming down, ma'am." He started to rise from his chair, picking up his crutches from where they leaned against the arm of his chair.

"As you were." She motioned him to stay seated. He turned back to the computer monitor. Sampson triumphantly pointed to a line that he had highlighted among twenty-five or so others. "Should I pull up a chair?" Wakefield felt her eyes go wide. Computer evidence would be a terrific asset to building their case.

"If you'd like." He gestured to a blue vinyl, wing back seat in front of his desk. Stuffing protruded from a split in the seat. "Sorry," he shrugged slowly. "I don't get too many visitors down here."

She pulled the lumpy chair to the corner of his desk. "Is that a list of IP addresses?" She blinked twice to make her contacts focus on the distant screen.

"It is not just any list of IPs. It is the list that coordinates with the people who ever visited the al-Qaeda recruiting site we talked about yesterday."

"You're kidding. And that is Tanner's number?" Wakefield moved her gaze to Sampson's face. He had a sharp nose and thin lips but a head of young-John-Travolta hair.

"His laptop at home. His number registered six times in the last three weeks. Should we go pick him up, ma'am?"

She cut her eyes toward him. "You know that's not enough evidence to charge him with anything. Keep digging. I don't want to ruin a man's career if his son found a website he thinks is cool."

"His son is ten," Sampson scoffed. He leaned back in his chair until the springs groaned.

"Exactly." Wakefield wondered briefly how Sampson would get up with a plaster-casted leg if his chair broke under him. He leaned forward and the chair back seemed to project him into straight-backed posture. "Good work, Lieutenant. See if you can get every email address ever linked to this IP and get his e-mail servers to forward a copy of every message sent and received by this IP number in the last two months."

"Don't we need a warrant?"

"Norfolk NCIS can help us with that." Wakefield paused. "The computer at his duty station is government property, start there. If he used time on duty for the United States military to coordinate a strike against us—or to get weapons into the hands of men who will—I want his butt rotting in Leavenworth for the rest of his life. A painless death is too easy on him."

"Ma'am, do we have any hard evidence yet?"

She looked at LT Sampson. His eyebrows nearly touched his hairline and his features strained forward.

"If there is no evidence on his office computer, get in touch with NSA. Scuttlebutt is they've been cataloging everything since the Web went live. We can use that." She heard her voice echoing around the room. She had overreacted again. Her emotions were getting away from her far too often recently. She'd hoped that Tanner was not involved in this, but more and more coincidences suggested his guilt. "No need for concern, Lieutenant." Wakefield read Sampson's face. "I won't eat him for breakfast," Wakefield smiled, "unless he is guilty."

Sampson's face did not break into a smile. "I hope not, ma'am."

She had really scared him. Wakefield leaned forward and touched his arm in what she hoped would be a reassuring manner. "Sampson, this is me we're talking about. You *know* me."

She watched Sampson's face closely for some sign of understanding. His hazel brown eyes tilted low on the outside corners and he inclined his head as he studied her face. "Permission to speak freely, ma'am?"

What was going on? This was supposed to be a consultation about a supposed terrorist among them, not a weighty conversation. She nodded and gripped the arm of her vinyl chair.

"I *do* know you, ma'am. I have been training under you or working with you for just over two years. And you're different now. Ever since you got back from Germany, with the president and all. Are you okay?"

"I'm fine," she snapped. She felt a tightening in her chest. I did not realize that I had allowed it to show. *I will do better.* "Will that be all?" Sampson bobbled his thin face up and down in silence three times. She could read the hurt in his brackish eyes. "Dismissed." She spewed the words. *Terrific, another overreaction.* I'm *in* his *office,* she pulled her mouth to the side in a disgusted grimace. "Sorry. I'll be leaving now." She grabbed the Tanner file from his desk and scooted out the door. She did not replace the chair; she did not close the door.

Alone in the elevator, Wakefield leaned the back of her head heavily against the wall and closed her eyes. "Lord, what is going on?" She felt the familiar heat of anger flow over her as she saw in her mind the poetic features and confident stance of James Yates. That was not his real name of course, but he would forever remain James Yates in her mind. He was her friend who had tried to kill the President of the United States and her. She had stood mere yards from him when he committed suicide in Berlin in January. "It's been eight months. I should be over this. Why is this one such a big deal?"

She curled her fingers into fists at her side, grateful that she was the only one going between floors. "Get over it, Wakefield," she commanded herself in a whisper. "You are bigger than this. People are going to start thinking you are a nutcase."

She opened her eyes to glance at her distorted reflection in the chrome elevator door. Her alter self, rolled her eyes at her. "When did I start caring what people think about me?" The door dinged and after a beat pulled open on her third floor.

She stuffed the emotion away, as she had done every day since January 25, and took her five-foot-eleven frame in Navy-issue heels back to her office.

The window glass rattled when she closed the door. "I have to get into his bank accounts." She snapped her focus back to her last five hours of concentration. She picked up the phone to contact Michelle Ryan, her liaison with Navy Federal Credit Union. "I have a suspect whose bank records I need to look at."

"Sure, Judah." Michelle's soft voice told Wakefield that the woman was smiling. "I just need the name and social." The two had formed a tentative friendship over the years, but had never met in person.

The commander read the number off Rivers' service record. "You sound happy today." Judah couldn't help commenting. It sparked a remembrance of easier days in her own life. She could feel the tension in her left shoulder loosen its talon grip as she massaged it.

"My boyfriend of six years, Hank, asked me to marry him three nights ago."

Judah's lips turned up. "Congratulations. It's time. Six years, wow." Wakefield heard the keys clicking in the background. A crackle sounded in the earpiece and Judah could tell the woman on the other end was still grinning. A new dimension had broadened Michelle's voice from the quiet woman that had begun faxing reports to her seven years earlier when Wakefield was stationed at Pacific Fleet headquarters.

"It's past time. But we're just going to Vegas. Three weeks from now" The clicking stopped. "Should I e-mail these to your office like normal?"

"Yes. ASAP."

Michelle chuckled. "It's always ASAP with you."

Judah looked down into her lap. "I can't help it. I deal with national emergencies." She knew she was falsely representing the problem. Morally, should she use her position and security clearance to track down a friend, a friend who obviously did not want to be found? Judah grimaced at her underhandedness. It was iffy.

Michelle gasped into the phone. It sounded like she cupped a hand to the mouthpiece. "You think this guy is a terrorist? He's an officer with the SEAL teams! I'll never understand what could make a man rat out his homeland."

"No. I didn't say that." Now she had given her NFCU contact the wrong impression about David. She softened her snappy tone. "He's *not* a terrorist." She swallowed. "I'm sorry I can't tell you more, but he is *not* a traitor."

"Well, I found some more. He just requested pre-approval on loan of $170,000. You may want to check into that. Based on the credit history I see here, it will probably go through. I'll forward the application with the other statement."

Confusion swirled around her and Wakefield was glad she was in her desk chair. "What did he state as the reason for the loan?"

"Mortgage. Okay. It should be there now."

Wakefield thanked Michelle for the information and hung up in a daze. *Why is Rivers buying a house?*

She scrolled through David's transactions. It was definitely a planned trip. *That's good; he wasn't kidnapped.* She saw the fund transfers to pay his utilities. "Five transactions on the thirteenth." The day before his last call. The check for next month's rent had already cleared his account. A cash withdrawal of $496.45 was made on an Italian bank. "Must have been 500 euros." Wakefield mumbled. The last transaction was a purchase with his check card for $87.35 with the Italian Rail Transit System.

"Great!" Wakefield blew out a frustrated breath. "What now? There is no way to track a single ticket purchase. You just go to a counter and buy it. They don't take names. Maybe I can track it through the amount and add back the difference between dollars and euros that day." The purchase was made on 15 September. Good for any day of travel.

Wakefield went to the on-line rail fare table. One way or round trip? North, south, east or west? Couldn't be too far west, he'd hit the water. He could have taken a ferry. She groaned and threw herself back in her chair. Too many variables.

She was almost relieved at another interrupting knock. "Enter." Her voice was weak as she straightened up her posture. "Ensign Drury." Wakefield's blood went cold. "I didn't expect to see you today. We didn't have a review scheduled," she scrambled to flip open the calendar on the far left side of her desk, "did we?"

"No, ma'am." The young officer was hesitant. Something was wrong. "It's Filasek. We found him."

Wakefield sighed and let her back collapse against the seatback again. "Close the door, Ensign. I put you on this case hoping that I'd never see you again."

His eyes jumped. She could detect hurt, but she didn't have the energy to deal with a junior officer who couldn't handle sarcasm. "We have movement," he said finally. "A large—very large—cash withdrawal and a plane ticket purchased from Athens, Greece to St. Petersburg, Russia."

Chapter Three

"Oskar Dabkowski, where have you been?" Helga yelled from the kitchen to her unseen husband coming in the back door. Her jiggly arms struggled to tie her favorite red apron. She fingered the embroidered elephants across her chest. Oskar had brought the gift back from a business trip to India. "I held dinner for two hours."

He stomped his boots twice, according to ritual. "I had a business call I had to take just as I was leaving." His deep voice surged from the back entry. He would be hanging his leather cap on the peg now, Helga pictured her husband. He was so predictable. After 28 years of marriage, she knew his routine by heart. He would walk in and kiss her, then apologize for making her prepare his dinner a second time. It was getting tiresome. Always some excuse. Always flimsy, with just a touch of validity so she couldn't count it against him.

Tonight will be different, I will not accept it. Helga sighed as she stirred the blackened sausage in her heavy iron skillet. *Of course I'll accept him; why should today be different?*

The pickled red cabbage he would have to endure cold; it had tasted mealy when she had nibbled at it at half past six. She watched the meat sizzle as she stood with her back turned, waiting for him to nuzzle her neck in apology. She could never hear his sock-footed approach. Every time a board began creaking, Oskar replaced it.

The sausage began to burn and Helga used a potholder to remove the skillet from the heat. She turned to the table where Oskar's empty plate sat with a plastic mug of milk that had not been cold for 90 minutes at the head of the table.

"Well don't just stand there, husband, come and eat." The floor needed a good mopping. *In the morning*, she planned. "I thought I told you to put those socks in my darning bag." Oskar's left big toe stuck out of his black wool office sock.

Helga straightened from the table as the heaviness of his familiar touch rested on her back. "I'm not hungry tonight." A paper bag rustled in his other hand behind her and his touch pulled her toward him.

His voice sounded low, as low as it had when they had gone to the hospital that last time with their unborn child. His tone sent her into the same hot sweat that she had felt when the doctor had told her that night that their dream of having children together would never be.

She twisted under his touch. "What is it?" She could feel the beads of perspiration forming on her upper lip.

"Helga, will you have a drink with me?" His blue eyes seemed tired, like he had not slept in a month and a week.

Without a word, she ambled to the cupboard and slid their two glass tumblers forward, one in each palm. It did not sound as though shot glasses would be large enough to contain this sorrow.

In the darkened living room with fingers wrapped around clear Russian vodka, he told her. "I sold the last of the chemical stock today. The business is gone."

Helga let out breath she didn't remember holding in. He wasn't dying. "We knew it would come. Now you will have time to do the fishing you drive me crazy talking about."

Oskar rubbed the top of his balding head and poured another three fingers of vodka. "It was my father's grandfather's business. Four generations of Dabkowski Chemicals and Pharmaceuticals gone." Her husband's strong bass vocals wavered. "At least I got a price we can live off of for the next few years."

Helga patted his hand that hung from the arm of the chair. It looked more liver-spotted than she remembered. "We'll survive. We always do." She sighed. She tucked her fingers inside the hollow of his hand. "We always do."

Office of Naval Intelligence, Suitland, MD
1137 hours EDT

"So Filasek's been hiding in Greece all this time." Her mind closed around a mental picture of herself and Rivers in the would-be presidential-assassin's hotel crow's nest. They had found a list and instructions for a hit written in Greek. "Now he is going to Russia?" Wakefield's hands stilled. "What's in Russia that would interest Filasek?"

Drury fingered the single half-inch gold braid on his black Class A uniform coat. He shrugged. The young man's shifting eyes did not fool her. He had given the matter some thought before bursting into her day. "They are still dismantling nuclear weapons leftover from the Soviet Union just a day-and-a-half train ride north of Moscow in Murmansk."

"Take a seat, Ensign." Wakefield leaned back in her chair and crossed her hands in front of her. Her head felt heavy as she let it drop a few inches toward her chest. "I did not need this today, of all days."

"I want to know what's been going on in Athens. What is there?"

"The Parthenon?"

She did not acknowledge his last. "Double check with the CIA. See if they have any unusual movements. People. Weapons. Drugs. Money. Anything in Greece. And I want somebody *living* at that airport. We are going to catch this sucker once and for all."

"Yes, ma'am. What are you going to do?" His eager expression showed his youth.

Judah sighed. "I am going to lunch."

**Langley, VA
CIA Headquarters
12:48 PM**

"It seems we have a new player in our little terrorism game. I don't recognize this man, let's run his face through the computer." Director Dietz committed the face to memory as he stood in the buzzing situation room.

Gibson, one of the field agents stationed in Athens, Greece, sent an e-mail with a picture of a man in local fishing garb on a pier in the Athens port, *Piraeus*. "Get me more information while the computer searches." Dietz walked over toward the semi-circular mainframe input center that had seventeen desk stations.

"This is all the agent sent." A girl barely out of her teens with cinnamon-colored frizzy hair shrugged.

Dietz halted mid-stride and searched her freckled face. "If you are incompetent in intelligence gathering, I suggest you go back to the Farm, or find a civilian career."

Even the girl's freckles seemed to pale. The Farm was the affectionate name for the intensive training ground for the CIA. Spy boot camp. Every agent started there with a class of men and women of all ages who were recruited for the business of espionage. "I'll get the field agent on the secure phone, Director."

"That's better." Dietz resumed his walk and dropped into one of the 32 chairs in a theater arrangement behind the mainframe desks

The red phone on the desk jangled. "Director Dietz here." He picked it up himself to save relay time.

"Uh, sir. I did not expect it to be you, sir."

Dietz rolled his eyes. *God save me from young agents.* "Drop the *sir* and tell me what is going on in there. What is your name, agent?"

"Yes, sir. Gibson, sir. Samuel Gibson."

Dietz rolled his eyes again. Gibson must have a military background. Getting ex-servicemen to drop the *sir* was as hard as trying to recruit suicide bombers in Catholic Mexico; he supposed.

"I've been tracking a man for the last seven days. He appeared out of nowhere and now it seems like he is a fly. Always hanging around the bad meat and humming an annoying tune," Gibson reported.

"Does he know you're following him?" Dietz stared into the blue-green eyes of the man they discussed on the giant screen at the front of the situation room. He seemed to be looking directly into the camera.

"I don't think so, sir, uh, Director. He probably would not care if he did. He has been careless, meeting with known thugs in broad daylight. He hangs out at bars where arms dealers and the *Mafiosi* are known to exchange information and deals. He travels to a different island every day in this little boat he rented. He has it for the next two weeks; I checked the rental company's records."

Dietz's mind whirled. "Does he ever change appearance?"

"He did once. The third day he was here, he blew up a catamaran belonging to one of the guys we have a watch on."

"What happened?"

"Our guys watched him go on board, set the charge and get out inside 50 seconds. He is definitely Special Forces. Whose, I don't know.

Every place he goes he just appears on the scene and then ghosts when he is done. There is no pattern to suggest what he is looking for. He seems to be working alone, sir."

Dietz flicked his finger at the center of the face on the screen as he made the connection he was looking for. "He is either selling something or looking for someone. I want fresh feed. Send a video through the live feed channel on your satellite uplink. ASAP." The longer Dietz stared at the blue-green eyes the more familiar they looked. There were hard lines around the edges, squint lines, as if the man spent too much time outdoors without sunglasses.

Dietz dropped the phone into the red cradle and gave the man's unmatched face a final glance. *We will figure out who you are and come after you if you are selling weapons to our enemies,* Dietz vowed. "Harris, ring me when Gibson sends the live feed. I want to see this guy from a different angle."

"Of course, and if the computer finds a match first, I'll be sure to send up a dossier on him."

Naval Intel HQ
CAPT Huntington's Office
1420 hours

"You wanted to see me, sir?" Wakefield reported in front of the desk of the man who was her immediate supervisor. Captain George Huntington was a man who looked better with his uniform cover on than off. He refused to shave his thinning hair, instead he kept parting it further and further down the side of his head. It was currently two inches above his left ear and a few black strands stretched nearly eight inches to cover the top of his head.

He looked up with a scowl. "An hour and a half ago."

"Sorry, sir. I picked up the newest version of German Translation software while I was at lunch. I had to wait while they unpacked the shipping crate."

That seemed to satisfy him. His sour expression melted as he opened the lap drawer on his desk. "We picked up a transmission right after you left that I need translated. Yesterday. The contents come directly to me."

Wakefield reached for the CD. It had no markings. "I'm on it, sir. What language?" It would be easier to know what to expect.

"The chief petty officer who recorded the conversation and sent it via satellite was in Baghdad, Iraq. From my rudimentary knowledge of Arabic they seem to be playing words games, not speaking in code, but in gibberish like our spoonerisms."

"Iay onay exactlyay utwhy ooyay eenmay, Irsay." Wakefield smirked at her superior officer. He shook his head and pointed at his door. She swallowed the smile and about faced on her heel and toe.

"I need a complete analysis of the conversation. I want to be able to assign bodies to go with those voices so we know who we are up against. There is a new attack underway. The traffic has picked up, and I can feel it. We have to route it. Dismissed. Thanks, Wakefield."

In her office, Judah spun the CD on her first finger. The need to find LCDR Rivers flooded over her again. Urgency electrified the air. "A few minutes on the computer won't make a difference to Huntington's project." She mumbled to herself as she slid the disc into her lap drawer for safe keeping and tucked her chair close under her desk. She keyed in her password to reactivate the secured desktop.

"Where are you hiding, David Rivers, and why did you go?" A niggle in the back of her mind said it had to do with her, but she disallowed the guilt to surge over her. *Sure we talk on the phone more than a little when he is in the country*, she shrugged as she pulled up the screens she had been comparing before. *But why would he feel trapped by that?*

At 1630 hours, she stretched her pinched back against the springy seat back. She was ready to scream in frustration. She settled for a tightly controlled, "Where are you?" which originated somewhere below her bellybutton. The track schedule for the Italian Rail and ferry routes left 184 possible destinations for the cost of his ticket. None of them stood out from the others as a place for a SEAL to hide from an impending marriage proposal. "Course, if they stood out, a SEAL isn't likely to go there," Wakefield assessed professionally. She glanced at her computer's time stamp. His C.O. would know he was missing or would have heard from him by now. She picked up the phone and dialed the administration offices at Coronado's SEAL training base.

She explained the gist of the situation to the enlisted yeoman who handled the admiral's calls and correspondence, and he put her through. "Admiral Johnson, sorry to intrude, I know you are busy, but I was wondering if you had heard anything from Lieutenant Commander Rivers."

"I can't imagine why I would." The older man's bass voice sounded as irritable as an old goat.

"But he is under your command, sir." She felt like her brain was sputtering even though her words came out smooth. "I thought you had him recalled from leave to do some training exercises." *Why would a C.O. not know where his subordinate was?*

"That is where you are wrong."

"Sir?"

"What?" he snapped.

Wakefield jerked the telephone away from her ear at his sharp tone. "Maybe I should explain who I am, sir."

"I know who you are, Commander. You are Rivers' girl from the Eastern Seaboard. The one he put in for a transfer for to move closer."

Wakefield was speechless. She could not even let her jaw drop as surprise smacked her in the chest.

"That is why I don't know where your precious commander is." Johnson cleared his throat deeply. "He is no longer under my command. If there is nothing else?"

Wakefield struggled to capture her thoughts. Why did she get a call from the re-called-to-duty service then? "Wait, one more thing. Did you know Rivers left the country? Do you know where he might have gone in the Italy area?"

"So you got him and then lost him, eh, Commander?" He sounded almost spiteful.

"Sir, this is important. You may not believe me, but I did not ask the commander to move out here. This is the first I've heard of it. However, that is not the problem." She paused to let him absorb the information. "He never showed up. He was one of your best SEAL trainers, don't you care even a little that he could be in trouble?"

A deep growl vibrated the phone lines across the 3000 miles that separated them. "Do not tell me what to care about, Lieutenant Commander Wakefield!" She felt herself shrink in her chair. "There is nothing I can do." His voice dropped several decibels, and Wakefield understood intuitively what the problem was. "Rivers is not under my command, and he is not due at Little Creek for two more weeks." ADM Johnson did not just lead the SEAL base, he was a former SEAL himself, and SEALs hate to feel helpless. Wakefield clinically assessed Johnson's growls, and her fear took a turn toward compassion.

In his volatile state, Wakefield did not know if it would be better to tell the admiral that she was trying to do something about the missing SEAL or if it would anger him that a woman, outside his loop of warriors, was going after his man. *Honesty above likeability*, she decided. "Sir. I'm with Naval Intel, and I will find him, and I *will* bring him home."

Johnson sighed long. "Godspeed, Commander."

As Judah replaced the phone in the cradle, it rang. She had missed the flashing light telling her she had a call on hold. "Lieutenant Commander Wakefield," she spoke coolly into the phone, though she felt irritated at the disruption. *I can't wait until my next promotion*, she thought. *It takes too long to say my name.*

"Commander, this is Sampson, calling about Tanner."

"Where are you, Lieutenant?" She tried to distinguish the background noises.

"Norfolk, ma'am. You sent me down here."

"I know that, Sampson. Where at Norfolk?"

"I stopped at the ship docks to eat an early dinner before I head back to Suitland."

That must be seagulls squawking, she determined. "What did you find?"

"He had some suspicious e-mails in his electronic recycle bin. Sounded like he is moving, setting up a new household, but he doesn't have new orders. Nothing concrete though. I played with the controls and every note sent or received, every website he visits, every entry on his computer will be sent as a copy to my mailbox. I want to catch him red-handed, ma'am."

"Go ahead and send me what you found before you make the drive back," Wakefield rattled her pen against the side of the telephone. "I want to take another look."

Chapter Four

Filasek stood before a 90-degree cliff wall and pressed his palm to a flat stone at his eye level. With a swoosh a shadowed entry way appeared and Filasek charged forward into the basement fortress of his unwitting octogenarian neighbor's house.

Four men and one woman scurried around in white chemical suits in the lab that appeared far too sophisticated to be located in a basement, even the basements of some of the finest homes ever built on the islands. A fifth man, Andros Spyros, sat covered in the same technical gear at a computer. Filasek could make out a colorful graph from eight meters away.

"Better put on a mask." The man at the computer said without looking up. "Just to be on the safe side." Spyros' voice sounded hollow as it pushed through his plastic helmet. Filasek slid forward over the natural rock floor, holding his breath, to snatch the white medical mask that Spyros offered.

"I will return in three days with the needed chemicals." Filasek spoke without greeting as he hooked the elastic over his ears. "Then you will have the next batch ready for distribution 21 days after that, correct?"

Steam hissed from a covered vat on his left. Filasek glanced at it as he smoothed his mask with his right hand and willed his heart to slow its beating. The steel and white porcelain equipment resumed its quiet hum. "Twenty-one days." The spacesuit-shaped head nodded once.

"Print a copy of the ratio of ingredients and the process you are following. I want to take a hard copy and a sample with me." Filasek contained his smile. Cooking up one batch a day for the next two months would cover the 500 largest cities in America with no problem. He would be ready for the November deadline.

The rest of the Spyros family busied themselves working in the back. They never looked at him, never stopped working. Finally, they had learned what was required of the employees of Arafeh Filasek. Autonomy and hard work.

Filasek climbed aboard his racy boat with his briefcase. His long-haired bodyguard, dressed in white loose pants and sleeveless shirt stowed the items and a change of clothes under the boat cushions. Filasek took the helm under the canopy. The salt spray that misted his face under the canopy all the way to the port of Athens refreshed him from his sleepless night. He would not sleep again until he returned from Russia and Iraq. Sadaam would certainly see him this time.

Dietz's office
1945 hours EST

Richmond Dietz adjusted the glasses on his nose and read the portion of the report again. "Excellent!" He grunted out loud. "It is perfect." He snapped shut the folder that had red and black security tape around its perimeter. Locking the top-secret file in his cabinet, he grabbed his umbrella from the peg by the door and secured his office for the night.

Dietz dismissed his driver for the night, walked to long-term parking on floor U6 of the parking deck, and he started his own vehicle.

He made a series of quick turns eight minutes into his drive home to liberate himself from his constant security detail before hitting the freeway in the opposite direction. It would not do to have an audience for this stop.

The breaks on his Towncar whistled as he pulled into the driveway and around back at a refinished row house in old Georgetown. He let himself in by tapping in the correct 15-digit code into a keypad next to the back door. All other doors and windows were welded shut. An electronic gurgle let him know that the system was deactivated for ten seconds.

"Dovlatabadi?" Dietz called out as he stood in the spotless kitchen.

"In here, Dietz. Did you bring those Little Debbie oatmeal cookies this time?" The English-accented voice emanated from the front living room.

Dietz's shoes clattered against the polished hardwood floor as he moved toward the sound of a baseball game on the television. "Not this time." He lowered his voice and stared at the man who, until January, had been a world-class assassin. His appearance of course was different. Plastic surgery on his nose, a scraggly but long beard and hair color prepared him for his next assignment. This time, he would work exclusively for the director of counterintelligence of the CIA. No one else knew he was alive. Including the President of the United States, his previous target.

"I have your directive." Dietz leaned against the inside of the arched doorframe. The room had been painted in colonial gray, blue and rose hues nearly a year before Dietz had moved Dovlatabadi in.

"One of our men in Iraq opened up a spot for you to apply for a place in Sadaam Hussein's body guard."

"Meaning that the CIA killed one of Hussein's guards and now they have to hire a replacement." Dovlatabadi's mouth turned down, but it was barely visible under the facial hair he had been growing for his mission.

"Actually, no," Dietz responded. "He was drunk on a vacation and wandered into Kuwait armed with a single AK-47 and two hand grenades. He's very alive." Dietz crossed one foot over the other and rested the toe of his dress shoes on the floor. "Your job is to filter information back to us concerning the whereabouts of Sadaam, any people he meets with, and if you have the opportunity, to kill him."

Dietz watched the man's eyes tighten. He recognized hatred there.

"There is no way I will make it out alive." Dovlatabadi turned to stare out the gauzy curtains.

"You already deserve to be dead." Dietz hissed. He adjusted his lean on the wall. "Any time spent alive since January has been a bonus. You were supposed to be the best assassin in the world. Surely, you can set it up." Dietz felt like goading the man. "Take as long as you need. As long as you send us information, I will keep feeding your mother and brother. If you can send back confirmation that Sadaam is dead, I will bring them to this house and the three of you can live out the rest of your life here."

Dovlatabadi snorted. "Some life."

"But you would be alive. And together." Dietz countered.

Silence reigned for a moment. "I will pick you up with your new papers under the name Katir Assef tomorrow morning for your flight. You can study your new history in-flight."

**Wakefield's office, Naval Intel
Thursday 26 September 2002
0605 hours**

The rush of fear was enough to keep her awake this morning. Wakefield did not even take time to fill her coffee cup, but pushed the power button on the desktop computer even as she was falling into her office chair. She unlocked her desk drawer and fumbled with the CD she was supposed to have translated the day before.

"God, this is so unlike me." She prayed behind her closed office door. "Help me get it done accurately and quickly." Her mind added a silent prayer that she did not dare voice, *and before Captain Henderson or Admiral Tamburillo arrive this morning.*

Wakefield typed as she listened to the CD on headphones. The information was disturbing, at best. She had to rewind three times in the first half hour of translation. The word game was easy to figure out; Arabic was second nature to her now. She'd been using it so often for the past two years, she had even dreamed in Arabic a few months back. The two male speakers switched the first and second syllables of each word and added an *eche* sound between them.

One man was better at it than the other, and the better speaker kept correcting the weaker one. Wakefield chuckled. She finished the first draft and listened from the beginning as she reread her transcription on her monitor. It felt strange today to read along as two Arabic speakers whispered in her ears. Perhaps the uneasiness was residue from her worry about David; maybe it was being wound so tightly from remembering that she had not completed—or even started on—this important project yesterday when she was ordered to. Judah shook her head to loosen the personal problems that were infringing on her work-life. "Unacceptable," she mouthed as Wakefield forced the thoughts into a little box in her mind.

"What is missing from this conversation?" Wakefield mumbled aloud. There were no names or dates. No actionable data. She was making her second correction when another voice startled her. A voice outside her headset. Her fingers pressed into the keyboard and jumbled letters appeared on the screen.

"I knocked." ADM Tamburillo said by way of apology for startling her.

Wakefield stood and tried to straighten to attention, but the headphones were still on her ears, attached to the CD player. It jerked to the floor with her movements. "Sorry, sir." She made no move to pick it up and felt the admiral's eyes boring into her.

"As you were," he finally directed.

She sat down in her chair and touched her warm cheeks with the back of her fingers to cool them as she stretched down to the carpet to retrieve the Walkman. She punched the pause button. What can I do for you, sir?"

Her heart thrashed. She knew why he was there, now that she had finally taken the time to do the translation.

"I hoped to see your translation yesterday before I went to see the SecNav, but I left early, and I came to get it now." The Black man was incredibly keen. Scuttlebutt had it that he had the highest IQ in the entire military. Though who had time to sit around and compare numbers, Wakefield did not know. She also did not know what to tell him.

"Still working on it, sir. I can print a preliminary copy." She touched the keys to print before he asked for a copy. "You might want to sit down to read it though, because it does not look good."

The squint of his blackest brown eyes chilled her liver. "Why aren't you done yet? Was the translation that difficult?"

Wakefield saw a stray glob of whiteout on her desk's top and forced herself not to touch it. "It was a tad more complicated than usual, sir." She misrepresented, feeling guilty even as the words tumbled out of her mouth. "As you suggested, they did use a word game that I had to figure into my translation. Plus, I got tied up with the Tanner case in Norfolk yesterday evening."

"Wakefield."

He did not have to say anything more than her name. The conviction sat like a white-bread bagel in her stomach. "Sir, I—" she could no longer look him in the eye. "I, I forgot about your project yesterday after Captain Huntingdon gave me the recording." She swallowed the lump in her throat. "The Tanner business does not look good for him. We may need to take him into custody in the next few days. It looks like he is trying to disappear into a new life."

Tamburillo settled his bulk into one of her chairs. "You want to tell me what is going on, Judah?"

Her C.O.'s use of her first name did not go unnoticed. He was not speaking about Tanner. "What do you mean, sir?"

"I mean you have been the best profiler that I have seen in many years, maybe as far back as WWII. Not to mention your language skills." Wakefield could hear the *but* coming. "But lately, say the past six months, something has started slipping. What is going on Judah? Are you unhappy here?"

"I am fine, sir." She tried to put extra emotion in her voice to convince him. "Really." Wakefield pulled the draft copy out of her printer and pushed it across her desk toward him. She looked him directly in the eye melting a few degrees inside. "I've been dealing with some personal issues, but I am *dealing* with it. You will not see any more slippage, sir."

"I hope not." Tamburillo picked up the paper between his first two fingers and stood.

The glass in her door rattled as the admiral latched it behind himself.

Judah Wakefield inhaled a lungful of air and held it tightly in her chest. Her face heated again. Nothing was worse than a compassionate reprimand from her commanding officer. It would have been better if he had yelled.

She returned to the CD, keeping a more watchful eye on her door.

An hour later, she began to relax as the final version of her translation spewed from the printer. Her one-page single-spaced assessment of the inflections, what was said, and what was not said, followed.

Wakefield hand-delivered a copy to ADM Tamburillo and CAPT Huntington.

Huntington motioned her to come inside his office. His head was bent to the left over the handle of his desk phone. His hair threatened to fall out of its precarious position covering his bald scalp. He must have felt it falling, for he smoothed his fingers over it to re-flatten it in place.

She tried not to listen to the conversation as she stood just inside the captain's door. "We'll be right there. Yes, she is in my office now."

Huntington dropped the receiver into its cradle. "That was Shaw. We have a new player in our arms dealings in Southern Europe. We have him in action now, courtesy of the CIA. They requested you to go down and check out the live feed in the situation room. They want to see if you can build them some kind of profile to help ID the man."

The pair endured a handprint identification and a retina scan before the metal doors slid open in front of them like an elevator.

The screen was split into three sections in the semi-lit room. Half of it was covered by a live feed video that looked to be taking place somewhere tropical, *probably a Mediterranean island,* Wakefield judged quickly by the vegetation, shoreline, and boats in the harbor in the background. The top section of other half of the screen depicted a close up of the man's face and the final quarter of the screen was the computer monitor that was racing through the faces in the data bank to find a match.

Wakefield felt captured by the man's eyes. The rest of his face, his large nose and dark sun-exposed skin were unremarkable. But his eyes, they looked familiar. "I have seen this man before," she announced within seven seconds of entering the room.

"Do you have a name?" A disembodied voice asked from a computer terminal somewhere to her left and forward.

"Not yet." She settled herself in one of the folding chairs normally stacked against the wall to watch the feed.

He seemed to sense the camera on him, she noted. The way he would play to that direction more than the others. The out-of-focus leaves that waved in front of the camera every few seconds suggested that the field agent sending the feed was hidden some distance from the action.

"This is Piraeus, the port of Athens," LT Shaw told the newcomers. The figure turned his back to the camera and bent at the waist momentarily.

Greece again. I don't believe in coincidence. "Tighten up on his face again when he turns back around," Wakefield told whomever was working on the live feed video. "Shaw, see if the CIA can get DNA or prints off this guy."

When the figure on the screen straightened, he tossed a stubby stick toward the water of the harbor, but it did not go far. He stared straight at the camera. *A perfect wanted poster.* Wakefield smiled. "Capture that. Now loosen up again." It was so much easier when she could run the controls with her hands instead of with orders. "I want to see his body language." *Come on, talk to me.*

As the camera panned out, the figure wiggled something white between his fingers on his thigh. It looked like a napkin.

"Tighten up on the white part." Wakefield instructed the officer controlling the view.

The block formed on the screen and then the rest disappeared as the picture filled in with a fraction of the detail that had been present. "Clarify, three times." Someone requested. Without effort, Wakefield assessed that whomever had asked had worked on the system himself, one clarifying sweep rarely made a difference.

"Is it a note? Does he know we are taking his picture? Shaw tell the agent to keep his head down." Was the arms dealer directing it at the cameraman field agent? Or someone behind him?

The computer beeped softly twice. "No match on the face."

Then the penciled block letters became clear, along with the thumb that held the note.

H-E-Y was written over J-A-W.

"Hey jaw?" The first disembodied voice asked. "I don't get it."

Wakefield felt her stomach plunge toward her toes. She knew exactly who the figure was.

People began to murmur and the officer controlling the feed panned wide again.

Wakefield stood. "Pull all of this feed and save it to CD for me."

"But—" Shaw said.

"I am going to see the admiral."

Chapter Five

Dietz felt mesmerized by the action on the screen. The as-yet unnamed figure was obviously in somebody's special forces. British SAS or Israel's Mossad, maybe even Iraq's Republican Guard. *Too tall to be Chinese though,* Dietz chuckled to himself. The director crossed his leg over his knee and slapped his shin.

"The man is good." Dietz asked the operator to zoom in on the white block at the man's side. He read the note. His blood lagged sluggish. "Somebody get me Naval Intel on the secure line."

"They are already watching the feed."

"That is not what I said!" He snapped. He tore his eyes from the screen long enough to search out the offending party. A 34 year-old profiler, Smith... Schmidt... "Smythe." The name came quickly. He should know better than to question an order. "You've been here since November of 1991." The spiky-haired blond man nodded mutely. "Well, you will not be here one more minute if you ever question an order again."

The man's jaw worked like a guppy. He shrank back and a mottled red crept into his cheeks that Dietz could see, even in the muted light. The room echoed his words like a mausoleum.

"*Somebody* get me Naval Intelligence on the phone!" Dietz strode to the red phone to wait while the action continued on the screen.

"Tell the admiral I am on my way in." Wakefield flew by Petty Officer Snow's desk. She rapped twice as she opened the admiral's door.

Judah could not quite catch her breath. "Sir. Sorry to barge in, but my partner has been missing for two weeks, and I may have just found him, and he is about to get himself in a lot of trouble—"

"You don't have a partner." ADM Tamburillo interrupted as he looked up slowly from his paperwork. He fixed his dark eyes on her.

She could not keep her fingers still. They jerked in an outward sign of what her intestines were doing. "Well, when I work for Director Dietz I do." She explained what she had seen on the screen, her vocal chords creaking with strain.

"Then I suggest you get on the phone with Dietz, so the CIA doesn't pop off and kill him in the name of keeping America safe."

"I want to go after him, sir."

Tamburillo's face tightened and his shoulders bunched in his black uniform with gold admiral's shoulder boards. "He's Navy, right?"

Judah felt herself nod several times in tight succession. "A SEAL trainer out of Coronado."

It felt like her C.O. was looking right into her soul. "Then use whatever resources you need. Here's my phone." He rose and motioned her around the desk to use his chair. "You better sit down before you hyperventilate. Now I see what your problem has been, Commander." Tamburillo's dark cheeks rose as he gave her a knowing smile.

She dialed auto-8 and Dietz answered the first ring. With no preliminaries she blurted out, "Dietz, that guy in Greece you're tailing, it's Rivers."

"Yeah, I know. I was trying to get through to your office. If you want to see your boy in action, better get down to the live feed."

"Is he okay?" Wakefield froze, slightly bent, with her hand flat on her C.O.'s desktop for strength.

"He is about to take out a cigarette boat with a little canopy wheelhouse on top."

She dropped the receiver into the cradle and rushed back to the situation room. Running the stairs three at a time in heels and a skirt was not as hard as she thought it might be.

She could hear Tamburillo calling her name behind her.

Port of Athens—*Piraeus*
4:47 PM local time

Filasek scanned the area for the man who had been following him at a discreet 30 yards all afternoon. He seemed familiar. Filasek checked his watch. He was going to miss his flight if he did not lose the guy fast.

There. The man stood next to a concrete picnic table for sailors' shore lunches. Filasek glanced past him, not lingering too long in any direction. His fingers tightened into the top-rolled paper grocery bag he carried.

He had picked up the man two hours before, as soon as he stepped off his boat. *It was as if he was waiting for me.* Filasek stilled at slip 27 on pier 5. His.

He glanced back. The man was still there. *Good.*

Filasek set down his bag of groceries and fiddled with the mooring line. *Come on in a little bit closer. If I can't shake you, I will try another approach.*

Filasek's bodyguard flinched as the boat's rocking under Filasek's weight woke him from his prone position laid out in the sun. "Wake up. I have a tail that I want to get rid of."

The muscled man with long hair took the paper bag from the pier and set it in the floor. "Did you bring back lunch or is this to take back to the cook?"

"That was a distraction to try to lose this guy." Filasek mumbled under his breath.

"What was that?" The guard cupped his hand behind his ear and leaned forward.

"Help me set the destruction charges." Filasek turned to the perimeter cushions and dug in the wells underneath. He flipped the radio-controlled explosives into the receiver-on position."

The guard stood on deck for a long moment before mirroring Filasek's movements on the starboard side of the boat. "When you had me rig this up yesterday, I never thought you would use it."

"You thought I was just being paranoid? Well, I don't pay you to think."

"Maybe not."

Filasek saw the man's dark eyebrows shoot up before he turned his back to set the last charge on the starboard side. *It is hard to find respectful help these days.* Filasek cracked his knuckles. He smoothed his short beard as he stood erect. *Maybe I should leave him aboard*, Filasek considered. *No, then the man following me won't go aboard.*

"He has to be the one who blew up my catamaran. That's why he looks familiar." Filasek left the groceries and whispered to his guard. "This is what we're going to do."

Filasek glanced in the man's direction. "I will take off all my travel things, then I want you to follow me. We will go up to the bait and picnic area and watch to see if he comes aboard. If he does, I will blow the boat, but I need you to buy another one—identical!—while I am away. If he follows me, you stay in town here and keep an eye on it. Sleep on the boat if you have to. You know how to disarm the explosives?"

"Same way you turn them on."

*****

David Rivers reached down and squished an ant that was crawling up his ankle. It was a different kind of stakeout than he was used to when spinning up as a SEAL. More casual. Though Rivers was still all-cylinders alert.

Filasek and his man rummaged around under the cushions on Filasek's speedboat looking for something. *Maybe they are going to have a barbeque with some of the food he just bought and can't find the lighter fluid.*

Rivers leaned back against the rough-concrete picnic table, wishing for a sandwich and trying to blend in with the slow-paced local fishermen who were readying their boats for the night's work.

The flap of his summer windbreaker fell open and he reached down to keep his weapon concealed. The last package of C-4 Plastic explosives that he commandeered, slept in his pocket. He had called in a favor from a CIA contact on his layover in Washington D.C. two weeks earlier in order to have the explosives at his disposal when he arrived in Europe. And it made nice fireworks. *Maybe I should wait until after dark this time.* He watched the men sit down and then rise suddenly. Filasek first, then the man with long hair. They both departed the boat.

"Where do you think you are going now, little man?" Rivers ran his tongue over his teeth. He was getting thirsty. "Not far." He chuckled without mirth. "Wherever you go, I will be right behind you. For as long as you live."

The men walked at an angle on pier 5 toward him.

The SEAL part of his being screamed a warning. He needed brush, camouflage paint, some way to become invisible.

Rivers forced himself still. He allowed himself only the cover of a casual people watcher. The pain of the concrete picnic table digging into his backbone and tailbone kept him focused.

They meandered closer.

The Glock at his side grew a heartbeat of its own. The metal throbbed in tandem with his pulse. The bullets cried out to him for freedom.

He forced himself to look at the men. A casual passing glance. *Look through them*, he told himself. They stopped four yards from his position.

Filasek's eyes found him over his guard's shoulder. Rivers felt his stomach turn as he nodded in greeting at the man who had filleted his partner's face nearly a year earlier.

Noting the suitcase and briefcase, Rivers wondered where the al-Qaeda man was going. He did not seem hurried. Rivers felt a bead of sweat start to trickle down his scalp under the wig he wore. The Grecian sun shone hot this September day. The latex mask would not melt until the temperature reached 112 Fahrenheit, but the jacket he wore to cover his weapon was not helping matters.

They were walking again. Filasek trailed his fingers across the prickly unfinished cement of the picnic table top as they passed within inches of him. Rivers could smell them. A mixture of the briny sea salt and cologne reminiscent of oriental spices.

Rivers rose and stretched his elbows over his head. The relief he gave his back muscles made a sigh rise up in his throat. He swallowed it.

All I need is 45 seconds. I can get in and out and be back to track them again before they are out of the parking area. Rivers began to move.

He took a slip of paper out of his pocket. A tip from the server at *Papandreou.* "Slip twenty seven," he read. The paper was gray from rereading. There was no mistake. It was Filasek's boat. Rivers glanced at the two men's backs as they walked toward the parking area. He stepped off the concrete slab in the direction of the water.

The concrete pier had miniscule ridges to keep people from falling when it was wet. The layout of the harbor reminded him of the Costa Rican port where he had participated in a drug interdiction on his second mission as a SEAL. *No, it was the third mission. Off the Florida coast was second, how could I forget that?*

He walked by six empty slips in a row. More than half of the slips were empty this afternoon. *Probably good for what I have planned. Less collateral damage that way.*

Slip 27. Rivers whistled low. *A very fine replacement. It is almost a shame to blow up this one.* "But worth it to dispose the world of such a hothead terrorist."

I hope the camera guy is getting this. Without looking around to create suspicion, he hopped aboard. The vessel bobbed in the turquoise sea under his weight.

Out of the corner of his eye, Rivers saw the man who had been trailing him off and on for several days angle for a better position. He had a palm video camera instead of the still digital camera he had used before. "When I get done here, I think I better take that guy aside and teach him a few things about surveillance." Rivers shook his head.

He strode across the luxury boat built for speed in three quick paces. Under the cushions in the seat wells would be the perfect place to plant the C-4. *Maybe a section by the wing mechanism to blow through the hull, too.*

He lifted the four-inch-thick red vinyl cushion that covered a long bench on the fore starboard area.

Get out! Get out! His mind screamed the order.

Even as his eyes took in the volume of the TNT, his mind calculated its devastation. It would be big.

They were set with both timers and a remote detonating device similar to the one he had planned to use.

It was a set up.

Get off the boat, his mind screamed the order at him.

His fingers would not cooperate. He tried to drop the lid to the seat wells with his right hand and loosen his grip on the explosive material in his pocket.

I'll go up like a cannon ball. Not enough left to ID.

He had time to straighten from the seats and take one step before his trained ear heard the slightest click of the detonator coming to life.

His body propelled through the air. *So this is what it is like to fly*, was his last complete thought.

Naval Intel Situation Room
Thursday 26 September 2002
0918 hours

Judah had to stop three steps into the room. Her feet suddenly felt disconnected from her spinal command center. There he was larger than life. "I don't know why it took me so long to recognize him before." She muttered. "All the signs are there. That cocky way he has of holding his head, that chin jutting thing he does." She had to chuckle. "That nose is terrible though." She pronounced to anyone listening.

She moved her eyes to look at the still picture she had asked for earlier. She could see the makeup and the lines of the rubber latex features now that she knew what she was looking at.

The camera stayed on him exclusively as he sat in a relaxed pose while people milled around him. "What is he looking at?" She asked.

"Based on the pan shot from earlier, I'd say something in the port. Maybe a ship or boat docking." LT Shaw filled her in.

She grinned as Rivers tossed his hair over his shoulder. *It's as long as mine, he's never going to live this down.*

She felt Tamburillo touch her shoulder and guide her further into the room. Now that she could see Rivers was fine, she began to relax. Wakefield pulled her eyes from the mesmerizing screen to find a place to sit. But who had ordered him to Southern Europe? She squinted at the screen as if somehow the orders were behind the video feed.

When she glanced back up her blood pounded in her brain, yet it felt as though her heart had stopped its steady rhythm.

The CIA cameraman had captured a new subject.

She squeezed the underside of the metal chair until her nails dug back into her nailbed in protest.

"Arafeh Filasek." She felt her lips quiver.

The name that had caused her eight months of hell. He had sliced open her cheek with a knife, shot her reputation by accusing her of a crime that nearly led to a court martial, burned down her apartment, and sent her murdered cat to her in the mail. She wanted to attribute the presidential assassination attempt to him as well, but she had nothing to substantiate the hunch.

Her breath left in a rush as she realized what Rivers was going to do. The tape of her nightmares played over again in her head.

"If you hurt her, I will kill you." She remembered the tone of his voice when he said those words. The inflection and intent in his eyes when he had made that promise to Filasek in the Afghan desert last December had scared her even then.

"No." The word came out strangled. She stood and held a fist to her breast as she tried to get to the communication desk without tripping. "We've got to get a line to that agent. I've got to stop him."

She knew she was acting like a paranoid, out-of-control excuse for an officer, but this was personal.

It was revenge. It was something that would ruin their relationship forever, if allowed to take place. He would be murdering for her. *What is he thinking?*

"I'll try to get through, ma'am. But the relay..." the red-headed young man shrugged.

She knew there was not a lot of hope. She could not tear her eyes from the screen. "What message do you want to pass on, ma'am?"

Filasek walked out of the picture just then. "Tell him...tell him his M&Ms are going to rot if they get blood on them."

Rivers rose from the bench and stretched. *Lord, don't let him mess up his life with this*, she pleaded. *God, you can get him a warning in time.*

Used to relaying coded phrases, Wakefield heard the tech relay her statement verbatim on the phone to Langley.

The camera followed Rivers' jaunt from its position behind the brush. His back was to the lens as he looked at the ground while walking the pier under the giant sign with the number 5 on it.

She whispered to her C.O. so that the entire room did not hear, "He knows he is on film. He must be justifying this to himself somehow. Probably because Filasek is a terrorist." *But this is a vendetta, not a mission.* She frowned. *The punishment would bearable. But I know Rivers, and he will live with the guilt of murder on his conscious for the rest of his life in some vain attempt to relieve his guilt for the scar on my cheek.*

"I told him it would only make things worse." She mumbled. She was past caring who heard.

The picture started in toward the movement on the pier. It was not just the zoom. The picture jolted around as the cameraman hurried toward Rivers. The message was on its way.

As the boat rocked under his weight, Wakefield could feel the roll of the sea in her stomach. *Sailors are not allowed to get seasick,* she reprimanded her insides.

The cameraman passed under the Pier 5 sign as an explosion rocked the harbor.

The picture dropped to the concrete pier. The lens cracked on the left side, one-fifth of the way into the picture. The sideways shot of a three-deck yacht filled the screen.

Judah's third grade teacher told her that there was never a time when the brain did not have some thought passing through it. Mrs. O'Reilly was wrong.

One second, two seconds, three.

There was a slight jiggle of the picture on the screen, but not the one in Judah's mind. Fixed there was the etching of a fancy cigarette boat exploding along with her future.

The room began to spin. *Snap out of it! Focus.* The only thing to focus on was the sea blue-green eyes of her larger-than-life partner on the left top corner of the screen.

"Wakefield. Lieutenant Commander Wakefield!" The deep voice of her C.O. and his tugging on her elbow broke through her muddled brain. "My office, now!"

"Aye, aye, sir!" It was the engrained response. When she could not force herself to breathe, training took control.

"Oh my God." She whispered. "I need you, Jesus."

There were 18 stairs between the floors, 14 steps to the outer office door. A long hall stretched to eternity. A light shown at the end. She counted every step.

Am I dead?

It felt more like floating than walking. Walled pictures of naval vessels at war moved from crisp contrast to fuzzy impressions and back again as she absorbed the shock on the go.

She followed the black uniform in front of her. She stopped when it slowed. "Sit down, Commander."

She obeyed the voice. As the cold leather touched the backs of her legs through her pantyhose, the steel of her backbone rose up. Her foundation was shaken, but it was not destroyed.

"Wakefield, I know you've experienced a shock just now—"

She interrupted her C.O. for the first time in her career. "Sir, permission to go to Greece and look into this matter?"

A look of duty descended over Tamburillo's features. "Denied."

"Rivers is a SEAL, sir. Was a SEAL," she choked at having to correct her tense. "He deserves a proper investigation."

"NCIS will handle it, Commander."

"But, sir." She stood.

"I said *no*, Commander."

"Then, permission to take emergency family leave, sir?" She felt her chin tremble. She was going with or without his permission.

"Denied!" It rang final in Wakefield's ears. Tamburillo walked to the side of his large desk. He made a precise quarter turn and leaned his thighs into the surface. He rested his hands in wide-spread peaks to distribute his weight. "I know it is hard to see your partner die in front of you. But you have to go on."

"Do I, sir?" She was sure no one had experienced what she had just watched.

"I was a lieutenant commanding an assault team in Ho Che Mien during Vietnam, August 10, 1974. My 2IC, who also happened to be my best friend, stepped in front of a bullet for me. He died with his face in pieces at my feet. Couldn't fix it for an open casket. His mother still calls me every year."

"I am sorry, sir."

"He was a hero, just like your Rivers.

"David Rivers was my fiancée." She held her right hand over her bare left hand in front of her body.

Chapter Six

Tamburillo snapped his head left to look at the woman under his command. Her uniform fit like a poster girl. Her light hair was in one of those braid things that reminded him of a spine down the back of her skull. But it was tidy. She was always tidy.

As she stood staring at the wall, he looked at her blue eyes. She had seen too much these past few months. It was tearing at her soul. Any other person under his command would have already teetered over the edge of a breakdown.

But not Judah Wakefield. She was of strong constitution. Good blood. Her valor was found not only in her military heritage, but stemmed from her spiritual commitment. She knew that her strength lay outside herself. *She taught* me *that.* He thought of the day she challenged him to meet Christ.

He could see the argument in her eyes. The one she was having with her spirit.

"Take a long weekend, Judah. But don't leave town. Let yourself grieve. From all I was able to gather, Rivers was acting as a civilian in this matter. He did not have proper authorization."

The pink scar on her cheek was not as blatant as it had been when she came back from Afghanistan in January. But now, as the blood rushed to her face, it seemed to highlight the damage. "Then I will act as a civilian, too, Admiral. You'll have my written resignation within the hour."

"This is a mistake, Wakefield."

"But it is my mistake to make, sir. If there is nothing else?"

He could see by her impatient stance that she was ready to be dismissed. Her knees locked and disengaged forward and then wrinkled into a locked position again. He wondered for one moment if he did not dismiss her, would she stay behind in his office instead of running off to Greece in pursuit of revenge against an international terrorist.

He sighed. His heart heavy in his stomach. "Dismissed." He heard himself utter. She was continuing the same vendetta that killed Rivers. Why couldn't she see it?

**Langley, VA
10:37 AM local**

The explosion on the screen rocked Dietz's core as if he had been in proximity of the blast zone. "This was not supposed to happen." The words trickled from his lips.

The picture blurred as it jiggled. The agent's face appeared in an upside down blur as he checked the lens for damage. He seemed to be muttering something and then the feed returned to the fiery boat. The picture zoomed in on the aftermath a few seconds later and panned the area. A piece of the hull that was burning sank below the water in a cloud of steam. Debris had landed on boats on either side of slip 27 and they were quickly catching fire as well. "Call the fire brigade, kid," Dietz whispered. "We don't want to burn down the entire port of Athens. It's older than Jesus."

"Not really, Director," a woman in her early thirties said as she stood at his elbow. "Jesus existed before he came to earth."

Her words sounded like something Judah might say. "Judah!" He gasped. He had piped the feed into her office. She had just watched her boyfriend blow himself up.

"Get Naval Intel back on the phone." Dietz bellowed. His tone dared anyone to stall even a moment.

The agent panned the water with the video feed. The wreckage was visible through the clear Mediterranean waters as it rested on the sand rock bottom of the port. Fresh green peppers and several citrus fruits bobbed in the disturbed sea.

The screen suddenly jerked to catch a blue sky and then turned to black and white fuzz.

Piraeus—Port of Athens
5:00 PM local time

"Raul, pull him out of the water." Filasek ordered. "I think he may have dived off the starboard side before the detonation." The guard was already pulling off his boots as he ran. "I want to know who this man is who has cost me two boats."

As Filasek watched, a self-satisfied grin rose on his face. He had finally found an employee who did not ask questions.

Raul pushed a man with a video camera into the drink on the opposite side of the wreckage and burning ship and boat. "Stupid tourists." Filasek grumbled. More and more people began to congregate and flood down pier 5.

He looked at the hands on his watch. If he did not leave in the next three or four minutes he knew he would miss the flight.

The man with the camera bobbed to the surface spouting water and American curses. "Terrific," Filasek sighed. He cursed under his breath as he resigned himself to catching the next flight to St Petersburg.

Filasek shuffled down the slight incline toward the pier. Flashing a leather wallet, he spoke in tired Greek. "Move along people. Medical help is on the way, fire control is minutes away."

The people stood gawking and jockeying for a better view down the narrow concrete strip. He pushed his way through the twenty-five or so gathered at the entrance onto pier 5. "Listen up," he snapped. "This is official business. Anyone left in the area in fifteen seconds, I will assume is a witness or an arsonist and I will haul you in for extensive questioning."

That thinned the crowd effectively. The American with the camera treaded water, holding his equipment out of the water.

Filasek pumped his short legs faster than he normally did. Kneeling on the concrete, he reached out his hand. The man looked very American and familiar, too. Assuming an authority in his voice again, Filasek told him, "You are doing a great job. Let's get you out of there, okay? What's your name, buddy?"

The man could obviously swim so Filasek motioned him over to the side. "Name's Patrick Mullion."

"All right Patrick, you held onto that camera like your life depended on it, so we will save it for you." Using this tone of convincing and calming irritated Filasek's skin. "Pass it on up first."

Filasek took the video camera from him and straightened his back to place it next to him on the pier. It was top of the line with a radio feed box attached to the tape side. Standard CIA, SAS, DIA, or NSA equipment. *This man is no tourist.* Filasek did not risk another look at the man's face, but curbed his own features.

Filasek reached into his pocket and touched the silver cylinder he never left home without. It was still intact. "All right, Patrick. I am going to haul you up. Give me your hand. When you get up here, I want you to just lie still and let me look you over."

A look of distrust passed over the man's features, but it disappeared so quickly Filasek wondered if he had imagined it.

The man's hand slipped out of his wet fingers twice. On the third try, Filasek grabbed his wrist and hauled him three feet out of the sea onto the pier like a giant fish.

Out of the corner of his eye, Filasek saw Raul floundering around with a bleeding limp body. "Lie still," he reiterated.

"I am fine."

"I want to make sure."

"Come on man, I am not even breathing hard."

"Turn over." Filasek demanded.

The man complied and Filasek ran less than expert hands over Patrick's neck. Reaching into his pocket, he removed the sample cylinder. The safety cap popped off with ease.

Filasek pressed against the side of Patrick's head, smashing his right cheek into the lined concrete facing away from him. He squirted a minute spray of the new chemical mix he had concocted toward Patrick's nose and mouth and held his own breath. Patrick's feet kicked up mightily as he tried to reposition himself.

Three seconds later Filasek noticed a weakening in the man's struggle. Eight seconds after that, the man was struggling to even breathe. Four seconds more and the man was no longer aware of his problem.

Filasek flopped Patrick over onto his back, and made it appear that he was administering CPR while he held his breath any time he was near the man's mouth and devised a plan for getting the two men back to his seaside villa, 31 nautical miles away with no boat or aircraft.

Rising from Patrick's side, Filasek smoothed the water out of his wiry beard. He went to help Raul.

Raul was treading water with their unconscious chaser's chin under his elbow. The man's bloodied face clouded the water around them.

Filasek did not have to study the man's face. He stood up straight and laughed from deep in his belly. "We seem to have caught ourselves a big fish." The latex-nose disguise hung by a thin line of glue off to the left side of his face. The make-up had melted off in the water.

"You know this man?"

"His name was Rivers."

"Is." Raul shook the rivulets of water running from his hair out of his eyes. "He's alive. I had to punch him to get him to cooperate."

Filasek's mind felt like it was exploding with new creativity. "Praise be to Allah." *So many ideas, so little time.* He beamed. "That is even better."

"It *won't* be better—if he comes to before he is in our custody."

Raul pushed from underneath while Filasek tugged on Rivers' arms. "He must weigh 250 pounds." Filasek gasped. His muscles were screaming in protest. He could not get enough leverage to ease him out of the water because he was not tall enough.

"Closer to 215," Raul corrected. It irritated Filasek. A mighty heave and a step backward, brought the man, face first, hanging by his waist on the pier. Then it was easy to transfer the legs topside. Filasek tossed a piece of mooring line down to Raul and anchored himself.

Filasek conscripted two oversized fishermen who had been watching from a distance to help carry Patrick and Rivers with the excuse that the ambulance was caught in traffic. "It will shave off a good eight minutes to take them in my personal vehicle," he told the bumbling fishermen. "Thanks for your help. They may survive because of you."

Filasek spit out his window as soon as the tires were rolling. It did nothing to rid him of the taste of concern he had had to use in order to calm the upset without an attention-grabbing massacre.

"So we have Little Officer Rivers in our custody," Filasek's chuckle bubbled from deep within. "Fortune's prospects are good to me."

Wakefield's Office
Naval Intelligence, Suitland, MD
1047 Hours

The letter sat on Judah Wakefield's desk, on top of an official U.S. Navy resignation form letter 1920-190. The edges tidily justified to one-half page. All it needed was a signature. *I just want to make sure the ink is good and dry before I sign it.* "I don't want to have to print it again."

Wakefield pulled the bag of M&Ms from her lap drawer and put them on top of her personal papers in the box she was packing. Rivers had told her on their first mission together that he was searching for the advertised promotional bag of all purple M&Ms. He had equated winning the treasure that the manufacturer was offering to finding the treasure of his wife. She traced the outline of the advertisement for the search for the winning bag of all purple candies on the brown bag. "I'll never eat them again." She dropped the bag into the trash can. The reminder would be too painful.

She forced herself away from the remembrance and back to packing. The ivy plant that was nearly dead, she also trashed. The four 2X3 pictures of her family she put into the take-home box. She fingered the one of her mom and dad—step-dad. He was in full uniform. It was taken the morning Admiral Graham had deployed to the Arabian Sea. "Wonder what he would have to say about this," she mumbled. She shook her head. She knew what he would say. Don't do anything in haste.

"Sorry, dad. I have to be hasty. There is not time for anything else."

She wrapped her empty crystal vase in the morning's paper and added it to the take-home box. Last was the porcelain-framed picture of Rivers. "God, if he somehow survived, please keep him alive until I get there."

Judah felt hope rise in her spirit, but was afraid to dwell on it, for fear of encouraging delusion.

One more glance around the bare office told her there was no more putting it off. She picked up the black Bic pen that the Navy provided for her use.

In heavy deliberate strokes she signed away her 12-year career.

I did not even pray about it, she froze, hunched over the tail of the final D in her name. *It is the right thing to do. Rivers would come after me, if only to retrieve my body.*

The single page felt encyclopedia-heavy as she marched toward ADM Tamburillo's office. "He said to go right in, ma'am," the petty officer stood when she entered the outer office.

*****

LT Shaw puffed as he climbed the final flight of stairs. He felt as if he had walked across half of Maryland in the hour since his last orders. In reality, he had not left the premises.

Shaw looked across the bullpen of secretaries, Wakefield's office door was ajar and the light was out. "I am either too late or I have perfect timing." Shaw spoke under his breath as he sped up his trot.

He leaned down and whispered to Petty Officer Jenna Casper, "Has she left yet?"

The young woman glanced up through her long lashes. "She's in with the admiral."

"Great. I wanted to say good-bye." Shaw entered the dark office. He flipped the light on and pushed the door closed.

Her purse sat on top of the cardboard box of her personal belongings. He fished for her wallet.

Unwrapping the half-inch round, mesh, tracking device that he had procured from downstairs on the admiral's orders, Shaw peeled off the paper backing. He stuck it to the backside of her visa card. "Never leave home without it," he quoted.

Placing everything back in order, exactly as he had found it. "Get a move on, Shaw," he ordered himself.

"Shaw? What are you doing in my office?"

Shaw felt his eyes widen and was glad his back was turned. "Coveting the space?" He turned and faced the senior officer, plastering what he hoped was a convincing smile on his lips.

"Scuttlebutt is fast." She was looking at the floor.

"Actually I wanted to say good-bye." Shaw lowered his head and caught her eyes.

She raised her head and a brief smile turned her lips up, but it did not reach her eyes. "It has been an honor to serve with you, ma'am."

"You, too, Shaw. If there is ever anything I can do for you..." her trailing voice did not sound like she was putting much hope into her future.

"Actually there is, ma'am." Shaw measured the thickness of the desktop with his first finger and thumb behind his back.

She straightened her back. "Name it, Lieutenant."

He paused for a beat. "Come back alive, ma'am."

He watched her swallow, the muscles in her throat tightening and loosening. Her neck reminded him of a swan's, long and white. He had never noticed that before. "I'll do my best, Justin." He let his gaze float up to find a knowing half-smile on her lips. It was early enough in the day that she was still wearing lipstick.

"Would you like to go out for drinks this evening?" He felt emboldened by her use of his first name.

"I have a midnight flight. But I'll let you carry my things to the car?"

Her look was so hopeful that he chuckled. "Of course, Commander Wakefield." He understood. She was not looking for a Rivers-replacement, but she needed a friend.

"It is just Judah now."

"Judah." Shaw tried out her name. It felt foreign on his tongue. Foreign, but delightful, like a sweet and spicy delicacy from the Far East.

Chapter Seven

"I want you to stay here until the new boat has been delivered day after tomorrow." Filasek held his briefcase in his left hand, car keys in the right with his overnight bag over the same shoulder. He stood in the doorway of Raul's sister's apartment shifting from one foot to the other.

"Give him one shot of that stuff every seven hours. It will keep him under until you can get him to the villa."

"I know." Raul sat on the rented chair with a television remote in his hand. "I have done this before."

"I just don't want to lose him. This is the big fish."

"I know. You said that already."

"I just—"

"Everything is under control. I will have your new boat in port to pick you up when you return." Raul sounded almost impatient.

How dare he, Filasek's breathing made a tight whistling noise. "Do you have something better to do than listen to your employer's instructions?"

Raul nodded once toward the television, his dark hair sliding forward. "The footie game is on."

Filasek stared at him half-lidded. Raul raised his hands and his eyebrows the same distance as if to ask, "Why are you still standing there?"

"Save tomorrow's paper for me. Finding a dead American spy in a fish hatchery should at least make the second page."

Filasek closed the apartment door behind himself, controlling his urge to slam it. The bodyguard was too confident. *I don't trust him. The apartment of a sister I didn't know he had was a little too convenient. But at the moment, I don't have a choice.*

Wakefield's Residence
1400 hours

The underwater feeling that overwhelmed her at the office had dissipated, leaving in its wake an intensity in focus that was reminiscent of the few hours of semi-sanctioned combat she had participated in over her career.

She could hear her downstairs neighbor's air conditioner kick on. The colors in her apartment seemed overly vibrant. She smelled the sour milk she had dumped down the drain the night before.

Even her spirit was hyper-sensitive. She had not felt so much activity in months. *Since January.* She felt her face fall.

How long are you going to hold James Yates' betrayal against me? She heard the words echo in her mind as if God had spoken them aloud.

"I'm not." She tried to dismiss the words that pained her like a blade. There was nothing else to occupy her energy though. The apartment was clean, daytime television without cable was less than tolerable, the refrigerator was cleaned out. She still had over nine hours before her flight. "You sure you want to get into this?" Wakefield felt her chest expand as she took a shaky breath.

No answer.

"Fine." She was surprised by the hostility in her voice. "You're right. *You* are the one who betrayed me. But, how could you not tell me who he was? You tell me all sorts of trivial things, but not the really important stuff. I could have fallen in love with him."

Could you?

She stomped her foot. She sucked in her lip. The sting tingled all the way up into her hip. "I hate it when you do that. Yes, I could have loved him. But *you* did not warn me not to."

No one warned me not to either.

"You're God, who would warn you? And don't you have to love everybody?"

No. I choose to. The same way you choose to love me.

"Sometimes, I wish I didn't. I wish I had chosen a regular life." An icy chill bit her heart.

The silence was daunting. Her neighbor's air conditioner chugged and stopped. *It is not too late.*

"I'm sorry." Judah pushed on her eyeballs until they hurt. "I didn't mean it." She sat heavily on the couch. It was hard, not like her old comfortable sofa before the fire. "No matter how angry I am, I can't help but love you. I just wish you had told me about Yates. And now Rivers"

What would you have done differently?

Judah was slow to answer as she considered the possible outcomes. "I don't know."

I do.

"How do you know?" That her question was illogical occurred to her after the words had left her mouth.

I know you.

The truth of the simple statement with every word emphasized surged over her heart. The words were gentle. A cry rose in her throat. She allowed, for the first time since January, tears to course down her cheeks. She melted over onto her side on the firm sofa cushions, drawing her knees up toward her chin. "Will you forgive me for ignoring you?"

Her shoulders curved toward her center. They shook as the pain loosened its tentacles from her heart. She had grown accustomed to the resentment that resided within her. "I said once that I could not live without David. But it is *you* I cannot live without. I know that now."

Saying the words aloud set off a new batch of tears. She had felt for a moment what life would be life without Him in it. She did not like it at all.

St Petersburg, Russia, International Airport
Friday 27 September 2002
3:03 PM local time

"You must understand." Filasek stood at the car rental counter of a company. "I must have a car." He shifted from foot to foot, his chin barely over the high counter separating him from the clerk. In his opinion, it was all that was saving the young man with unwashed hair from his temper.

"Apparently, *you* don't understand." The 19-year-old boy narrowed his eyes as if Filasek was being difficult. "I have no cars left. Not one. I have nothing to rent to you." He shook his head in small motions and jutted his chin forward dumbly.

"I must get to Moscow to pick up my sister's wedding trousseau." He tried a new tactic and a new tone of voice. He pulled his lips down into a deep frown that, he hoped, looked like he was pleading for help.

"Sir. I am sorry. I don't have anything until day after tomorrow. You are too late."

An idea stung Filasek in the back of the head. He slapped an open hand at the pain like it was a mosquito. "What about your personal vehicle, son? Would you rent that to me? I would pay you well."

They clerk's shoulders dropped and his mouth pulled to one side. "My personal vehicle is a bicycle with a rear tire that goes flat every third day. I don't think you'd want it to get to Moscow." Grimy teeth poked through his grimacing lips.

Filasek felt his mouth turn down. He swallowed as he scrambled for an idea. He had to meet his seller in Novgorod at 6 PM and it was an hour's drive. "How about your father's vehicle? Your employer's vehicle?" Filasek folded his hand together and brought them down on the counter hard enough to send pain stinging into his elbows. "Find me a car."

"Does it have to be a *car?*" the boy looked slyly from behind slit eyes. Filasek felt buoyancy return to his sinking soul. The young man had an idea.

"At this point anything with an engine will do." Filasek smoothed his beard with his right hand in anticipation.

"My father has a truck. It runs real good." The boy bobbed his head to some inaudible beat.

"Excellent!" Filasek exploded. "Take me to it."

"How much will you pay me for it?" The clerk stepped back from the separating counter.

"One hundred pounds sterling."

The boy ran fingers through his matted hair and showed his yellowed teeth again. "Each day."

"What?" Filasek scowled. He reached toward the young man with his fingers itching to throttle him.

"It is a seller's market, man. There is one vehicle for rent. Who knows how many people will need it by the day's end. I need to recoup my losses from renting it to the first one. Besides, it will cost me to exchange pounds to rubles. It is a dying commodity."

"What are you, some business school reject?"

"Absolutely not. I finished at the top of my class, two years ahead of those my age. This is my shop."

Filasek blew out his breath between lips swollen from pressing them together in anger.

"Fine, 100 pounds per day. I will need it for two days.

At 4:45, Filasek was his own driver in a 1956 rattling, communist-made truck that looked like a knock-off of a Ford. Understanding what was being said over his SatFone was next to impossible, but he tried as he pressed it into his ear.

"Would you just listen to my idea?" The irritability that he had more and more trouble controlling in his voice sounded through again.

"This is not your area of expertise." The normally marble-smooth voice snapped over the connection. "You stick to the San Francisco Bridge. It is a sound idea."

Bin Laden was the most recognizable terrorist in the history of the world because of all the world-wide television coverage by the Americans. Filasek knew him as a fervent-tempered, passionately religious man whose devotion to Allah surpassed his long-ago family responsibilities. His inspiring voice sounded soft and strong at the same time. "Please," Filasek tried keeping his tone more neutral, "Don't let the pressure of American dogs keep you from hearing what I have to offer."

"Infidels do not control anything I do or think. Speak, friend of Saddam. I will listen."

Filasek grinned. Bin Laden still had no idea who he was. He switched the SatFone to his left hand, so he could maneuver better around the potholes in what used to be a black-top road. "In our Endeavor," Filasek spoke shadily, "perhaps we could use our contact to replace the backup exploding bolts with a set of heavy exploding bolts. Pack them with say, five times as much power as normally used to release the...uh, pack. The secondary equipment will cause an explosion significant enough to ignite the oxygen on board."

"It is a night launch. That would make nice pictures."

"And it would take care of the problem of spontaneity. No matter how often the wind or weather sets back the launch, the bolts will still be waiting."

"How would we get the crew to replace the original bolts to the secondary set?" Filasek had a hard time distinguishing bin Laden's tones. He sounded only slightly interested, and Filasek had thought he would be rejoicing that someone had finally come up with a feasible plan for the theoretical idea of the next big strike on the Great Satan. Bin Laden's initiative was to perfect the cleansing techniques against the Americans and then purge the Holy Land of Jews. Filasek wanted to help. For now. He was angling for the number two position, currently held by one Abu al Zarqawi. It should have been his, by rights of the firstborn, but he wanted to earn it on his own merit. Then soon after, he would surpass his father's fame.

"Fake some test results, spray some acid on the bolts once they are on the launching pad, chip the enamel. Whatever. They check everything a million times after the *Challenger*. It should be no problem getting the backup bolts to the launching pad, only getting them through the intensive scrutiny."

"Not really, that is the area where our contact works."

"And he doesn't mind exposure? The American press will be all over him." Filasek warned.

"Unless we start a rumor that someone higher than him coerced a cover-up." The suggestion came over the line.

"That could be fun." Filasek rubbed his beard. "And believable because of Enron and HealthSouth."

"It is a den of corruption over there right now. We will help purge them of their sin." Filasek did not think of himself as religious. He would take the good parts, Jihad, heaven and women, and leave the rest. He did, however, believe in his ability to manipulate religion against others. If he found someday that he had to make a choice, Filasek had determined to go with Allah. That god offered the best post-life retirement plan.

"What about our Jell-O plan? Is that able to shift with the weather as the bridge and the other endeavor?"

"Our? It is not *our* plan; it is *my* strike. You are participating." Bin Laden cleared his throat, obviously waiting for contrition.

It seemed that 12 months of living as a nomad were beginning to wear on the religious leader. *It should be natural for him.* Filasek jerked as the truck hit another pothole. Since he was a boy, he had heard bin Laden boast that he could trace his heritage back 4000 years to Abraham's eldest son, Ishmael, the son of promise. The one who should have received the blessing instead of being cast out when the second son came along. It was the seed of the father, not the mother, be it servant woman or wife, that dictated a son's place. Ishmael and his descendants had wandered in the wilderness for years. They set up cities and villages and then were slaughtered by the Israelites, the second-born Isaac's sons.

"I apologize. *Your* plan, which I am helping to facilitate."

Filasek could almost hear bin Laden clucking his tongue and nodding through the bad connection. "The plan is flexible." The terrorist confirmed.

Filasek knew enough about the plan to know that the location for the third leg of their tri-pronged attack would be Fort Knox, Kentucky. Home of the gold reserve of the United States government. It would take generations to recover from that strike. San Francisco's Golden Gate Bridge would wipe out a historical landmark, Fort Knox would take out their present financial security and *Endeavor*'s destruction would cripple America's prideful future.

Filasek jerked the wheel to the right, narrowly missing another vehicle that dared share the road with him. "Are you interested in buying a diamond mine with me?" He planned to remove his money from the American market just before the strike. With Fort Knox's gold decimated, the trade value of diamonds was sure to skyrocket.

"I already own a diamond mine."

Filasek tucked in his chin. He had not expected that response. "Good. You will need it," he finally said. "I will buy one on my own." He cocked his head to the side. A wooden sign announced in Cyrillic that Novgorod was three kilometers ahead.

It's about time. I am ready to be out of this horrible truck. The fifty-year-old seats were sunken into springs that overreacted to every movement of the wheels. The first drops of rain splattered the windshield as he entered the outskirts of the ancient town that in the fourteenth century had been the largest city in the known world.

Filasek looked at the six-story dirt-white buildings and the Cathedral of St Sophia through the useless windshield wiper movement and decided that it had probably not grown much since then.

Chapter Eight

Shrouded in stifling darkness, Wakefield stood on an unfamiliar dock. She reached into the water again to try to find Rivers. She brought up another handful of seaweed instead. It slithered through her fingers and the slimy water dribbled down to her elbow when she held up her arm.

"Where are you, David? Come back to me." Wakefield's voice sounded guttural to her ears. Her hand that she had been searching with transformed as if being eaten with acid before her eyes. The fingers elongated with the nails growing out into talons. The skin and muscle disintegrated in some places and bunched up in others. It looked grotesquely demon-like.

Rivers' body floated to the surface and she reached out with her claw to save him. The acid began to chew away at his body the moment she touched him. She turned him over on the dock. His eyes were open, hollow and staring, but alive.

"My God! What have I done to you?" Wakefield screamed as he disappeared before her eyes.

"Watch out for the wolves." David's face crumbled into ashes.

"No!" Wakefield's shrill scream welled up in her chest. A hand closed over her shoulder. She tossed her body around to loosen the numbing grip.

The back of her hand smacked a hard surface, shoving pain signals into her brain. She forced her eyes open and found herself in her living room at home; the dock melted into the mist of her mind.

Her shoulder tingled from lack of circulation as she pushed it into the sofa cushion. The back of her hand was red. She had slammed it into the coffee table. "Thank God it was a dream." She sucked in new breath while shaking her head as she tried to exorcise the horrible image of David Rivers with a half-dissolved face. "I hope this was not a warning from you, God." Wakefield glanced at her watch. "I can't believe I slept five hours." She scrambled around to call a taxi and prepare her luggage for her flight.

"If it was from you, does that mean he survived?" Judah was afraid to hope, yet found herself unable to stop the bubble forming in her belly.

Langley, VA
CIA Headquarters
0029 hours EDT

"I have her frequency on the move." A little blinking red dot moved slowly over a line drawing of Connecticut. "Good work, Admiral. We are tracking her now." Director Dietz hung up with Judah Wakefield's commanding officer and prepared his office paper work for an extended absence. *A week should do it*, he nodded as he reviewed Ms. Cravits' arrangement of schedules and transportation. "I've not been out of the office for more than four sequential days since I came to the Agency."

He downloaded the real-time data for tracking down Wakefield from his computer into his PDA. "Just don't do anything stupid until I get there." Dietz frowned. "If you wait, we can do something stupid together." He had never personally chased down one of his agents before.

In the course of his career, three of his men had gone rogue to extract their own revenge. After the first man, Dietz made it office knowledge that he cut off men like that. That they all three had died within days of their diversion was a much-speculated topic at office Christmas parties.

Dietz sat on the edge of his seat to touch base with Dovlatabadi one last time before he left. The man had gotten the security job immediately and was training with Hussein's bodyguard now, only two days after touching down. There was one e-mail in the special address box. "Expecting important company next week." Dietz read it out loud twice before saving it for his return.

Sadko Hotel, Novgorod
16 Gagarin Prospekt
Friday 7:00 PM

Filasek grunted in surprise as a knock sounded on his hotel room door. *A Russian who found timeliness important—rare indeed.* As Filasek opened the wooden door, it creaked. *How long since this place has been remodeled?* The mildew smell from the bath down the hall hit him in the face in the open doorway. *At least a century.* He rubbed his nose and slid his hand over his bearded chin.

"Comrade Filasek?" A graying blond man of heavy girth stretched out his hand. "Oskar Dabkowski. It is my great joy to meet you."

"Come in, Dabkowski." Filasek shook the man's hand. It was wide and thick. "I have to pick up my coat and I will take you to dinner." Filasek turned on his heel leaving the door ajar for Dabkowski to follow.

"Please, call me Oskar. And my wife has prepared a Russian favorite for us tonight. I insist, you must come dine with us this evening at our farm." The Russian's voice lilted with the invitation. "It is not far. Then we can send my Helga to the parlor while we discuss our business like gentlemen, over vodka."

Filasek turned to gauge the man's motives. His light eyes were crisp and clear. His ruddy cheeks held a measure of hope. Filasek saw nothing to fear in the openness of Oskar's countenance. "I accept your offer." Filasek took his pea coat from the wooden hanger in the tiny hall. He hoisted his briefcase. "Let's go." Filasek nodded for Oskar go to the door first.

A woman stood in the doorway of the farmhouse where Oskar pulled his 1998 Mercedes SUV into the paved driveway. "There is my Helga." The woman waved at them.

"You are a man of surprises, Oskar." Filasek chuckled at his own notions of what he expected the farmhouse to look like. This was anything but. With vinyl siding and bay windows and ironwork on every balcony it was the most modern house he had seen from St Petersburg to Novgorod.

"Come on in. Supper's getting cold." Helga called from the porch after Filasek and Oskar had opened their doors.

Over reindeer meat in a thick brown sauce, cucumbers in vinegar, and shredded, pickled red cabbage Filasek said, "This is the best meal I have eaten in years, Mrs. Dabkowski." He was serious, too. *It is just too bad I have to kill you to keep my chemical buying under wraps*, he frowned.

"It is too bad you don't have good food where you live. This is just a regular meal. You should taste Helga's food when she's had time to prepare a fancy meal."

Oskar's wife blushed at the compliment and glanced in his direction. "Where did you say you're from, Comrade Filasek?" she asked.

"Here and there," he skirted the question. *Though I suppose it doesn't really matter to tell them I am Yemenite.* "I am hoping to make your husband an offer that will allow you both quite a bit of extra time in the kitchen or anywhere else you would rather be."

"Before, when you first made the offer, we were sad to see our business die. Now, Oskar and I are quite happy. You see there are no children to leave the place to, and we think it will be nice to spend some time on ourselves."

"After dinner, please. I am trying to digest, not conduct business." Oskar shot a teasing look at his wife. Then the look was directed at him.

Filasek smiled and nearly laughed out loud. *How long has it been since someone teased me?* He could not recall.

El. Venizelos Athens International Airport
Friday 4PM local time

Wakefield looked at the pad of paper where she had taken notes about Rivers' endeavors while he was abroad. She told the cab driver in Greek. "Marble House Pension, south of the acropolis, please." She grimaced at her garbled accent. "Forgive my words, I am a little overtired."

"It happens often on flights from America," the driver answered in English. "It is a long way to come." He pulled away from the curb and Judah leaned her head against the cloth bucket seats in the back. "You have surely not come to our enchanting country alone. Not one as beautiful as Helen. You are meeting someone here. A man."

Judah left her eyes closed and felt a smile play at her lips. *Helen of Troy? How did I draw the romantic cabbie?* "You could say that." She deliberately fudged the details. It would be nice to dream for the ride to the hotel that she was on her way to meet David here. That she would not have to comb the city and the sea for him or his body. That he was waiting for her. *Nice dream, Wakefield,* she scoffed at herself. *You had better wake up before you start your quest tomorrow.*

Heathrow Airport, London
6:30 PM local time

Dietz checked his PDA for Wakefield's location one more time before boarding his flight to Athens. "Good. Just stay put, woman," he whispered. She had not moved in 42 minutes. A fanciful thought fluttered through his mind. "God, will you keep her still tonight so I can get to her in the morning?"

It gave him shivers to pray, even about such an important subject. "I don't expect you to do *me* any favors, but she doesn't know she needs help, so she won't be asking. I am asking for *her*." Dietz hurriedly explained under his breath.

Dietz buckled himself into his seat for the second leg of his flight. Even in the wide, adjustable, first-class seats, he felt permanently creased at the hip and knee. No one was next to him and he allowed himself to think of what he had just done. "Praying wasn't so bad. I might be able to do that again sometime. Later though," he qualified softly to himself.

I would like that.

Dietz whipped his head around. *Who?* A lithe woman who looked like a singer he had seen on a televised concert he had flipped past one night was the only one within range. She was stowing a bag in an overhead compartment three rows back. *Nope, not her. Besides, it was too deep for a woman's voice.*

"Was that—" Dietz was almost afraid to ask such an impudent question, "you?"

Did you think that though I created you to speak, that I don't?

Something Judah once told him about God ran thorough his mind just then. He could hear her laughing inflection. "When God asks a question he is not fishing for information."

A blanket of anxiety swathed over him. "You are not going to kill me on this flight are you?"

You have not yet fulfilled the destiny I planned for you from the foundation.

The craft strained against gravity and lifted. Dietz's fear lifted with the same trumping of the law. Aerodynamics rose above gravity. Love overcame fear. "Destiny? Planned?" he repeated the words under his breath. "He created me. The foundation of what?"

Suddenly all the hokey things he had dismissed as foolish settled into his spirit. They arranged into tidy rows.

"Oh, my God! The foundation of the *world*. You were there." The satisfaction he had never been able to identify as missing in his life was suddenly dangling before his eyes.

"It is time for a new chapter," Dietz whispered aloud after the flight attendant passed.

Chapter Nine

Filasek stood in Dabkowski's office, chewing his lip and window-watching Dabkowski's men load his chemicals into a giant shipping container. Filasek had arranged an evening pick up by rail that would deliver his goods to the sea. After sailing to the Mediterranean, the container would transfer by truck to a warehouse three miles from his home and two blocks from the water on Poros.

Every arrangement fit perfectly except that Dabkowski and his wife could ID him.

Dabkowski nodded to his men and sealed the container after the last man cleared the door. Filasek watched him secure the door and suddenly felt giddy. He wiggled around the room waiting for Dabkowski to return from shaking his men's hands. *Get on with it, man. Save it for the retirement celebration tonight.*

Filasek decided as he watched Dabkowski interact with his group of men that the husband and wife's deaths had to look like a murder-suicide, or he might never get out of the country. Dabkowski was a well-liked man. The big, jolly man who shook his hand now, used both hands and looked as though he might dislocate his boss's shoulder. The men dispersed as Oskar Dabkowski entered his office building for the last time.

"Grab your samples and come to my house to wait for the party time. You have time before your return flight, no?"

Perfect. "No, no. I could not possibly intrude on your party." Filasek stroked his chin and looked at the carpet on the office floor.

"Yes, I insist." Dabkowski reached over and jogged his shoulder with a rough hand. Filasek almost jumped out of his skin at the touch.

"You are the one who made this all possible. You have been generous with the up-front cash, so that my men do not have to worry about going hungry while they look for other jobs."

"I gave you fair market value, that's all." Filasek wished Dabkowski would just shut up.

"We will celebrate doing business together."

Filasek nodded with what he hoped looked like reluctance. "But I will drive the truck I rented. I will have to leave by 9 o'clock to catch my flight. I don't want you to have to leave your party to bring me back to town."

"Fair enough." Oskar gave a belly laugh. "You would probably not want me to drive you anyway. I plan to drink a boatload of vodka by 9."

When Filasek arrived, the Dabkowski kitchen smelled like hot yeasty bread. Inhaling the sweet smell made Filasek's stomach rumble. Helga appeared from the direction of the living room with an English magazine folded in half, her first finger marking her place.

"Welcome. Did you get the warehouse emptied?"

Oskar nodded to his wife. "I wasn't sure everything would fit into one container like Filasek said, but he was right. There was even some room to spare." He chuckled. "We could pack ourselves in the container if you feel like a cruise to Greece."

Filasek watched with amusement as Helga drew her brow into wrinkles. "Thanks for the offer, but I'll take my cruise to Greece with a proper stateroom and feasts every night." From behind Oskar, Filasek watched the man's shoulders imitate the bunched up response that Helga's forehead had made. "It was your idea, husband. You can afford it."

As he watched the pair interact, Filasek hoped that the police in Novgorod did not have a forensic team capable of measuring endorphins in the blood. These two were the happiest people he had ever had the displeasure of coming in contact with.

"Would you two care for a bun? I took them from the oven not five minutes ago." Helga did not wait for a response, but stepped over to the counter where a pan of crusty brown bread lay cooling.

Filasek hung his coat on a fish-shaped coat peg in the backdoor entranceway. Helga handed each of them a saucer with a portion of steaming bread. "Butter and honey are on the table."

Filasek took note of every surface he touched. The chair back when he pulled it out. *The saucer, the knife. The doorknob. I don't want to forget to wipe anything down.* As good as they smelled, he swallowed the bun without tasting it.

Helga disappeared back into the living room with her shiny magazine.

Filasek cleared his throat. "Excuse me one moment, will you Oskar? Where is your toilet?"

"Through the living room." Oskar tried to speak around a mouthful of bread and honey. "Down the hall, second door on the right."

Filasek let the swinging French doors between the kitchen and living room close behind him. Helga sat engrossed in reading and did not look up. Her legs were folded under her on the couch like a young woman. Her green eyes scanned right and left as she ingested the words on the page.

Filasek withdrew his six-inch snub-nose pistol from his belt under his untucked white dress shirt. He stood four feet from her, hoping to avoid the spatter. The woman raised her head slightly to acknowledge her guest's presence, but her eyes still scanned the page. "Can I get you another bun?" she asked, finally tearing her eyes from the words.

"No thanks." Filasek pumped the trigger once. Aiming at her left breast. For two seconds, the same length of time it took Oskar to rush through the swinging door, Helga sat without moving. The bullet in her heart stopped its function. A red stain spread across her chest as she began the bleed-out process.

"Have a seat next to your wife, Oskar." Filasek could see the man frozen in the doorway out of the corner of his right eye.

"Helga, don't die on me." Oskar rushed toward her. Filasek felt the breeze of his passing on the hair of his arms. Oskar kneeled in front of his wife and took her face in his hands.

"Good-bye." Blood spilled down her chin.

"It is not good-bye, but see you later," Oskar corrected with tearful voice.

"Sooner rather than later." Filasek grabbed the back of Oskar's neck and forced him to sit side by side with his dying wife. Filasek moved his grip around to the front of Oskar's neck and cut off the windpipe. Oskar gaped like a fish for air. There would be some bruising noticeable in an autopsy, but it wouldn't be ruled cause of death.

Filasek jammed the nose of his weapon between the teeth with a tinkling porcelain sound. He pulled the trigger.

Wiping down the hot gun, he placed it into Oskar's left hand, picked up the dead man's hand to where his mouth had been and let it drop to a natural position.

Oskar's right hand held his wife's left.

Filasek left it; it looked ordinary for a man to seek one last ounce of strength.

He picked up the suitcase of cash he had delivered, the bill of lading that gave the delivery address, and the sale papers he had signed. They were stacked on the side table with a triangle of blood droplets pointing to his name.

He washed his knife and plate and put them in the dish drainer to dry. Picking up his coat and taking the yellow rubber gloves from the kitchen, he left with everything he came with except the gun and two bullets.

Athens, Greece
Marble House Pension
1027 hours local time

Wakefield rolled to a sitting position in the rented bed of the ample hotel room. Her eyelids felt scratchy and her head throbbed in a dull ache at the back of her skull.

She remembered arriving at the beautiful hotel covered with bougainvillea the evening before. She glanced at her watch. "Have I been asleep all this time?" She held her head between fingers and massaged her scalp to alleviate the pain.

She looked down to see she was still wearing the rumpled clothing she had worn on the flight. She rubbed her eyes and flopped forward over her crossed legs on the bed.

"Well, I am here. Now what am I supposed to do?"

"I recommend a shower," came a voice from the anteroom.

Wakefield jerked up straight and was standing next to the bed on high defense without thinking. She heard the squeak of chair springs and took a step forward.

A dark head appeared around the corner of the half-lit room.

"Stand down, Judah. It's just me."

"Dietz! What are you doing in here? What are you doing here period?" She screeched "You almost gave me a heart attack!"

"You look as thunderous as Judge Pella when he got the paperwork dismissing your Afghanistan charges in open court." Judah watched Dietz hold a purposeful wince, giving her a chance to reassess her circumstances as she was more fully awake from the adrenaline charge. "I thought his cheery red cheeks were going to explode. You're not going to explode on me, are you Wakefield?"

Dietz looked disheveled, as if he had slept in his clothes too. It made sense; he was in her room.

Wakefield relaxed her posture, rolling her stiff shoulders back in wide circles. "What are you doing in my room, Dietz?"

He had a day and a half's growth on his chin and cheeks and his little black mustache was bent upward on one side. "I prayed." Dietz spit it out like chicken liver. He stepped inside the bedroom with Wakefield and dropped his weight against the doorframe.

His shoulders sagged. "Do you think he is still alive, Judah?" Dietz voice sounded fatherly for the first time since she had known him.

She smiled. She knew he was determining her psychological state, so she bounced back down on the springy bed with one leg folded underneath her and a bracing foot on the floor. "I have some hope." She felt her eyes water again. "But, whether it is just his body or we find him alive, I need some closure." She would not allow herself to dwell on the possibility of a future with a man she loved being lost a second time.

Dietz was past his phlegmatic mood and dressed when she came out of the bathroom. "What are your plans for the day?" He asked, his voice too bright. He adjusted the buttons on his Polo shirt.

"You never answered my question." Wakefield put it to him again. "What are you doing here?" She stared at the yellow shirt Dietz wore. She was not sure she had ever seen him out of a three piece suit unless he was in a tux.

"I took a vacation."

Wakefield felt something stir in her belly. "So you *did* have something to do with Rivers' mission."

"There was no mission, Judah. He did come to Langley and talked with one of his buddies who used to be a SEAL. He got some of our gear and took off on his own. That is the best I can piece together. I never talked to him, never gave him instruction, never gave him information."

"So why are you here?" She rocked back on the heels of her brown boots. She was getting tired of asking the same question.

"I," Dietz paused as if he was considering it for the first time. "I like Rivers. And I know you love him. And I like you, so." He shrugged as if the answer was apparent.

"So you came because," Wakefield shook her head, "you wanted to help me find him?" It was like pulling teeth from a tiger to get answers out of this CIA man.

"I suppose I didn't want to see you get hurt. I have lost too many men in the past year. I couldn't stand to lose you, too." Dietz frowned. His mustache still stuck out funny on the left side.

Wakefield sat down on the bed and pulled out her make-up bag. *Powder and mascara*, she decided as she glanced in the tiny mirror. "Are you planning to share this room with me, Dietz?" She rubbed a light lotion into her skin and concentrated on the pink line of a scar on her right cheek. It ran from a thumb's width underneath the middle of her eye at a slight angle to her jaw.

"Why haven't you had plastic surgery on that cheek, yet?" His voice sounded careful. "If it is a money thing, and the military won't cover it, I can have the Agency take care of the costs and any wages you miss in recovery."

Wakefield found Dietz's eyes on her and his Adam's apple bobbed as he swallowed. "Does it bother you, Dietz?"

He fidgeted with his fingers and Wakefield could read his discomfort no matter how he decided to answer. "I, uh," she let him flail about. "I suppose," his voice lurched, "I feel a measure of guilt every time I look at you."

Compassion fell over her and she turned her lips up sadly. "It was not your fault, Richmond."

"But you were beautiful before."

"Beauty is more than a flawless complexion. My desire is to be full of beauty inside and attract people through that." She paused as she assessed her current state of inner peace and beauty. "Unfortunately, I am not doing too well at the moment." She frowned.

"You'll do, Judah Wakefield. You're dealing with a lot."

Wakefield shot Dietz a thankful glance and finished brushing her eyelashes black. "Say, I couldn't possible have looked as scary as Judge Pella that day."

"Oh yes, you could have, Missy. I saw you both." The pair exchanged a little laugh.

"It wasn't my fault my apartment burned down under suspicious circumstances, and I had to find a new one and get some furniture to sleep on before setting a hearing date. All my paperwork was smoked. Uniforms, everything."

"Yeah, even though under-cover ops won't really be an option for us anymore, I thought all the press coverage of your actions in Berlin would be good for your court case—"

Wakefield interrupted with a groan, "But the coverage meant Pella knew exactly when I got back to U.S. soil. I so regret that last on-camera interview. I told Admiral Tamburillo I didn't want a big to-do. But he thought the PR would be good. Good for the Navy, sure, but I thought Pella was going to eat me alive." Judah shook her head at the remembrance.

"Did you have a plan for how to find Rivers once you got here?" Dietz changed the subject abruptly.

Wakefield shot Dietz a thankful glance and tucked her mascara back in the tiny clear bag.

"Not really. I have all his movements on the CD in my laptop. I thought I would copy off a photo from his service record and flash it around at some of the bars around town." Wakefield frowned. "That was as creative as I got. In the back of my mind, I guess I was hoping to find him safe in his hotel room when I got here." She sighed and traced the flowers in the bedspread. "I used to pretend the same thing right after my father died. I would dash into his bedroom and hope to find him laughing, folding his BDUs and saying that it was all a big joke." Judah looked at Dietz. "It never happened." She added needlessly. "It is scary how you revert to a child's behavior when you're afraid. Have you had any word from the camera man?"

Dietz offered her a sad smile and disappeared into the other room without a word. Wakefield stared after him as she brushed the tangles out of her long wet hair. He had a newspaper when he reappeared.

"I picked up an evening edition on my way in last night."

"How did you know where I was, by the way?"

Dietz's expression said, "Don't ask." He flipped open the black printed pages to the third page on the top half. He tossed it at her, picture-side up. "Samuel Gibson, a.k.a. Patrick, will be of no help. He's dead. He was filming when Rivers," Dietz broke off, "uh, did his stunt. I don't believe a word of the local story, but it was picked up by the Associated Press and is being distributed in the States in the morning. It makes for interesting reading."

Piraeus, **Port of Athens**
Saturday 28 September 2002
2:45 PM local time

Filasek parked his vehicle in the secured lot at the Athens ship port, *Piraeus*, and scanned the area for Raul. The briefcase stuffed with the advance money equally balanced the chemical samples he was bringing back and he carried one in each hand, but they were both heavy. "Where are you, man?" He topped the little rise that shielded the view of the parking lot from the in-coming ships and boats.

Pier 5, slip 27 was cordoned off with yellow crime tape. Two buoys floated ten meters out to hold the square of the slip from being contaminated. There was no boat to take him home.

Filasek dropped the two cases in frustration. "Terrific, now what am I going to do? I already bought two cigarette boats and an airplane in the last two months."

Filasek picked up his cases again. He scanned the area. "Finding a boat for hire in a busy port should not be a difficulty."

A ferry bell clanged as it pulled away from Dock 4. Filasek squinted to read the writing on the top billboard. Destination: Poros. He groaned and shook his head. He found himself sweating. Coupled with carrying the two cases, the sun beat down on him. "It is too hot to be September." He growled in Farsi. "Nothing is going right today."

"Oh, sometimes it gets far hotter in September." An unfamiliar voice chided him from behind in Farsi.

Filasek whirled around. A bleached blond man in his early twenties whose skin looked as though he worshipped the sun daily stood there grinning with white teeth.

"Are you here on vacation? I could set you up with a taxi boat anywhere you want to go. Show you the sights on the islands, take you to the best place for seafood that is minutes out of the water. Where are you going, Farsi-man?"

The young man was certainly a salesman. "Allah smiles on me today," *finally,* Filasek added critically in his mind. He improvised. "The house where I am vacationing this month was to send a boat to pick me up. However, I do not see them. Do you know Poros?" Filasek played the game, while still scanning for Raul.

"Oh, sure, about 40 nautical miles from here, a short trip. I could do it in 35 minutes. Only 70 euro for you, my Farsi-friend."

"I thought the guide book said 35 miles." Filasek cocked his head to one side.

"Who are you going to believe? A guidebook made of paper or me, I have been sailing the waters of Greece for sixty centuries. I know where the fish live and where they die. I hear the cry of siren." The blond man raised his eyebrows in question. He obviously saw nothing strange in his statements.

Filasek stepped back from the young man. *What ward did he escape from?* When the man reached over to pick up Filasek's cases, Filasek smacked his hands away. "I will carry them."

"This way to my boat. I am on pier 5." The man with his wispy curls hanging down his back sauntered toward the water. "It is the same pier where a boat spontaneously combusted just two days ago. I will take you by the site. People are saying that it was a drug boat, but I know better." Filasek sped his pace and leaned forward to hear this man's take on the explosion. "I can hear the spirit of the boat crying. It felt rushed by the engine and wanted to float over the seas and enjoy life at a slower pace." The man's bright teeth glinted again as he turned and smiled.

Filasek hesitated a step. He began to wonder if he should get into a boat with this psycho.

Pier 5 contained more foot traffic than Filasek remembered ever seeing. It took all his concentration to avoid ramming anyone with his heavy cases as the blond man plowed down the middle of the pier.

A whistle pierced the air stopping everyone in their tracks. Filasek traced the sound to his right and behind him.

It was a welcome sight.

Raul stood on the bow of a shiny white cigarette boat waving both arms over his head. Filasek looked furtively around to see whose attention he had attracted. Everyone on the pier. Thankfully, Raul did not call out any names.

"That must be him. The man who was to pick me up." Filasek carefully stayed in the character he had created. He pulled a five-euro bill from his wallet. "For your trouble," he pressed it into the sun worshipper's hand and he scurried over to Raul. "Where have you been?" He snapped.

"Right here, Boss. You wouldn't look up. I did not think it prudent to leave the boat after what happened last time."

Filasek looked at him with scorn. "The man who blew up the last one is in our custody now—or he had better be." Filasek questioned Raul as to the outcome of his assignment.

The man nodded once. "You want me to get those?" Raul gestured to the pair of cases.

Filasek dropped them on the concrete pier and scrambled down to scrutinize his third new boat.

The young water-taxi driver wandered over to observe as Raul loaded the cases one at a time and lashed them to the deck. Filasek cringed as the two men began to talk. He did not have to strain to hear the young man's loud comments. "You need correct your guide book. It is 41 nautical miles to Poros, not 35."

Raul's face crunched up, and for a moment Filasek wondered how he would react. Raul reached out with both hands to shake the strange young man's hand. "Thank you. I will be sure that the boss does just that."

Filasek sighed with relief. He was not sure what the mental hospital escapee would have done.

"Let's get going," Filasek bellowed, *before anything else happens.*

Forty minutes later, Raul tied the boat off at the dock under his villa. "Take this up to the house, I am going to put this one away." Each of the men took one briefcase. Filasek wandered down the rocky beach and to the plant entrance in his neighbor's vast basement.

He pressed his palm into the correct rock and the six-foot rock that sealed the entranceway slid back.

A steam whistle blasted at his ears as a chemical burning smell assaulted his nose. The Spyros family was buzzing around frenetically hitting buttons and yelling back and forth at each other. "What is going on in here?" Filasek bellowed.

"Shut the door. Quick!" One of the chemical-suited men yelled at him in an agitated hollow voice. He could not distinguish which Spyros it was. "Don't breathe! Get a mask on. We'll have this under control in a minute."

The alarm blasted on. His brain pulsated along with it as he held his breath and slapped a mask over his mouth and nose.

"What is going wrong now?" He muttered.

Filasek slumped into a cold metal chair by the door.

Chapter Ten

Filasek took tiny breaths until the alarm finally abated. He watched in wonder as the Spyros family began congratulating themselves, hugging each other and shaking hands.

There was no mistaking their smiles. "What is going on?" Filasek roared through his mask.

Andros Spyros removed the white chemical suit's hood and his voice sounded normal again. "Everything is fine. You just walked in at a critical point in the process. At the end of the third cycle, all of the newly formed compound has 6.85 seconds to be put inside the airless containers where it will stay until distribution."

Andros's wife, Maya, spoke as she removed her mask too. "Which means that we can take a break from 24-hour watches this evening. The next batch is complete." Her grin appealed to him. Her curly brown hair was frizzed from being under the protective chemical suit. "The last batch will wait until tomorrow."

"Actually, I've brought a sampling of the chemicals I purchased abroad. The rest will be arriving by ship in the next three to four weeks." Filasek pushed the case in front of him with his feet. "We may have one or two days overlap, but it should be timely." Filasek saw two of the brothers exchange sidelong glances in the back by the computer.

Andros opened the case. "Good brand, very pure elements." He commented.

"I want another sample to take with me day after tomorrow. I am going to see if I can find a test market for it, and maybe a sales market for its use after this run is complete."

"Should not be a problem. I have 18 batches divided into 126 units ready for distribution in the deep freeze room now." Maya knocked her head toward the back of the basement where she tracked the finished product.

Filasek entered his own leased villa by the downstairs kitchen door that overlooked the water. He ate a handful of hulled strawberries on his way to the basement.

David Rivers lay shirtless on his side in the small cell. Filasek leaned against the metal bars and saw bruising on his ribs and head. A nasty gash on his forehead looked like it was beginning to heal.

"Has he been out the whole time?" Filasek asked Raul without looking back at him.

"He started to wake up on the boat ride yesterday, but I stopped on the water and gave him the next injection. Except when I went to pick you up, I have been with him the entire time." Raul walked over and stood on his left and held onto the cage. "It took as much to put him out the first time as it would a horse."

"Go ahead and let him come to next time. I want to begin our negotiations." Filasek felt his lips turn up at the prospect. He smoothed his beard and mustache with his right hand. "I hope he resists for a while. I picked up a new technique that I would like to try on someone of high constitution."

Raul's chuckle sounded deep. "Let me know if you want help."

"For this wounded lion? Don't count on it."

Athens
Monday 30 September 2002
1834 hours

Wakefield sipped her tonic water with almond syrup in the eighth bar she and Dietz had visited that day. "I have to use the ladies room before we leave this time. I feel like I am floating away. I've never had so many drinks in three days in my life."

Dietz chuckled, his mustache turning to the side. "You don't actually have to drink them, you know. Just order them. You might as well take that break now." Dietz nodded to a blue-lit hallway by the door leading to what had to be the kitchen area. "I can't imagine that we are going to get many more people to look at that photo until they get some more customers. And that won't happen for a few more hours."

As they walked down the congested street, the streetlamps began to pop on. "Where to next?" Wakefield was dragging. "Not a single real lead in three days of talking to people. This is my record low, I think." She frowned. Every day without a lead it was more likely that David was dead. But where was his body?

"Did I ever tell you about the time that I tracked a man in Saigon for eighteen days?"

Wakefield grunted. "I didn't even know you were in Vietnam." She looked at him. Wrinkles around his eyes and mouth, his lined forehead and cheeks were visible where she had not seen them before. "My father served during the Vietnam Era."

"I've been around a long time." Dietz's smile did not reach his eyes.

She smiled softly. "Not *too* long."

"I was one of the youngest field agents at the time, and the CIA was in country under the guise of The Phoenix Program. Some people called us assassination squads. The VC were brutal, but I wonder if we were worse." Dietz looked to the ocean horizon beyond the Athens streets, and Wakefield could almost see Dietz take himself back to the jungles of Vietnam.

"What I am about to tell you is classified, and I'll deny it if you tell anyone."

Wakefield nodded as she walked shoulder to shoulder with the director.

"Ho Chin Dang was a North Vietnamese Viet Cong. One of the cruelest men I have ever come across, even today." Dietz shook his head in his faraway place. "He had set up the execution of a group of American P.O.W.s and let the information leak to our boys. When the Americans came busting into the bamboo camp to effect a rescue, Dang's men ambushed the team of 37 PRUs (Provincial Reconnaissance Units) and strung them up by their wrists in trees, just two feet off the ground. All but one man. That man they tied higher. They had exactly 37 strands of rope. When the animals came that night, they chewed up the bodies of the men and their cries haunted him. The silence by midnight was worse.

"In the morning light he could see that the animals had left the heads. Some of the men still had shoulders and chests left. By 10 AM the crows had finished their work with the eyeballs and Ho Chin Dang came back with a friend.

"He took pictures of everything and then cut the living man free and handed him the roll of film."

Wakefield laid a hand across her churning stomach. "I need to sit down a moment." She swallowed and melted into a slatted wooden bench in front of a bakery that was closed for the evening. The yeasty smell that lingered around the shop did nothing for her nausea. "Someone on our side betrayed the plan. How else would they have known how many PRUs were coming?"

"That is what I figured at the time, too. Ho Chin Dang was on the top of the list of wanted men. I was sent after him with every resource at my disposal. I spent seventeen days tracking him down to a Catholic Church just outside Saigon. It felt as though I was in one of those carnival funhouses with mirrors and uneven floors, and I couldn't find my way out." Dietz stretched his feet out in front of him on the bench.

"I don't think I slept during those seventeen days. When I spotted him inside the walls of the church grounds, I called in an air strike. Of course, it took a bit longer in those days." Dietz's shoulders shook as he tried to chuckle, but could not seem to push the sound past his vocal chords. "The place went up in smoke. Even back then our flyboys were the best. Still, Dang managed to escape."

Wakefield tilted her head to look at Dietz. *How does one manage to escape an air strike?* she wondered.

"His mistake was fleeing in my direction. I was watching the entire church compound through my scope on the far side away from the city. Three snipers were with me. I assigned two of them a leg and the last one an arm. I wanted to talk to Ho Chin Dang."

"I think you wanted to torture Ho Chin Dang." Wakefield softly spoke.

"Very perceptive."

"You were sent because you were the only one who had seen his face, aren't you? You were the man they left hanging alive."

Dietz's nose flared. His body stiffened beside her, but he did not speak.

"I don't blame you or condemn, Dietz. I don't know what I would do in a similar situation. I imagine I might want to set the man on fire and give him a preview of hell."

Dietz turned sharply, his eyes dark. "I did." She could barely hear his words.

Wakefield was shocked silent. The hard lines in Dietz's face came into focus in her mind. She grappled with what God was revealing to her. It had been months since she been quiet enough to focus on what God was saying to her about anyone else.

She softened her voice. "That is when you put God out of your worldview, isn't it? The world was just too ugly for it to have been created by a loving God."

"And if God is not loving, I decided He was not worth believing in."

Wakefield held her tongue a moment longer as her spirit quickened.

"Until the other day," Dietz whispered. She was not sure she had heard the words at all and she leaned closer to him. "On the airplane coming here from my layover at Heathrow. I could have sworn I heard God speaking to me." He shook his head.

Dietz shifted his weight forward on the bench and rose with a straight back. Wakefield watched him walk off in the same direction they had been headed before. She decided after about 10 steps that he was not coming back, so she scrambled after him.

"…Strangest thing." She heard him mutter as she threaded her arm under his elbow.

"Let's go back to the Pension. We can rest up and go back out tonight when there is more action."

Marble House Pension
Odoszinni 35A, Koukaki
8:50 PM

Dietz tossed his arms heavily into the bedcovers. He rolled over onto his left side and faced the window for the third time, or was it the fourth? "God why won't you just leave me alone?"

I did leave you alone. For 25 years. You are the one who started talking to me again, remember?

"This is too weird. God is not supposed to talk to humans?" Dietz buried his head in the pillow and tried to block out the words. "When did I concede that God was real?"

Did you make up the rules?

The question coming from the One who did, was not pleasant. "Look, I just want to rest. I am tired and I need to rest." As his voice echoed back into his ears, the whine grated on his spine.

He flopped over to his right and stared at the bathroom light.

Rest is exactly what I am offering you. You have carried your memories, your guilt, your shame, too long. I have already paid the price for your sin, you just have to give it to me.

Dietz lay still for what felt like hours. The words churned in his mind. The travel alarm beside his bed began to chirp. "Finally," he sighed and rolled out of bed.

He picked up the phone next to the clock and rang Wakefield's room.

"Hello?" her sleepy voice traveled over the wires.

"It's time."

"Oh," Her chuckle sounded almost embarrassed. "Dietz. I think I have spent too much time in bars. Now I am dreaming about them." She was quiet a moment. It sounded like there was something she wanted to add, so he waited. "Does the name *Papandreou*, mean anything to you."

Dietz paused; he could almost feel the synapses energy charging in the electrons of his brain. "I can't believe I forgot."

"Forgot what, Dietz? I rarely dream in specifics like a name? Did you know about this?"

"Gibson mentioned that name as a place he had tracked the man he thought was an arms dealer at the time. It turned out to be Rivers. It is located a rather squalid neighborhood, if I remember correctly."

"I am scared to rely on your memory now, Director." Wakefield said.

"Sorry, Commander." Dietz knew he did not sound sorry at all. "It is not my fault that I forgot and did not connect the two."

"I am not a commander anymore," she whispered. "Dietz, this is what you do for a living. Forget it, let's just go." He heard her bed squeak as she stood up and sighed. "There is no use wasting time arguing."

Papandreou
Kantara 11348
2130 hours

Dietz held open the door to the bar and food shop. "Just a second," Judah pulled back after a glance inside.

Dietz let the glass front door fall shut. He pulled them out of the traffic pattern. "What is it?" His voice had dropped low.

Wakefield laughed. "You don't have to be so spy-like about everything. I just wanted to say I am sorry for being so hard on you earlier. It's not your fault you did not connect this bar faster."

Dietz shrugged in acknowledgement of her apology. "You're on edge," he said. "It can't be helped." Judah thought it should be helped, but did not say it. "Now," Dietz continued. "I would like you to appear alone when you enter. Be extra cautious. This is the *Mafiosi*'s favorite place to arrange arms deals."

"I can handle myself. Besides," she squinted her eyes in a teasing manner, "I have you *and* God watching my six this time."

Dietz's eyes rolled over and she guessed what he thought of that idea. "Let's see what we can find out."

Wakefield grimaced as she ducked around a smoked side of beef that hung near the doorway. Haunches of cow and ham hocks swung from the ceiling in the cool, dark outer room. *The entrance to the Mafia bar is a meat hall? How appropriate.* Every mob movie she had ever seen came creeping back into her consciousness.

She could see a portion of the beer hall in the back room from where she stood. Thick glass thunked as a toast went up somewhere in the room. Silverware clinked and the lights rotated from blue to yellow to green. An American hard rock song functioned as the buzzing bottom layer of sound and all the patrons sounded as if they were competing for the prize for talking the loudest.

Judah felt conspicuous walking in. Men were the majority of the customers and they all looked as relaxed as regulars. Too many heads followed her progression to the long mahogany bar that dominated the right side of the room. She cautioned herself against showing any anxiety and stiffened her neck in an effort to appear more confident.

"What can I get for you?" The man tending bar asked. His head was as bald as a newborn opossum, and he had squinty black eyes that matched the animal-like appearance.

She realized she was not doing a very good job undercover when he addressed her in English. "I am looking for someone." She took one look at his wrinkled lips and decided, "But I'd like a drink as well. I don't suppose you can conjure up any hot tea back there?"

"We have everything drinking." He boasted. "Got a picture?" the man's bushy Greek eyebrows rounded upward.

While she took her folded black and white copy of Rivers' service picture from the inside pocket of her blue fleece vest, the man dug under the counter for a cup and saucer. "English Breakfast or Herbal Lemon?" His voice sounded muffled from its buried position under the wooden length of counter.

"English Breakfast with a dollop of cream, please." Wakefield could feel the eyes of patrons on her back. She understood, *I'd stare too, if some foreign woman walked into my favorite bar and ordered hot tea.* She decided she would just have to ignore it and get on with finding Rivers. She smoothed the lines out of the white paper and spun the picture around for the barkeep to study.

"Have you seen him?" She had to force herself to watch for the man's reaction instead of studying the picture with him.

He plunked down her hot water and the teabag. The paper-wrapped teabag slid to the edge of the counter and stopped against her belly where she leaned against the mahogany. "Maybe I have, maybe I haven't." His words came out slow and contemplative, but she couldn't decide if he was playing her or he was really trying to remember.

He picked up the paper and held it under a light that did not change colors behind the mahogany bar. Judah dipped her tea bag slowly and held her breath.

"Yeah, yeah. I think I see him. He here three nights past or four maybe. He from the States too." Wakefield did not bother to affirm the comment. It was obvious from his naval uniform that he was American. "Yeah," the man's head bobbed, his chin pushed his lips into a frown. "But that wasn't the first time. He came in, let me think, two other nights, too."

Wakefield finally breathed. *We found him. At least he was here.* "Did you talk to him? Did he say anything about where he was headed or what he was working on? Did he look healthy?"

The barkeep ran his wet rag over the counter and tossed the paper back to her. He ran his tongue between his top teeth and lips. "I not know." His left eye closed and reopened. "Maybe if you sit at booth and order good food," he shrugged, "I have time remembering."

Wakefield saw the extortion for what it was, and hoped her wry smile told him that she did. The information was more valuable than any price he would charge for his food. "Bring me the best meal of the house. I'll wait right there." She pointed to a red vinyl booth set with napkins for four.

"Very good." His grin choked her insides. It looked as though he knew something she did not. She stiffened her back and walked as elegantly as she could on the sticky concrete floor to the corner booth. She wished she could sit with her back to the crowd so she did not have to watch them stare at her, but that was not an option.

She saw Dietz walk in behind a couple who both had long black hair, body art and facial piercings. She squinted trying to determine if there was one of each gender or not.

She sipped her tea and let her eyes roam around the room. A foursome poker game occupied the opposite corner from her. Two men watching a television with closed captioning sat at a table toward the middle of the room. She did not recognize the actors but it must have been a comedy, because the two men kept punching each other in the arm and laughing. A round table of eight men dressed like thugs sat listening and nodding to a man in a gray suit with freshly trimmed hair. The other five tables in the middle held two groups of two and one table each of three and four. One empty. She could see the bulges of handguns under the majority of the men's shirts.

The barkeep brought her a refill of hot water, but no new teabag after he served the newcomers. He slid into the booth with her. His knees grazed hers. "Meal be around 40 minutes from now. But I guarantee, it will be one you'll never forget. You do like fish?" He turned up his nose.

"I can eat it." Wakefield smiled for appearance. *Ugh, I hate fish.* "What was Rivers doing in here?" Wakefield asked.

"Ah, his name is Rivers. He did not mention it while he was here."

"What *did* he mention?" She leaned over the table, not wanting to miss a word.

"He was also looking for someone. A man named Arafeh Filasek. The gentleman has a house on Poros and sometimes comes in to recruit new help. Your man was asking about him."

Wakefield dropped her back against the red vinyl seat. "Do you know if they ever connected?" She had seen on video that eventually they did, but she was searching for information from before the climax.

"I think, I don't know. I must go stir." He slid out, grazing her knees again.

"You are doing the cooking yourself?"

"But of course. I am the best." He shot a cocky grin in her direction.

Wakefield followed him with her eyes until he disappeared behind a pair of swinging white doors. At least she thought they were white. "Who can tell with these stupid lights changing colors all the time?" She muttered.

Dietz sat at the bar with his back to her at the bar, sipping his cocktail through the stirrer and reading a newspaper.

Wakefield worked hard to keep from rolling her eyes. Let's see if we can look more out of place, Mr. Director of Counterintelligence.

Chapter Eleven

Filasek touched the hot wand to the American's ribs again. The man squirmed against the bonds that strapped him to the table. Like the previous two days, he would not cry out. "Tell me where your lovely friend is and I will set you free, even take you back to the Athens airport myself."

The man clamped his lips stubbornly. He stared straight ahead.

"Come on, Rivers," Filasek baited the man. "She can't stay squirreled away forever. I *will* find her, but it would make me happy," he touched the wand against a steel wool pad in his gloved hand to create the desired effect of sparks and heat, "if you would tell me sooner rather than later."

"Lieutenant Commander David Rivers. United States Navy. Service number four six four three four seven seven eight one."

Filasek growled. The man was maddening. But he was also the perfect bait to getting to Wakefield. If he could secure pictures of her talking to known terrorists and then release them to the American press after the November strike, it would avenge the havoc she wrecked on his household and ten years of weapons stocking in Afghanistan.

"Water," Filasek called out to the idiot who was supposed to be helping but kept getting in the way.

The man in his early twenties gestured with his foot to a five-gallon paint container that was just over half full. Filasek was beginning to wonder if the man really was off in the head. "I am surrounded by imbeciles," he muttered remembering the water taxi man from whom he had barely escaped days earlier.

The bucket was heavy and awkward as he hoisted it above the American spy.

"Perhaps you should get a lower torture table so you don't have so much trouble lifting." Rivers sniggered at him. It was the first words he had uttered other than his name, rank and serial number.

Filasek dumped the entire three gallons on his face. As the man blew the water out of his mouth and nose and shook his head, Filasek taunted, "I thought you were coming after me. I am disappointed. You said if I hurt your whore, you would kill me." He breathed in deeply, pumped his chest with a closed fist and let out the air in a sigh. "It still feels like I am alive."

Filasek leaned over him and saw Rivers' nose flared white. "Does that make you angry, Lieutenant Commander David Rivers?" Filasek thought he performed a good imitation of a shrink. He laughed as he pulled back and reached for the steel wool. *The man is too stubborn to let me go easy on him.*

He dragged the hot and charged metal pad down Rivers' leg. The singed hair sizzled. It stank. "All you have to do is tell me one thing today. You tell me if she is still living in the U.S. then I will bring you a meal of fresh lamb and vegetables and hot buttery pita bread. Mmm that sounds good. Now it is simple. Just tell me if she is still in the U.S."

Filasek leaned in over the sailor. He could see the pain compounding in his eyes. He was right the table was too high.

"No thank you." Rivers coughed the last of the water from his windpipe. "I am fasting."

Raul clattered down the stone steps just then with a cordless telephone. "You are not going to get very good reception down here, but it is my brother on the phone, and you are going to want to take his call." Raul shook the black house phone like he was trying to entice a dog to take a snack from his hand.

Filasek felt his upper lip curl at the gesture. He nodded to Raul who bounded back up the basement stairs. Filasek leaned over Rivers again. "Even your Jesus only lasted 40 days," he whispered.

*****

Rivers held back the relief he felt when he realized his captor was taking a break. Hostage training was hard in Basic, but there was always a built-in safety, if only in his mind. The trainers were not actually going to kill him, just make it feel as though they would.

He closed his eyes to keep the instruments of torture out of his sight so he could build his resistance back up. "Jesus, if you will give me the same strength you had for those 40 days in the wilderness, well, I don't know what I could give you that you don't already own, but then I can feel I put up a good fight against this enemy."

Rivers forced his shoulders to relax against the table and let his wrists take some of the pressure for a moment. "I am nowhere near breaking yet, Father, but I also know that day will come. Please pour your strength and hope into my heart. Build a reserve in me." Rivers let the muscles in his back take over the stretching pain again and relieved his wrists. I could not bear to know that Judah was going through this nightmare. Help me be like you, my Lord, a lamb and even when led to slaughter, you did not open your mouth.

Filasek's tread sounded again on the stairs. Rivers found him quickly as he descended. The short man's smile scared him more than the sparks that the horrible steel wool threw off. Rivers arrested his imagination. The cat would boast about his canary soon enough.

"I just got a call from Raul's brother," Filasek gestured upstairs and then clasped his hands together in front of his chest. "But you know that don't you." His chuckle stirred anger in Rivers' chest. "What you don't know is that he owns *Papandreou.* You remember the bar over on *Kantara,* in Athens.

Rivers felt his heckles rise. Of course he remembered the place. He had spent most of three nights there.

"It seems your little whore is in town looking for you and she is waiting for her meal at the bar." Filasek came closer, gliding over the concrete floor like a snake. His head, shoulders and top of his torso never joggled as he came.

Rivers could smell Filasek's odor over his cologne. He kept silent and breathed through his mouth.

"I am thinking of delivering her a goat sandwich instead of the fish she ordered."

Reacting out of instinct, forgetting his current state of rest, he blurted out, "How do you know about that?" He snapped his jaw tight realizing his blunder. He and Wakefield standardly joked about becoming jam on somebody's goat sandwich.

"I know everything." Filasek leaned over his face and Rivers could see the root follicles of his beard. "I can read your mind, Rivers." The man circled his first finger above Rivers' eyes, but Rivers kept his eyes in a strict military glaze. Sixteen years of practice don't die easily. Filasek touched down his circling finger right between David's eyes, made the shape of a gun, and pulled the thumb trigger with a smirk. "See you soon."

Filasek told the young man to leave him on the table before he disappeared upstairs. Rivers squinted his eyes in the dark room and flexed his back muscles against the metal cuffs on his wrists again. *It can't be her*, he told himself, *she hates fish. Her father told me so. She would never order fish, so Wakefield is safe.*

Papandreou
Kantara Street, Athens
10:20 PM local

Filasek entered the familiar establishment and nodded to Raul's brother, Racine. He catalogued the place as safe as he made the rounds with his eyes. He recognized nearly everyone in the place. Most had been in his employ at one time or another.

The man sipping a drink and reading a newspaper was probably with her. He had CIA written on his posture. Filasek couldn't see his face, but the man was too alert for a bar patron.

There she sat. The object of his desire.

She looked just as he remembered: arrogant, American and decidedly female. His remembrance that he had carved on her face was fading into her skin. *Maybe I will give her a matching pair.*

He felt more giddy than when he had gotten bin Laden's approval to help with the November strike on the U.S.

She sat studying a piece of paper and sipping out of a coffee mug. *Enjoy it while you can*, he thought.

Racine held up a platter behind the bar.

Filasek nodded and trod over to pick it up. "Mm, looks like a good red sauce."

"Cranberry salad." Racine smiled.

He stuck his finger into the pulverized berry and nut concoction. He brought it to his mouth. "Nice and tart." He grinned and could not help adding, "Just like your customer." He took a plastic bag from his pocket and crushed the two pills that were inside between his fingers. He stirred it into the food with the finger he had just licked.

Filasek slid the plates in front of her without saying a word and waited for her to look up.

*****

Wakefield kept her head down to stare at the food privately. It would not do to insult the man after he went to the work to prepare the fish for her. It looked interesting. The saucy red salad looked sort of like the cranberry stuff her mom made during the holidays. Deep-green asparagus stalks rested like Lincoln Logs in a pool of white sauce. A little overdone for bar food but normal enough. It was the fish that made the meal unappealing. Its single black eye stared at her.

She noted the man still stood at her right shoulder, waiting for some comment for his trouble. "Well, it looks good enough. But what took an hour to prepare?" She looked up then with a teasing grin.

Her blood dropped cold and her heart choked.

"We had to catch the fish." Filasek leaned toward her. The words, she knew, did not apply to the fish on her plate.

Oh God, please help, she prayed as she extended her hand to sweep the opposite side of the booth. "Won't you sit down, Mr. Filasek? I trust the veil is not a problem in Greece." She cocked an eyebrow.

"Thank you, I will." Filasek slid onto the red vinyl. His knees did not brush hers. As he moved Wakefield took the time to look at the barkeeper. He grinned in her direction as if he mistook her look as one of gratitude.

"So, to what do I owe the..." She could not force herself to say *pleasure* of the visit. Her lips mutinied. She compromised with, "...this visit." She pushed her plate back. This fish and company stank in three seconds, not three days.

He pressed his fingers to the rim of her plate and pushed it back toward her a fraction of an inch. "Don't let me keep you from your meal."

It felt strange to have someone stare at her while she ate. The asparagus was excellent; she scraped the last of the sauce up with her fork, stalling for time. The cranberry salad sauce tasted of brown sugar. She made note to add a pinch to her mother's recipe.

Wakefield searched the library of her mind for some neutral topic of conversation. Even baseball would not work. *The weather?* She wondered.

Just when she was about to open her mouth, Filasek leaned in. "I knew Rivers would be the perfect bait."

She felt her heart stop and start again. If the surprises kept coming, she thought she might need to have a pacemaker installed. "Is he still alive?" She held her breath as Filasek leaned his head to the left and then right.

"Depends on your definition of life."

"So he *is* alive." *Thank you, Jesus.* Judah tapped the pan-fried fish tail with the tines of her upside-down fork.

"That is up to you." Filasek pushed back from the table and she felt like a specimen under a microscope. He licked his lips and stroked his beard.

She remembered him doing that in the desert. It made her want to shave him then. Now, she thought, *I might take pleasure in plucking that beard out.* She sighed and tiredness waved over her. She stared at the fish's eye. *Forgive me, Lord.*

"How is it up to me?" She touched her forehead. The sinus cavity above her eyes was beginning to pound.

"I will exchange your life for his."

Filasek's words tangled in the neurons jumping from one brain lobe to the other. The room was beginning to spin. The flashing lights. *Why won't they just stay one color?* Her brain begged for mercy.

Drugs...I've been drugged. Stupid.

Filasek's sneer drew closer and fell away as her focus diminished. With her last savings of energy and coherence, she pushed the plate toward her enemy. *Move legs*, she commanded. *Stand up.*

The world shrank lower as her body tried to comply. "Take me to him, now." Her words sounded too loud in her ears. *Shh*, she begged the swirling people.

Black fog edged into her intermittent blinking vision. When the world tilted left and did not right itself, the blackness closed to a five percent tunnel of vision. Enough to see the floor rush up to meet her.

*****

Dietz sat at the bar, his back side beginning to numb while he contemplated how to play out the charade. Filasek he recognized in the bar mirror as soon as the man entered the doorway.

Dietz did not want to let Wakefield out of his sight, but he knew he might get more leads to the terrorist's activities and contacts if he trailed them with the tracker on Wakefield's credit card.

He only heard the people approaching from behind one second before hands gripped his upper arms. It did not appear he would have a choice now. "Unhand me!" Dietz thought he had better play an offended American now.

The crash of a body, her body, sounded above the din and he squirmed around to look. "Hey! What's going on here?" He yelled in English. He added a loud string of curses for good measure and tried to shrug out of the men's grasp.

In the mirror, Dietz saw Filasek motion a man over from the doorway. Dietz recognized him from his brief performance on the waterfront video. Filasek's man picked up Wakefield from the floor. Dietz heard her hair slap the man's jacket as he slung her midsection over his shoulder roughly. "Hey, what are you doing to that girl? You can't do that." Dietz protested and squirmed again. "What's wrong with the rest of you people?" Dietz accused raising his voice more. "Don't let him get away with this!"

Patrons at the table either watched with passive attention or ignored the altercation altogether. One of the men pointed a remote and turned up the volume on the television.

One of the detainers loosened a hand from the bruising hold on his arm and Dietz felt a palm on his scalp. The powerful digging fingers made an unmistakable suggestion that he turn his head and mind his own business.

Filasek passed behind Dietz on his way to the door. "Take care of the loudmouth after we leave," Filasek ordered the two Sampsons.

"*Outside* my establishment," the barkeeper stressed. "It was too hard to get the blood off the concrete last time." The two thugs chuckled a little too hard.

"Don't forget her purse," the dark-skinned man playing cards called out.

Filasek walked back to pick up the bag. "How much does she owe you, Racine?"

"Eighteen euro." He did not look at her tab. Dietz stared the man down, but the barkeeper didn't even bother to glance his direction.

Terrific, Dietz slumped on the barstool, feeling every minute of his 64 years. What was the CIA motto that was drilled into the head of every wet recruit on the Farm? Never get caught.

Filasek rummaged through the bag that Wakefield had so meticulously packed that morning. "Cash or credit?" Filasek joked.

Time stopped for Dietz as the barkeeper finished wiping down the spotless counter and threw the rag into the stainless steel sink. "I'll take cash if she has it. Saves me two percent."

Filasek threw a twenty euro note on the counter. It slid over the edge onto the rows of double-stacked clean glasses. "Keep the change." Filasek waved and disappeared through the doorway.

Dietz counted five seconds before the two thugs picked him up bodily and dragged him outside. Just to annoy them, Dietz let his heels drag and made them support his weight. *Make them expend as much energy as possible before ol' Diet-man gets ahold of them*, he thought with enthusiasm.

He sent up thanks to whichever director before him had implemented mandatory physical readiness reviews once a year. He was up to date on his punches, throws and kicks and would not embarrass himself as a relic fist-fighter from WWII.

His nose smarted at the putrid smell that permeated the meat locker. He did not remember it smelling as pungent on his trip inside the bar. *I was a bit preoccupied, I suppose.*

As if by some silent signal, both men dropped him at the same time.

The ancient stones that pushed through cracked concrete also tried to push through the skin on his shins, elbow, and shoulder. He used the time down to reach into his breast pocket. From behind came a racking kick to his kidneys. Dietz kept up his American tourist mutterings. "Can't even go into a bar for a drink on vacation any more. Europe's getting worse than New York." Finally, he wrapped his fingers around the cold pen.

Dietz rolled up to his knees. "Guys, guys. I'll go home now. Just leave me alone."

The kidney kicker shouted a Greek phrase that Dietz had never heard. *Maybe it is not Greek*, he thought as they hauled him the rest of the way to his feet. But he understood it to mean his new home would be hell.

The second man's fingers dug into his shoulder as he backed him up against the alley wall of the bar. It would be a perfect place to kick off. Dietz rebounded into the man on his right. Reaching forward, the silver pen caught the man's attention and his eyes followed it to his black T-shirt.

Dietz kicked the other man away with his left foot. He pressed the pen over the man's heart and twisted his fingers.

A blade like a hole-puncher pressed through his shirt and skin and deposited a round pellet of nerve agent into the flesh above his heart and lungs. The gel casing dissolved on contact, spreading deadly poison into the man's nervous system. Then to his pulmonary system. Then his respiratory system.

When the circular blade retracted into the silver pen a puff of gunpowder tattooed the skin. It would appear to any coroner that the man had been shot by a .9 mm at close range and the bullet had simply vanished without an exit wound.

The man fell over dead in three seconds. His brain did not have time to register more than the sting of a paper cut. Too bad.

The second man, however was now back on his feet and wary of the silvery pen. When he aimed a long-legged kick at Dietz's pen hand, Dietz loosened his grip. The pen flew from his fingers, and the man's attention followed the arc of its flight. Dietz did too. He would have to know where to retrieve it in a minute.

The second thug shuffled forward with an open-mouth grin. Dietz could see rotting teeth even in the lamplight. "What will you do now?" he asked in rocky English with an evil laugh.

Dietz answered as he made his move with the practice of eighty-six hours in the past six months. "I don't require instruments—" he chopped across the man's Adam's apple crushing it with a powerful hand, "to kill you."

The man leaned forward trying to suck air into his lungs.

Dietz brought a more precise blow with his right hand between the first and second vertebra in the man's neck. The bone broke and severed the central connection between the man's head and body without the mess of decapitation.

The body dropped face-first on the stony concrete. Dietz examined him without touching the body. "Lugo would be proud." Dietz pronounced to the night air. Lugo was the 280-pound, bald Italian-American CIA trainer who had worked overtime perfecting Dietz's right-handed blow.

Dietz collected his pen and scurried to the end of the alley to track Wakefield. He walked a little taller than when he had arrived. But glancing left then right and left again in the street, only a few people milled around. No Filasek. No Hulk. No Wakefield.

Chapter Twelve

Richmond Dietz let his beard growth stay for a fourth day. He stared at his reflection as he brushed his teeth. Even on vacation he drew the line at personal cleanliness. He could not remember a single four-day stretch since he turned 15 that he had gone without shaving. Well, maybe in country, but he couldn't be sure.

His yellow button-down smocked shirtsleeves billowed around him, hiding his slight paunch about the middle as Dietz transferred his suitcase and shaving kit to Wakefield's room and sat down at her desk to track her and, hopefully, Filasek.

The PDA tracking software created the outline of the Greek Islands, including the mainland that contained Athens. A dot blinked on the northwest shore of an island not too many miles away from the Athens port.

"Poros," Dietz muttered to himself as he connected to the Internet on Wakefield's laptop. "It sounds familiar, but at my age, everything sounds familiar. Let's find out," his fingers clacked on the keys.

He wanted to get in, break Wakefield out, then send in a SWAT team to take out any others. The likelihood of Rivers being alive—it wasn't worth calculating. Dietz scratched his scruffy chin. He would take the rest of his time off to rummage through Filasek's personal effects for leads to the man's partners. He was tired of being in the dark about this man's movements. Filasek was becoming more and more an international player. Dietz, as head of counterintelligence, could not afford to overlook that.

"I guess Greece is as good as any place to hide as a fugitive, but I want to know why Filasek choose here."

The computer listed the first 10 of 4692 references to Poros, Greece. Dietz sighed and scratched his chin, "Might as well start at the top. Wakefield is not going anywhere." At least her visa had not moved in the last 9 hours.

Dietz scanned the page and pictures. "Lemon groves and the Temple of Poseidon from the sixth century B.C. scattered beneath pine trees on the Plain of Platia east of town," Dietz read. "Sounds like tourism central," Dietz groaned in disappointment. "I will stick out like a brick in a bag of feathers." He clicked back to the list and chose the fifth site. "Hmm," he leaned back in the ladder-back chair until it squeaked, "I wonder if this is a coincidence?" Dietz did not believe in them. More than 30 years as a Company man superseded coincidence.

The island of Poros was the home of a naval training school.

A blinking icon appeared in the top left corner of his PDA map next to the keyboard. "I have mail?" The only address he had connected to was Dovlatabadi's contact address. Dietz felt a sinking sensation. Dovlatabadi was not due to report for two more days.

He dotted his pencil-wand against the screen mailbox. After decryption it read:

Meet set for 2/10 PM with bL+2 big fish. S.E.
wing of pres. palace on riverside. bL here now.
A-7188914661.

"Bin Laden is there!" He felt his insides tighten in excitement." It was the first reliable and up-to-date lead he had heard on bin Laden's movements.

His chest fell. "Great," Dietz moaned. "If we turn the Iraqi presidential palace into an inferno, we can guarantee a war for which we are not yet fully deployed. Saddam would probably retaliate by sending the Republican Guard into Kuwait and Israel again. Maybe ol' Osama isn't as backward we we'd hoped." Dietz lauded. "It is the safest place he could go. Right out in the open."

The U.S. could deploy troops from carriers and ships in the Fifth Fleet that was whirlpooling up the Arabian Sea. However, they would not be enough to finish the job as completely as the president had instructed. "We could just bomb the palace," Dietz shook his head, "but how many civilian casualties would that incur? Even a handful is too many these days. The world would turn on us as the schoolyard bully." He knew he should send the decision up the chain.

Then there was Wakefield. He weighed his quandary. She was being held by a known terrorist and was counting on him. But if he could eliminate The Terrorist, then it would reduce the organization of terrorism itself. "Not to mention be a huge boon to my career which has just about topped out," he muttered.

Dietz could feel the chase, could taste the victory. With the new equipment available, even Iraq's underground labyrinth of tunnels, which had been fashioned after Rome's catacombs, would not be a safe place for enemies of the United States.

"Duty is duty," Dietz jutted out his chin with determination and Judah's blue eyes floated through his mind. *Which is duty?* He felt a tearing inside.

"Forgive me, America." Dietz whispered his fingers trembling around the pencil with his tight grip as he composed his reply.

Subdue as many as possible with as much risk
as you are willing to assume. Same as original deal.
Calvary will not be coming. D.

Filasek's Villa, Poros
1245 hours

Judah squeezed her eyes shut against the light. She tried to avoid the brightness that pierced her fogged-in brain, but her neck would not comply.

She was alert enough to classify her headache as past pounding and into the stabbing stage. A distant feeling of familiarity distracted her as she swam to the surface of consciousness.

She tried to pinpoint the remembrance as she forced her eyes to open into slits. Her mouth tasted like a cotton boll. *Ah, yes. This is why I promised myself I would never get drunk again.* The thirst and the discomfort of waking up and having a piece of life missing. A sinking feeling burrowed into her stomach as the last activities she could recall formed shape in her mind.

It was effort to open her dry mouth that had sealed with the sucking motion she had repeated in her need for water. *But I wasn't drinking.* More of the sequence of events came back to her.

As the memory of Filasek hovered before her, she cracked her eyes open wider. At that moment, danger felt more threatening than pain.

The room's overhead lighting filled the area, but the stinging light, Judah traced to a small window five feet above the carpet. The window framed the sun as it blinded her momentarily. *A little slow, Wakefield,* she chided herself.

She checked the rest of the room as well as she could without moving her head. *I think I have decided that I don't like not knowing where I am when I wake up.*

The last time it had happened, it was a self-induced hangover after Stewart Bailey broke her heart the summer she turned 20.

It was not helpful to draw clues from the bedroom where she lay. The walls were stucco white, no pictures. The two pieces of furniture she could view, besides the bed, were made of rich, dark wood. The rest of the room was swathed with a combination of white and cream fabrics.

It was tasteful, but more bland than she would have chosen. She did appreciate the quality linens.

Her roaming eyes snapped back to the top of the four-foot dresser. She had missed it the first time. A crystal bulbous pitcher of water with ice floating in the top sat next to a cut crystal glass.

Move it! She ordered her body.

After draining three-quarters of the pitcher, Judah shielded her eyes and looked out the window. It was midday, based on the sun's relationship to the horizon which was a flat seam of blue water and blue sky. But what day? Her huge thirst made her think it was more than one.

Judah stretched up on her toes to look down. A small white Cessna bobbed on water floats across a wooden dock from a long skinny boat. She didn't see any people.

She turned away from the window, her headache had reduced some. A white door stood opposite of the window in an alcove. Two brushed chrome deadbolt locks balanced over the matching handle. "I didn't even try the door," she ridiculed. Twenty-three paces from the window, avoiding the end of the bed to the door handle.

It turned one centimeter to the right and stopped. Same to the left. *Well, what did you expect?* She shook her head gently.

She felt a strange peace fill her chest cavity. Judah poured the last of the water into the glass on the dresser. The ice spun in the pitcher.

The peace surprised her and she tried to analyze it. It was stronger than hope for freedom. It was more sure than faith that she would have her old life back. It was a surety that she would accomplish the purpose of God for her life. In life or death.

She drained the glass of cold water.

Filasek's Basement
1310 hours

Rivers rolled to his feet from the wooden slats they called a bunk as footsteps sounded at the top of the basement stairs. Filasek had been gone for 15 hours according to his calculation.

An eternal 15 hours.

"On your feet." A familiar voice called before Rivers could see who it was.

Then he recognized him. "Oh, it is you, Brutus, I mean Raul. What does your master call for you to do today?" Rivers found a source of amusement in taunting the man. He obviously would not pound him and keep his employment. He figured that if Raul momentarily lost control, as long as he could get to the man's neck, it would be an even match.

Raul dangled the key on the iron ring in front of the ancient rusty lock of Rivers' cage. Raul's lips sneered at him through the bars and the key swung like a time-keeping pendulum.

Rivers waited. He saw a hint of challenge in Raul's brown eyes. The key ticked. The man in terrorist-employ did not know who he was dealing with.

Rivers remembered waiting for one shot while functioning as his SEAL team's sniper. It took six days in 95- to 113-degree weather watching a Haitian village through his two-inch scope. That captor was dead now and the captive a lawyer in Montana. Rivers stepped back into parade rest; he had patience of steel.

"Come on, Sailor." Raul twisted the key and the lock released with a deep metallic clank. "You've been assigned new quarters."

Rivers intuitively catalogued from some clue in the pronunciation of the words that Raul had been formal military for some country. He also detected a hint of respect in his mannerisms. *Interesting*.

*****

Filasek ciphered while relaxing on his white stone and iron balcony. The blue water beckoned him to risk more, to be more daring. His solar

104 ~ K.J. Frolander

powered calculator lay abandoned on his knee. He could figure down to the gram how much of his new chemical weapon he could produce with the shipping container of chemicals that were underway.

"The trick is," Filasek stroked his beard with his thumb and first finger as the other fingers curled into his palm, "balancing the amount I need to destroy the United States and how much money I can skim from Hussein by selling him my overage before selling him the formula." He wanted no residue left in his lab or storage facility to point to him in the new world that would emerge after November.

"Of course," Filasek chuckled deep in his belly at the irony, "who is going to come searching for the killer of the world's policemen? No one." He gleefully answered his own rhetorical question.

Filasek tapped his foot on the stucco balcony floor. If he sold the first 18 batches that were already complete to Saddam Hussein for Kurd control then he could raise the money to finance the perfume bottling and transportation costs of getting 500 units to the U.S. and to the cities in time for the *Endeavor*'s night launch.

Filasek rose from the end of his cushioned lounge chair. "It is past time to see Hussein." He looked at his watch. "But it is right on time to have my fun for the day. The Americans are in place by now." He curled his lips in anticipation.

Wakefield's Room
1403 hours

Judah Wakefield stood in the tiny all-white bathroom refilling the water pitcher when she heard it first. She turned off the tap and listened for the sound to repeat. "I must have imagined it," she shrugged and dumped the last glassful of water into the crystal pitcher. As she set it back on the dresser top, the lights dimmed and went back to normal. Then she heard it again. It was a small sound in volume, but deep in pitch. It sounded like an animal growl. A large animal.

She tried to analyze it. She had nothing to compare it with except a trip to the zoo. When she was 10, and her mom was dating her step-dad-to-be. Then-LCDR Graham had taken all three of the girls to the San Diego Zoo. The man responsible for feeding that morning had decided to tease the lion. The lion had made a deep-throated warning sound just before he pounced toward the feeder slot with a ground-shaking roar.

That growl sounded the same as what she was hearing now.

Her eyes darted all over the room. It seemed to be coming from behind the wall that her headboard stood against. *Why would there be an angry lion in the next room? Where am I?* She wondered again. She tried to judge the strength of the wall.

The lights dimmed momentarily again. She counted the seconds. *One, two, thr*—she could not even finish the number in her head. The sound came again. Much louder. The growl pitched into a feral scream.

It formed a recognizable syllable. "NO!"

It was no angry lion. The sound was human.

A tortured human being.

"My God!" Wakefield froze in place.

"NOOO!" The scream came again. She could not distinguish it as male or female, but it reverberated through her ribs. She gripped her stomach. What caused someone to make a noise like that? She didn't want to imagine.

Then music started. A deep thump, thumping of bass clashed with out-of-sync drums and high-pitched symbols that carried no beat, only a continuous cacophony of clashing. Electric guitars screamed while whomever played overused the waa-waa pedal. A sound that had to be a voice shrieked lyrics above the rest of the racket. The volume increased and Wakefield held her hands over her ears to protect her sore head.

She squeezed her eyes against the intruding noise and finally understood the term thrasher music.

The light fixture in the center of the room had 15 crystals hanging from its circumference. They jiggled with every boom of the bass guitar.

As suddenly as it started, it stopped. The silence echoed with thundering reverberations.

Wakefield forced her shoulders to relax and peeled her fingers away from the side of her head. Slowly her body uncurled. Another animal scream tore through the air. A deadly quiet followed.

She had just stepped away from the bathroom door when the thrashing resumed. Just as loud, just as demanding as before.

She moved to pound on the wall as she had done in her apartment before her noisy neighbors moved. "What good would that do?" she stopped. "They couldn't hear my pounding above the music." She looked at the bouncing beads on the light fixture in amazement. "I cannot even hear myself talking." She knew she was; she could feel the air passing over her vocal chords. What must it be like next door?

When the lights dimmed the next time, so did the music. Blessed relief. Then the heaving scream. Judah felt like a monster for looking forward to the brief moment of reprieve. It could only mean one thing. The energy to run the lights was being diverted into the body of the one crying out.

An hour later finally it was quiet.

The bolts on her door turned. She could not hear it, the sounds pulsed in her ears. She just happened to be looking in the direction of the door.

It opened in a rush. She tensed. A small form filled the exit. She frowned as she recognized his shape. "I had hoped that you were part of the nightmare," she said. Her voice sounded strangely outside her body.

Chapter Thirteen

Baghdad, Iraq
Tuesday 1 October 2003
5:45 PM

Dovlatabadi unfolded both antennae to his American satellite up-link. He was three minutes away from the optimum connect time. It would last seven minutes, then the link would be severed. In twelve hours, he would have the same link available to e-mail without interference from the regulations regarding outside influences on Saddam's people.

He remembered studying the rise and fall of Adolf Hitler in Germany when he was in school. Saddam shared many character qualities with the Furor. Kurds, Jews, did it matter? They were people who were supposed to be under their leader's protection not his curse. Dovlatabadi had met Saddam only long enough to swear his allegiance to the man so he could be accepted into the elite bodyguard.

The man's heavy black brows threatened to overrun his face like summer kudzu. With his eyes, the Iraqi king seemed to be able to reach into the newcomer's chest and grab his heart to check its color for loyalty.

Dovlatabadi studied his own darkened skin. He still was not used to it. The CIA had supplied a weekly dose of pigment stimulator when he had left house arrest. The small pill was the only factor that kept him from being noticed as an infiltrator on sight. His accented Farsi made him sound as if he was from northern Iraq. Not a bad quality, since that was where the fiercest fighting had been taking place in the last three decades. His thin build and smooth poet-like curls had instigated a number of challenges from men who didn't seem to think he deserved a place among the elite. Daily target practice with the Guard helped quiet them a bit, but in the week that he had been on staff, his fear of being uncovered had caused him to allow himself to think only in his secondary language.

The computer clock counted down the last few seconds to 5:48. His shift was coming up shortly. The dead man he had replaced had held the 7PM to 3AM shift. So, that was the one he had inherited. In the bodyguard of Saddam Hussein, however, he was always on duty.

He read the message a second time. He cursed under his breath and straightened his long fingers above the keyboard. "What does he mean he is not coming? I thought that this is why I was here." He cursed again. "You get your man, and I get freedom." Dovlatabadi knew better than to believe that would ever happen.

He spent his nights after duty trying to plan a way to outsmart Hussein and Dietz, so he could go after Filasek. *If only there was a way to get all three men together*, he wished. "I would pick them off one at a time with a decent scope." Hatred clung to his patrician lips like honey.

A double rap sounded at the door, and he wondered how loud he had spoken those last words. The former world-class assassin shifted in the metal folding chair in his mouse-sized apartment and disconnected the satellite link. His brown uniform was stiff and itchy. He pulled at the collar then at the zipper as he went for the door.

His contact within the company of soldiers, Zee Jasiq, stood stiffly with his hat in his hand. "We are recalled early again tonight." He sounded impatient. "When will your telephone arrive?"

"Soon." Dovlatabadi repeated the answer that had been given him in the Office of Communication. "Whatever *soon* means."

"Well," Jasiq cleared his throat, "at least you're dressed. How long will you be? I don't want the kitchen duty. Again." The last people to arrive for each shift's briefing got stuck with the worst assignment, keeping watch over the kitchen staff as they prepared food. Which in itself sounds ideal, except that if you were caught sampling, you were up for a dawn execution. Hussein had almost been poisoned when one of his bodyguards had stirred in a lethal dose of arsenic when the guard asked if he could take a taste of a dish in 1994.

"Sorry about that." Dovlatabadi reached for his own cover lying stiffly on the threadbare chair beside the door. "I am ready now, just let me grab my keys. Though why I bother to lock the door is beyond me."

"You are not supposed to know about that." Jasiq lifted his thin eyebrows into peaks.

"How could I miss the scratches on the door handle and a dusty boot print on the carpet? One of them even drank one of my Coca Colas and left the can on the counter."

Jasiq let out a chuckle. Dovlatabadi shook his head and turned the key in the lock behind him. "Those jokers get worse every year," Jasiq determined. "If new recruits are hiding anything in their background, the idiots they send to find it would have to trip over their own boots and land on it face first to see it."

"Let's hurry. I have not eaten tonight." *And I won't until I figure out how to get my life back*, he vowed as the two jogged the two blocks to the palace's west entrance.

Filasek's Villa, Poros, Greece
Tuesday, 1456 hours

"How are you finding your accommodations, Miss Wakefield?" Filasek shut the door behind himself.

Judah thought his voice sounded as if he had gargled with snake oil, but then she decided maybe she was a mite prejudiced. "I was troubled to find the locks on the doors. Do you always have to imprison your guests?"

"This is not prison. Prison is downstairs." Filasek's eyes jumped from place to place in the room. He looked at her in between each jerking glance. It made her feel dizzy just to watch him. His pupils were tiny black dots and his hands had a detectible tremble. He seemed high on some drug.

"Well then, I would like to complain about the noise my neighbor is making," she decided to act as civilly as possible.

Filasek's furry eyebrows extended wider. "I thought you would appreciate my efforts. But then I guess there is no pleasing you people."

Judah turned her back to him and went to lean against a wall. She would have preferred to sit, but she was not going to sit on the bed. That was an invitation in any culture. "So we are back to the issues of women and Americans. It is too bad we cannot move past that."

"Very well. What would you like to talk about?"

"I would like to see Rivers. I believe you made me a promise."

"I never have been good at keeping promises." The easy, almost apologetic, shake of his head angered her, and Wakefield squeezed the outside edge of her thigh tightly between her fingers to choke it down.

"Shall I have some food sent up? I know that RHB can make you ravenous."

"No, thank you. I am fasting." It was pure instinct that drove the words from her mouth. She was starving.

"By the skin of Allah! What is with you people?" Filasek advanced toward her as he cursed.

"What?" Judah felt a smile growing on her lips. "Is that what Rivers said, too?" She knew it had to be, to cause such a reaction in Filasek. It was satisfying.

Filasek grasped her shoulder. Judah thought it looked funny that he had to reach up in order to touch her, until the pain set in. He found the nerve. "Come, sit. We need to talk. Soldier to soldier."

"You are not a soldier," Wakefield followed him and sat warily at the foot of the bed while he took the head.

"I am a soldier of the jihad, commissioned by Allah himself. But that is of no consequence." Filasek's eyes roamed over her body.

God, please hurry Dietz up, she prayed.

Filasek must have detected her fear, for he snorted, making the bed springs jiggle. "If I had wanted that, I would have already taken it. I have a trade to propose."

Judah swallowed. She did not know if she felt better or not. "I already tried trading with you." She tapped into her reserve of courage and sat up straighter.

"Your people do not know where you are. The man following you is dead. No one will ever find you here. They do not care about you. I want to know what the largest cities in the U.S. are and where they are vulnerable."

What was he talking about? "Look at a map." She squinted her eyes and shook her head. "That's no secret."

"No. I want your help. And you are going to help me." Filasek's eyes told her he was the player with the trump card.

Wakefield pursed her lips in what she hoped looked like a stubborn manner. "There is nothing you can do to make me help you." Filasek made a guttural groan deep in his throat. *How dare he be impatient with me? He is the one who kidnapped me! Does he really expect help with anything?*

"Woman, you don't even know what I want the information for." He gestured with an open hand in a logical way that felt demeaning.

"It doesn't matter." She tossed her blond hair emphatically. *Mistake!* screamed her pounding head. "I will never help you."

Filasek stood up from the bed with his jaw set, "We'll see." His voice sounded calm and it scared her.

He shut the door behind him. The bolts slammed into the doorframe. One, two.

The torture began again next door. A horrifying feeling began in her innermost being. Her unseeing eyes moved back and forth on the unstained carpet as she encouraged her brain to kick into motion.

Chapter Fourteen

Dietz checked the PDA display and looked back at the white adobe house in front of him. The pinprick blinked in the X of the crosshairs. "This is the place," he muttered.

The expansive villa was spectacular. A brilliant white diamond set against a blue velvet sea. He was disappointed that the ridge where he had counted seven other homes already occupied the highest point on the island. The only underdeveloped space with a view of the villa that he had encountered was one 200-foot by 10-foot roadside swath of an estate lot between his current hiding place and Wakefield.

Dietz kneeled on the rocky ground and brought the infrared goggles to his eyes. He swore, "There are bodies everywhere." He counted eighteen red-lit heat sources moving around in the house. *Not unrealistic for the square footage of the villa but,* "Come on Filasek, which one are you?" Dietz spoke with his teeth clamped together making his sounds hiss.

He pulled the binoculars away from his face to switch off the infrared mode. He scanned the estate again, looking for a place to close in.

The back of the house dropped off a cliff into the sea below. The only backyard to speak of was a staircase that offered a safe passage between the height of the home and the sea. Dietz repositioned his angle. Filasek's front lawn was bright grass that looked as well-kept as a Master's Tour golf course. Only a few palm trees surrounded by shrubs and flowers interrupted the emerald carpet.

On the side nearest him there was a possibility. A cascading stacked brownstone fountain bubbled. "It could be six or seven feet high," Dietz decided, "but who can really tell with the magnitude of the house I have to use to compare?" He scanned once more. "Nothing else to consider."

He hung the binoculars around his neck and pulled out a nature trail guide pamphlet that he picked up at the tourism office where the ferry dropped him off. He had the German version in case he got caught. It had been a long time since he had done fieldwork, and he would take every precaution. A grounds-man still wandered around on the property between him and his goal.

Dietz settled into the tall weeds of Filasek's neighbor to wait.

**Rivers' Room
1 October 2002
1710 hours local time**

Thy Word have I hid in my heart that I might not sin against Thee. At what time I am afraid I will trust in Thee. Why am I thinking in King-James English?

That is how you first memorized My Word.

That makes sense then.

Rivers watched Filasek come toward him again with the electric wand and the steel wool throwing off sparks as he touched them together.

What is this guy's fascination with fire?

Rivers remembered how Filasek stood nearly howling at the moon outside the giant fire in the butte in the middle of the desert. He watched sparks reflect in the man's dark eyes as the lights dimmed slightly and the pounding music lowered one blessed moment. Filasek's eyes seemed to light up of their own accord.

Creepy.

Filasek and his minion who handed over tools had their ears protected with modern-looking sound-attenuating headphones. They didn't quite look like anything David had ever seen on the shooting range though.

The tongs came closer clasping the fire-red steel wool pad which was coming untwisted with its prolonged use. A few coils had escaped the original round form completely, sticking out from the sides like a woman's wayward curls.

The muscles in Rivers' waist flinched away from the heat without his consent as the glowing scouring pad got closer and closer. He held his breath.

Rivers looked back at Filasek's eyes as the steel wool burned hot. He felt his molars grind and his lips pull back as he fought the pain by sucking in breath through his teeth. He knew next would come the smell. A fresh layer of the unforgettable, horrible stench of burning flesh. It clung to the room even after the animals had left both previous times.

I wonder if I am actually able to feel my skin melting or if I am imagining it. Ugh. There it is. Rivers swallowed the bile that rose in his throat at the reek of his burning skin.

I can't quite remember any scriptures about bad smells, Lord.

There was one right on the edge of his mind. Oh except, "Surely by now he stinketh." Or something like that. That was Lazarus. He was dead four days when one of his sisters said that. Hmm. I never got a chance to have any sisters. I would have liked to have a sister, Lord. Even if she told me I stink. Oh wait! Mollie, Sam's wife. I have a sister-in-law, and that's almost as good. Thank you, Lord, for Mollie and the joy she brought into our family, good times and bad. She was fun and never told me I stink. Even that time when Sam and I came back from five days in the woods when it rained on day one.

Filasek was yelling something at him, but Rivers didn't even try to surface from his constant inner dialog anymore. He couldn't have understood him anyway. The music, if you could call it that, assaulted every atom of the room.

Filasek re-lit the heat on the pad and touched it to the same raw, melty spot on Rivers' waist.

Lord, I keep thinking of sweet aroma verses, of things that please you. That we are a sweet aroma to you because of Jesus. I remember that the smell of a burnt offering is a sweet smelling savor to you. I don't know that I am an offering, but I am certainly burnt.

For a moment the thought was rather disconcerting in a paradoxical sort of way.

Rivers had just focused his gaze on a joint in the badly re-plastered ceiling, and so he felt Filasek coming toward him before seeing him. But even that was not enough to prepare him for the bare wand touching the arch of his left foot.

A scream tore through his clenched teeth and he pulled his legs up and away from the electrical current and jerked his head up to see what had happened, wrenching against the chest restraint. Each leg was held fast with inch-and-a-half wide leather straps, so he only managed to jar his knees. The cartilage screamed at him to stop. The force of the electricity through his body slammed his head backward onto the metal table and muscles knotted that he didn't even remember having.

The music stopped abruptly.

Time was not normal. Though Rivers couldn't tell if it had slowed down or speeded up.

"What is it you want from me?" Rivers worked at evenly modulating his voice and his breathing.

Filasek walked up and stood at his head. Rivers had to turn his head to the side to see the small man.

"So many, many things," Filasek whispered. "Mostly I want your soul to wither away before I send you to hell. And so I shall. All you have to do is show Raul here how to rig up a bomb capable of blowing up a bridge without being detected. It won't take much time and then after the bridge is destroyed, I might be convinced to let you go. Are you ready to offer a little bit of help yet?"

"Lieutenant Commander David Rivers, four six four three four seven seven eight one." He used the same pitch, cadence and monotonous tone he had learned from his instructor during Basic's hostage training. It did bolster him strangely. There was a connection to an ancient brotherhood and a strength supporting him. Why in the world would Filasek need help with explosives? He had been gathering war-material since he was a boy. And what bridge? Why had he stopped pestering him about where Judah was?

Filasek chuckled. "Name, rank and serial number. Yes. I've seen your American movies. You think you're so tough."

Rivers said nothing.

"I want nothing from you." Filasek gave a single laugh and shrugged as his eyes blinked closed. "I will have satisfaction for 10 years-worth of weapons storage gone in seconds at your hands. I want you to feel the pain I felt that night. I will have revenge and satisfaction, and," a tight-lipped smile showed through the man's wiry beard, "your little whore has already satisfied me."

Rivers remained silent as he struggled with what part of the man's speech to believe, if any. There was something to the bridge, it was too specific, and perhaps the wanting to kill me was truthful, too.

Filasek kept jabbering and then gestured to his cohort to turn on the music as he replaced his ear protection, but Rivers decided to dismiss everything as a lie. Even as the torture changed back from psychological to physical again, Rivers quit listening. On the outside at least.

Inwardly, he spoke to the Lord. *What is another word of wisdom, your strength in Scripture that I can apply in this situation?*

A picture formed in his mind at the same time he heard in his spirit, *As dead flies give perfume a bad smell, so a little folly outweighs wisdom and honor.*

The words which came so immediately gave him pause.

I don't remember that one, Lord, but I have a feeling you brought it up for a purpose.

And so David Rivers waited as his mind processed and his spirit listened. And a scene rushed back to him. As he stared at the white lumpy ceiling in Greece he saw it as clearly as if he were living it.

Months earlier in Germany as he sat in Herr Faulkenburg's office eating breakfast surrounded by Wakefield and Nelson, he doubled-down on his vow to kill Filasek. The force of the vow had pushed him back in the chair, but as he looked around the scene again, it didn't seem anyone else had noticed. He and Judah and several others had teamed up to eliminate a threat on the sitting U.S. President. They had been up to their chins in figuring out what ended up being their final move in the situation, before Azure Tiger sprang. After being found, the would-be assassin had jumped from a hotel window before he could murder the president. Azure Tiger initially survived, then died during his medical extradition home. It had been rather anti-climactic.

But, the first time he had made the vow, Rivers had been standing in the back of a transport truck in the middle of the Afghanistan desert on his first mission with Judah.

He had warned Filasek that if he hurt Judah, Rivers would come after him and kill him. When Filasek had brought her back, there was a knife slice down her cheek and a somewhat shrunken soul, though Judah would be loath to know he saw the difference in her.

Filasek started this path. "It's my job to finish it," Rivers said. "I am a man of my word, and I will finish this. I will finish him."

"What's that?" Filasek yelled. Rivers assumed he yelled because he could barely hear the taunt over the continuous roar of sound.

Rivers looked around the cinderblock room painted white. He had traveled a long way between two large goons when they moved him from the basement. Shackled, there had been no opportunity to escape. But Rivers knew the facility was fairly large.

Will it be like Sampson? That I take out more in my death than in my life? You made me strong for this.

Not for this, came the still small voice once more in his heart.

Everything stopped for Rivers.

Chapter Fifteen

Rivers' head swam as things in his heart shifted uncomfortably. Everything he had known felt untethered. His inner self bumped into the edges of truth like a cross between a billiard ball and a SCUBA bubble.

You don't have to end the way Sampson did. You can let me hold your identity in my hand.

I don't understand, Lord. You're the one who made me like this. A SEAL who never gives up. Are you saying there is something wrong with me?

You made a vow I did not ask you to make, and it has come between us.

Rivers knew exactly which vow. It had been poking at his head the same way Filasek was poking at his body. But I thought you would want me to—I don't know—defend her honor, or follow through on my promise...it sounded silly now that he had assigned language to the thoughts that had tied him in double knots for almost a year now.

Rivers felt tears slip down his temple at the kind correction. I guess, I must have known deep down that revenge wasn't right. I was just so angry and it felt like righteous anger. I see now it was not. I'm sorry, Father. Would you forgive me? Would you cleanse me of all unrighteousness so that I am following you with a pure heart?

That same moment a woosh of water splattered icy daggers across his chest and up over his neck and face.

Rivers' mouth had thankfully been closed, but there was nothing to stop the water from rushing up his nose and down the back of his throat. Don't breathe, don't breathe, he commanded himself.

He could hold his breath just a few seconds shy of four minutes, when he had properly prepared. But he had not. Filasek's man dumped a second and then third bucket over his face.

This isn't what I had in mind for cleansing, Lord.

I forgive you, my dear son.

Rivers nose began to sting, and as he focused on it, he realized every open wound above his waist was sending emergency messages to his brain. What was the liquid? Acid?

Then the taste of brine finally registered as it trickled through his sinus cavities and down his throat. Seawater; it was just salt.

Will you let me handle this circumstance and do only what I tell you?

Of course.

Breathe.

The instruction was the last he expected to hear. It felt like his God was asking him to commit suicide.

A moment's hesitation as he processed what obedience would cost was all he took. Rivers gasped for a huge lungful of air just as the fourth bucket released its contents.

Everything in him rejected the seawater, and he gave great heaving coughs as he fought to clear his respiratory system. Again and again. Oh how it burned.

Rivers struggled, hardly able to think, for maybe a minute, but it felt like days.

"Release him," Filasek told his man.

Rivers processed the words, but as black closed his vision to a doughnut hole while he hacked up only the smallest drops of seawater, he wondered if it would be in time.

Rivers felt his left arm and leg released almost simultaneously. He rolled to his right to let gravity help him clear his lungs.

Rivers moaned as the stale pita and tea he'd been given for breakfast followed the expiration of the water from his lungs onto the floor.

Filasek sighed heavily. "Nothing I hate worse than men crying like stupid dogs. Suck it up, Soldier, you disgust me."

But Filasek turned around and left, just like that, turning off the music on the way out.

The stifling blanket of sound lifted and Rivers could breathe once more. But hearing felt like trying to swim through Jell-o.

Still, it was something. He had survived.

"I repent of making that vow, Lord." Rivers whispered. "Of trying to bring vengeance in my own strength and timing, rather than repentance. Of not trusting in you. I cancel my words and evil thoughts toward Arafeh Filasek, and I make null and void my promise to kill him." David Rivers swallowed hard and spat his pride out. "I give Filasek over to you, Lord, to bring justice yourself. You are the only one worthy.

"I am a bleeding, broken man, inside and out, Father. Would you come and heal me?"

Naval Intelligence HQ
Suitland, Maryland
Tuesday, 1 October 2002
1034 hours EDT

Admiral Tamburillo rubbed his forehead. It was days like today that he hated his command position and wished for civilian life. What kind of business sent its employees to prison for helping another person in danger? He knew she was in trouble. Her marker had not moved in hours. "Who am I kidding? I don't even remember what civilian life is like. But this whole mess would not be an issue, because my people would be safe."

The admiral pushed the speakerphone button to page his yeoman. "Get me Captain Huntingdon."

"He is right here, sir," came the tin reply. "I am sending him in." The words mixed with a rap on his door.

"Captain Huntingdon reporting as ordered, sir." The man stood stiffly in the doorway with a file folder tucked under his arm. It had top-secret striping along the edges.

"At ease, have a seat, Captain." Tamburillo did not rise. "Do you normally flutter outside my door?"

Huntingdon chuckled. Tamburillo thought he detected a bit of nervousness in his laugh. The captain smoothed his thin hair back across his head as it began to fall forward. "Only when I am trying to get an appointment to see you."

Tamburillo stilled his hands.

"What is it?" he asked his competent subordinate.

"As you know I have taken on most of Lieutenant Commander Wakefield's work since her...departure. I thought maybe you should take a look at this file."

Tamburillo nodded and moved his coffee cup to make room for Huntingdon's file. He pulled back the manila cover. "What am I looking at?" The tone in which Huntingdon delivered the suggestion made him wonder if he was about to hear something he would rather not know. Like Wakefield was a double, or—*no, there is nothing worse than that. But she would never sell out her country*. He was confident.

"This is the case against Petty Officer Tanner, an enlisted man out of Norfolk. She has an entire case against him. It is obvious that he was stealing weapons from the arsenal and stockpiling them somewhere to sell to the highest bidder. Lieutenant Sampson said that on Wake-field's last day she told him she would authorize the NCIS office at Norfolk to search his computer. Everything pointed to his guilt, but she never moved on it, sir. She had time, and now he is missing." Hunting-don's voice dropped. "All the signs were there that he was going to bolt."

"She has always been one to give a man the benefit of the doubt. One more chance before she takes away his life. I don't understand your point." Tamburillo spat gruffly and looked at the captain instead of the folder. He knew the man would come to it soon, and he knew he was not going to like the accusation.

"Petty Officer Tanner disappeared on the same day Wakefield left the country, sir."

Tamburillo curled his fingers. "Don't tell me you are starting to believe the scuttlebutt about her being involved in the Afghanistan mess." Tamburillo's deep voice resounded low to warn Huntingdon not to answer in the affirmative.

"Look, Admiral, I liked her, too." Huntingdon leaned forward and Tamburillo thought he looked like he was pleading with him. "But there has been so much speculation. She has been present when so many things have gone wrong recently. The assassination attempt on the president, plus all the stuff that came out during her Article 32 and congressional hearing. She has been different lately, and," the captain shrugged, "have you considered that maybe where there is smoke there is—"

The anger that began bubbling with the officer's first whisper of wonder, reached full boil. "Don't finish that sentence, Captain. Leave the file and do not let the hatch hit you on your way out!" he bellowed.

The captain stood. "Aye, aye, sir." He about-faced and fairly jogged to the door. He turned with a sad expression and his hand on the knob. "We all have our price, sir. Maybe they got to her."

Then he was gone. The words rounded in the admiral's mind like a psychedelic carousel. He threw himself back in his leather chair and closed his eyes. "Not Wakefield. There is just no way. Is there?"

Tamburillo unfolded his half-moon glasses, slowly perching them on his nose. He balanced the precarious information on his left palm and flipped the file open.

Chapter Sixteen

Wakefield lay curled on her bed with the pillow over her ear. Her stomach grumbled at her for dismissing the offer of food. The noise and dimming lights had been going on for over two and a half hours.

She would not allow herself to think about what was going on next door. The cries were still strong, but she knew that they would weaken shortly. *When will they be coming for me? It has to be more than one person, right?* The action was too continuous to be just Filasek. Her thoughts felt jumbled and her body tense.

The poor soul, didn't he know that if he would show a weaken-ing that they would lighten up. "Please give out soon. The noise is deafening me." She pleaded with her unseen neighbor.

And it stopped as abruptly as it started. The sound seemed to continue its echo in her brain. She tried to shut it off, by forcing herself to concentrating on forming each syllable of Psalm 23.

"Already talking to yourself, woman? I have not even started in on you, yet." Filasek's voice boomed next to her.

She jerked the pillow away from her ear. He must have seen her lips moving. *How did I get so lax? Pay attention!* She jerked away from him, rolling off the other side of the bed. He held a syringe between his fingers like a cigarette.

"I've come to see if you have reconsidered. It is only names of cities. Like you said, I could get the information from a map." He slowly advanced toward her.

She backed away, then her heel touch the wall. Why did he need the names from her? And badly enough to use drugs? She couldn't make sense of it. "I will never tell you."

"Never say never," he chuckled.

Judah's stomach churned as she flashed back to the stunning moment when Filasek had struck like a snake tossed into a fire in Afghanistan, marring her face. And her soul, in those moments when she could admit the fear still lingered deep in that cut.

"Are you not even interested to know who your noisy neighbor is?" She instinctively turned her head toward the wall.

Wakefield felt her throat constrict as she swallowed. She would not ask, would not show interest.

"That's all right. I can see you're dying to know." He laughed again. "Your Rivers is not much of a SEAL. He doesn't even like water. He flails like a kitten every time we dunk him."

Rage that she had not known existed in her pounced on him. Judah rushed forward with a primal shriek. She grabbed his hair and tried to bring his face down into her rising knee. But that was when she felt it. The needle punctured her arm. *How did I forget? He was only baiting me. He has been baiting me the whole time. Rivers is dead.*

Why am I still conscious? She wondered, but could not form the words. Filasek peeled her off of him and then caught her just before she collapsed onto the carpet.

"I brought you a tape to listen to, before you make up your mind." Filasek pulled out a silver 3 X 4 inch tape recorder from his loose cotton shirt pocket. He depressed the play button.

"It doesn't matter. I'll never help you." She recognized her own last words to Filasek on the tape. Then Rivers' voice streamed into the room, strong. He repeated his name, rank and social security number. She had never heard him say his own name before. It pulled on something deep inside her.

A buzzing sound came from the tape, it sounded as if the tape had caught and snapped apart. Then a grunt that escalated into a scream followed. She recognized the pitch from a minute before.

Filasek allowed the tape to continue rolling. He adjusted the volume of liquid in the syringe by adding to it from a half-ounce bottle of clear liquid from his pocket. The tape rolled for an additional eight seconds. There was no denying that it was David Rivers' staccato breath and groan on the tape.

She knew she should feel something, but she did not. Her emotions were as numb as her body. "You have control over what happens next door. In case that tape is not convincing enough," Filasek tapped the bubbles to the top and pushed the air out with the plunger until the liquid erupted two inches into the air, "I have another cocktail for you. The effects of that watery dose will only last another minute or so."

She began to feel the muscles in her chest first. "The deal is, for every name you give me, your man gets one minute of reprieve. You should be able to feel your shoulders now."

Judah moved them and then could move her jaw and tongue. But her extremities were not there yet. "What is it going to be?" Filasek leaned over her with the full syringe. "Just ten names and you buy yourself some time and your boyfriend some relief."

Her fingers began tingling. She would not make the same mistake twice. Giving him names of large cities in the U.S. was not privileged information. It was not wrong. She filled her lungs to capacity. "L.A., New York, Boston, Philadelphia, Chicago, San Francisco, San Diego, D.C., Houston, Miami." She rattled off the first ten names she could think of before she could change her mind.

Guilt pulled at her like a riptide.

"See that wasn't so hard." Filasek backed off and put a cover over the needle tip. "I'll be back in ten minutes."

Rivers' screams still echoed in the silence of her mind. She knew it was no longer real, but she also knew that the sound would never be deleted from her mind.

The time was up and Filasek was back before she had even decided how she would proceed. The second time she bought twenty minutes. She was down to Indianapolis, Denver, and Atlanta. She was not sure how many more she would be able to name with her mind as groggy as it was.

You haven't told him anything he can't get from an atlas. She repeated the words to her soul as her mantra.

But she knew better. She felt him winning.

She heard a tapping sound on the wall near the bathroom divider. Her cryptilogical mind automatically decoded the taps and spaces. GUNSMOKE IS THAT YOU

Then the tears came. No one called her Gunsmoke except David Rivers. He really was alive. Or was she hallucinating from the drugs?

She moved as quickly as she could to the sound of the tapping. The feeling in her feet had not come back completely since the injection.

They felt tingly, like they were asleep. She could barely make out the shapes in the room through her watering eyes.

RIVERS HI. She tapped back in Morse code. She could barely make her fingers stay in a fist to tap with her first finger knuckle. Thank God for the instructor who had drilled the dots and dashes into her head. It had seemed like such an outdated communication, but she had used it numerous times. Seemed like it was more often with Rivers than any other time.

PROVE IT. Came the next transmission. Wakefield stepped back. Her overloaded emotions felt like she had been slapped. It makes sense, her logical side argued. Mind games would not be beyond Filasek. He would take pleasure in psychological tinkering. *How does one prove that she is herself?* Wakefield asked.

THINKING. She tapped to give herself a minute. Then it occurred to her. A smile found her lips and she leaned one hand against the wall for support as she knocked with the other. "I can't believe I am smiling at a time like this," she murmured. "But he won't mistake me for anybody else." WHY WONT YOU KISS ME.

There was silence for a moment. It was Rivers. No one else was privy to the Gunsmoke nickname. HA. The taps began again. HOW ARE YOU.

OK DRUGGED. She paused to wipe her face and neck. The tears, now that they had started made her feel like a faucet in need of a plumber. YOU OK. She knew even as she asked that she was making him lie to her.

BEEN BETTER, Rivers tapped. She felt herself chuckle as she saw a glimpse of David Rivers' character. He would not lie to her. He never had. BE STRONG.

She sank to the floor. She was anything but strong. I TALKED. She admitted.

His taps lowered too. NEW BEGINNING.

She wondered how he even had the strength to tap, much less offer her encouragement. David Rivers would be an amazing husband. *But not mine.* She leaned her head onto her hand that pushed against the white wall. *I cannot go through this again. I will not join myself to a man who I constantly have to worry about.* "You can't ask that of me, God." She whispered.

JUDAH YOU THERE.

She pawed the wall as if petting a puppy. She wished she could touch him. She would give Filasek a hundred names if she could hear his voice—and not screaming in pain.

JUDAH

DAVID WE HAVE TO GET OUT STOP I AM BREAKING.

A lonely tear tracked with the admission. She had faced ten minutes of threats, had not even been touched. "I don't deserve to be a naval officer. I sold out."

PRAY STOP AM PRAYING FOR YOU.

"God, please help me. I see more clearly now than ever that I am helpless without you." Wakefield let the wall support more of her weight. "God, let only your words flow out of my mouth from now on. Forgive…" She broke again as she realized she had not offended God, only herself and her country. "Help me forgive myself." She swiped at the tears again. DO YOU THINK HE IS COMING BACK. She tapped.

JESUS

She looked at the wall and shook her head. It was hard to communicate without punctuation. She laughed as she realized how Rivers interpreted her question. NO HA FILASEK STOP I KNOW JESUS IS COMING BACK STOP I WISH TODAY.

Filasek's Neighbor's Yard
1 October 2002
6:27 PM local time

Shoeing a spider away from his face, Dietz remembered now the advantages of an office job for a body over 50.

He had enjoyed the first few hours of thinking time, but the numb bum he could forego.

Moments later an unobtrusive European-mini SUV charged out of the driveway and turned right. Two passengers.

Dietz didn't even need to lift the binoculars to ID Filasek's head low on the passenger side. He followed their progress from his hiding spot until the road turned them out of sight. Then he recorded the license plate number on his PDF.

Less than thirty minutes later, the driver returned at a slower pace and an empty passenger seat.

Dietz smiled as he stretched his legs. Very fortuitous.

He inched his way through the wild tree line to the road and began to walk back toward the little village he'd seen on the way in.

Filasek was gone for a while, Dietz needed to report in at the Office, find a place to clean up, and visit an art store for a little idea that had percolated while sitting in the field.

Baghdad Presidential Palace Gate
Tuesday 1 October 2002
11:30 PM local

Filasek spoke in impatient Arabic to the large pair of armed guards at the iron gate in front of Saddam's impressive Baghdad Palace that stretched for nearly a mile along the Euphrates River. "Look. Just call him. I flew in especially for this meeting. I know he will see me."

"We already did. He said to come right up." The guard who was smaller by perhaps fifteen pounds seemed to be the one with seniority. Filasek addressed the rest of his comments to him.

"Then why do you keep me waiting like a common peasant? You wish to displease your commander?" Filasek leaned forward; his eye level reached the man's third button from the top.

"We were told," The guard bent down and Filasek could smell his pretzel breath, "to have a little fun with you."

Filasek did not respond aloud, he merely pushed the guard aside with the back of his hand. *You will take me more seriously after tonight*, he vowed silently to the leader of the Arab world as he marched across the marble pavers that led to the massive palace doors.

Floodlights lit the palace and created interesting shadows on the walls. He stood in front of the closed doors looking for a bell to ring. Why was no one there to greet him? A whistle sounded to his left.

Filasek whipped his head to locate the sharp sound. A man was walking toward him, waving arms in the traditional robes of a Muslim cleric. "Come," the man motioned him. "We use this door."

Anger rose in Filasek's belly. Being reminded that he was unaware of palace protocol also reminded him that he was a nobody. A nobody who should have been a somebody by his birthright. He followed the cleric's black flowing robes and round pillbox hat, keeping a distance of four steps back to insure respect. And add an extra second of response time if he found need of it.

The man opened an unframed white door, and Filasek followed him inside, securing the door behind him. Servants in black and guards in uniform with guns holstered at their hips milled like picnic ants in the palace hallways the two men traversed. "The men are eating a late supper and have requested you join them there." The cleric stopped in front of another door, similar in style to others they had passed.

There was not even a second's pause to collect himself as the religious leader nodded for the duty-guard to open the door and announce him.

"Arafeh Filasek."

Filasek heard his name echo in the cavernous room. The room was pillared to support the wide arched ceiling. It shimmered like Solomon's fabled temple in gold leaf.

Five men sat on pillows around a low table on the far side of the room. A guard stood behind each man, ready to assist. Two of the seated men wore brown military uniforms and the other three traditional Arab garb. "Filasek. Join us." Saddam threw up an arm in greeting and Filasek wondered how sincere the invitation was. To make his voice travel the distance to the door where Filasek realized he was suddenly alone, Saddam had to shout, covering any vocal nuances that Filasek could have used to ascertain the situation.

Filasek could feel the cylinder of poison liquid in his pocket hit against his thigh with every step. The guards had not even searched him. He could feel the eyes of the men assessing him on his trek across the marble floor. He could feel their irritation at being interrupted singe through the atmosphere.

Filasek's glance took in all the men and committed their faces to memory. Thin, stringy-haired bin Laden he would recognize anywhere. Though he looked more like ancient paper than he remembered from the photo his mother had given him years ago. Saddam's cruel older son, Qusay, sat at his father's right hand, and both men dressed as soldiers. A French advisor to Saddam sat on a scarlet fringed pillow next to the place Saddam gestured for him to join them. The fifth man, Filasek did not recognize. Of the guards, Filasek categorized them all together, one caught his attention a fraction more than the others. Something about his posture made him seem more aware than the others.

"We were talking about the plans for November. How is your part unfolding?" Saddam reached for a clear jeweled goblet of amber liquid and slurped a mouthful.

"Everything will be in place in three weeks for an attack any time after that. I will need only a few hours' notice." Filasek was relieved that he had positive news to report. The side of his foot tapped the floor as he sat cross-legged under the table. "What about the others?"

"Why no details?" bin Laden's tongue slithered out to lick his lips. Filasek saw the challenge in the old man's dusty eyes. Filasek was exhausted of the game, and threw his plan to the side.

"You do not trust the son of your own loins?" Filasek set his shoulders firmly against the years of indifference from his run-away father.

"You are not my son." Bin Laden's tone carried a dripping layer of hate.

The small talk among the Husseins halted.

"What is this?" Saddam's fleshy face jiggled as he looked back and forth between his two guests. "My brother Osama, do you have a son?"

Filasek saw unease waver in the king's dark eyes. As if the man were questioning his life hero about his moral life and the hero had been found wanting.

Filasek felt frozen under bin Laden's unswerving gaze. "I had a son. Once." He told Saddam. "This little man killed him."

Hussein rose to his feet and gestured his guard to be alert. "Answer these charges, Filasek." His low voice rumbled through Filasek's soul stirring up anger at the accuser. He could almost feel the bullet in his brain that would be literal if he did not hold this snake with care.

"I was four at the time." Filasek appealed wide-eyed to Saddam. After a full three-seconds hanging in the balance, Saddam called his men back into formation. Filasek moved his plea across the table to his father. "I was not even there when the American soldiers came. It was they who murdered Soli with their guns."

Bin Laden's back was still stiff with opposition. "You were not my son, even then. You are the son of my brother and my wife."

Filasek felt like he had been sucker-punched. "It is untrue."

"You were married?" Saddam questioned the religious zealot. "You told me you were married to Islam."

Filasek snuck a glance at the king. His jaw was slack with the same shock Filasek felt.

"This really is no concern of yours," bin Laden shot at Saddam whose chin jerked back in surprise. Bin Laden's even-temperedness was his trademark, even under the most severe battle plans and attacks. But Filasek remembered the anger the man was capable of. He had often wondered if the beating the man had given him the day before he abandoned them had cause his short stature. His back and both legs had been broken, taking half a year to heal enough to walk again.

The silence in the room only blew on Filasek's rage. "All I ever wanted from you was for you to like me. But you, sir, the great religious leader, had only hate for me, not even indifference." Filasek knew he should stop, but the bottle inside him seemed to be exploding on its own. The audience followed as if the conversation was the Wimbledon championship march, but he might never again have an opportunity to see this vile man face to face. "You gave *my* love to Allah, and can't even lay down your contempt long enough to appreciate the qualities in me that I inherited from you."

A low rumble came from bin Laden's throat. "The only thing you took from me was my name and my son. You inherited the worst qualities from my wife and my brother. You are out of this attack." He spat on the marble floor. "You are as unworthy as the Infidels." The man whom Filasek had alternately abhorred and tried to impress sealed his lips like a used bottle of Gorilla Glue.

"Gentlemen," Saddam began. "I think we need to cool our heads. We can revisit the topic at a later time." Filasek felt the king staring at him, so he nodded in what he hoped looked like submission. "Omer, why don't you go ahead with your report."

The man Filasek did not recognize when he entered spoke in subdued tones that sounded incongruous with the topic. "Omer Asheed." He introduced himself. "My explosive gold is being weighted in Chechnya as we speak and will be ready for transport on time. I have Barhai working on it, and I already have a tentative pick-up scheduled with Agent Kenworth at Fort Knox." The Arab had an unusual accent to his Arabic that Filasek had a hard time placing.

"The explosive replacement bolts are already in the warehouse for the shuttle." The Frenchman smiled as he wiggled his fingers noiselessly above the surface of the table. "We just have to wait until we are closer to the launch date before we substitute for the originals."

"So why are you here?" Qusay threw the question at Filasek. He had always been the bold and impetuous son.

He would have to play this just right. "I have a new product that may interest you." Filasek addressed the youngest man in the group. "You and your father." Filasek glanced at Saddam and saw his mustache twitch. He was not sure if that signified interest or disinterest. He figured either way he had about 15 seconds to sell his new chemical weapon before they went on to a new topic. He kept his eyes deliberately away from bin Laden. "I realize that more and more whole people groups are threatening our way of life. It is not feasible to gas them all into submission."

Filasek saw Qusay bristle at his words. "I have found a new compound that is most effective, and it's cheaper to produce than sarin or mustard gases. And it does not have a bad odor."

Filasek saw eyebrows raise all around the table and the guards startle closer as he pulled the cylinder out of his robe pocket. "This is a tube inside a metal casing. It contains exactly one milligram of the new liquid compound. This amount, once activated, will feed on the oxygen in the air and spread to cover an area of approximately one-fifth of a square kilometer."

The silence told him it would be an instant hit.

Then the questions began. He fielded each one.

"Let's try it out," Hussein finally spoke in guttural tones.

"When and where?" Filasek stilled his hands. He was sweating from the excitement.

"I have a prison with an overcrowding problem." The king pursed his lips through his thick beard and mustache.

A deep chuckle made its way full circle around the table.

River's Room
2 October 2002

It had been hours and hours of uninterrupted quiet and Rivers felt strength returning to him. Everything still hurt though, even breathing. Sometimes he dozed on the hard floor—he was not getting back on the torture table for any reason—and other times, he prayed or tapped out conversations on the wall with Judah.

Father, I do like and appreciate that you were able to stop Filasek's sick plan to kill me, but did it have to be so painful?

I didn't make it painful because I'm mean or punishing you. Of all the ways I could stop your pain, this was the most merciful.

You could have just struck him dead.

Yes, I suppose I could have struck him dead, but I love him and would like to give him some more time to receive atonement by accepting Jesus' sacrifice.

Oh. Rivers pursed his lips. There was nothing else to say.

He saw himself as a single person in the sea of all the people God knows and has ever known and felt very small, and very big in his own eyes.

Two tears from each eye rolled in heavy drops toward his scruffy chin. "Father, forgive me?" He mumbled under his breath. "I see finally that my actions and decisions, made in rebellion against you, are what landed me where I am right now," he mumbled. "That vow was unrighteous. And I again declare it null and void right now. Since I made the vow twice I strike it down twice. I declare those words are powerless and dead in my life, and all its rotten fruit I reject and cover in the blood of Jesus."

Rivers didn't really feel anything different, well maybe a little lighter. Consequences were still consequences, there was no casting those down. It was God's law of sowing and reaping. He knew that well enough. "But Lord, if there is any way of minimizing those consequences, I'd be ever so grateful." Rivers slowly and deeply shrugged his aching shoulders to try to push out the pain and tension.

Chapter Seventeen

Wakefield lay on her bed with chandelier light shining in her eyes. Normally, brightness would not have affected her ability to sleep as her captors had planned. It wasn't now. It was her mind turning over like a rotisserie chicken set on high speed that prevented sleep.

She wished she had not sent Rivers to get some sleep. Her knuckles were sore from knocking out messages, but it helped her feel not so isolated.

She lay face-up on top of the white coverlet and stared at the light fixture hoping to tire her eyes into closing. She lifted her left leg with a pointed toe to a controlled 115 degrees and lowered it slowly for the twenty-fifth time. Then she started with her right leg. When she counted, it helped keep her imagination at bay.

At number 17, Wakefield slowed her descending leg and then let it fall from the knee. The crystals on the chandelier threw off wiggling reflections as someone walked on the floor above her.

"Why didn't I think of it sooner?" She mumbled to herself as she stood on the mattress and then balanced on the circular horizontal post of the wooden bed. "It is not a ticket out of here, but it is something."

Wakefield jerked on one of the three-inch crystals from the window-side of the fixture, so it would not be noticed from the door. It came free of its wire and fell into her palm. She lost her balance and jumped to the carpet, sending stinging pulses through her bare feet.

She kneeled next to the headboard and began to scratch on the wall. She went through layers of paint with the pointed crystal. The sheetrock began to score away in curly fragments. Widening her work area to a square two inches, Wakefield scratched and blew the chalky dust away and scraped some more.

"Boy, will Rivers be surprised in the morning." Wakefield felt her lips curl upward. Life was beginning to feel like a roller coaster ride.

Some minutes she felt ready to dissolve into a puddle of salty tears. Other times, she found joy in the simplest of things.

She smiled knowing that she would be able to touch Rivers' fingers when he next woke. Then tears threatened because she knew she was leaning on a man whom she was not sure she trusted any more. The Rivers she loved and had been long-distance dating would never throw away his principles for revenge. It was not in his character to be moved by petty vengeance. Her hand stilled in its quest to the other side of the wall. "Except that he did." Wakefield rested her head against the side of the mattress. Her feet were numb from her hour's work on her knees. "I just don't know. I can't risk having that in my life, Lord. I can't risk my heart to include vengeance in my other half." She prayed as her lower lip quivered with the pain inside. "I feel too close to breaking myself these days."

She had never considered herself a china doll to be handled gently, but she could see that was exactly how she was sheltering her heart.

Judah snorted softly as she began scraping away the sheetrock again. "Maybe I should concentrate on getting us out of here before I go crying over having to break up a non-engagement with a man who is next door literally dying for me trying to avenge a cut on my face. But who sends stupid M&Ms rather than actually say he wants to choose me."

And there it was.

A single tear rolled down her broken cheek. With all the other things that had been pressing on her for months, even working through the guilt of killing her friend—albeit he was a bad guy trying to kill the president, and *he* made the choice to jump, she didn't shoot him—and the house fire, the court appearances, none of it had weighed on her like loving and wanting and feeling put off and undesired.

Presidential Palace, Baghdad, Iraq
2 October 2002
1:40 AM local time

Filasek followed Saddam and his son through a musty underground passageway. "Is it much further?" he finally asked. They had walked briskly for more than 20 minutes. They could be taking him to his own execution for all he knew. But even with the twists and turns in the passage way he figured they had to be under the river by now. The damp air seemed to confirm his suspicions.

The Frenchman and bin Laden mumbled behind him as they walked no more than two wide. "A little ways." Hussein's voice from in front of him echoed in the stone chamber. "Are you tired?"

"It is nearly two in the morning, of course I am tired." He snapped. Then he thought better of wielding a sharp tongue with a man just as likely to cut it out as not. "But I am more anxious to demonstrate the effectiveness of this new weapon so we can come to agreement as to its usefulness in the November Endeavor."

Filasek's eye was drawn to a gas-burning torch mounted on the stone wall, one of hundreds they had passed on their jaunt to the prison. This one leaned into the passageway in an L shape and no longer carried a flame. He had passed it minutes earlier.

Filasek stuffed his sigh into his footsteps. They were walking, practically jogging, in circles underground in the middle of the night. He suddenly stopped short. The men behind him narrowly managed to avoid a collision. Before speaking, he waited for the Husseins to turn to see what was going on. "I know you don't trust me yet," Filasek appealed to the other men. "But if I was planning to kill you, don't you think I would have tried by now. We are on the same side. The side of Allah and of Islam. The winning side. Let us set down our differences for the sake of time, yes?"

The senior Hussein retraced his steps to square Filasek in the eye. It was a silent assessment. Filasek counted three breaths while Saddam stared into his soul. He bent his neck upward, too scared to look away.

Apparently, Saddam was satisfied. He broke the contact and resumed walking, never acknowledging Filasek's words. Filasek swallowed hard and brushed a shaky hand over his wiry beard.

Four minutes later Filasek followed the men who ducked under an overhanging and crumbling arch. The odor of unwashed bodies, urine, and fear hung in the air. They had arrived at the prison.

Qusay clanged on a metal triangle next to the doorway where the six of them stood. Four crashes echoed through the tunnels. Then the young man repeated the signal. Six brown-uniformed guards toting large black weapons that Filasek could not identify in the flickering light entered the area and crisply saluted their commander. "You are relieved of duty here. Report in with the assignment roster desk." Qusay ordered the men. None of them questioned the strangeness of leaving a prison unguarded mid-shift, but ran to follow orders.

The six men fixed gas masks with double charcoal filters over their faces. Saddam nodded. "You may begin the demonstration." His voice sounded tinny through the round snout of the mask.

Filasek pulled the safety ring out of the nozzle. He depressed the atomizer and a thin puff of chemicals nebulized in the dank air. It was lighter than a mist and thinner than a cloud. Filasek hoped there was enough oxygen to properly display the power of the weapon.

It began to spread at an increasing speed. After the puff dispersed to about a six-inch circumference, it became invisible.

Fourteen seconds later the first prisoner slumped to the ground with a choking sound. His cellmate hit his knees, then before his back locked, and he went face forward into the filth on the hewn rock floor.

The five others had seen enough. Saddam led them away and sealed off the prison compartment to allow the poison to complete its work. He took them back to the palace by a less circuitous route. The hollow sound of masks sucking in filtered air echoed off the clammy underground walls.

Filasek was the first one to take off his mask. One by one they followed his example as they walked.

"What is going on in there?" Filasek asked. A well-lit alcove buzzed with activity like a New York office building. Desks with computers and telephones spread in neat rows. About 15 men in Islamic robes and turbans worked in near silence.

"They are Afghans who sought refuge here during the American siege on their homeland." Saddam replied evenly. "They are working for me now, tracking the chemical and biological weapons that we must keep transporting to keep them away from the U.N. inspectors. They keep up with inventory and trucking expenses in exchange for room, board, and exile." Saddam shrugged. "It is a good trade."

"What about those three?" Filasek pointed to three men separate from the others that he had missed at first glance. They stood studying a wall map and pinning certain locations. One man shook his head, adamant about something.

"Those three are former Afghani Taliban. They are helping to organize our Army's strategies, and camp locations for the coming P.O.W.s." Qusay offered.

"If America dares come here, she will not leave." It sounded like a slogan that the men had repeated often as it flowed off Saddam's tongue.

Rivers' Room at Filasek's Villa
Wednesday 2 October 2002
0346 hours

Rivers rolled to his right on the concrete floor in the small room. He stifled his groan. "I've been in worse places," he tried to encourage himself. But at that moment, he was not sure he had. At least the music was off. He dug his fingers into his ears and increased the pressure to get them to pop by moving his jaw. He hoped the hearing damage was not permanent. "I do not want to walk around in a bubble the rest of my life."

Rivers felt his body protest every breath he took, but his mind was clear. He had not moved the entire four hours he slept, now his muscles hurt. "I've got to figure a way out of here." He rolled to his feet. "Suck it up, SEAL," he told his body. "I think better on my feet, and that is where you are staying."

Rivers took inventory of the room as he paced. The man helping Filasek had packed up all the electrical equipment, so rigging a surprise shock when someone walked into the room was out of the equation.

A coil of wire lay on the floor in the corner of the concrete room. Maybe strip off some of the plastic casing, join one end to the electrical outlet and the other to the door handle? But that won't get me out of here. He shook his head, "I would still be inside and the keys would be outside," he mumbled. Even the echo of his own voice in his cranium was off in its sound.

Rivers looked at every crack in the walls. Three of them were concrete block; the one plaster wall joined Judah's room. There were no light controls, no windows, no bathroom. Nowhere to hide.

Rivers paced. *I wonder what day it is? Will anybody come looking for me, for us?*

He stopped and bent over at the waist. His back screamed at him and he knew bending down had been the easy part. Straightening would be a nightmare. Putting off the inevitable, Rivers twisted his hanging upper body in a shoulder-width figure-eight to help oil his stiff lower back and realign his spine. Then he first spotted the anomaly.

A dark spot speckled low on the wall. He blinked once, and when it was still there, he shuffled over, with his body still folded in half. There was a gash in the wall.

Rivers ran his fingers over the hole in the sheetrock. Dust particles drifted to the concrete floor. He had not had time to inspect the place when he'd first arrived, but this had to be new. "Did Wakefield?" He could not form the question so he slumped further down to his knees and tried to peer into the hole.

A sphere of light about the size of a silver dollar shone through. He could only see whiteness. "I wonder what she used to break through." He smiled. She was certainly an officer with ingenuity, especially for a woman who sat at a desk most days.

He decided to let her sleep. He straightened one vertebrate at a time.

Renewing his pacing, his bare feet slapped the floor. Rivers wondered if they could widen the hole until it was large enough to climb through. Once it was large enough, he ought to be able to break it off in chunks with his hands. But where will that get us? We will still be in adjoining cells.

A question bouncing to the forefront of his consciousness was taking every ounce of his concentration elsewhere to keep at bay, broke through every few minutes: When will the torture start again? "God, please don't let them start in on Judah. I could not handle that."

Do you trust me, David?

The question skittered around in his head like a pool ball. "I thought I did." He finally said as his humanity hit him full in the face. "God, after all this time, how could I not trust you to do what is best for me? Is anybody else as dense as me?"

Oh, you'd be surprised.

Rivers chuckled. He could almost hear God laughing along with him.

You still can't grasp how much I love you, son.

Rivers jerked his head back, offended. "I know you love me. You sent Jesus to die for the sins of the world. He was your Son and you let him go. It was one of the first things I learned about you." Rivers felt his brow wrinkle and smoothed it out with his fingers.

Have you ever considered how much I love you, individually?

"I suppose if you are asking, then I haven't." Rivers leaned against the wall and lowered himself down painfully. He drew his knees into his chest and wrapped his arms around them. "Help me understand." He bowed his face.

Take off the mask, my David.

Rivers looked up. The voice sounded soft and yet clear enough that he had to see if the Father was standing on the concrete floor beside him. When the Father called his name, never had his meaning been more pronounced. Beloved.

Rivers let his guard down. Pictures of the men he had killed came into the focus of his mind's eye. They did not taunt him or even appear accusing. Their faces were just in front of him. The two women and the child occupied the foreground as the men flashed in the mid- and background.

There were so many.

He remembered the lies and deceit, and he was no longer able to assign it to his job. It had become part of who he was. Rivers felt only slight remorse for his deeds.

He tossed his head, scratching his prickly beard on his shoulder. He did feel guilty for not feeling bad. They were people, too. "I should have cared more. But I didn't."

I see the full revelation of who you are, David. I can stand it. You think you hide the ugliness from me. But you cannot.

Memories slapped his face. His hatred of Filasek for his arrogance and his slicing Judah's face. Anger surged in his soul at the injustice of having to stuff down his knowledge of good and evil because of his job.

He stayed with the Teams because he liked it. He liked the power, the pride that came with his title: SEAL. The killing had become first nature. It no longer touched him. He exuded to others the importance of discipline, but now, it was control. He wanted to control everything around him, because... "Because it makes me feel that I matter."

Rivers gasped as saw the depravity of his own heart.

"How could you love me?" He swiped at a tickle on his neck. Pulling his hand away, he expected a mosquito, but his fingers were wet. When did I start crying?

There is no logic in my love for you. I just do. My one compulsive behavior.

Rivers dropped his head against the plaster wall and let his feet slide out away from him. He was absolutely depleted. "Please don't stop."

I won't.

Presidential Palace, Baghdad
2 October 2002
7:54 AM

Filasek entered the giant dining room where the men had eaten the night before. A table full of breakfast fruits, breads, salads and meats had been spread. The five men stood talking in two groups, one Hussein with each group.

Filasek stretched his neck high as he glided toward the men. The guards on duty looked like they had been up all night. Filasek's eyes flickered over the familiar one again. The man's mouth puckered and he looked away too quickly.

"He's arrived. Let's get to business." Saddam had on a less wrinkled uniform this morning, but he still looked dusty. But then, he usually did. Filasek was moved to sit at Saddam's left and Qusay still occupied his right. Bin Laden sat overly close on Filasek's right. Filasek caught a whiff of Chinese soap whenever bin Laden moved.

"I want to include this new chemical in our three-pronged attack," the terrorist leader said silkily. Filasek was concerned about the overnight change in his father's demeanor.

"I would also like to have as much as possible delivered to me." Saddam crossed his legs under the table." I have Kurds stirring up trouble in the north and Turks poking their spears over the borders too." Saddam reached for a crusty roll and one of the bowls of soft cheese spread. "Not to mention American troops beginning to muster in Saudi Arabia."

"I hoped this would be the case." Filasek could not keep his lips from turning up. It felt strange to his facial skin, and he rubbed his hand over his tight cheeks and beard.

"Can you do it?" Saddam sounded almost like his patience was being tried.

"I have 18 full batches I would like to sell to you for personal use," he addressed Saddam and had to glance past Qusay in order to address bin Laden on his right. "I will have enough to cripple 500 American metropolises by the last week in November."

Saddam leaned over and whispered in his son's ear and the man nodded once.

Qusay's face darkened. Filasek could feel the young man's jealous streak rising. "How do you propose to get it inside?" He sneered.

Filasek, if nothing else, had learned to be quick on his feet. "Actually, I think you would be the best man for that job. Would you consider getting 500 bottles of perfume to the 500 largest cities in America for our jihad?"

The man's arrogance flared his nostrils. "It will be simple for me."

"Excellent. Thank you. I knew you were the best." Filasek felt his stomach lurch. He despised catering to arrogant royalty.

The guard shift changed and Filasek watched the familiar man walk away. Suddenly, he identified him.

"Do you normally keep traitors in your bodyguard, your Majesty?" Filasek asked after the former guards were gone. He opened his eyes wide with innocence. It was a perfect setup to get Saddam on his side completely.

Chapter Eighteen

The tall man rushed into his apartment and turned on his computer. Filasek had recognized him, he was sure of it. He had to get an e-mail off to Dietz before something happened. He would not wait for a secure channel. He loosened his boots while the computer came to life.

He double bolted the door and returned just as the signal connected. He typed, not taking time to correct mistakes.

Filasek is here. Peddling a new chemical weapon. Saddam will be sending someone to check on the plant security in Greece. You must do something soon. There are three attacks planned on America in November, and they will use the gas on 500 American cities. I've been made. Care for my family.

Dovlatabodi's mouth went dry as he heard a dozen sets of boots treading up his wooden stairway outside.

"Come on, let me in." It was Jasiq's voice on the other side of the pounding.

He punched the send key and then began the deletion process on his hard drive by the second crash against his door.

The door splintered in two as Dovlatabadi closed his laptop's cover and stepped away from it, hoping against hope that it would complete before the men thought to check it. "What is going on?" he yelled at the uniformed men breaking into his house.

"Why did you not answer the door?" A man with coal black eyes asked.

"I was in the bathroom." Dovlatabodi shrugged. "That's why I ran home."

Even as he gave the excuse, he realized they had not accused him of anything yet.

"I think not." He recognized Filasek's voice before the shrimpish man rounded the corner to join the storm troopers who had just wrecked his door. "Hello there, Dovlatabadi. Have a new job now, I see."

There was no use feigning innocence. The world-class assassin focused sharply. The man he had once vowed to take out was finally standing before him. If he did not act now, it would be never. He could not live with that. *How ironic*, he thought, *I can't die with that either. The CIA had better live up to their promise to free my mother and brother.*

Dovlatabadi stood as still as he did when he waited for a shot with his scoped sniper rifles. Filasek moved in closer; he could feel the tiny punk's arrogance reach him before he could reach Filasek. The rest of the Republican Guardsmen, Dovlatabadi counted nine without breaking eye contact with Filasek, each stood with a pistol trained on his head.

No one flinched, save Filasek who slithered ever closer.

Filasek was hissing some nonsense. He ignored it as he waited to pounce.

Five feet, three feet, two feet. Now. Dovlatabadi struck like a python.

Filasek's neck was soft in the crook of his elbow. The small man was pawing at his arm as he gasped for breath. Both of Filasek's feet shot out in front of him as he squirmed like a strung minnow. Dovlatabadi held him dangling off the ground.

Saddam Hussein walked inside the door last.

Dovlatabadi swung around to spot the sound. "What is wrong with you people?" Saddam barked at his soldiers. He cuffed the nearest one on the back of the head and grabbed the pistol out of his grip.

Dovlatabadi tightened his hold on Filasek's neck and felt the squirming slow. It had not been long enough to kill him. But maybe he had small lungs for his small body.

Saddam did not even glance at his troops again before holding the pistol to the base of Dovlatabadi's skull.

"You can still choose me." The voice he dreaded was back, inside his head.

"Not you again!" Dovlatabadi howled aloud. "Get out!" He shook his head; he had enough going on without that crazy voice coming after him again.

That the coin-sized muzzle was cold was the last sensation he registered.

*****

Filasek griped his throat and tried to massage out the deep pain. "Why," he asked Saddam on their way back downstairs, "did bin Laden suddenly accept me this morning? After last night, I half-expected him to slit my throat while I slept."

"I encouraged him to put away his bitterness at least for the time until the Endeavor." Saddam paused and the entire entourage behind him followed suit. "But after it is over, I'd watch my back if I were you. I've never seen him like this. When do you leave?"

Filasek's chest swelled with pleasure. King Hussein cared for him. Suddenly his whole future—a future with him ahead of his father—dangled enticingly before his eyes in the dank hallway outside the flat of assassin he had once hired to kill the president of the United States. That decision was finally paying dividends.

"I've got a first-class ticket reservation in just over two hours, your majesty." Filasek pinched his thigh. Stupid! He shouldn't have boasted about a first class ticket to a man who owned a fleet of jetliners.

Island of Poros, Greece
Ridge near Filaseks Villa
2 October 2002
0745 hours

Dietz pushed aside some overhanging brush to view the house next to Filasek's. The infrared goggles still showed eighteen warm bodies milling throughout Filasek's villa as it had every 15 minutes for the last 9 hours, since his return from that quick trip into town. Wakefield's visa card had not moved in a day and a half. "I hope that's a good thing," he muttered as he sighed. Flexing and releasing each muscle group, Dietz felt every year of mileage he had put on his joints. The moist morning air did not aid him. He just felt cold, stiff, and sticky.

He caught a movement with his naked eye. A man dressed in loose white pants and a wife-beater undershirt wandered from behind the white pavilion in Filasek's neighbor's yard. The gardener was back. "Don't they give you any time off?" Dietz wondered in a whisper.

The gardener wiped the dirt from his hands on the seat of his trousers, kept the small trowel and began walking in a straight line. Toward him.

Dietz held his breath and tried to make himself as small as possible.

"Ahoy there!" The gardener called out in English.

Why would he speak English? Dietz wondered. *How can he see me?* He decided he should have asked himself that question first.

The man in white pointed a deeply tanned and muscled arm at Dietz's face. "You there. What are you doing?"

Dietz pushed the infrared-equipped binoculars under the long grasses and rose a little from his place in the underbrush as he pointed to his own chest. "Me?" His mind raced to come up with a cover story that would include the English language and the German handout he was still carrying.

"How many other people are hiding out in my grass? Stand out here so I can see you." He sounded like an old seadog barking orders. The squint deep lines around his eyes indicated that he might be.

Dietz rose slowly with his hands out.

"Who are you, landlubber?" When the man was close enough, Dietz could see that he was probably nearing 75, but his body appeared as strong as a young mule.

Dietz adopted an English accent. "My name is Richmond Dietz. I am with British Intelligence. On assignment with the German Embassy in Athens." Dietz looked at the gardener's squinty captain's eyes and wondered if he would accept the story.

"Then why are you hiding like a manta ray in my grass?"

That was the second time he had implied owning the property. Dietz reevaluated the man. He held his shoulders high and the set of his tanned jaw seemed to hold aristocratic leadership. There was something appealing about a property owner of his obvious wealth who tended to his own landscaping with pleasure.

"I am investigating your neighbor." Dietz watched the man's eyes for a reaction. "What can you tell me about him?"

The older man shook his white hair and lowered the trowel to his thigh. He blew out his breath. "There is something not right over there."

Dietz took a step closer. "What have you observed, Captain?"

The man drew his neck back. "How'd you know I was a captain?"

Dietz smiled with closed lips and raised one eyebrow. He felt it unnecessary to remind the seadog of his profession. It could be such fun to catch people off guard with knowledge.

The captain raised a gnarled hand and with a codger's smile gestured in a small circle as the information came to him. "That man next door, he has owned the place for nigh on 15 years. In that period, he visited three times, until 8 months ago when he moved in. Now he comes and goes at all hours of the day and night. He unloads cargo out of his plane in the dead of night and carries it, himself," the captain emphasized with a cocked brow, "to a doorway into the cliff basement of the neighbor on the other side." He pointed past Filasek's shining villa to the blue roof of the next house.

"Guess they don't realize what I can see from the top deck balcony." Dietz turned to look at a turret that sat aloft the captain's home like a maintop platform high in the rigging of an old clipper ship. He shaded his eyes with his hand.

"Looks like it is probably your favorite place."

"Besides the garden."

"Besides the garden." Dietz agreed. The sea captain had spent hours putzing in the flowerbeds the night before. Dietz had left at a quarter to eleven, stiff from waiting for the old man to disappear. Now he understood. The captain had no restrictions on his life. *I hope my retirement is as freeing.*

"That man is smuggling something." He sucked on his teeth. "I just don't know what. He had a monster alarm system installed about a month after he moved in. Don't know what he needs that for. Nobody bothers anybody else's business up here."

Dietz's PDA pinged once. He withdrew it from his inside breast pocket of his jacket. "Excuse me a moment," he turned toward the sea to read the e-mail.

It was a lot to take in. The e-mail was written with obvious haste. He reread it. If Dovlatobadi talked to get himself out of trouble in Iraq, Dietz knew he would end up in the hot seat at Langley, probably forced retirement or worse. But if he did not talk, he was most certainly dead in the next few hours. Either way, it was very bad.

Dietz studied the horizon absently as he tried to determine the best course of action. Filasek was in Baghdad. Now would be the best time to grab Wakefield. But he still did not have any leads on Filasek's contacts. Except Saddam Hussein.

The revelation surprised him. Filasek did not seem to be far enough up the food chain to be able to get in to see Saddam. Maybe the old soldier was feeling desperate.

He cut his eyes back to the blue roof and decided to leave Wakefield for a little while longer while he looked into Filasek's new cliff warehouse. He felt a pang of disappointment at losing an expensive, well-placed snitch. He shrugged. *Nothing I can do from here. I don't have anybody else inside.*

Dietz turned back to the captain only to find him under his right elbow, staring at the classified screen. "What in tarnation is that contraption?" He scratched his scalp and smoothed down his wiry white hair.

"Tarnation?" Dietz could not keep a straight face. "I haven't heard that word in a while."

"Picked it up from my first mate. We sailed together 28 years. He taught me English. Great man, that Spires. Too bad about the great white that took him." The man's sea eyes stared far away.

Dietz had a feeling the captain was already packed for a trip down memory lane. He excused himself while the old man mumbled about First Mate Spires' Tennessee in America.

Dietz slipped the PDA back into his pocket and wandered over toward Filasek's estate more anxious than ever to make arrangements back at his hotel. He would definitely need a shower.

Rivers' Room
1002 hours

Rivers did not even feel himself start drifting off. He opened his eyes again and knew time had passed. But how much?

The annoying sound that brought him back from deepest sleep squeaked again. More dust fell out of the small hole in the plaster.

"Wakefield, is that you?" His jaw was stiff and he rubbed the hinge as he opened and closed his jaw.

"Rivers? I can hear you!"

Rivers had to smile. She sounded as giddy as a six-year-old on Christmas morning. "It is good to hear your voice, too, Judah," he told her softly. He calculated; it had been over three weeks since they had last spoken. "Do you think you can hold off on the destruction until morning?"

Her laugh tinkled through the tiny hole. It was refreshing to hear, even if he could not see the way her eyes almost closed and little wrinkles formed at the corners of her mouth and eyes. He missed seeing her face. "It *is* morning, sleepyhead. The sun is five inches off the horizon."

She had a funny way of describing time. "You have a window," Rivers sighed with the realization. "What is it like outside. I have been inside for a week."

He heard her giggle again. It sounded again like the six-year-old, not the resolute naval officer he was used to. She sounded happy. Happier than in Washington or on any of the assignments they had been given together or individually. How was that possible?

"From where I am sitting, I can see the sky as blue as the topaz in my grandmother's necklace. There are a couple of little pouffy clouds. And there must be a decent breeze out, because they are changing shape constantly."

"Pouffy clouds?" Rivers smiled again. Her voice was infectious.

"I thought that more descriptive than 'cumulous clouds.' Um." She hesitated. "Rivers, will you do me a favor?"

She sounded young. "Anything." Rivers scooted on the floor as close as he could get to the hole where her voice drifted to him.

"See if," she cleared her throat. Was she embarrassed about something? "Um, see if you can reach my fingers through the wall."

Rivers pushed the first two fingers on his right hand into the ragged sheetrock hole. He ran into soft insulation before touching the tips of Judah's slender fingers.

His skin twitched at the human touch. "I've been starved for you, Judah." He sighed and rested his forehead against the wall.

"You are real." He heard her voice crack as if she was crying. He wondered if he was supposed to be hearing her whispers. "I thought I dreamed you, but you're real."

"As real as that sunshine out there." He could not see it, but he knew she could. "Thanks for coming to find me. I am sorry I didn't stop to see you in Washington. I thought I would be home by now."

"Let's not talk about it right now, okay?" Her voice was weak.

He wanted the laughter back. He needed the laughter back. But he was too raw to think up small talk. Finally, she spoke again. "Tell me your earliest childhood memory." He heard her sniffle.

"The earliest recollection I have is getting my three-year-old birthday spankings at my party in front of my friends. My dad thought it was funny—"

"Hey, someone's coming," she interrupted. "Don't let them find the hole." Her fingers slipped out of his grasp. Rivers rubbed his thumb over the fingers that had touched hers. They felt softer just from having been next to her.

Chapter Nineteen

From the protective cover of the tree line and over the garden fountain, Dietz watched his mark disembark from the backseat of a taxi. Dietz stood and stepped forward to make his move while Filasek's back was turned. Suddenly Dietz dropped back to watch. What held him back?

He wasn't sure. All senses were firing on full-auto. It had been years since he had done solo field work, and yet the hesitation he knew was not a false start, but a sixth sense of knowing in his knower that the game was about to change. He needed to wait for the next entry point.

The short man disappeared behind the villa door. If he had been a cartoon, there would have been smoke leaving a trail behind his heels.

The whole exterior of the villa was quiet. No lights, no servants, no body guards ventured a nose to the outside, or even to lift a curtain.

Dietz now observed 19 heat sources inside, rolling about the hallways and rooms like billiard balls, coming together for moments and then knocking away just as fast. Word of Filasek's return spread quickly.

The rattling lock alerted her in time to flop back onto the bed covers. *God give me strength and your words*, she prayed. *New beginning*, she remembered His cleansing words from the night before.

Filasek breezed in. A small grin lit his lips. "Why are you in such a good mood?" she asked, dreading the answer, but still curious.

The short man rubbed his hands together in short movements. "I am glad you asked." He smoothed his beard. She sat up and scooted against the headboard. Filasek moved to stand at the footboard and caress the eight-inch round finial of the post. "It seems our plans have been successful again. All of our television stations have gone to cover the story with live news."

Wakefield felt her stomach drop. "What. Did. You. Do."

"I hope you did not have any relatives in Alaska, Miss Wakefield. The news is reporting a zero percent population survival in and around the Anchorage area. Even better than we had hoped for when we set the charge." Filasek's chuckle was sickening.

"How do you blow up a city?" Judah felt her mouth grimace and her eyes widen as she pictured the destruction.

"We did not blow up a city." He spoke down to her. "We blew up a mountain covered with snow and ice where the city sits at the base. The biggest avalanche ever recorded buried the city. Like Pompeii except cold." He roared at his own joke.

Wakefield shook her head at the horror of it. How many people lived in Anchorage? Certainly not as many as the LA basin, but still, it was horrific. She had not heard any rumors or vocal traffic talking about Alaska as a possible target.

"What is even better," Filasek stroked the wooden finial as if it was his crystal ball, and Wakefield cringed. *There's more?* "We managed to get a small hand grenade into Camp David where your president was taking holiday."

Judah's chest heaved without her permission. *Not Bush.*

"We doubt we hit anything, but CNN is speculating, because the cowboy president is not showing himself. However, the funny part is that your vice president has locked himself in a room while America drops into chaos." Filasek looked quite self-satisfied. Judah wanted to scratch his eyeballs.

She closely controlled her voice before she let herself speak. "What is it that you wanted, Filasek?"

"I want your password to get into the Naval Intel web site."

"It is secure." She scoffed. "It is not accessible from outside. Even with a user name and password." It was not strictly true, and she forced herself to look him unflinchingly in the eye as she said it.

"That is a lie. I have already gotten past the firewall. If you tell me, you can save your friend some pain. But I'll get in either way."

Judah clamped her lips and looked away in defiance. There was not a chance that she was giving this terrorist access to all the super-secret material her password was cleared to read. She steeled herself against what she was pretty sure would be coming her way next, even as she prayed, *Lord, just in case, please remind them to change my clearance ID to inactive so the password is invalid.*

Filasek's phone chirped. "Yes?" he held his elbow out as he held the phone to his ear. His eyes narrowed and she could hear rapid words on the other end. He glanced at her and then to the door. "I'll be down momentarily."

"Cheerio." Filasek charged for the door. "Give it some thought. I will return for your answer."

Before the second lock clicked in place, Wakefield was down on the floor on the other side of the bed. "Rivers? Rivers did you hear that?"

"Stick your fingers in here." His calm voice wafted into her room. She complied, anxious for his touch.

"Did you hear about Anchorage and Camp David? How did they get inside?" Her breath was coming in spurts. She held her air as long as she could so that she could hear any reply Rivers had and then sucked in a new lung full.

"Lieutenant Commander Wakefield!" Her spine straightened of its own accord at his tone of voice. "He was lying to you. No avalanche could cover the entire city of Anchorage. President Bush was scheduled for Africa this week, if I am not mistaken. And does it sound to you like Dick Chaney hiding in the back of some locked closet? No. Think about it Wakefield. He is trying to skew your worldview. It is the first step to brainwashing. Do not believe a word that comes out of the man's mouth unless it is something that you knew before you got here."

"Like Dietz?"

Rivers' reply was slow in coming. "What about Dietz?"

"I didn't tell you? Dietz was shadowing me when Filasek came in the bar where you first connected with him. Filasek sic'd a couple of his goons on him. I was nearly out from the drugs when he instructed it, but I remember the men's faces; I didn't dream it."

"My God! Dietz is dead because he came looking for me?"

"And, um," Judah paused to consider phraseology. She did not want to make him feel responsible, but he would find out eventually.

Better sooner. "By the way, I am not a Lieutenant Commander anymore."

"You got a promotion? But you haven't even been in rank a year and a half. Oh." He choked on the word. She could picture the way his face scrunched on the left side the way it did when he got unfavorable news. "I am sorry, Judah." His voice was small. "This has turned out to be a worse idea that I thought."

"You knew it was a bad idea and came anyway?" She felt her jaw drop incredulously. "Are you insane as well as having a death wish?" She accused. "Excuse me," she folded her knees under her to get up. "I need to think."

**Filasek's Neighbor's yard
2 October 2002
3:19 PM**

The slight squeal of old brakes behind him broke the peaceful sound of surf and seagulls. Dietz turned in time to see a man hoist a shoulder bag to rest on his back as he leaned in the front passenger window of a dusty, peeling taxi. The man stood and slapped the roof with an open hand, and the taxi U-turned and disappeared over the rise in the road.

Dietz didn't move a muscle as the man took inventory of his surroundings. He looked down to what appeared to be a phone in his palm and looked back at Filasek's villa and began walking with stiff shoulders back. The man completely overlooked the unmoving lump of Dietz crouched next to the large stone fountain in Filasek's neighbor's yard.

"Thank you." Dietz whispered a prayer. It was strangely becoming easier.

The man would have to walk directly next to the hedge in the old captain's yard in order to get to Filasek's villa. Dietz had no question as to where the man was headed.

As he sauntered closer, and just before he disappeared from view for a few seconds behind the hedge, Dietz noted that he was younger than he had originally thought at a distance. He was definitely carrying. Twice inside 60 seconds, the young man had reached back to pat his lower back.

Who was he?

Dietz decided to find out.

Dietz scurried silently over manicured lawn to the hedge where the roadside gravel crunched under the man's shoes. Dietz matched him pace for pace.

The end of the hedge drew closer and closer and Dietz's body tensed as he prepared to pounce.

He waited one beat behind the hedge's curtain for the man to get fully in front of him so he could remain outside the man's peripheral vision.

As he sprang Dietz fairly flew for the man's neck with the crook of his left arm while reaching under the man's jacket to disarm him with his right hand.

The pair went to the ground. They tussled until Dietz got the man's air cut off in the choke hold.

"Be still," Dietz said in English. He tightened the hold.

"Who are you?" The young man choked out in accented English, pawing at Dietz's arm.

"Security." Dietz improvised. "Who are you?"

"Zee Jasiq. Please. Release me. I am a business associate of Mr. Arafeh Filasek.

"What business?" he asked. This had to be a man sent by the Husseins.

When Jasiq did not respond, Dietz bent at the waist, taking the man's head quickly down to Dietz's knee. "What is your business and where are you from?"

Still silence. Dietz wished he could see the young man's eyes. The eyes spoke volumes when the lips would not.

Dietz decided to try something different.

He loosened the choke hold and cocked the man's Glock and pressed the muzzle to the side of his head.

"I've not seen you here before. Are you expected?"

The man seemed to melt to the ground gasping great breaths, and yet keeping his hands very visible and his head very still against the muzzle.

Definitely law enforcement or military trained, Dietz assessed. That accent, even in a few words, Dietz identified it.

"Look. I didn't mean to cause a problem. I was sent by mutual business acquaintances. We needed to verify certain things after Filasek's recent visit, so I was sent to follow him home."

"So you are from Iraq?"

The man still stared at the ground unmoving, but the rapid tensing of his muscled neck told Dietz he was correct.

Somehow Dietz's guess of where Filasek had just flown in from gave him credibility in Jasiq's eyes. It was like popping a cork. The whole story spilled out.

Dietz lifted the man by his arm pit, the Glock he moved to the base of his neck. The man's dark hair brushed his shoulders and covered the muzzle. "Stand up. Let's walk."

Dietz turned him away from Filasek's villa and crossed the road to the ridge's cliff across the street from the sea captain's hedge.

They moved at an angle back toward where the taxi had dropped Jasiq off. Dietz wanted to keep out of the line of sight from the villa.

"All right. Hold it there," Dietz jerked back on his arm and removed the gun from the man's head.

"Is there some sort of secret entrance?" Jasiq asked twisting his head left and right and then leaning over the cliff to search.

The man was certainly an optimist. "Something like that," Dietz nodded slowly. Dietz spun the kid around and they finally made eye contact.

Dietz adopted a casual stance, which relaxed Jasiq greatly. He released the clip, tucked it in his armpit. Pulling back on the slide to de-cock the Glock, he popped the unspent bullet out of the chamber to the grass. Replacing the clip, Dietz stuffed the gun into his waistband and put a hand on the Iraqi's shoulder. They were of equal height and weight, but Dietz's weight was centered in his middle with the old-man paunch that he loathed, while Jasiq's weight was equally balanced between muscular thighs and shoulders.

"Never give away information." Dietz said while reaching into his breast pocket, and before Jasiq had a chance to adjust his stance or even go back on the defensive, Dietz had brought out his pen of death.

With the extra time to aim, Dietz brought it up to the young man's freshly shaved throat. Dietz could see little nicks and a line of sun tan there from a recently shaved beard.

Dietz hadn't needed to spend the time at the village arts shop buying the false beard and keeping the disgruntled owner late after all.

Dietz twisted the pen. The small puff of gunpowder tattooed the skin and as Jasiq went down. The younger man's eyes had a single moment in which he registered the betrayal.

"Sorry, kid. It was unavoidable."

Dietz caught and redirected Jasiq's fall toward the edge of the cliff. The body flopped and bounced once before becoming dead weight that picked up small stones and cascaded the whole pile down the side of the cliff into the treeline 300 plus yards away. Jasiq disappeared into the tall grasses at the edge of the trees.

Dietz dropped to his knees on the roadside, the gravel pressing into his kneecaps as he studied the trail and waited to see if there was movement from where the newly blazed trail ended.

Nothing for more than three minutes of staring.

Dietz rose when the rock impressions dug in too far for his knees to bear any longer.

As Dietz turned toward Filasek's house with his way of entry now secured, he saw the old seadog standing in the tower of his house, not looking out at sea, but staring straight into Dietz's heart.

Chapter Twenty

A man with dark straight hair in Western European dress trousers with knees that had seen better days stood in the entrance of his home. Filasek observed him from the shadows of the upper level. The visitor did not look like one of Saddam's men as he had been advised on the phone. This man with a small mustache that seemed to twitch and a scruffy beard held his shoulders with too much confidence.

Filasek cleared his throat to draw the man's attention upward. The man's dark eyes found him too fast. "Dempski, show my guest up." He turned on his heel and walked to his receiving room.

It had been aired while he was gone and smelled like the fresh sea air. He looked out the six-foot windows with his hand behind his back. "It will be a disappointment to return to the desert." He was surprised at how much he enjoyed living by the sea. But his home was the wilderness of Afghanistan. He would rebuild. *My ancestors were forced to be nomads, but no more. I will establish a kingdom not bested since Solomon.* The first step was the sale of the chemical weapons to Saddam.

Filasek heard the two men enter the room behind him. He stroked his beard. It felt smoother today. "Have a seat. Close the door on your way out, Dempski."

The latch clicked softly. Filasek turned to face the man. He placed him in his early sixties. "You look familiar. Who are you and what can I do for you?" Filasek formed the words in English, not knowing what language the man might speak. His skin appeared too light to be middle-eastern and his features were pinched as if he needed glasses.

*****

Dietz sat on the hard chair in Filasek's light pink and sea green parlor. He held the terrorist's gaze as he repeated the name on Saddam's man's passport. "You probably recognize me from the king's bodyguard. I lead the guards. I saw you there a few hours ago. I am Zee Jasiq. Saddam ordered me to follow you and check the security of your manufacturing plant."

"And me." Filasek's eyes narrowed under his furry brow knowingly.

"I hope you don't mind." Dietz adopted a humble approach. He formed a small smile that exposed his teeth to Filasek. "He can't be too worried about you though. He did send the old man." Dietz pointed at his chest.

Filasek bobbled his head and politely chuckled, but Dietz knew the terrorist was still determined not to trust him.

"You understand I have to call and verify your identity." The man shrugged his diminutive shoulders almost apologetically.

Filasek was a master, Dietz assessed. He asked for no papers. Those were so easy to forge these days with laptops and color printers.

The man pressed only two buttons to place the call. Dietz chuckled inwardly but kept his cheeks from moving as he stayed in character. How many people in the world could actually say they had Saddam Hussein on speed dial?

Dietz listened as Filasek spoke. It sounded like he got Hussein himself. Filasek described him as medium height and build with a mustache. He kindly left out the aging bit. Which was good. There were at least 30 years difference in age between him and Jasiq.

Dietz looked down at his folded hands. *Is that a bit of blood under my thumbnail?* He asked himself studying it with his peripheral vision. He ran the jagged nail on his first finger under his thumbnail to get at the crease of rust red that lined his nail bed.

"Very good. I will send Jasiq home to you as soon as he is satisfied with the security of my facility." Filasek was eyeing him as he crooned his farewells.

The phone clunked into its plastic cradle. "You may go out on the balcony for an afternoon tea." Filasek gestured to the terrace off the next room that was visible through the panes of glass.

"But..." Dietz started, confused. He left his nail and stilled his fingers.

"Are you in a hurry to get back?" Filasek seemed condescending, but Dietz had no idea why he would be.

"Well," Dietz stalled, "I was hoping to spend the weekend with my son." *Oops*! He remembered too late that Filasek had just lost his sons, wives and daughter in the air strike in December, not a year earlier.

Filasek eyes tightened just the slightest bit at the corners. It was barely a reaction at all. "I will allow you to observe when it is convenient for me." He spoke slowly as though to a dunce. It was no wonder Filasek had few friends.

Dietz hauled himself to his feet, first leaning over and then lifting his backside before straightening. The small of his back had not recovered from the swath of woods and overgrown grass he had dozed in for 15 minutes at a time the night before. At least that's what he decided to attribute the stiffness to, certainly not to tossing a grown man's body off a cliff.

Dietz paused at the doorway. Apparently, he would be going unescorted. Filasek was looking far away. Maybe the terrorist contained an ounce of human emotion after all. "Thank you for your hospitality. May Allah be with you." Dietz bade him adieu.

When he received no response, Dietz turned and walked away.

Wakefield's Room
1621 hours

Wakefield curled her knees closer to her chest as she listened to Rivers recite. "But thanks be to God who made us his captives and leads us along in Christ's triumphal procession. Now wherever we go he uses us to tell others about the Lord and to spread the Good News like a sweet perfume. Second Corinthians 2:14."

Wakefield smiled as she considered her next verse. "As the deer pants for streams of water, so I long for you, O God. I thirst for God, the living God. When can I come and stand before him? Day and night I have only tears for food. While my enemy continually taunts me saying, "Where is this God of yours?"

"What's the reference?" Rivers voice challenged her through the two-inch hole."

"Psalm 42:1-3." She grinned. This was a game fit for a starving soul.

"What does it have to do with my verse?" They had been playing for over an hour.

Wakefield squinted her eyes as she tried to remember what had sparked the verse she quoted. "You talked about being captives, and I talked about my enemy taunting me." She shrugged. It was not a hard connection.

Rivers chuckled a slow deep chuckle until he began coughing. Hacking would be more accurate. It worried her. "I was talking about," he loosened one final cough, "being *God's* captive, but it will do. I have another one, but there is no way I can ever win this game with you. You have a photographic memory." His sigh sounded long-suffering through the hole.

Wakefield pouted out her lips even though there was no way for him to see her when she sat this close to the hole. "Oh, poor baby," she teased. "I know being a SEAL and all, you probably have no concept of playing anything for the sake of fun and refreshment. Everything is a competition with you. It is time you learned to have fun."

"You have always been fun and refreshing to me. So is competition." He sounded so matter of fact.

"Only when you win." She teased, but there was truth behind it. His competitive streak had caused more than a few tiffs in the year they had known each other. "But go ahead with your turn." She was having fun and did not want to let it dissolve into a bashing session.

"When the poor and needy search for water and there is none and their tongues are parched from thirst, then I, the Lord, will answer them. I, the God of Israel will never forsake them."

"God, I hope not." Judah leaned her head back against the wall and sighed. She chuckled again. "We are back to a water theme. Are you thirsty, Rivers?"

"Aren't you?"

"Not really."

He sounded puzzled. "Have you been given water or something?"

Wakefield pulled her head away from the wall; concerned she stared at the hole in the sheetrock. "I have a bathroom with a faucet. Have they deprived you of water?"

"I had a drink when I was in the basement yesterday morning. Or was it the day before?"

"My God, David. We have to get you some water. Do you have anything over there we can use as a straw?" Wakefield paused as a familiar sound registered on the back of her brain. "Wait! Here he comes again." Wakefield scooted away from the hole.

How could they be so cruel as to deprive a man of water? Filasek rattled the door and appeared in the room. The man was a snake, lower than a snake. But if she showed him her rage, he would know about their communications. She was not going to risk that lifeline for anything.

"Are you ready to help out?"

Wakefield tightened her lips. *I am going to get wrinkles if I keep this up.* She smoothed out her lips and gave him her serenest of smiles. *Mask it, Wakefield,* she commanded herself. *It is time you began acting like the naval officer you are, instead of some emotional babydoll.*

She walked casually over to the dresser with the water pitcher. She leaned her back against the wall and her forearm on the dresser top. She had no particular plans, but felt lightheaded and was going to prop on some support.

"Have you heard of the phrase 'name, rank and serial number,' Filasek?"

Filasek rolled his eyes, looking very Western in his mannerism. "I got it from your pimp, too. We'll see how long it lasts now that the two of you are on speaking terms again." Filasek slammed the door behind him.

"Good girl. Do not give it up for me, Gunsmoke." Rivers voice of encouragement filtered through the air before Filasek arrived next door.

He knew about their talking. She looked around the room for possible hiding places for listening devices and cameras. "They are so tiny now, it would take a team of people days to go over this room." She whispered as her practiced eye caught three-dozen prime spots on her first spinning glance.

When the screams resumed, she did not care if she was being taped or bugged. The naval officer sat on the pillows at the head of her bed and put herself as close to Rivers as she could with the wall between them.

She prayed.

It lasted two hours and forty minutes.

Wakefield could not feel the blood in her palm where her fingernails had sliced a pattern of four holes.

Filasek's Balcony
2 October 2002
5:25 PM

Dietz sat drinking his fourth refill of apple tea. Filasek knew how to hire good help, he admitted begrudgingly. The woman had remained unobtrusive, but exceeded Dietz's every expectation of an afternoon tea. After she cleared his plates, Dietz browsed through a selection of periodicals and hardback books she had laid out for him.

It would have been a perfect afternoon on the deck, had he not been anxious about his people, his host, his character portrayal and the itchy old-man beard, and of course, his mission. Oh, and that infernal cat. It sounded like it was in heat with its yowling screams. "Someone should put it out of its misery," Dietz mentioned to Yolanda as she poured the last of the pitcher of tea into his tall glass.

Her round cheeks jerked but she refrained from comment this time. She had practiced witty English replies to his other remarks.

Dietz reopened the musty Irish poetry book, but he did not read. He stared through the ironwork of the balcony to the cliffs and sea below. The waves gently lapped against the rock cliffs and the pilings of the pier. The boat and plane rose and fell with the rolling water that lapped against a miniscule beach.

The surface was fairly flat today.

Like trying to break out of hypnotism on his own, he struggled to tear his eyes from the view. He had to find a bathroom.

When he returned to the balcony, Filasek was waiting with his back to the villa. "I trust you are ready." The villa's owner seemed to have the same draw to the compelling water. Filasek seemed calm to his core. Dietz, in all his years of service, had never personally seen this particular quality displayed in his enemy. He had only read about it.

Placidity was too human. Dietz averted his eyes before he succumbed to the connection. "I will follow your lead."

Filasek led him through a series of stairways and tunnels through the rock by flashlight. "Excuse the lighting. I am planning to put in gas torches like the tunnels in Baghdad soon."

"They are convenient, sir." Dietz wiggled his mustache back and forth in the dark behind Filasek. He hoped the information was not a trap. Every minute he was with Filasek, he hoped the man would not recall exactly where he remembered him from. Dietz had never considered the lighting source of the Iraqi Catacombs. It made perfect sense. He would update the military and intelligence databases with the information and mark it "plausible" when he got home.

Filasek removed a key from his pocket and fit it into a large reinforced metal door. Then he punched a code into the keypad beside it. A series of secondary locks disengaged.

Dietz nodded as he was sure that Zee Jasiq would have done. His security at Langley was much more sophisticated, but it was also in the open. This door had the added security of a secret location. Until now.

Filasek was beginning to remind Dietz of a mole. Not the kind connected to his profession, but the animal who lived underground. From the intel he had collected when Wakefield returned from Afghanistan, the terrorist had developed a system of corridors in the rock of the butte in the wilderness. She had mentioned a sublevel anthrax lab in his last home. Now they had spoken of the tunnels in Baghdad and toured some more under his basement here in Greece. A mole was too slick-skinned. Maybe Filasek was more of a groundhog than a mole, Dietz thought as he took in the high tech equipment and the six people busily trying to ignore the tourists. Yes, Filasek was stubby and furry like a groundhog.

"Where are you keeping the supply you intend to sell to us? And what are your access protocols?" Dietz raised his eyebrows as he did a second sweep of the large room.

"I sent it before I knew you were coming. It has been shipped for five hours or more." Filasek shrugged and blinked leisurely.

Dietz allowed the terrorist to win this round. He knew the man was lying because he had not been home for five hours yet, and had not left his villa to send anything, nor had any courier come or gone from the ridge. Dietz had been watching with the infrared binoculars that he left in the grass when he had approached Filasek's front door.

Dietz approached the man entering data on a computer. "Walk me through the entire process, will you?" He had the time. "Might as well get Saddam's money's worth before getting back on that airplane home." He returned Filasek's shrug and smiled, pleased with himself. How many opportunities did the CIA have to take a guided tour of a WMD lab?

Wakefield's Room
2 October 2002
1824 hours

Judah paced from the window back to the door. *Why won't he answer me?* Almost two hours had passed since Filasek left Rivers' room and stopped to ask her once more for her password. She paused and kneeled next to the hole again. "Rivers. Rivers! Come on, wake up, David." She pleaded into the next room. The other side of the hole appeared as black as roof pitch this time, instead of the super bright LED lighting she'd seen in the morning.

Unless he had been taken away, he had certainly passed out from the pain. She did not know which finish she preferred. She called to him again. "Lieutenant Commander Rivers, get yourself up out of that bed right now. That is an order, mister!"

She put as much energy into it as she could.

After a moment, a stirring as quiet as a roach scratching inside a wall sounded in her ears. She didn't think she was making it up.

Then it came again. A guttural groan followed.

"You're alive!"

Another groan. Her heart cringed at the pitiful sound coming from the SEAL. Did she want to know what they had done to him because of her refusal to talk?

"Mom. Is that you?" His voice trembled.

"It's me, Judah."

"Am I dead, mom? It is so dark. I always thought it would be light."

He sounded so child-like. He had retreated into a hallucination. Tears swept down her cheeks unchecked. "It is good Filasek is not here," she whispered low enough so that she would not be caught on tape. "I would tell him anything just to be able to hold you." Her chin quivered and she pawed at the wall.

The whiteness of her room compared to the blackness of Rivers' room made her shake her head. There was a contrast that ran deeper than the color, but she was loath to catch it.

Digging the small crystal from between the box spring and thick mattress Judah gouged the hole larger with vengeance. She had to get to him.

"Rivers." She continued talking as she enlarged the hole. "God has not given you a spirit of fear, but one of love, power and a sound mind." She did not know if she was speaking to him or to herself.

He did not speak again for 25 minutes while she carved the hole to almost four inches on her side.

"I am not on a bed, Wakefield." Came unexpected words from the other side. "And I am the senior officer. You can't give me orders."

"David. David. You're all right." She hated the tearful edge in her voice. It was fine for when no one could hear, but not now.

"Well." He huffed and she heard a sliding on concrete sound. "I would not go that far. But I am alive." His voice sounded so scratchy. She remembered the water.

"Listen, we need to get some water into you. Is there anything you can use for a straw?"

"It is blacker than night over here. You are my one star in the universe."

"Nice wooing technique," Wakefield snorted appreciatively, "But seriously, can you remember the layout of the room. What can we use to move water from me to you?"

"Lemme think." Rivers hardly even used contractions, and he always spoke with newness, not using trite phrases or verbiage. His slurring worried her.

She made her eyes take in every item in her room individually. *Come on, Wakefield. Be creative.* The shower curtain was cloth. If she stuffed the corner into his room and the wet the fabric, he would be able to suck some moisture out of the material. A pillowcase was more manageable. She reached up to strip her white pillow.

"Try this." Rivers coughed. A stiff red plastic wire poked its head through the opening.

"Are you planning to use it as a straw, Commander? Because I should pull the wire out of the casing first."

"Uh-uh." He grunted in the negative. "It is like in elementary science."

"What are you talking about?"

"Hold the wire tight and then drip water onto it, slowly. It will follow the course of the wire through the hole, as long as it is not touching anything and drop into my mouth."

Wakefield would have looked through the hole to check his eyes for sanity, if she thought it would do any good. "I guess I went to a primitive elementary school. I never learned anything like that." She was skeptical, but what could it hurt. She grabbed the half-full crystal pitcher and trotted back to the wire.

She poured. "It's not working. It is just puddling on my carpet.

"You have carpet and water? Try pouring a trickle."

She adjusted the angle of the water pitcher and raised the wire so that gravity would not play as heavy a role. A few drops at a time. "Goodness! It is working. Open up, Rivers. Here it comes." She chuckled in relief. It was weird, but nice to be doing something.

My way would have probably been easier. She didn't say anything though. It would have ruined the delightful sound of Rivers' swallowing.

Chapter Twenty-one

Dietz stretched back from the computer in the cavernous basement lab. "You'll have to get that fixed." He pointed to the screen. He had broken through the firewall password in a matter of minutes. "Then I think we can do business." He was enjoying the tension that had been mounting in the lab for the last four hours.

Dietz wondered how far he could push the terrorist. It was obvious from Filasek's stifled sighs and incessant pacing he was near the brink. "Do not forget the shipping and loading problems you pointed out." Filasek's voice tinged with barely concealed frustration.

"Yes." Dietz nodded and pushed his borrowed chair back. "You'll want to have that door reinforced and the refrigeration temperature regulated. It is imperative that you drop it below -10 degrees for the stability of the product."

"I told you before." Filasek scratched his fuzzy chin and smoothed the bristles back into order. "Temperature has nothing to do with this weapon. That is old-school. It is all about the propellant."

"Which can be set off prematurely if the gasses get too warm." Dietz emphasized his point with a single cocked eyebrow as if he were talking to a petulant student, not a terrorist trying to break into the inner circle.

Filasek set his jaw. He jutted his chin toward the computer monitor. "How did you get into the system so quickly?"

Dietz offered a lazy smile. "I used to freelance for the American CIA. You'd be surprised what secrets they share with their own." Strictly, it was untrue, but Filasek had never been on the Agency payroll. How would he know?

Dietz gestured the oldest worker over. "You need to add symbols instead of just letters and numbers to your passwords to buy more time to shut out intruders. And pay strict attention to the pop up messages that tell you that you are being monitored. The Baghdad Palace values privacy."

The man nodded and exchanged places with him not speaking a word. Filasek probably had him scared to open his mouth.

"May we go out by way of the water?" Dietz loved the control he felt. Filasek would not risk the sale by upsetting the waters of their tenuous relationship.

"You are ready?" Filasek seemed genuinely surprised. Dietz's mind raced. Had he forgotten some aspect of terrorism sales that he should have demanded to know? He could not come up with anything so he clamped his lips tightly and nodded with a quick up and down jerk.

"I did not think we would make it to the evening meal while it was still warm." Filasek told him caustically as the nasty snarl reappeared on his mouth. He was being sarcastic after all.

Filasek's phone chirped in his pocket. It was the first time since they had been in the cliff basement. "Excuse me while I take this." Filasek moved away from the group around the computer, but no one else was talking so they did not miss one cryptic word. "What do you mean a setback?" Filasek's face noticeably paled even under the halogen lighting. "No. I don't care about the cost. You get us back on that road. Hire anyone you have to." It did not escape Dietz's notice that Filasek was speaking in perfect American English.

Dietz stared at the floor and studied the cracks that disappeared under the table where the computer sat. He savored every word to ruminate later.

"I will see what I can find out from the warehouse tomorrow. No, thank you. I will never step foot in that country of accursed infidels again." He spit on the floor.

Dietz looked up sharply. And returned his eyes to the floor. Only the United States or Israel could procure such a distasteful reaction from a good Muslim.

"Until tomorrow." Filasek clipped the phone shut and muttered under his breath while flying for the door. Dietz watched him move like lightening.

Filasek looked over his shoulder at him as the seaside entrance slid open as if to say, are you coming or not?

At the edge of the dock, Dietz commented appreciatively, "Beautiful boat. You don't see many of those at home."

"It is a week old." Filasek smiled. Dietz found a weakness in the desert man. Of course, he already knew it was new. He had watched the old one blown to the sky. "I can return you to the airport in it in the morning if you like."

"Don't go to any trouble." Dietz waved off the suggestion. "You can direct one of your men to drive me back to the ferry." Dietz looked at the sky. It had a funny greenish cast to it. No clouds marred the moon reflection, on the smooth waters, but Dietz noticed the drop in air pressure.

"Believe me," Filasek sighed. "It is no trouble." Dietz could almost see him salivating to drive it.

They began climbing the stairs to the villa towering above them. "What do you think of Americans and Israelis?" Filasek poked.

Boy, that came out of the nowhere. "I uh," What answer would be acceptable? "I believe that the average citizen, like the average Kurd, is too cow-like to realize that they are being anesthetized to true life."

Filasek seemed more fanatical than that. He was looking for more. Dietz gave it to him. "However, the leaders of those countries are servants of Satan, elected by his demons to destroy the principles of Islam. There is no God, but God, and Muhammad is the apostle of God. God did not debase himself to father a son. Jesus is a lie."

A strange sadness descended over him as he spoke the words into the air. His spirit rejected the announcement. He did not believe it. In fact, he found he believed the exact opposite. *When did that happen?*

"Do you believe in the righteousness of Allah's every word?" Filasek asked.

"Doesn't every Muslim?" He looked over at the small man.

"What I mean is, do you live by the creed and rightness of jihad?"

"I do." Dietz tasted iron in his mouth as he bit his tongue. "I would not have served in Saddam Hussein's bodyguard if I did not believe in the promise of glory in the afterlife." *Thank God for the two-week Islam course I enrolled in last June. Here I am praying again. Strange.* "Surely you do not wish to discuss the finer points of our religious differences." He was anxious to move to a new topic.

"No." Filasek's furry brow moved together as he tightened his forehead. "I want to recruit you."

They reached the second plateau in the staircase. He could not have been more surprised if Filasek had drawn a gun and shot him. "Recruit me? For what?"

"The head of my security team." Filasek smiled, and it seemed sly to Dietz. "I am reorganizing."

"But I already have a job." Dietz rubbed his neck. He could feel the noose tightening. Something big was in the works. "Perhaps we could talk again after I make my report to the elder Hussein, hmm?"

Filasek's Villa
Dietz's overnight room
3:10 AM local time

The Grecian wind billowed through gauzy white curtains at the tall, single-paned window. Lying in bed, Dietz discussed eternity with the face on the moon. It was a much better bed than the previous night. He rolled to his back. It was probably safe now.

Soundlessly, the CIA counterintelligence director booted his PDA. The LED face glowed like a cyclops. Dietz tapped the table while he waited for the mail icon to appear. He bridged his fingers. He put his hands in his lap. He tapped with his pencil wand and accessed Wakefield's locater. "The problem is not the Internet," Dietz formed the words with dread. "There is no news." Dovlatabadi should have written again with the next satellite pass, if he was still breathing.

Dietz glanced at his watch. "He's had time for two notes." Dietz composed a short note and hit send to request an undercover SEAL raid at Filasek's address, including the basement next door. He sent it Eyes Only to his boss Edward Hammond, the Director of Central Intelligence. "That ought to send them scrambling." Dietz smiled. He figured the time difference. Eight in the evening. Ed would be just about ready to head home and he would check his e-mail one last time while he re-sharpened the pencils he had used that day. Hammond kept a more rigid schedule than Big Ben.

Dietz knew he could count on the Team to arrive any time after noon tomorrow, but being SEALs they would probably strike in 24 hours, during the dead of night. They would work around the moon that was three days past full by beginning their offensive after the moon set. Dietz shook his head. "It is amazing what you can predict when you focus on the big picture instead of trying to figure out the details."

Dietz changed programs and centered on Wakefield's tracking device. She was approximately 140 feet from his room. The opposite end of the house. He could not wander that far plausibly looking for a bathroom if he got caught.

He held the binoculars to his eyes in the darkness. It was dizzying as all the walls were stripped from the house. He looked at the carpet. All the floors were concrete. They showed up differently than the two-by-four studs in the walls. Dietz pulled his face back to blink away the sleepy blurriness. He swept the structure from one end to the other.

The house was at rest.

He hid his equipment again and lay down to join them.

*****

Judah Wakefield awoke to a screaming bladder. She wiggled uncomfortably as she sat up from the side of the bed where, last she remembered, she had leaned to rest her back. Her right arm was numb as it hung through the hole she had gouged out. She measured it at eight inches in diameter on her side and perhaps six inches on Rivers' side.

Judah rocked from side to side. Her tailbone told her she had fallen asleep hours ago. Her hand rested on Rivers' heart. He slept leaning against his wall with one hand on her elbow and one on her wrist.

Disentangling herself, she wondered how they would handle the arrangements when Rivers' needed to use the facilities. She stumbled slightly in the dark room. She decided to worry about it later. He had been dehydrated, and it would not be a problem for a while.

"God, won't you rescue us soon? Show us the way out?" she prayed before resettling herself on the floor next to the damp patch of carpet from her earlier experiment with the wire and water.

Sparks tingled in her fingers as the circulation resumed in her arm, but she needed to feel Rivers' breathing more than she needed relief.

Thursday 3 October 2002
5:50 AM

Filasek took his yogurt and fruit breakfast sitting on the balcony off his room as the sun rose. "Raul, please see that Hussein's man is escorted to the ferry and that his every need is anticipated." Filasek raised his spoon of vanilla yogurt.

"He did not join you for breakfast?" the large man asked. Filasek squinted against the hazy morning sun to look at Raul. It was obvious that no other body occupied the table.

"I turned on the monitor to check on him twenty minutes ago. He was sleeping like a baby. A very loud baby." Filasek cut his grapefruit in half and sawed around the edges to loosen the fruit. A spit of juice spurted onto the glass table top.

"When is his flight? In case I need to wake him."

"I don't believe he has reservations yet." Filasek moved the serrated knife between the thin membranes to create bite-sized pieces. "Keep an eye on Jasiq," Filasek glanced at his employee mid-slice, "without smothering him. You may work with him soon."

"Where will you be going, sir?" Raul stood stiffly, far enough away to avoid the projectile citrus juice.

"It is none of your concern. That is all." Filasek finally got the first bite of grapefruit to his tongue. The vibrant tartness woke him like the strongest coffee in the world could not.

The door clicked with Raul's departure.

"I am going to have to change our morning briefings to evening. I like quiet in the morning too much to be bothered." Filasek pried loose another bite with his deep-bowled silver spoon.

*****

Dietz smiled while looking at his watch. Precisely noon. Surely Filasek had given up on him as a companion today.

He had not heard a single sound from the hall all morning as he lounged in bed and went through his checklist for the day's plans. Break Wakefield out, check Filasek's office, steal a boat, head back to the Athens airport by way of the Pension Hotel, call the Office to confirm the raid.

"A busy day," he whispered to the mirror as he smoothed his pencil-thin mustache then twisted his neck this way and that checking for glue residue. He rubbed his hands over his fake-fuzz cheeks. Pretty solid. It looked so staged to him, he shook his head at his reflection in the mirror. It was probably only because he knew what his real beard looked like. He was looking forward to a smooth face again.

He glanced left to the window for perhaps the tenth time since waking. The putrid green sky was becoming more pronounced. A small pile of angry clouds sat on the horizon.

Dietz pulled open the heavy bedroom door to search out a meal. Filasek's lead man hovered in the doorway. What was his name? "Raul?" Dietz raised his gaze to look the large man in the face. "I wonder if you can tell me about the weather."

"Cyclone coming." Raul gestured for him to follow. "A brunch is being kept warm for you." They traipsed through the corridor and walked past several other bedrooms and offices that Dietz had observed hours earlier in stick form. "I expect it will make landfall in two to three hours. They come in pretty fast around here. Only last a half-day or so though. Filasek will be back by then, I am sure."

He did not sound sure at all.

So, Filasek was gone. Perfect timing

Dietz ignored everything else his escort said.

"I will leave you to your breakfast then." Raul turned to leave and then added, "If there is nothing else?" The man did not seem accustomed to this function. Dietz waved his babysitter away.

Dietz gobbled down a tasty quiche—for having no bacon—and breakfast bread with an unidentifiable meat spread, but he slowed to relish the chilled grape juice.

He placed his linen napkin on the tabletop. He had a fairly good idea of the villa's layout now. "No time like the present." He took a right out of the small dining area.

Chapter Twenty-two

Wakefield's Room
Thursday 3 October 2002
1244 hours

"Do you think I will ever look back on this experience?" Judah intoned as she gouged out more of the sheet rock. The hole was just about large enough for her to start scoring and pounding it out with her hands and feet. "I don't care if I look back and see some epiphany in my thinking process or regret everything I did here. I just," she stilled her hands to readjust her slippery grip on her third crystal. "I want to look back. I want to button the brass buttons on my winter class A's, and return to duty." Her hands slowed as she realized that the uniform was out of the equation.

"I understand completely." Rivers was laying on the floor. She was glad he was finally acting on her suggestion to rest and boost his resistance. Filasek had been to visit just after sunrise, but had not returned for nearly six hours now.

Judah was proud of him; David had not uttered a sound for the entire half hour. Too bad she could laud herself for the same silence.

The bright lights were on again, and with the growing size of the hole in the sheetrock, around ten hundred hours she had taken her first look at the nasty burns on David's bare chest, neck and arms. She could not see his legs, but she could tell his shoes were gone. His feet sounded like raspy old men on the dry concrete.

She touched the scar on her right cheek. If David had any unresolved guilt over that incident, he should be able to sleep with the fact that they were even now.

She did not expect to ever sleep normally again.

A strange scratching sound came from the door to her room. She had not heard anyone approach this time.

There it was again. She put the crystal down and dusted her hands on her black pants. "That's not noticeable at all." She chided herself.

"Rivers, I think Filasek is back again." She whispered. "I hope you're up for it." The scratching came again. "I'll pray for you all the way through."

Her door creaked wide. A figure slunk inside. *What is this?* The figure stood straight. Judah blinked. She narrowed her eyes and blinked again as the face became more clear.

Her dry contacts made changing distance in her focus difficult. She had not cleaned them in too many days.

"Rivers?" Judah slumped downward and reached for her connection to her partner. "I think I am hallucinating."

"You big kidder." The sound came from the doorway.

It was definitely Dietz's voice. He chuckled. She remembered the first time she had heard Richmond Dietz laugh. She had not even known his first name then.

She felt a gurgle in her stomach. He had an aroma of food around him that had already reached her. "Dietz?"

"Yep. The cavalry is here."

She tripped over the toe of her own shoe trying to hurry toward his arms. She hurled herself like a puppy the last few feet.

"I thought you were dead. I thought those goons from the bar killed you."

Dietz caught her under her arms. "And I thought you were passed out when you went by us." His arms came around her back.

"I was close to gone. I sure could not speak. Let's get out of here. I will be happy not to spend another minute."

Dietz pushed her slightly away but held onto her upper arms. She was glad because she thought she might just fall over with excitement. "Were you talking to Rivers a moment ago? Or was that…"

Judah felt a bubble of happiness float higher in her gut. "No, I was not hallucinating. Rivers is next door. But he is in bad shape." She directed her voice toward the hole in the wall. "Hold on, Rivers. We're coming to rescue you."

"So I hear. Hop to it, Commander!" David's voice wafted in softly.

"You are not 'rescuing' anybody." It was the tall dark-haired man from the first day. His wide girth filled the entire doorway. A drawn gun looked comfortable in his right hand, cellular phone in his left.

CIA Headquarters, Langley, Virginia
Thursday, 3 October 2002
0602 hours EDT

Ed Hammond hung his damp umbrella and more damp pea coat on the cherry coat tree left behind by his predecessor, ten months earlier. He had been promoted from within after serving for eighty-two months as the head of counterterrorism. Old Bill Stennis had committed suicide after 18 years with The Company. Hammond did not wonder why now that he sat in Stennis' vacated seat.

Too many secrets.

Too many lies.

Hammond checked his watch for the forty-fourth time since rising. The SEALs would still be in the air. Their flight seemed to take longer than if he were crammed into coach or lashed into a jump-seat himself.

Hammond ran wide fingers over his shiny scalp, fresh shaved yesterday, as he walked to his clear fiberglass desk. He tossed the newspaper onto the chair side of his desk.

"Lou, lots of coffee this morning." He begged into the intercom as he twisted around the desk to sit. With the remote, Hammond switched on the television that would update him on the last five hours of what the world knew in an inter-company newscast.

He flipped open the newspaper to full size and leaned over it. He would read it from cover to cover like a book, flat on his desk while he listened to the news briefing.

Page four caused him pause.

Not removing his eyes from the grainy picture, Hammond reached to his left for the top drawer. It still squeaked, he noticed. His black coffee mug with the CIA emblem in gold clunked as he absently set it aside. He maneuvered the paper closer so he could study the middle section of the top of the page with his magnifying glass.

He swore colorfully. His ability to curse well was the only thing he had taken away from his public high school in the inner city of Chicago. The story that ran with the picture came from Reuters, the British version of the Associated Press. Reporter G.L. Johns had adapted his story from an *al Jazeera* television broadcast.

American spy discovered and hung, the caption stated. "This face *is* familiar," Hammond angrily tried to place it. It was not one of his men, he was sure. He searched the rest of the picture under the round glass.

The fuzzy background looked like downtown Baghdad. "Those are military uniform pants and boots." Hammond looked up at the television without seeing it. "It had to have been a quick trial and punishment if they didn't even remove his boots." Hammond glided the magnifying glass back and forth over the newsprint picture. He remembered where he had seen the face before.

The counter intelligence unit had forwarded one picture along with DNA and fingerprints to complete the file on Azure Tiger, the assassin who had committed died in custody after taking a shot at the president in January.

Hammond studied through narrowed eyes the features of the man's face again. "He is remarkably well preserved. Which means…"

He slammed his fist into the desk and cursed again. "Dietz." He pounded three more times, picturing his subordinate's head beneath his meaty fist. "I am going to kill him when he gets back. It is fine to keep secrets from them," Hammond gestured outside his window, "but not from me. You do not keep secrets from the head of the CIA!"

He folded the page back to emphasize the picture. With a black Sharpie marker he circled the dangling body and printed next to the text, "My office, NOW! E.H."

Hammond's heels thumped on the marble floor as he stepped three doors down to Dietz's office.

"Ms. Cravits." The brown-haired woman looked up in surprise as he punched his code to open Dietz's inner office door. "Be sure this stays in the center of his desk. I want his first appointment when he—" Hammond was not sure how much she knew, "returns from vacation."

Island of Poros, Greece
12:55 PM

Filasek looked at the sky over the lemon groves as he drove the winding cliff road toward home. The green cast matched his mood. "A completely wasted morning. Now I'll be stuck inside for the rest of it." He cursed. "That storm will be here by two o'clock."

"I suppose," he looked out the left window of his yellow MR2 to watch a flock of black birds getting out of the path of the cyclone, "it will give me more playtime this afternoon." Twenty minutes from home he began to smile as he considered ways of forcing the American woman to talk. She would beg to tell him more before his evening meal. Her reprieve had gone on too long.

His phone chirped in his breast pocket. These Western clothes were good for something after all. Pockets that are not buried in layers of fabric. He flipped the speaker open. "Filasek."

Only static sounded on the other end.

He flipped it shut with a vile curse.

The engine roared in response to his heavy foot on the accelerator.

Filasek's Villa
Wakefield's Room
1255 hours

Wakefield's stomach dropped at the sight of one of the men who had carried her out of the bar. The exhilaration of escape morphed into the expectation of death.

Dietz whipped around to the intruder.

Wakefield had spent her emotional margin on the roller-coaster of the last few months. Now as she stepped forward to make her appeal, she found that her supply was depleted. She reached inside as far as she knew how. Empty. She continued forward unsure of what she would say when she got to him.

The stringy-haired fellow was talking, but she was not listening. He was probably just warning her to stop coming anyway. Only eight feet now.

He would have to move his arm to shoot Dietz behind her. That would take time. If Dietz had a weapon, she hoped he was going for it.

"You look like a smart man," she stated. Another step. Her voice was flat and she blinked several times to refocus her vision on his eyes. Despite his rag-tag appearance, he did seem to have an awareness about him. He was more than a half-witted man hired for his bulk, she realized.

"What do you think Filasek will do to you," her ankles felt week as she enlarged her step this time, "when he discovers that you have killed his star hostage?" Only three feet from the muzzle, but she did not release his eyes. They were a strange combination of light brown and olive flecks.

She felt Dietz behind her before she heard him. Training drill took over as the man in front of her seemed to be considering her question.

Judah moved her left hand behind her hip. She marked off a signal with her fingers. On three, she collapsed to the carpet. Her fall was less controlled than she had hoped.

Dietz attacked over her falling body.

Wakefield heard a single blow and then a gasping gurgle.

Filasek's second-in-command hit the floor precisely three seconds after she did. A look of surprise froze his wide jaw, and his eyes somehow broadcast a desire for help and fear simultaneously. His fingers were wrapped around his own throat.

Wakefield heard the snap of plastic before two pieces of what she assumed used to be the man's flip phone went skittering in opposite directions on the polished wood floor of the hall.

"Let's get out of here. If he got Filasek on the phone..." Dietz shook his head and reached a strong hand down to her. "That was quick thinking."

All she had the energy to do was nod. It was nice of him to say so, but she had not planned anything.

Dietz stepped over the guard first. The man made a single-arm attempt at tripping him. Dietz offered his hand back to her. "I need to get my purse." She stepped to the bathroom door where the sling bag hung on the handle. "A lot of good it did me here. I did not have a single snack. I always bring food with me." Wakefield took Dietz's hand and stepped over the large downed man while staring at his face.

His lips hardly fish-gasped anymore. His eyes half-lidded, told Wakefield that the man's fear had been well placed.

"Which way to your partner?" Dietz voice interrupted her thoughts.

She pointed left as she bent at the waist to take the man's pulse. "He's nearly gone." She looked up sideways as Dietz told Rivers to back away from the door.

Dietz unloaded a gun into the doorframe. The sound was so jarring Judah reached up to protect her ears. Her brain felt like it would explode. The fall of the handle echoed with the eight gunshots.

The sharp smell of cordite punctuated the blast of sound. Why had Dietz not shot the guard?

Judah lost the man's wrist pulse and dug with her first two fingers for movement in his throat.

Nothing.

She smoothed an open palm over his eyes. She hated dead eyes.

A pair of dusty feet appeared in her peripheral vision. The left one had an oozing cut. She followed a long pair of legs up to what used to be khaki pants. The hem of a wrinkled blue shirt with two buttons left spread into wide shoulders.

And there was David Rivers' devil-may-care smile. He jutted his chin at her on the floor. "You staying with this one or coming with us?"

Sweet relief prickled over her scalp. "I haven't decided," she offered him a small, closed-mouth smile. "Depends on you."

Rivers' eyes narrowed. "What about me?" His words sounded cautiously optimistic. Typical Rivers.

"Will you promise to take better care of your *next* birthday present?" She pointed at the frayed shoulder, missing buttons, and torn collar of the blood-soaked shirt she had painstakingly picked out at Macy's in August.

His grin grew impossibly wider. "If *you* promise no more clothes as birthday presents."

Dietz stepped between them, replacing a pen in his breast pocket. "He promises," he looked at her. Dietz turned to Rivers, "She promises." He used his shirttail to wipe down the gun. He tossed it on the dead man's chest where it balanced precariously then slid down toward his arm pit. "Can we go now?"

"Please." Rivers breathed. She was surprised that he was actually on his feet and moving without help.

"We both need something to eat if we are going on the run," Judah dictated.

Dietz hesitated, his face a blank mask. She wondered what he was thinking as he twitched his tiny mustache back and forth. He obviously came to a decision as he reached back for the empty pistol.

"Kitchen is back this way." Dietz took the lead. "Grab what you can and eat on the run. I don't trust that sky."

"The sky?" Rivers asked as they charged through the corridors behind Dietz.

"A cyclone will be making landfall in the next hour or two." Dietz told them both over his shoulder.

Wakefield increased her pace. If it came to a question of death by Filasek or death by a cyclone, she chose the weather.

They walked into a deserted downstairs kitchen. Something bubbled on the stove, but not a soul peeked out. Wakefield devoured a banana while still picking out an apple and filching loaf of cooling bread from the sideboard.

Rivers picked up five of the hard-boiled eggs that were also cooling on a dishtowel next to the bread. A watery pudding sat on an orange stove eye. It smelled like rum and coconut to Wakefield. "You need some carbohydrates too, Rivers." She tossed him an apple.

Dietz tucked the empty gun into his waistband. He was looking out a rectangular window over the industrial sink. "Guys." His voice sent a chill of fear through Wakefield's spine. "I don't think the ferry is going to be running by the time we get there, and it took me three hours to walk up this far."

"We'll be going downhill." Wakefield said, eyeing Rivers' tattered body. "What about Filasek's boat or plane?" She wondered aloud. She pulled open a door onto a back patio 40 feet above the pounding surf. The wind whipped her hair into her face and mouth.

"Now why didn't I think of that?" Dietz pounded on her back excitement in his voice. "Between two U.S. Naval officers one of you can steer a boat right?" Dietz edged over to the railing to look down on the dock he had seen from Filasek's neighbor's backyard.

She followed him. "Uh," she searched the rocky coast line, "where's the boat?" The lone Cessna bobbed on waves of growing intensity.

"Can either of you fly a plane?" Dietz asked hesitantly. He did not turn back to them for an answer, only stared down at the aircraft below.

An incessant honking came from the front side of the house. A pair of brakes squealed. "Filasek is back." Wakefield gave language to the uh-oh demeanor on the two men's faces.

A thunderous roar sounded out to sea. The storm blasted away some miles to the south headed straight for them on its way to the mainland.

"I have a flight simulator on my computer at home. How hard can it be?" Rivers' smile was full of confidence. He started down the stairs. "It is now or never," he called out. Judah felt like a mannequin, unable to move from the deck.

Judah looked at Deitz with wide eyes. "Maybe he won't have to take off. Maybe we can just taxi on the floats all the way to Athens." She pursed her lips. "Is there any place to shelter between us and Athens?" She reached up to calm the hammer in her chest.

Rivers slowed on the first landing of the steep staircase. He waved them down with a smile. He was such a bad faker. She could see in the set of his shoulders that he was scared. But it put him ahead of her on the fear scale. She was terrified.

Chapter Twenty-three

Filasek threw open the front door. "Where is everybody?" He did not care if his voice sounded shrill or if his movements came in jerky bursts. He turned in a complete circle in three twisted steps, tossing his head around. "What do I pay you people for?" He shrieked.

The air seemed thick and timid. Something was definitely wrong.

He scrambled up the wide carpeted staircase. His first thought was for Hussein's guest. Filasek took half a dozen steps in the direction of the guest suits where Zee Jasiq had been sleeping a few hours earlier.

As suddenly as the wind changes direction, Filasek about-faced. His gut told him to check on his other guests first.

He swept through the corridors to the southwest wing. He cursed as he became winded. "Where is my staff?" he grumbled. He flashed his eyes in every direction at all three intersections before arriving at the Americans' quarters. Not a single person had appeared in his hallways.

He saw a reflection of light shining on the hardwood of the hall. It seemed to come from the room where he had stashed the Wakefield woman. *That's impossible.*

A lump on the floor of the otherwise dark corridor came into view. As Filasek scurried closer, the lump became an arm. Filasek did not try to contain the growl of rage that rose from his belly as he identified the owner of the arm.

Raul. And he looked very dead.

Wakefield's room was open.

So was Rivers'.

How did they escape me again? A wildcat shriek echoed with his stomping heel in the corridor.

He knelt down to touch Raul's skin. It still felt a normal temperature. It couldn't have been long. "No blood." He commented.

Filasek's instinct for escape told him they would head for open water. He continued running. This time to the lower level and out the back door.

There they were.

He could see his plane bobbing on the growing waves. They were already untied from the dock. He strained to hear the sound of the engine. The only noises were natural. Wind and waves. Even the birds had run from the impending storm.

Filasek's breath came in regular torrents as he collected his thoughts and priorities. Two white streaks formed in the turquoise white-capping water behind the craft as it picked up speed moving out to open sea.

A snarl of a half-smile formed beneath his beard as he remembered. He had put off refueling the plane after returning from Athens on his last trip. The Cessna had less than a quarter of a tank left. Barely enough to make it to the city.

His smile dropped abruptly. The aircraft also contained a radio.

The realization rearranged his order of business. Taking the stairs down two at a time, he burst into the cliff-side loading area of the chemical lab. "We have a possible security breech. I need this lab cleared out in a half hour. I do not want to lose this stuff. The truck is in my second garage."

He tossed the keys to the woman. "Follow the protocol I set in place exactly. If you disappear, I will hunt you down. Load all the equipment and raw materials. I will meet you in four days at the rendezvous point."

No one said a word. There was no time. Boxes seemed to materialize from the air. They had practiced the complete drill twice before. It took 47 minutes the first time, 38 the next time.

He grabbed an AK-47 and three clips of ammunition. "Lock the door behind me." Filasek scurried back toward his house and felt the first drops of rain hit his face.

Standing on the end of the pier, he shielded his eyes against the wind and light rain. He did not see the plane on the water or in the air. His new boat would pick up the slack. They had not had enough time to get above the cloud cover.

With the remote start button on his keychain, Filasek fired up his boat that was nestled in his neighbor's boathouse. The ramshackle shed's only redeeming quality related to its shingles.

Open Sea between Poros and Athens
1331 hours

Rivers scanned the instrument dials in the cramped cockpit. Wakefield fidgeted in the co-pilot's seat. Her skeptical grimace made him want to prove his worth even more. "You all right back there, Dietz?" The CIA man had graciously accepted the cargo hold smaller than a car trunk as his riding space.

"Just hurry, Commander. My legs are already going numb."

Wakefield laughed beside him; she had so many different kinds of laughs. This high tinkling giggle was her stress-relieving laugh. The lady had had to use it far too often in the ten months he had known her.

Rivers jogged the throttle, maneuvered the flaps, adjusted the heading by moving the nose attitude. All the parts seemed to be unobstructed. "Going to do my best and hope that is good enough. Buckle up."

He pulled back slowly on the steering column. The engine responded with a growing roar of power. The floats began to cut through the waves instead of being tossed by them. The cabin immediately felt more secure.

Rivers scanned the gauges one more time. Hydraulics, temperature, altitude, speed, all the indicator hands looked to be in familiar ranges for take-off. The fuel was low, but it would get them away. He tapped the face of the indicator with his index finger just to make sure.

The green swirling horizon sat on gray-black water. When had the blue patch of sky been swallowed up? *Storm is moving in fast now.* He tightened up on the throttle. The engine kicked harder.

In the tiny mirror mounted outside to his left, Rivers saw their wake. "We are kicking up a spray." He felt pleased with his progress. Unfortunately, even playing with a flight simulator taught him that take off required a fraction of the skill that landing did. And he had never even simulated a float plane landing

The speedometer indicated 50 knots. That was probably fast enough. He adjusted the attitude of the nose to pull them up from the resistance of the waves. He felt the rise. Then they dropped back into the water with a jarring bounce.

He brought more air under the wing by tipping the nose higher in the air. He kept the airspeed increasing by easing the throttle closer to his body.

The second time they stayed aloft.

"We're up. You did it, Rivers!" Wakefield patted the top of his hand.

"You doubted?" He threw her a wide grin.

"I hoped you'd be able to start the engine."

"You're not supposed to tell him that." Dietz corrected from the back seat. Rivers did not think Dietz sounded very confident either.

Rivers pushed the nose higher to gain altitude. Thirty feet was just not acceptable.

The weightlessness was different than in a jumbo jet or helicopter. It was more satisfying, more freeing to be at the controls himself. He felt his back relax against the seat. *I wonder why I never pursued a pilot's license.*

He took his left hand from the small wheel and touched the cabin pressure dial.

"Don't even think about it, Commander." Wakefield's soft warning voice interrupted his daydream.

He turned his most innocent eyes on her. *How does she know what I am thinking? It is supposed to work the other way around.* "Think about what, Commander?" He jerked his eyes away from her hers, which were currently much bluer than the sea.

"That you like the control of flying your own plane much better than you like riding in the back seat." He snuck another glance at her. He was caught. Her eyes were still on him. "You can't control everything all the time." Her words were soft and she seemed to understand his need.

Maybe another time or place they could pick this back up. "And here I thought I was doing so much better at that," he chuckled. She was doing so much better now that she had some food in her. *Come to think of it, I feel a lot better myself.*

Dietz spoke up from behind him. Do you know where you are going, Rivers?"

"Away." Rivers told him. The CIA director didn't laugh. "Roughly we're heading north by northeast." He tapped the compass for Dietz to read.

"That will take us to Athens?" Dietz questioned.

Wakefield cleared her throat. "I thought we should go to Piraeus, the port, so we can tie this thing up."

Rivers decided he could not take his concentration away from keeping them in the air to figure out where they were going. "Commander, go ahead and get on the horn and tell the authorities we are coming in."

She coolly reached forward and squawked the radio. "Port of Piraeus, this is U.S. Navy 3767. Do you read me?"

"Where did you come up with that number?" Rivers turned his head slightly. He was flying at 1020 feet and the craft was bucking in the turbulence.

She rolled her eyes at him. "It is on the tail, oh observant SEAL."

The Greek authorities came back before he could devise a reply. "We read you, Navy 3767. Don't get too many of your kind here. What can we do for you?"

"We are flying in from Poros and have a rookie pilot at the helm. We need a heading and for you to begin clearing space for us to set her down. And perhaps arrange to have someone available in a few minutes to talk us down. Over." Uncertainty watered in her eyes when he dared to dart a glance at her again. Did she think he would not appreciate some instruction on how to get them out of the air?

"Navy 3767, you certainly know how to throw some excitement into my day. Not too many people out today. What is your position?"

Rivers pointed to the GPS for her to read to Piraeus.

"All right, I am tracking you now. But you are registering as a boat."

"Sorry. We are definitely aloft. Trying to stay out of the clouds." She told him. "We have a low ceiling out here. We are currently at 850 feet."

"Climb to nine or drop to seven and hold her steady." The instruction came over the speaker. She shrugged at looked to the pilot's seat. "We don't want you to run into anybody going the opposite direction. You really are a rookie, aren't you?"

"I am not at the helm. Lieutenant Commander Rivers has that distinction. He has made the correction. We are at 900 feet. Over."

"Very good. Continue on current heading. You should run right into us." The tinny voice spoke into the tiny cabin.

Wakefield's features pulled to one side. "How'd you do that?" She asked, wonder filling her voice.

He shrugged as he held onto the column. "Lucky guess?"

The Greeks came back. "How many people on board, Navy 3767?"

"Three of us."

"Do you have personal flotation devices?"

Wakefield turned in her seat, her shoulder pulling at the 3-point harness. "Dietz, poke around and see what you can find." She twisted back as Dietz began bumping against the bulkhead in his search. "We are looking now."

A giant thump sounded in the tail of plane and caused a rocking of the entire craft. "I got it." Came a hollow voice from the back. "Two of those blow up life vests." Dietz shoved them between his shoulder and Wakefield's shoulder as proof.

"Port of Piraeus. This is Navy 3767. We have two life vests."

The hum of the engine was the only noise.

The first drops of rain hit the front glass.

DCI Hammond's Office Langley, VA
Thursday 3 October 2002
0744 hours EDT

"Richmond Dietz on the direct secure line for you, Director." Hammond's intercom buzzed.

"His ears must be burning." Hammond rubbed his one hand over his smooth head as he reached for the red phone with his other. How does a man with so much seniority manage to screw up an operation, a presidential assassin who was supposed to be dead, and a vacation to boot? Hammond blew a chest full of air through a tiny hole in his pursed lips as he waited for the decryption system to patch the line through.

Hammond did not even wait for the man to say hello after the five ascending beeps that told him the line was listener-free. "Dietz. I am not happy with you. What do you want?"

"Sir, I don't know how long this line will hold out. Just listen." Hammond could hear a rush of background noise. The man was cocky.

Hammond determined to help the deflation process when Dietz returned to Washington.

"I'm listening," he told Dietz shortly. Dietz needed to understand that arrogance did not sit well with superiors.

"I am in a Cessna, driven by a man who has never flown before."

"Were you kidnapped?" Hammond reached for a pencil to take notes, even though the call was being recorded.

Dietz's snort carried over the lines. "Just listen, sir. I have Lieutenant Commanders Wakefield and Rivers with me, but a cyclone is rolling in on our tails. I need to forward intel to the SEALs in case we don't make it. You did get my message right, sir?"

"Is it okay for me to speak now?" Hammond rolled his eyes at Dietz cloak and dagger mentality. "Yes, I got your e-mail and deployed a SEAL team to your location. They should be touching down in two hours."

"Forward the following information." Dietz commanded.

Hammond began to scribble as Dietz relayed the most twisted story he had heard since the unfolding of 9-11.

"And the worst part," Dietz paused and Hammond heard an unsettling curse through the line. "Sorry. We just picked up a tail. This one is in a cigarette boat. The worst part is that 18 batches of Filasek's new chemical weapon have already been shipped to Saddam Hussein."

"Dietz you are as bad as a run-on sentence. You should have called in counter-terrorism. Take a breath. Who is chasing you and where are you headed?" Hammond pressed the #2 pencil into the paper until the lead tip broke and skittered across the desktop. Dietz frustrated him to no end.

"Arafeh Filasek. Athens' port of Piraeus. We're in a skid plane. Gotta go. We're taking flack."

"Dietz." Hammond called loud before the man could hang up. "Azure Tiger was hung this morning. In Baghdad." There was silence on the line, but Hammond could hear the plane's straining engine. The channel was still open. "We will reckon when you return to D.C."

Hammond replaced the red phone in its cradle. And pressed the intercom button connected to his secretary. "Mr. Phillips, secure a line to the pilot who is flying our boys out to Greece. ASAP."

Twelve Nautical Miles out of Piraeus
1350 hours local

"Get the Port Authority back on the radio." Rivers ordered.

Wakefield reached backward over her shoulder to get the radio head from Dietz. The curly cord bounced in the turbulence.

Dietz pushed the plastic squawk box into her palm as DCI Hammond spoke again. Wakefield felt like her arm was frozen. In the chilling numbness, she could not move her hand from above her shoulder.

Azure Tiger was dead. James Yates was dead. Four long seconds passed before her brain kick-started with a roar like a motorcycle. "I had a moment of suspicion when I read the autopsy report." She yanked the radio mic forward. "But I can't believe you would falsify a legal document, not inside the States." She twisted back to pierce him with her eyes so he could feel the full effect of her anger. The motion combined with the bouncing plane turned her stomach inside out. "I thought better of you, Director Dietz."

"Look," his voice was soft and appealing, but she would accept no contrition now. He was too late. "I know you had some trouble concerning Yates' death."

"You have *no* idea!" She spat and flounced in her seat.

She heard a sound start out of Dietz's mouth, but Rivers interrupted him. "Look can the two of you pick this up later? After we are out of the air?"

"And if we don't make it back to the ground?" she asked.

Rivers arms were taut as he fought with the steering column. He threw her the strangest look of unbelief. "We *will* be reaching the ground. One way or another. If ends badly, will an un-won argument matter?"

She found the decency to bite back the remark that struggled against her teeth.

Another burst of flack skimmed around the shaking craft. In the mirror Wakefield glimpsed black oil smoke begin to stream from a hole in the fuselage.

Rivers saw it too. "Get the Port Authority on the horn," he reminded her, and then caught his breath as the Cessna bucked and then nose-dived. "Now."

Chapter Twenty-four

"Piraeus, this is Navy 3767. Come in. Over."

A garbled squawk filled the cabin. Wakefield saw Rivers tense in the pilot's seat. He pulled hard against the steering column, leveraging his feet against the floor.

"I can't read you, Piraeus. Come again." She shouted into the mic.

Another distorted noise came back.

Wakefield made the mistake of looking down at the blistering sea below while trying to make any sense of the noise-message she had just heard. The swells rose 12 to 15 feet. The boiling gray stew got closer by the second. She swallowed the bile on her tongue three times.

She wondered that she was able to even put together two syllables.

"Piraeus. We are unable to understand your message. Navy 3767 has a cigarette boat tailing us, one with an automatic weapon. We have been hit and we are declaring an emergency." She broke contact and looked at Rivers. "Do you think they can hear us?"

"Maybe." He gave a mighty tug on the half-moon wheel. The jerking craft responded. While they did not begin climbing, they had at least stopped the horrible falling sensation.

Wakefield checked the altimeter. She swallowed again, but her throat was dry. "Piraeus, Navy 3767. We are still on course for you. Altitude 330 feet. We cannot pull up. Please advise any other craft in the area."

"I don't think anyone else is stupid enough to be out in this mess." Dietz yammered from the back. Wakefield blew out her breath through her nose. She did not need extemporaneous comments.

"I can't look back. How far away is Filasek now?" Rivers gestured with his elbow for her to find the boat behind them.

Wakefield was not sure she wanted to know, but she turned in her seat again, her stomach rising to her throat. She angled against the glass to follow the wake that pointed to Filasek's speedboat.

She spotted him taking aim again. He was less than 60 feet off their port side. "Incoming." She yelled as a spray of bullets slammed into their undercarriage. How was he even staying afloat in this sea state—much less firing at them?

More smoke poured out of the engine compartment. Wakefield felt the bump of all 15 slugs. She watched Filasek jerk his drifting boat back on course. At least he had to release his speed and heading to take shots. "How much more of this can the plane take?" Wakefield flopped back around in her seat.

A whistling sound that had not been present before now sounded throughout the cabin. "Oh, no." Dietz's tone scared her.

The plane dropped 60 feet in three seconds. "That last spray must have broken through into the cabin." Rivers told them. "That sound is wind resistance."

"We definitely took a bullet." Dietz offered.

"Are you hit, Dietz?" Wakefield snapped her head to the opposite direction. All this turning was making her hope she would empty her stomach of the food she had needed so desperately a few minutes earlier.

"No." Dietz held up one of the orange inflatable life vests and pushed his first finger through a .44 caliber hole. Wakefield caught her breath.

Wakefield met Dietz's black eyes. She identified certain resignation there.

She turned slowly in her seat to face the low green clouds again. *Shouldn't there be land in sight by now?* "We are down to one life preserver," she advised Rivers. She looked at him when he did not reply.

His arms quivered with the effort of holding them in an even flight pattern. She reached over before she could reconsider and smoothed her palm over the trembling arm muscle.

"Try duct tape," he finally spoke.

"Where am I supposed to get duct tape?" Dietz sounded highly sarcastic and his voice was too high.

"Look around, Dietz. That one is yours." Rivers sounded ultra calm next to Dietz's shrillness. "Be creative."

Rivers looked at her out of the corner of his eye. It was the first time she remembered him taking his eyes off the instruments or windscreen. Then he winked. Just once. The way he did in the desert when he promised to make sure she was safe.

She acknowledged by tapping his shoulder three times with the tip of her first finger. Peacefulness settled around her as she knew that he was taking charge. The naval officer in her had done all she could. It was time to submit. The giving in did not reflect gender weakness, only told that independence and self-reliance were not the best ways to accomplish goals. Not the goal of staying alive anyway.

The altimeter read 120. With the Mediterranean's rolling water, sometimes that left only 100 feet between the aircraft and the sea. At least Filasek was having to cover twice as much distance. He had to drive up and down the swells. When Wakefield looked back, they had gained about 30 more feet away from him.

A warning bell dinged five times. Wakefield turned from the window to see Rivers scanning his instruments. His jaw tightened. "Out of fuel."

Wakefield allowed herself a one-second prayer. *Lord, I have had enough adventure today. I'd like to get back to my desk job. I hope that is what you'd like too.* "Should we buckle in or bail out?"

Open Sea
2:07 PM

Filasek pounded the dash in frustration. "How are you still in the air?" he bellowed. He shook the same fist at his airplane wafting 100 feet overhead, with a stream of smoke trailing from it. The first shot at his first personal aircraft had been difficult. Then he had no problem with the sacrifice. It offered the satisfaction of taking down the Infidel woman who had caused him grief since he had come into contact with her.

Filasek struggled to maintain control of his boat as he slid sideways at a 50-degree angle into the trough of the wave. The rain had not started in earnest yet, a few buckets here and there. But it was coming. He could feel the storm looming behind him, snapping its jaws and licking its chops.

He motored up the next crest and rode it a moment while he popped off a few more shots. The left float gaped in the rear. It seemed polarized to receive his bullets. He had torn a wider hole with each burst he had managed.

His long boat slid into the next trough.

Filasek wrestled for a breath. The storm seemed to have sucked all the air backward into its lungs as it prepared to blow.

The sky dropped lower. The waves rose up to meet it.

A second plume of smoke erupted from the Cessna's engine. Acrid black. They began to lose altitude again.

"Yah!" Filasek cheered and kicked his vessel faster. He wanted to see the destruction as the plane tore bolt from bolt with the Americans inside. It would be like a sign to him of the destruction that would overtake all the Americans come November.

He cautiously kept a 50-foot buffer. He was not keen on causing his own demise.

The plane went out of view as the sea kicked up. The water was now more dirty white than green or black. The cyclone loomed on his backside. Its cold breath drove him forward.

He looked at his watch. He had been on the water for 36 minutes. Factoring in the waves, he figured he was still four to five miles out of the harbored port of Athens. He would need to take cover soon.

"Come down!" he cursed his plane as it appeared above the waves again when he crested. "I should have bought the cheaper one." Filasek wished.

He could see seaweed in the water as he slid to the trough again. His hands slipped on the wheel. Too much water.

Airspace four nautical miles from Piraeus
1421 hours

Rivers watched the outside. It was getting more difficult to see every second as the storm moved in from behind. All of the alarms on the instruments blinked fast red-light warnings. He stopped inventorying them. The plane was going down. Where, was the only question. Thankfully, the blasting dings stopped.

Rivers pulled against the waves and rode every tailwind he could catch to take them closer to land. He blinked a stinging bead of sweat out of his right eye. The plane vibrated violently. His arms ached with the effort of holding the stick back to keep them out of the drink.

A vague shape appeared at the crest of one of the sea swells a quarter mile ahead to starboard. He felt the impact of another string of Filasek's bullets. The shape was gone in the swirling water.

"Watch at 1:30, about 400 yards out." He gave Wakefield directions based on a clock dial for where to look for what he hoped was a boat.

"I think it is a fishing boat."

Rivers cut his eyes to the shape.

The brown bow was more obvious now. A tiny wheelhouse sat in the middle of the 40-footer.

He could not see how many men were aboard, but it usually took three or four to handle a boat that size with fishing nets. *Plenty of men to rescue us.* "Get into your life vests. I am going to set her down." His words came out more terse than he had intended, but he did not have time to correct it.

"I can't get the tape to stick." Dietz's voice wavered in the back.

Wakefield squirmed to turn backward in the seat beside him. Her arm brushed David's skin again. Her touch, even accidental, soothed him. *God, please cradle us in your palm.*

"You don't need to tape the entire vest, just the part with the hole." Wakefield remarked as she reached for the second vest. "Tear off the excess or you'll get tangled and rip it off completely." She pulled the orange vest over her head and touched the nape of her neck. He wondered if she might be getting seasick.

He could see Judah tugging the one-inch nylon belt around her waist in his peripheral vision. She moved too slow. She breathed in little puffs in through her nose and out through her mouth. *Definitely a sailor trying to control nausea.*

"Don't inflate it yet, Dietz. You'll never clear the plane." She told him.

"Fifteen seconds to impact. Hopefully. Get strapped in, Judah." The fishing trawler disappeared between sea swells again.

"Impact or touch down?" Wakefield teased and snapped the buckle in next to him and pulled on the belt to tighten it. He felt bolstered by her confidence in him. Her fingers reach inside his seatbelt strap and tugged it tighter against his thigh.

"Thanks." A smile touched his lips, but he could not break his eyes off the water. "Get on the horn and radio our position."

"Aye, sir." She warbled the microphone, "Mayday. Mayday! U.S. Navy 3767. We are going down. Last known position—" she slid her finger over the display and repeated the numbers on the GPS.

"You a praying man, Dietz?" Rivers called to the backseat.

"I am now."

Rivers wished he could see the expression on the DCI's face that accompanied that wobbly voice.

"I do so much better with an emergency when I don't have time to anticipate it." Dietz loosed a nervous chuckle from the back.

The water was only 20 feet below them now.

"Anticipation is over." A bump pushed the tiny craft from behind. It felt as if a hand had come up under them. Rivers let the wheel retract toward the console. A wave slammed into their port side, throwing them off course and into a spin.

The swell moved underneath them. Rivers could feel the might of the storm as the plane skittered sideways. But they were down and still in one piece.

They rode the wave and it flipped them backward as they slid into a trough. Walls of water loomed above them in all directions.

They were at the pit of the trough, yet still seemed to be sinking. Rivers reached for his belt the same second he knew what was happening.

Filasek's shots must have gouged a hole in the floats. They were foundering.

"Time to bail," he yelled to his crew. The rain began in torrents. The pellets hitting against the metal sheeting of the aircraft's body, made it hard to hear anything. He gestured to the outside.

Wakefield's eyes widened and her face blanched white. When she was scared, whether or not she admitted it, her scar always stood out pink against the delicate white of her cheek.

"We're sinking."

"I've got water back here!" Dietz yelled.

"Everybody out." Rivers commanded. He was surprised they were still there to receive the order.

Rivers tried to take his bearings with a last glance out the windshield. It was impossible. They rode an out-of-control natural Tilt-a-Whirl, spinning in the choppy waves with the sea undulating in giant rolls underneath the waves.

Cold water swirled in around his feet. He stepped onto the pontoon and turned in time to watch Wakefield leap into the sea. Her side of the plane stuck up high like a cowlick. They were sinking at an angle. Dietz had scrambled to the front and followed Wakefield out starboard.

The intensity of the storm's sound reminded him of some of the raids he had participated in during the Gulf War when quietness had not been a requirement for his SEAL team.

The water crashed against his waist and then slapped his back. The typhoon screamed in his ears.

Are they clear? He couldn't see them.

The plane shuttered on its way up another hill of water. The port wing dipped into the boiling soup once. He watched it go under again as a breaking wave devoured it like an appetizer.

The cabin burped as trapped air was forced to the outside. It was dropping fast now.

Rivers let go of the door and pushed himself out of the vortex of the sinking Cessna. Survival leapt foremost in his mind.

He could not tell which way Athens or the fishing trawler were. He did not want to swim toward open sea.

A wave cuffed his face. The salt stung his eyes, but he forced them open. The burn wound on his waist shrieked and clawed at every nerve signaling his brain.

Filasek's cigarette boat topped the crest in front of him. Twenty feet above and forty feet to his right.

Rivers could read the hatred on the terrorist's features even from that distance. He knew with dread that the fight had just begun.

Maybe this was not such a bad way for a SEAL to go. Drowning in a flume of glory while protecting the woman he loves. *If only I could guarantee she would make it out alive.* He began to crawl through the choppy tropical water that had turned cold toward where he had last seen Judah. Oh, and Dietz.

Chapter Twenty-five

Three nautical miles outside Piraeus
1440 hours

Filasek topped the choppy sea. He squinted and could barely make out the shape of his white Cessna against the white water. A solitary wing jabbed out of the water like an iceberg. She was going down. Filasek searched the water for surviving prey.

One orange vest bobbed like a carrot medallion in soup.

The downpour broke for a breath. Filasek spotted an old wooden 40-foot trawler on the crest across from him. He squinted against the wind and water to clear his vision. The orange vest lay in the trough, equidistant between the two boats.

The dogs faced off. The trawler started down the swell as the sea rolled under her again. Filasek hung back. A second vest near the first caught his eye before the storm caught her breath and began screaming again.

He tugged the steering wheel right to stay on course. His boat pitched forward as a wave broke directly on top of the life vests. Filasek slowed his engines, whipping his head in the rain. He reversed his throttle. He did not want to get close enough to be identified by the fishermen.

Wiping the water from his eyes with an equally wet fist, Filasek gripped the wheel again. He could not tell with all the rain and wind, but he thought the vests looked too solid to be empty.

He brought his binoculars to his eyes.

Pieces of kelp-like hair dark from the water covered the face of the victim he zeroed in on.

Filasek cursed in Arabic. "Why won't you just die, woman?" he screamed. Desire to exact a more swift revenge swelled in his chest. "I can still implicate the Wakefield woman after her watery demise."

Filasek licked his lower lip and braced himself to wait. He would let the trawler close in on them. When they pulled his prisoners out of the water, he would pick them off, one at a time while the fishermen were busy.

The Cessna had disappeared under the waves when he looked for it the next time.

He throttled back his engine to hold his place against the surging waters. He looked again through his binoculars. The woman waved her hands above her head as a wave doused her thoroughly. "One way or another." Filasek shrugged as the woman disappeared under the water again. He wanted the Americans dead.

*****

Judah Wakefield spit out the water that splashed into her mouth as she gargled out Rivers' name. She had not seen him since she had jumped into the water.

She kept hoping he would swim up beside them so they could share the life vest's buoyancy. "Hold on to me, Dietz." She had to yell to hear her own voice above the din. Dietz floundered beside her. The black electrical tape he had used to secure the hole in his vest had already come off. Second-hand tape and water don't mix. Only one side of his vest remained inflated, which left him nose deep in the drink instead of chin deep.

Her eyes stung and she kept feeling pockets of cold water stirred up from the ocean floor flow over her body. "I am two for two," Wake-field muttered through chattering teeth. "I may never go up in a small aircraft again."

"I wouldn't fly with Rivers again if it were the last flight back to the U.S. ever." Dietz agreed from behind her.

"If you will hold onto me, I can share some of my buoyancy." Wakefield grasped Dietz's hand. "How're you doing?"

"I am ready for a towel." Dietz's left arm encircled her waist from behind. "You always were a skinny little thing." He remarked with a smile.

Wakefield felt herself sink into the water with his added weight. She took two deep breaths to control the rising panic. Dietz tried to wipe the water out of her face. With just as much water dropping out of the sky as they were floating in, the gesture did not help. She tried to smile, but another wall of water crashed over them, filling her mouth with salt water. They tumbled upside down with the force of the storm.

Just hold your breath, she instructed herself. She could not tell which way was up. The life vest would eventually surface, she knew, but it was a struggle not to fight the waves.

Dietz's arm tightened around her. He wrapped his right arm across the front of her vest and held onto her left shoulder as they buoyed up to oxygen again.

She could feel his chest inflate with hers as they broke the surface. "That was a deep one." She puffed and wiped her eyes.

Dietz pulled her head toward him and kissed her temple. His chest stilled heaved. "I didn't think we were coming up that time." He kissed her again as their heads bobbed just above the water. "I must have been saved by a mermaid."

"Richmond Dietz, we are drowning and you are flirting with me." She admonished.

"We are not drowning. The boat is almost on us." He pointed forward." The fishing trawler rode the intensity of the storm to their advantage.

"Yes, and where is Rivers?" Wakefield tried to see him above the undulating waters. It was impossible.

Two sailors stood on deck and Wakefield could see a third in the wheelhouse. The shorter fisherman tossed a lifesaving ring into the water and held onto the rope. The boat was 25 feet away. The wind pushed the ring toss short.

Wakefield groaned.

Another wave broke on their heads. It came unexpectedly from behind and pushed her under the water again. Dietz squeezed the life out of her fingers until they resurfaced.

When Wakefield's vision cleared, the ring was flying from the fisherman's hand. He was right on his mark. The white circle landed two feet from them.

Wakefield floundered in the jumbled water trying to swim with Dietz on her back. "Work with me, Dietz," she tried to shrug him off, "or we'll never get out of the water."

She could feel his legs begin to kick with hers. Wakefield grabbed the edge of the circle. The solidity of the device surged hope through her soul.

The rain renewed its strength with fury. For a moment she could not see through the density of the weather to the trawler now only 20 feet away.

Dietz was yelling something she could not decipher and motioning her into the life preserver. Even as close as they were, the roar of the storm drowned Dietz out. Wakefield shook her head as if she did not understand his very urgent request. She would not leave him alone in the water with a half-inflated life vest.

Wakefield pushed the round life-giver into his chest. "Hold on!" she yelled. "They are going to pull you up." She waved her hand forward and back above her head. The fisherman must have seen her, because Dietz began to move away from her and toward the trawler.

Temporarily safe, Wakefield turned her attention toward finding Rivers.

She could not see more than 15 or 20 feet in any direction. She spun around in the thick boiling stew. Her legs twisted in the water. Another wave dragged her under and knocking her upside down under the surface. Kicking, she felt her heels break the surface of the water. Judah considered rolling her eyes at the stupidity of her predicament, but she was seasick enough without her own body rolling against her. She held her breath until the life vest did its job.

"Daaa-vid!" she yelled. She twisted again floating over the wave before it broke on her again. "Daaa-vid!" She screamed with more intensity to the opposite direction.

The wind stole the words the moment they left her tongue.

"Where are you?" Her words twisted into the depths of the cyclone. She circled in the water again. She did not see him anywhere.

The fisherman hauled Dietz's rope hand-over-hand. She followed the CIA man's progress. When a small wave overtook him, Wakefield winced. It hit him squarely in the ear.

"Daaa-vid!" She continued her summons in all directions.

She felt something close around her upper arm. A cold chill, unrelated to the water, skittered up her spine.

"Looking for me?" A masculine voice rang in her ear.

Wakefield jerked in the bulky life vest at his voice. "David Rivers, you almost gave me a heart attack." She yelled over the weather ruckus. She held her arms wide and launched herself unceremoniously at his neck.

They both went under in a tumble of sighs.

*****

Filasek readied the scope on his rifle. He held tightly to the wheel with his left hand and flipped open the protective lens cover with his right thumb. Rain soaked though every layer of clothes. He wondered if it had penetrated his skin. He felt soggy enough.

A quick glance down showed water rolling over his canvas boat shoes. He would have to start bailing soon, or attend his own watery funeral, alone.

Stretching forward around to the front of the steering column box, Filasek slapped at the bulkhead. *Where is that accursed switch?* Finally his pinky brushed a metal pump switch. He flipped it up.

There was no sound of the motor and no visible difference in the water depth. But it was not getting deeper.

Filasek straightened and locked the long-barreled gun between his knees. He pulled with both hands to maneuver the boat back on course.

Filasek looked across the water to locate the fishing trawler. Fifty-five feet, he estimated. They had reached the apex of another rolling wave. He grabbed his scope. Focusing on a target was more difficult than he had imagined.

Short black hair and long arms stuck up out of the life preserver. "Rivers. Good job, man. Finally taking the rights you deserve to go first." Filasek's one chuckle came from deep in his throat. *I didn't think he had it in him.*

He put the scope back between his knees, and steadied his craft. He still was not ready to be observed, and he eased back on the throttle, just as another wave capped into his boat. Filasek wiped the water out of his beard. He cursed the raging sea with a snarl.

Filasek steadied his feet and scoped the woman bobbing like flotsam. He picked out the back of her head, a dark pin against the white swirling sea with that orange beacon of a life preserver from his own airplane. He moved the scope to clarify the letters on the bow of the dingy fishing trawler. *Siren Helena.*

204 ~ K.J. FROLANDER

His finger itched with anticipation of the larger target her body would make as she hung beside the hull of the boat.

He squeezed the rifle with his knees again to correct his position and close in a few meters.

Filasek's sight was only for the Infidel woman.

The donut life preserver from the fishing boat sailed out over the waves to her and began reeling her in.

She kept pointing to something over her shoulder. Filasek could not see anything in the water. *Is she talking about the Cessna?*

He did not have time to wonder further. Soon she dangled from the rope, two feet below the boat's railing. Waves nipped at her feet.

He took aim and fired a trio of bullets with a single pull.

Twice, for good measure.

A body flew through the circle view in his scope from top to bottom. "What the..." Filasek trailed off. He blinked and looked again. The black-haired man flailed in the water. "That's not the SEAL."

"Turn around," Filasek urged the man.

He gasped as Saddam Hussein's aide's face—minus his beard—appeared clearly in his scope. The man's jaw gaped open in a silent scream before a wave crashed over him.

Filasek squinted hoping to clear his vision. "What is Jasik doing out here?" The scope flopped to his side.

Chapter Twenty-six

"Look out!" Dietz yelled as he spotted Filasek with the rifle to his shoulder taking aim. His words eddied away never reaching his charge. Wakefield dangled at the end of a rope like an effigy at a homecoming bonfire. Dietz jerked his head up to find the second boat again. The sky was dark enough for him to see tracer bullets race toward Wakefield.

"Nooo!" Dietz screamed. He launched himself over the side. His voice sounded animal-like as it resounded in his mind. The waves and wind drowned out all other noise.

The moth-eaten blanket a deck-swabber had wrapped around his shoulders fluttered like a Superman cape against his ankles in his fall. It ripped from his fingers.

A bullet ripped through his chest. His brain did not have time to register the pain before a second shot pummeled his right shin.

His body felt as if he had been tossed into the fire. The waves smashed into his face. Below the surface, he cooled. Quietness, deeper quiet than he had ever experienced, washed away the topside disturbance.

The waves dug down deep and uncovered him. He opened his eyes to see Wakefield bent over the top rail of the boat's side. She was screaming something.

She is safe.

Dietz could not hear her words. The noise deafened him.

He needed to escape.

He sank below the surface. The deeper he went, the quieter it became. *Blissful tranquility.*

His chest burned. His leg burned. His lungs burned. He could follow the line of his nerves from his leg to his brain.

206 ~ K.J. FROLANDER

The lower water became cooler and cooler, soothing his burns. "Swim," he commanded himself. His right leg would not respond to his orders. He kicked with his left. "Got to get to the colder water before I burn up."

The pain stopped. Dietz sighed in relief. I feel so tired. I need to rest just for a second. One second and I will fight back to the surface. One second. One....

*****

"David, get him!" Judah screamed and pointed at the pink cloudy water. "He's right there."

Rivers dove under; his feet shot through the chippy surface waves.

Wakefield tore her eyes away from the pink foam and twisted on her rope to find the source of the shot. In the coves of her mind, Judah knew that Dietz had taken the bullet for her, but she could not comprehend it.

Filasek's speedboat topped a wave 45 feet from their bow.

A scroungy young man pulled her over the railing and dropped her in a heap on her knees on the wooden deck. He tossed a blanket over her back and picked up a long-nosed rifle beside her. She jerked to her feet at the noise of the shot. How does that break through this howling storm?

Filasek's windshield split into a spider's web of lines. His lips moved in slow wide motions. He shook his fist in the air and pointed straight at her.

It shook her core.

Filasek whipped his wheel, hand over hand. His boat turned on the crest of the wave and disappeared behind its protective covering.

A deep belching horn blasted through the torrent of weather sounds. Wakefield glanced down at the water on her turn toward the blast. No sign of either man yet. But Rivers, she knew, would not return to the surface without Dietz.

The second blast cut through the storm on the starboard side. Looking across the fishing trawler, Judah recognized the sleek lines of a gray-hulled government ship tossing lightly on the water. "The Coast Guard!" She waved her hands above her head as if they could not see her.

The blue cross and stripes of a wet Greek flag flopped in the wind atop the large cutter.

"Put down your weapons. We intend to board you." Wakefield recognized the Greek words and the tone of authority.

A pair of .50 caliber guns mounted above the ship's railing were manned and aimed below the water line of their boat.

Wakefield's wet hair slapped at her face, stinging her eyes. She elbowed the young man aiming out to sea. He stumbled backward two steps. "Sorry." Her sodden blanket fell to the scarred plank deck. "Get rid of the gun. They're coming over." She yelled through the rain.

The young man slipped on the wet deck, and he left the gun down when he straightened up. His ragged hair hung in black dripping clumps in his face and over his large ears. He didn't look a day over 12 years old.

She offered him a hand up. "Nice shot though. Keep a watch out for that man."

A boarding party left the Coast Guard ship in a black RIB. It looked like four officers and a driver, but it was hard to count as they bucked on the open sea.

Wakefield turned back to port. The pair of men who had helped her over the side, vigilantly watched the water. That their backs were rigid and their hands motionless, gripped her.

The pink-tinted foam had washed away. The boiling white water showed no evidence of Dietz or Rivers.

It had been too long.

Judah pushed her hair out of her eyes. She stuffed it into the back of her collar. "Any sign of them?" She yelled and touched the white knuckles of the hardened fisherman who did not seem to be having much luck that day.

"The younger one came up for air. Once." He did not take his eyes off the water.

"He can hold his breath a long time." She reassured the man with a firm nod. She was speaking just as much to herself.

The simple white ring with *Siren Helena* imprinted in fading block letters bobbed on the surface. It tugged against the constraining tether.

The Zodiac RIB rounded the pitching bow of the *Siren Helena* eight feet below where Wakefield stood. "Two men under the surface." She yelled down and pointed to the water. Wakefield held up her first finger and pinky to show him the count.

Two of the Guardsmen were dressed in black neoprene wetsuits with air tanks, masks, and fins. The bearded man who sat next to the man guiding the tiller held a bullhorn to his lips. "Men in the water?" The tinny sound heightened Wakefield's emergency state.

She nodded and held up the count on her fingers again.

The Guard leader motioned the two suited men over the side. As their fins disappeared over the side, Rivers surfaced, wheezing for air.

"Where's Dietz?" Judah screeched. "Did you find him? You have to find him!"

The SEAL either ignored her or could not hear her. She was grateful to see him so she gave him the benefit of the doubt. While Rivers tried to suck oxygen back into his body, the two divers swam around the raft.

They exchanged words. The pair dove, and Rivers allowed another officer to pull him into the boat.

Wakefield gripped the railing until she could no longer feel the pain in her fingers. Rivers just lay in the Zodiac boat. *What is wrong with him?* "David, did you see him? You've got to go after him. You can't just let him die!" She yelled at him.

The wind whipped her words from her lips. A brief flutter of Rivers fingers in her direction let her know that he could hear her. *Why isn't he doing anything?* "God, make him get up and go after Dietz. Don't let Dietz die. He saved my life. Have mercy on him."

Wakefield felt a tug on her shoulders through her distress. When she focused on it, she remembered feeling the sensation for more than thirty seconds. The first mate pulled on her right arm. "Ma'am, you must come away from the side. Please, come away." He kept repeating it over and over.

What does he think I am, some kind of imbecile? Judah shook her head. "Not yet! Not until I see that Dietz is okay." Her escapee hair slapped her face like a cat-o-nine-tails. She deserved the flogging and did not brush the pain away.

"Ma'am, you're not doing your man any good out in this weather. Please! Come below decks." He pried at her fingers. "You'll make yourself ill."

"No!" She elbowed him away. "Leave me alone." She could not get the leverage she needed. Her grip on the rail seemed stuck with glue.

She had to concentrate to loosen them. The first mate's grip on her arms dug painfully into her wet skin.

"No, no. I have to see that he is safe. He is my responsibility!" Judah twisted away as he held onto her upper arms. Her shoulder jerked and she doubled over in pain. "Let me go!" She repeated.

Her strength was failing. Her voice faded weaker, and she could not force her body to comply with the movements she needed to get to Dietz and Rivers. "Help me, David. You have to save Dietz. Can't let him die."

*****

David Rivers lay face up in the rubber craft. He allowed his body to sink into the floor and move with the raging seas. He loved the smell of Zodiac crafts. *How many of my missions have involved these crafts?* He could not focus his thoughts. *More than half, not all of them, though. Maybe three-quarters, no, perhaps two-thirds.*

He rolled his head from side to side to clear his thoughts. *Who cares? Relax and get oxygen back into your brain, SEAL.*

"Rivers! David." Rivers heard his name. He forced his eyes open. The trawler was close. Wakefield stood, still wearing the orange fully inflated vest, fighting with someone dressed in wet white pants on the deck. She looked like she was crying. She was definitely yelling. *That man should know better than to make her mad. He is going to end up with a bloody nose.* Rivers let his eyes drift closed again. And felt his lips turn up at the corners. "That's my Judah. I'll come help you straighten him out in a minute," he called up to her. It did not sound any stronger than a mumble, even to his own ears.

He felt the bump alongside the rubber craft. "We got him, sir." Rivers heard. He let himself relax then. The snarling sea had given up Dietz.

David sank into the comfort of blackness where the cyclone was silent and the waves were a rocking cradle.

Chapter Twenty-seven

"Doctor. You promised me." Judah Wakefield projected her best command voice.

"I am concerned about the puncture marks on your hand. I would like to give you an IV of antibiotic."

"It'll take too long. You wrapped them. Give me a pill or something." Wakefield started wiggling down from the paper-wrapped exam table in the Athens emergency room. Its crinkle irritated her blasting headache. "You promised I could see him now."

"So I did." The doctor looked a bit like Judah's aging grandfather on her real father's side. The slippery silver hair fell to one length in a crown of sorts from the bald spot that circled the top of his scalp, and his deep brown eyes had the same tilt that mixed kindness with concern. "That medicine will kick in soon, and your head won't hurt so much." He offered her his wide hand to step off the exam table's stair.

The hospital corridor could have been anywhere, save the lyrical and loud Greek language that swirled around her, untranslated. The cream and green walls reminded her of every hospital she had ever been in. "Where did you attend medical school, Dr. Patamos?" Judah threaded her arm through this offered elbow for the trip to find Rivers' room.

The doctor let out a jolly laugh. "Are you concerned for your care, or the care of your husband?"

Judah's chest tightened. *My husband.* It turned the lining of her stomach inside out. She could not decide if it was a good mistake or a bad one. She did not correct him. "No, sir." She forced a chuckle. "I was going to commend your English. My brain is so frazzled that I am not sure I could put together a single sentence in Greek right now. But I don't need to, because your English is perfect, doctor."

"Thank you. I went to school in Cairo. I did study English there, but, I did my internship in New York City, 1959."

"I see." Judah could feel herself weakening. How far back in this hallway had they placed Rivers? She leaned harder on Doctor Patamos.

He rattled on about New York while she counted doors. *Small goals*, she coached herself, *just to the next door. It can't be much further, the hallway dead ends. I hope that is not a sign of his condition.* Her chest contracted again.

"Here we are." Dr. Patamos patted her hand before unwinding it from the crook of his arm. She was sure he could not have missed the increased pressure of her weight; she could see concern grow in his squinting eyes.

The doc picked up a chart on a metal clipboard in a plastic holder to the right of the door. She could not wait any longer and pushed open the standard hospital door with a creak.

Rivers' eyes were open, and he was propped up on several pillows. She felt her lungs expand with the first full breath she had taken since the plane crash separated them. Judah let the wetness flow down her check unchecked.

"Mr. Rivers." Doctor Patamos cleared his throat and looked up from his chart. "I am glad you decided to stay with us. My nurses noted that you gave them a hard time."

"Sorry about that, sir." Rivers mouth turned up in a lazy grin. His speech was slow. "They did not give me much choice in the matter, though." Judah decided he must have been drugged.

"Were you looking for this?" The doctor's hand pushed her lower back, and she stepped forward. "Your wife is even more stubborn than you are. She insisted on being here."

Rivers' eyes jerked slightly at the corners. It almost looked like fear.

"I do need to examine you though. She can wait in the hall, now that she has seen that you are indeed alive. That I was not lying to her." Patamos' chuckle sounded forced. The doctor had seen the fear as well.

Rivers held out his hand. "No, she can stay, Doc." Rivers folded his fingers, motioning her toward him. Her feet dragged like wet concrete as she plodded to his bedside. *Was it the wife comment? Surely, he knows I needed to see him and wouldn't get in under any other circumstances. Otherwise, I would have corrected the assumption.* She hated that she had already started justifying her actions. The lines of truth and justice were too gray on this mission.

His hand swallowed hers. Even though he was the one lying down and she was the one standing guard, the gesture made her feel safe. "My wife," he seemed to choke on the word, "is the most stubborn woman in the world." He brought her hand up to his lips, and kept his blue-green eyes locked on hers. "You did well not to argue with her, Doc." His chapped lips dragged across the tender skin on the back of her hand.

Judah wiped at her eyes, though it did little to stop her tears. It was only the second time he had kissed her and she had to share it with a stranger.

She melted into a ladder-back cane chair at the head of the bed and held onto his hand. Around his wrist, an inch-wide red welt swelled like a cuff. *Why didn't I see that in the air?*

"What is a young couple like you doing in Greece? Are you on your honeymoon?"

Rivers chuckle rolled like a bass drum from deep inside. "I have not been called young in over a decade, Doc." He winced and pressed his right hand to his chest. "And today, I feel like I am closing in on 90 real fast." His left hand squeezed Judah's fingers and then relaxed.

Patamos pulled back Rivers' hospital gown to inspect the damage. He gasped unprofessionally. Wakefield zeroed in on his face before he had time to hide his horror.

"What's wrong?" she could not stop the question.

The gray-headed Greek looked up from Rivers' torso into his eyes. "What happened to you, son?" His slow words were compassionate.

"It was not your average vacation." Rivers fudged. His voice dragged from the pain medication.

Judah swallowed.

"We were in a plane crash, doctor," she told him.

Patamos did not look away from Rivers' face. "I've seen plane crashes. These wounds are not from a plane crash."

Rivers blinked slowly several times. He opened his mouth to speak. No words of explanation came out. He swallowed and tried again. "I'm sorry. I'm just so tired."

A double knock sounded on the door. "Doctor Patamos," a white-clothed nurse with a stethoscope around her neck intoned at the doorway. "I have the x-rays back on Mr. Rivers."

Patamos stepped back from Rivers' bedside. "Why was I not called immediately for this patient?" Judah watched the tense line of the doctor's shoulders. The young nurse's face blotched red.

"Sir. We had to clean him up before you could even see to his injuries. There was so much blood, sir. That gash in his side," she shook her shorts dark curls.

It was not until that moment that Judah realized they were speaking in Greek. They used the same words for blood that described Jesus' blood and gash in her Greek Bible.

She felt compelled to look.

Rivers' eyes were closed. The lines in his face had smoothed out, and he looked like a young boy napping from a day at play. His grip on her fingers did not diminish though.

Wakefield felt her pulse rock her body as she leaned forward in the hard chair.

Burns marked Rivers' upper body. Pin-prick white blisters looked like large ant bites over his chest. She moved the gown to the side and the blisters continued over his shoulders and onto the base of his neck. Ugly black and red bruises marred the area around his ribs. He had broken them. Again. She traced the line of knuckles in the muscle under his broken ribs with a feather touch of her first finger.

Rivers sighed.

She snatched her fingers back as if his body were a hot oven. In shame, her eyes flew to his face. He was asleep. His lips moved a fraction of a centimeter, and he exhaled another sigh over his vocal chords.

Someone had knotted black silk string to thread his skin back together. The gash the nurse mentioned. That could be from the crash. But setting down had seemed so gentle. Her head pounded as she tried to make sense. Did Filasek stab him in that torture chamber? It looked meltier than a knife wound.

The room began to spin. *God, please wake me up from this nightmare. I can't take any more.* She slumped forward in the chair and rested her heavy head on the side of Rivers' bed.

"Mrs. Rivers." The doctor's voice called her back from the swells of sleep. "The police are here to take your statement."

She levered open her eyelids. The nurse was gone, and Dr. Patamos was examining her partner's foot.

"I suggest," he looked at her with piercing eyes, "that you come up with a better story than a plane crash. The ER took two bullets out of the other man who came in with you."

Wakefield jerked upright. "Dietz. I forgot about him." Her eyes roved around the room. *How could I have forgotten Dietz?* "How is he? Can I see him?"

Patamos slowly straightened his back from his exam in silence. He did not let go of her eyes for a second.

Apprehension tumbled upside down in her stomach. Her muscles contracted. Judah felt her lungs empty of air. All the sounds of the machines monitoring Rivers' health subsided while she waited for the inevitable.

She knew, but she needed to hear the words.

"He did not make it. I thought you knew." Patamos' voice was soft. "He was DOA."

Just like my dad. The thought echoed in her mind.

"Can I—" her voice cracked. *Suck it up, Navy,* she commanded herself. *I don't have to, I'm not Navy anymore,* her alter-self argued. "May I see him, um, his body, anyway?" she asked Patamos.

"He is already in the morgue, but we do need someone to ID the body." Patamos' slow nod slid his hair back and forth.

"I will go there first and then meet with the police." She rose from the chair. Her knees buckled once but she caught herself before Patamos said anything.

"Are you sure that is wise, Mrs. Rivers?"

"Probably not. But I am going anyway." Anger stirred in her midsection. Everybody was pulling at her. She looked at Rivers' face. The police questioning would probably go on for hours. Then they would call the U.S. consulate and she would have to go through the whole thing again. The CIA would get involved for round three. *Oh, the CIA notification!* And Rivers just lay there. *You started this. Now I have to clean up the mess.* "A good man lies dead, and you nearly got yourself killed, all to have your vengeance."

She shook her head and loosened his fingers from her hand. "It's never worth it," she whispered sadly and walked out the door.

The frigid hall to the morgue had odd little jogs right and left where additions had been made to the hospital over the years. She thought about asking for a wheelchair. No, she would do it on her own. Judah pursed her lips as she trudged one foot forward and then the other. She kept a list. Rivers would hear about each inconvenience and strain he had caused with his careless, emotional tactics. *Oh, those horrible burns on his body.* Heaviness sat on her chest. "I am going to set Dr. Patamos straight on my name, just as soon as I see Dietz." Judah mumbled under her breath.

"What was that, ma'am?" The young male orderly leading the way asked.

"Mind your own business," she snapped. "Sorry." She regretted her words immediately. "No matter how difficult this is, it is not like me to take it out on others."

"Not a problem, ma'am. I know a person who can take all your pain and wash it away like the tide." His voice sounded inviting.

"I know him already." Judah lowered her face, chastised. "Thank you for reminding me." *You never let me sulk,* she accused God. *Other people can do whatever they want, but never me.*

You gave your life to me, came the immediate reply. *You told me I could do whatever I wanted.* She recognized the voice easily.

"Whatever," Judah mumbled and threw her hands into the air. They slapped against her thighs. "I am tired of fighting."

That is exactly how I like you.

She heard the words resound in her mind, but could not muster a smile for God's witticism.

A man dressed in a white gown, mask and gloves opened the third drawer from the bottom, on the second of five rows. He peeled back a white sheet.

Dietz's skin was too pale. His mustache looked like a black marker slash above pasty slack lips. Judah reached up to touch his neck. He was CIA. They were not above faking a death.

The skin was hard like cold silly putty. Too cold. Dietz's death was no hoax.

She shuffled backward, her hand hung mid-air.

"His name is Richmond Dietz. Please prepare him for transfer back to the United States. A military liaison will claim his body as soon as I can arrange it, and I will escort Dietz home."

Judah's hand dropped to her side as the pathologist re-covered Dietz's face. The shape of his features pushed out the white shroud like an ancient death mask.

"I am ready to talk to the police," she told the orderly. She ordered every ounce of military training to the forefront, and she walked away with straight shoulders and a tall neck.

Island of Poros, Greece
12:24 AM

The sea sloshed like a great bowl of uncongealed Jell-o salad someone threw onto a refrigerator shelf. Arafeh Filasek glanced at his blinking gas gauge. "I'll go in a minute." The engine's soft hum reminded him of the desert crickets' serenade from his boyhood. He touched the webbed windscreen with smooth fingers as he remembered those simple days, before Soli was killed and his father ran off. "I guess he is finally fulfilling his dream." Filasek bobbed on the water in the dark. "I could have helped him."

He swept his fingers down his damp beard. "Enough melancholy. He will discover my worth soon enough. I will get the Wakefield Infidel later. If it is the last thing I do, I will keep her from happiness." Filasek snarled. He geared up the engine. He whipped the wheel starboard to a heading of 290 degrees.

When he puttered up toward the pier at his home, an eerie feeling encompassed him like pea-soup fog. Keeping himself as still and small as possible, Filasek searched the black choppy water behind him. He scanned the hillside all the way up to his house. The light in his bedroom shown over the rail of the seaside balcony. The kitchen porch light glowed brightly. He frowned. That should not be enough to set him on edge.

A slight movement at the left corner, outside his house. Then it was gone. A reflection from the porch lamp? But what was doing the reflecting? There was only a square meter of dirt and stone at that corner. The light glistened again, then went dark.

The whole house plunged into darkness.

Filasek pulled the boat's gear into reverse. A few meters out would be safer.

Filasek kept his squatting position in the well of his boat. Little green lights seemed to swarm over the exterior of his villa. A similar one flashed on the water, 20 meters to his left.

Night vision goggles. He recognized the distinctive color. Only the U.S. special forces had resources to outfit that bevy of men. "If I saw them, they saw me." Filasek cursed under his breath.

He powered up his craft and flipped the nose forward. He sped southwest around the island. "Have to stay near heat sources. They'd spot me on the open water like a flashing beacon." Filasek mumbled.

He sliced through the residue of the storm that floated on the water's surface. Passing a small cove to his left, Filasek turned toward it and cut his engine. They would never expect him to stop running after a half kilometer.

He tied off to a low-hanging tree branch. Filasek grabbed a torn Styrofoam cup floating in the water and dipped it into the cold Grecian water. He poured it over the hot engine, to eliminate the telling glow of a heat source.

Filasek ducked behind houses and trees as he drew closer to his villa. Sweat beaded on his forehead. It was almost impossible to maintain a safe distance. He flattened himself on the ground and used a flowerbed in his neighbor's yard to cover his image on the SEALs' goggles.

There were not as many now. He counted eight still outside. Two by two, they ran to the edge of the cliff that overhung the water. They backed over the edge. Filasek shook his head as the last two repelled away.

"Couldn't even tell they had been here, if I hadn't seen it with my own eyes." The house had to be wired, either with bugs or explosives. "I am not idiotic enough to care which." Filasek belly crawled backward a hundred meters before standing.

As he took his first step in the direction of his abandoned Cigarette boat, the ground trembled under his feet. The night sky lit like the dawn in erratic orange and pink.

Filasek turned on his heel. "Not again," he moaned. He did not care who heard or saw him. He ran back.

His pier was engulfed in flames. An accelerant was the only explanation.

The grand white house, now a glowing red inferno with smoke ascending in a gray line to heaven. All the charges had been set to discharge together. The house had imploded on itself. The SEALs had cut the gas line. They were thorough, he could afford them that respect.

Except for the initial boom, it was a quiet burn. He appreciated not having to share his third loss with nosey strangers.

Filasek felt the familiar anger possess his belly. He dropped into the grass like a frog to watch his beautiful villa smolder.

He muttered his plans as the fire wafted inspiration.

Marble House Pension
Friday 4 October 2002
0140 hours

The rain still dribbled from the black sky like a baby's forgotten drool when Wakefield stepped out of the taxi empty-handed. A nurse's assistant had pressed the cab fare into her hand as she stared at Rivers' sleeping form 30 minutes before.

She trudged up the stairs to her second-floor hotel suite. She let her hungry eyes roam around the room. Her computer still sat on the desktop. Her clothes still lay in neat rolled rows in the open suitcase. Dietz had moved his suitcases into the room. His PDA cord lay plugged into her laptop.

She sank onto the mattress. Everything was too familiar. Yet strange because so much had changed since last viewing this room. Her things lined up against the bathroom sink and Dietz's were scattered across the counter. It felt like she supposed an ended affair would feel. She closed her eyes. Her hollow belly ached. "What is Dietz experiencing right this minute?" she wondered softly into the moonlit room. "I guess there is no time wherever he is."

Chapter Twenty-eight

Doctor Patamos stood watching in the doorway as his patient rolled to his left side for the nurse. "You'll be smug as a fly in carpet in a few days." She patted his shoulder and helped him lie flat. "The doctor will be in soon."

"Is that soon enough for you?" Doctor Patamos walked into the tile-floored room carrying the metal chart holder.

"Hi-ya, Doc." Rivers grinned. "I love this stuff you're giving me. Your nurses sure do talk funny. When is my girl coming back in? Did you know we're married? I don't remember that, but," Rivers shrugged carefully, "I have trouble recalling a lot of things right now."

Patamos laughed. The large American, despite his injuries, was in a good frame of mind, albeit slightly altered frame of mind. "She went to make some arrangements. But, she is not your wife. She told me yesterday. Ms.Wakefield just said that so she could see you. Apparently, you are just partners." Patamos waggled his eyebrows. "Though if I were you, I would correct that ASAP."

Rivers leaned his head against the pillows. "That's too bad." He frowned. "You have to let her come back anyway. Her hands are soft and cool. It will help me get better faster." His eyes shifted to the right and then returned. He blinked and seemed to have trouble focusing.

"Maybe we ought to tone down the pain meds a hair." Dr. Patamos clicked his false teeth with his tongue. "How are you feeling, Mr. Rivers?"

Rivers lifted his head. "Oh, I feel fine. Why are you here? Actually," he tried to illustrate with his hand but could not disentangle it from the tubes, "my head is a little heavy. Can you fix that?"

"I am a doctor, Mr. Rivers. We can fix anything."

"Oh, good. Fix Judah's cheek. I can't fix it. I'm going to sleep, but just for a minute." The patient's lids slid closed.

"It sounds to me," Patamos said to the sleeping American, "like there is more that needs fixing than just Ms. Wakefield's cheek."

U.S. Embassy, Athens, Greece
91 Vassilisis Sophias Avenue
0943 hours

Judah Wakefield saluted a Marine colonel as he walked out the embassy gate at the same time as she walked in.

"Do I know you, ma'am?" the dark-haired senior officer stopped mid-stride and turned on his toe.

"No. Sorry. Force of habit." Judah quickly turned away as she felt the blush creep to the roots of her hair. Not only was she out of uniform, but she had forgotten she was no longer required to stand at attention or salute a senior officer.

She quickened her step to the large entryway.

Ambassador Kilbourne himself waited for her. "Ms. Wakefield, you're early. I just sat down with my coffee."

He was young to have drawn such a prestigious position. She smiled and tilted her head to the side, willing the traces of pink to disappear from her cheeks. "I am afraid I am chronically early. Please, go on with your coffee break."

His wide smile dimpled his cheeks. "Won't you join me?" he patted the stone bench in the shade of the archway next to him. "I can think of much worse character flaws than being early." He paused and turned slightly toward her as she smoothed her black skirt under her legs. "The morning after a storm has the most glorious atmosphere, don't you think?" He did not give her a chance to reply. "What's that old phrase, 'Joy comes in the morning'?"

"Um-hmm," she nodded. Judah didn't see any difference in today and yesterday. Her life was still a mess. The air felt just as humid as it had before the storm to her.

"Has your joy come yet this morning?" He turned soft brown eyes on her. A spattering of freckles trickled across his nose and cheeks. "I read the police report this morning. I am sorry for your loss."

"You are kind, Ambassador Kilbourne. Has the embassy been able to make arrangement for Dietz's transport?" She crossed her legs and stared at the veins of pink in the marble patio to avoid his eyes. She felt his interest.

Kilbourne cleared his throat and rolled his coffee around in the paper cup he held. "I talked to State this morning, too. They suggest that all three of you come home with the SEAL team tomorrow night. There is plenty of room on the DC-10."

Wakefield snapped her head back to look at him. "What SEAL team?"

Kilbourne leaned in toward her. His coffee hand went to rest the cup on his knee. "SEAL Team Seven was diverted here on their way home from Chechnya to mop up the Arafeh Filasek problem." Kilbourne's brow furrowed into five tiny lines. "They destroyed his villa, though he was not there. The pair who stayed in the Zodiac extraction boat spotted him, but could not pursue. He disappeared in a cigarette boat with a cracked windscreen, according to the reporting officer."

Wakefield sighed and returned her gaze to the floor. "Yep," she said with a light frown. "That was him. However, there's something I did not mention in the local police briefing that you need to know."

"Should we take this upstairs?" Kilbourne dropped his voice. Only one guard was within earshot.

Wakefield shrugged. Kilbourne rose and handed her up. He tossed his coffee cup into the metal trashcan on the way inside.

Seated in an opulent but decidedly tropical office, Kilbourne questioned her. "Go ahead. This room is swept for bugs on a daily basis."

She looked the young ambassador in the eye. "The man who needs transport home." She swallowed hard, "The man who is dead is the current Director of Counterintelligence of the CIA, Richmond Dietz. The Director needs to be informed. And probably the president."

Kilbourne sat back in his wide, cane-back chair. "My," he said, his eyes wide. "That certainly changes things." He brought his fingertips together in a peak with his elbows resting on the chair arms. "Not just a woman missing a passport are you, Ms. Wakefield?"

222 ~ K.J. Frolander

"Is that what they told you?" she leaned forward and covered her knees with her cool fingertips.

"No, no. I was briefed that you were tangled up in the Filasek mess."

"You could say that." She leaned back again. "He's been trying to kill me for almost a year now."

Kilbourne stood and walked behind his desk. He stood with his finger poised above the intercom call button. "Get me the Director of Central Intelligence on the line, A-SAP, but be kind, remember it is the middle of the night in the States." He came back around and reclaimed his seat next to her. "I don't know how long it will take for my secretary to find him." He explained his hasty movements.

"If we can uniform those SEALs, this flight could actually work. Even with all the press that will be on hand to tape the arrival ceremony." Wakefield licked her lips trying to work out the logistics.

"What about Lieutenant Commander Rivers?"

"He will not be ready to fly by tomorrow." She offered no further information. Wakefield looked from the palm tree in the corner behind Kilbourne's desk to the pair of prints depicting sunsets over the tropical waters. She shifted in her seat. She should volunteer to stay at Rivers' bedside. He was her friend, her almost-fiancé, the reason she was here in the first place, which was the problem.

She also felt duty bound to escort Dietz's body home. Who would meet him? Who would take care of him? The thought of home called her. Ideally, she would like to disappear beyond the water and not be anybody to anyone. But that was not Judah Wakefield. Military officer or not, she would do her duty.

But which one was her duty?

El. Venizelos Athens International Airport
Friday 4 October
9:40 AM

Filasek stood in front of the check-in counter at Delta. His finger clenched into fists at his sides. "Please, ma'am. I've got to be on the next flight."

The attendant looked about 21 years old. Her long brown ponytail lay across her shoulder and hung to her waist. She picked up his blue American passport and studied his name. "I am sorry, Mr. Jacobs. All international flights must be reserved two days ahead. Company policy." She shrugged. "I can get you on Sunday's flight." She clacked her fingers over her keyboard and moved her eyes to the screen.

Filasek reached up and placed his hand on her forearm to still her movements. She startled at the touch. "Sunday will be too late." Filasek took a deep breath in four ragged sections. "Look, I know about the restrictions. I am on the Homeland Security team for San Francisco County. I helped put those guidelines in place. Two day waiting period for flights into the U.S." He pushed his lower lip out and hoped he sounded like he was quoting a manual. "It is imperative to do background searches on everyone these days. But my daughter is lying in a hospital bed in San Francisco, dying from a motorcycle accident. I have to set things right with her before she goes."

Filasek pulled the attendant's hand toward him and covered it with his other hand. "I am not a terrorist. I have never killed anyone. I promise. I help people, for goodness sake." He thought he might even be able to squeeze a tear out if he kept up his performance much longer. "I have to get home to my little girl before she dies. Please help me, Rachael." He read her name badge in his peripheral vision as he held her hazel gray eyes captive with his.

"Mr. Jacobs." The girl tilted her head with watery eyes. He had definitely reached her. "I can't." Her words were slow. She was not completely committed to her negative answer.

"Look, I don't have any luggage or anything. So, I am not carrying a bomb." He stroked her hand again. "I came straight from the conference center as soon as I got the call about my daughter's accident." He looked at the scarred countertop. "You know," he sniffled, "It's all I can do not to break into tears right here in front of everyone." There was no one in line behind him and the other desk attendant was busy checking-in a lady of considerable age. "You look just like her. That long, beautiful hair."

He felt the tear work its way to the corner of his eye. He squeezed tight and it fell. What a strange sensation. *I have not cried since, well, maybe never.* "I have to get there before she dies. Please. No one has to know. I can show you how to change the date."

He looked into her eyes again. "I know how, Mr. Jacobs," she said.

224 ~ K.J. FROLANDER

"Then you will do this huge thing for me?" he stroked her fingers.

She glanced left then right with the minutest of head movements. "Just this once."

"Oh, thank you, Rachael. I knew when I saw you that I could count on you. I am forever in your debt." He removed his hand to let her issue the ticket.

He wiped the wayward tear from the crease of his nose and brushed his hand down over his beard.

As he sat in the boarding area for flight 1783 to San Francisco, Filasek licked his lips. Another 18 hours and he would be on the west coast in the United States. He would oversee the placement of evidence of Wakefield's involvement. He would see that all the dynamite was placed correctly on the bridge for optimum advantage. He would insure that the chemicals were delivered to the appropriate parties within the cities. He would be sure this round went off without a hitch.

It would be magnificent for all three attacks to prevail, but the bridge was coming down whether the shuttle came apart or Fort Knox exploded. And the Infidel woman would be clearly implicated and imprisoned for the remainder of her miserable, privileged life. If it was the last thing he did.

U.S. Embassy, Athens
91 Vassilisis Sophias Avenue
1018 hours

Wakefield reclined in Ambassador Kilbourne's leather desk chair. She stared at the reed-like paint finish on the walls in the empty office while DCI Hammond droned in her ear from thousands of miles away.

She could barely reach the floor with her toes from her position, and she twirled herself back and forth as the director let off steam. She held the receiver a few inches from her ear.

"Director Hammond." She waited while he continued his thought. "Director." She used a sharper tone. "Please let me get a word in."

"Go ahead, Commander Wakefield." He was curt.

"I think it would be best if we leave transportation plans as they are, sir."

"I did not ask you."

"I realize that, sir." Wakefield told him dryly.

"What the heck is going on over there, Wakefield? You are required as a Naval Intelligence officer to comply with the CIA, and I want full disclosure *now*."

He was pushing her patience. "Actually, I am no longer in the service. I am a civilian." Judah told him evenly. "And I am trying to help you bring home one of your own who displayed the finest courage and bravery I have seen in the Agency. He died with honor and in the service of his country." She cleared her voice and softened her tone. "I think if it was not 3 AM, you would see that, sir."

"Dietz was not authorized to go after you, Wakefield." He still sounded terse.

"I did not ask him to come after me. I am not responsible for his death. But," her voice wavered as she said the words for the first time, "he did die to save my life."

The line was clear with no crackles, no words.

"Director Hammond, are you still there?"

"Yes." He cleared his throat and she heard squeaking, like bedsprings, in the background. "Bring Dietz home, with full military honors." His words were slow. "Lieutenant Commander Wakefield, I expect you in full dress uniform when you step off that plane."

Wakefield cupped her cheek in her hand. Her hands felt soothingly cool against her face. "Aye, aye, sir. We will be at Andrews Air Force Base Sunday morning."

"So will I." Hammond signed off.

Evangelismos Hospital
Ipsylandou Street
1403 hours

"Rivers, you're awake." Judah forced a happy face.

Rivers' body looked like he was spilling out of the tiny hospital bed. "Where have you been?" His face lit boyishly.

His eyes were glassy black, nearly all pupil. She walked over to take his outstretched hand. "I have been doing some walking and thinking." Wakefield admitted softly.

"Did you bring me some French fries?"

"What?" She narrowed her eyes and sat on the edge of his bed. "You don't even like French fries."

"They won't let me see you. They won't let me see Dietz. But now you're here. Where's CIA man? He follows you everywhere. Is he in the hall? Come on in, Dietz. Don't be shy." Rivers raised his voice and his neck reddened with the effort.

"Rivers, hush." She tightened her hold on his hand and smoothed her fingers over his arm. She smiled sadly. "What kind of stuff do they have you doped up on?" She could not read the tiny letting on the IV bag across the bed.

"I don't know. But you should try it. Then you would not be so sad. Why are you sad, my Judah?"

The endearment struck her heart. Guilt assaulted her for avoiding him. She pulled her feet up to rest on the sideboard of the bed and scooted further onto his mattress.

Rivers eyes widened as she squirmed. "You cannot get into my bed, Judah."

Judah chuckled mournfully. She stopped herself before the laughter turned to tears. "Don't worry. You are safe with me." She patted his chest. "David, can you focus for a minute? I need you to hear me."

He blinked several times and straightened his shoulders against the pillows. "You have my attention."

He did sound more coherent. Maybe he would remember the conversation. "David, Dietz is dead. He died when Filasek shot at us in the storm. Do you remember the plane crash and the Coast Guard rescue?"

Rivers closed his eyes. His hair had grown in the three weeks he had been gone. She liked the length and longed to reach out and touch it. "I remember. I wanted to save you." He opened his eyes and looked down at the white sheet folded at his waist. "I remember everything," he whispered.

She looked at his eyes and knew the truth.

Wakefield refused to allow disappointment on her face. She had hoped he would be spared the details of that room of horror. "I have been ordered to escort Dietz's body back to Washington." She withdrew her hand into her lap.

"I am going to be gone for a little while, but I will come back and get you." She tried to catch his downcast eyes.

"That is just what Jesus said." Rivers mumbled miserably.

"Well, then. You know you can trust it." Wakefield sighed. "Dr. Patamos said it would be at least four or five days before he would release you. So you work on getting well, and I'll be back in time to get you something better than a hospital gown to wear on the plane."

Rivers' mouth turned up. "I thought we decided you would not buy me any more clothes."

"That was clothing as presents." She teased. "This isn't a present. I'll be using *your* visa." She raised one eyebrow and could not stop her broadening grin.

Chapter Twenty-nine

The ground crew secured the door to the aircraft and Wakefield strapped herself into one of the eight seats at the front of the deep-bellied DC-10 transport jet. She looked over her shoulder at the SEALs who were seating themselves on the benches that ran the walls of the craft while the engine warmed up.

A jeep had been chained into place at the back left of the rounded-top, flying warehouse. The white casket was roped in three places to the bulkhead.

She turned forward and tightened her lap strap. It felt like she was on the set of a surreal movie. The 38 men who had risked their lives to destroy terrorist assets all made it out. Here they were on the plane together with her and the spymaster who had given his life. They cajoled each other and she could hear them excitedly talking of a home-cooked meal.

She closed her eyes dismissing her normal planning of her first meal stateside. Placing a hand on her rolling stomach, Judah tried to keep her Sprite and toast down. *This is no movie.* She pushed her thumbnail into the fresh bandage around her hand. *No bad dream I can wake up from either.* "I wish I could remember the last time I was in control of my life." She breathed softly.

The hatch on her right and behind her rattled. "Probably some poor idiot who almost missed movement." She let her hand flop down on the armrest and hoped he wouldn't sit next to her. "I don't want to be civil; I don't want to be kind," she murmured.

"You don't have to on my account." A deep voice whispered in her ear. She could feel him leaning over her shoulder. She did not turn around to look at him, even in her surprise.

"David Rivers! What are you doing out of the hospital?"

He slid smoothly into the seat next to her. The plane's engines revved and they began to taxi toward the runway. "Doc let me out on good behavior. Didn't seem sensible to let you make two trips to rescue my six."

She slid her eyes toward him. "Well, just as long as we've got the details straight." It came out sounding more sarcastic than she had meant to reveal.

He bristled in his seat. The roar of the engine waylaid any further conversation. Rivers loosely placed the lap belt around his hips. She saw the wince he tried to hide. He must have done some fast talking to Dr. Patamos to get himself sprung three days early.

"I needed to be at Dietz's service."

Wakefield was not sure she heard the admission right until she saw the far away zoning on Rivers' face. He was so insistent on doing things his own way. "It is gonna be a long trip," she sighed and crossed her arms over her chest.

*****

"What is that supposed to mean? Rivers turned his neck instead of his torso to look at Judah. He was in a lot of pain, but he did not think he was imagining her hostility.

Again, she sighed. "Nothing. It will be a 10-hour flight to Andrews that's all. Don't get so uptight, Rivers."

"I think there is more to it than that." He pushed. If they were going to make it as a couple, they were going to have to start communicating better. And he was taking the responsibility to make sure it happened.

The plane banked left to maintain the flight path north. "So what if there is?" She would not look at him.

"Then you need to tell me what is going on." Agonizingly, he turned toward her and rearranged his legs so his burns and scraps a la Filasek mellowed to a tolerable level of pain. *I should have taken that Loritab Patamos prescribed.* Rivers closed his eyes while he waited for her to decide to talk. She was right, it was going to be a long 10 hours.

Four minutes of silence were too many. "Judah, you can't not talk to me until we get to Washington," he told her.

She turned toward the wall of the craft where her black dress uniform hung under plastic. "Who says I am planning to talk to you in D.C.?"

Rivers felt his eyebrows rise without his permission. "Judah, you have to at least let me apologize." He tried a soothing tone of voice.

Judah turned to stare at him. Her pale face was taut and unmoving. "Go ahead," she invited and shook her blond hair in the smallest movement. He suddenly felt like the fly in the old adage about the spider and the fly.

Tread carefully, he admonished himself. "I am sorry that things got so out of hand. Nobody was supposed to die. I just wanted to set things right and make certain Filasek was not going to come after you again. I was not planning to get trapped in his torture chamber. I didn't plan on any of this happening. Please forgive me."

"Nobody was supposed to die?" Judah's blue eyes turned icy. "What did you *think* Filasek was going to do when you confronted him, turn around so you could spank him and then change his life?" Her eyes narrowed as she took a breath.

"No, but—"

"Oh, no you don't," she interrupted. "You wanted me to talk, and I am not finished yet." She brought her hand down roughly on the armrest, her voice even louder than the engines' roaring.

Rivers took a quick glance in the back to see if anyone had been disturbed.

She shook her head at him, "Now you are worried that your buddies might hear us arguing?" She rolled her eyes. He could see her resentment churning and he kept his mouth shut, bracing himself for the crosswinds.

"All of this is your fault." She gestured over her shoulder, he presumed to Dietz's casket. "What makes you think you have the responsibility to right all wrongs? To control what Filasek does? Oh, that's right," she slapped her forehead, her sarcasm at an all-time high. "You are incapable of thinking with your head. You think with your hands. Always-take-control-Rivers, that's who you are."

Rivers felt her words sting his face as if she had slapped him.

"Well, I hate to be the bearer of bad news," her voice waned low, "but you don't always get to be in control. Sometimes things just happen. And you don't get what you want. Sometimes, and sometimes," her voice quivered and dropped even softer. "Sometimes you have to give up what you want most."

The water that had been building in the wells of her eyes as her voice softened, dropped down her cheek. One tear sought refuge in the channel of her pink scar. Unconsciously, he reached out to wipe it away.

She flinched and turned toward the wall again. "Don't touch me, Commander."

Suddenly things were clear in his mind. "You are angry with me because you think I forced you to quit the Navy and come looking for me. I am so sorry. I will do everything I can to see that you are reinstated. Please, won't you forgive me for—" He paused to seek out the root of her offence.

"You still don't get it." She turned back to him with a smile full of pity. "It's you. You are the thing I wanted most in life. Not the Navy."

"You've been through a lot." He tentatively touched her white fingers that gripped her upper arm closest to him.

"Yes, I have. Now the one person who was supposed to keep me safe has put me in the most extreme danger. That I can *forgive*, but I cannot *live* with it. I would be in a constant state of worry, waiting for a phone call to tell me that I was a widow."

"Wow." Rivers pulled his mouth into a little O. He stared at the empty seat in front of him. "I don't know what to say." *It is too bad that soul numbing does not extend to my skin.* He reached to his waist to loosen the drawstring of his hospital scrubs. The fabric felt like it was cutting him in two, right at his stitches.

His future was falling through his fingers like hot butter. There was nothing he could do about it. She was right. *I am responsible for Dietz's death. He would not have been in Greece if I had not come on my fool's errand of revenge.*

But her complaint went deeper than just this excursion. She would relive her fear every time he shipped out with his team.

Even giving up being a SEAL would not change the quirks of his personality that had made him become a SEAL in the first place. The control, the order, the fast-paced strikes, they would always be there.

Maybe this was God's way of getting his attention again. If they would not complement each other and enhance each other's gifts and callings, then what was the point? *I was so sure, God. I will not try to change her though, not for my pleasure. Judah would not be the woman I am in love with if I change who you have made.*

"I am going to go sit with the guys for a while. If you need anything, let me know, okay?"

"See, it is just who you are. You still try to—"

"I was just being polite, Judah. Don't read things that are not there. I am trying to give us both space to deal with this." He slowly stretched to his full height, his side protesting all the way.

Andrews AFB
Sunday 6 October 2002
0404 hours

Director Hammond stood with his knees locked watching from the inside shelter of B Hanger as the DC-10 circled the airstrip and glided like a whale onto the tarmac. The predawn gray of the sky served as a perfect backdrop for his mood. He hated to lose an agent, especially a good one, and especially a high-ranking one.

The pilot taxied toward the hanger, instructions he had given the tower to relay. Four news crews were on hand to tape the arrival and interview him and the new arrivals. As if by some inaudible cue, everyone moved out of the hanger as one.

He watched a couple of heavy-set camera men jockey for the best position while a blonde who looked like she had not slept that night dusted her face with an enormous powder puff, and two other reporters argued over something he could not quite hear. It didn't matter. They were just background noise until the plane pulled up.

The long wide body of the craft rolled to a stop in front of the open doors of the Butler-building hanger. Three ground crew members rushed forward to brace the tires with triangular wooden blocks.

The back hatch slowly lowered.

Thirty men in khaki U.S. Navy uniforms filed out somberly. They made two lines, forming a corridor between themselves.

The engine cut off. The dead calm was more striking than any Taps bugler had ever been.

Even the reporters ceased their whispers.

Hammond stared, waiting for the casket, waiting for Judah Wakefield and David Rivers.

A man in loose-fitting, too-short hospital scrubs hobbled out next. He walked through the corridor of warriors, the men saluting him. He stopped at the end and became the odd 16th man in the left line.

Two more men appeared stiffly at the open tail section. They led six others, four men on each side of a glossy white casket.

Their cadenced footfalls sounded harsh on the concrete. There was no calling of the rhythm or turns. These men had carried a casket before.

Judah Wakefield looked like a widow in black following a precise eight steps to the rear of the men. She kept perfect time.

Each khaki-clad SEAL saluted the casket and held the salute as the procession marched through. When it was past, the 31 men, turned as one and followed in the same step. A crunching one, two, one, two.

The lights hazing in orbs from the runway and the early mist lent a celestial quality to the atmosphere.

"Company, halt." A deep voice instructed.

Dietz was a good man, Hammond thought as the sailors slid the casket into the black SUV hearse. When the door slammed shut, the reporters unleashed their questions.

"Can you tell us the circumstances surrounding the death of Director Richmond Dietz? Did it have any connection with terrorist cells in the States or outside the country?" The blonde who questioned him looked more awake now.

"I cannot comment on the exact nature of his death. But it is nothing mysterious. He was in a plane crash while on vacation at the beach. Nothing to be alarmed about. No terrorist connections." Hammond spewed his rehearsed story.

"Which beach?" It was a black man in shirtsleeves and a blue tie.

Hammond swallowed. He never got through to the North Carolina State Police to cover his story. "I wouldn't want to influence tourism negatively. You understand." He forced a small smile. "No comment. Dietz will be mourned by family and friends in a private ceremony Tuesday." He waved them back toward their vehicles. "Thank you for coming. The Agency will release more information as we are made aware of it."

Chapter Thirty

Judah Wakefield wandered among the white headstones of the military burial ground of section 11 off McPherson Drive. In the three years she had lived in Washington, Judah had never made time to come back here.

"So many men." She pushed out her lips and let them fall back into the frown that had felt as natural as breathing for the last 56 hours. "So many heroes have given their lives to our country."

A rumble rolled in the distance. She glanced up at the low steel sky. It did not look as though it would hold through the funeral at 1300 hours.

Judah reached inside the breast pocket of her black uniform for the strip of paper where she had written down the location the man at Arlington's office had given her yesterday on the phone.

Section 11. The area was correct. She kept scanning headstones. Where was he? A little shiver crept up her spine as the wind danced across her face. Her stoic bun released a tendril of hair that blew into her lipstick.

Henry Jorgensen, Jonathan Marksley, Kenneth Adams, Roman Spiff, James Wakefield. "Dad." Judah's breath left her body. She felt 9 years old again, here for her father's funeral. She could almost hear the bugler playing that mournful melody. The guns discharging their salute to his life. The marine uniforms, black and blue, with their proud red stripe. The cotton flag with its sewn stripes. Judah tugged at the collar of her black Class A uniform.

She touched the top of the cold marble. "Did you know I slept with your flag under my pillow until mom found it three weeks later?" Maybe talking to a gravestone was not as foolish as she had thought.

She walked around the back of the stone in the thick, cropped grass. She could vaguely remember the few minutes the family had spent here the summer Judah turned 12 when Graham had brought them to Washington for a vacation in conjunction with his promotion. "He was becoming a full Commander that year I bet. My age now." She was suddenly fatigued.

Judah sat on the top of the headstone and cupped her chin in her hands. "You had a full family by my age now, mom, Melia, Penny and me. What am I waiting for? Why can't I have that? Rivers is a fantastic guy. Most of the time he seems to really understand me. Sometimes it is like he can read my mind. It's freaky." Judah tittered. "And we seem to have this weird unspoken understood future." She shook her head. "But he's never actually said he loves me or what he wants from me. I wish—" she broke off as visions of some grand gesture and declaration of love played out in her head.

Judah brushed away a pair of yellow fallen leaves with the toe of her dress shoe and frowned as she realized she'd never risked saying out loud how she felt about David either. What he would think of her played into every decision she made. And she was a better officer and human being for it.

Judah let herself create a perfect future with David Rivers in the mist of her mind. Still she couldn't shake an obstruction. Something was foreign was amiss in the puzzle.

She couldn't identify it, she could just feel it.

She looked around at the sea of white sheep on the brown and green grass dotted with snaps of color from leaves that had not yet been gathered this morning.

"This is fear," she mouthed the words as she realized it with dread. "I'm afraid." Judah smoothed her wayward hair behind her ear and fidgeted with her cover to secure the hair from blowing in her face again as she wiggled to a new position on her father's headstone.

When she stilled herself again, Judah could only visualize her dad's face from the pictures she had studied as a child. He seemed to gently ask, "What are you afraid of?"

"Of loving and not being loved in return. Of being locked forever in a relationship with a man who cannot ever express his love for me," she began working at the answer aloud, but was still not satisfied.

"No." She shook her head and closed her eyes, searching the cavities of her soul. She recognized the excuses. She knew she could live with never being loved. She had 33 years of experience being single. It was something more. Something deeper. She opened her eyes and quickly closed them again, not able to bear what she saw as it penetrated to the core of her being.

"This." She gestured to the cemetery full of war heroes. "This is what I am afraid of. And don't tell me it won't happen because it will. It did." As the knowledge bubbled to the surface, it connected to a weight that sat in her belly too deep even for tears.

"Everybody dies, Judah." The picture in her mind said.

"Yes, and most soldiers go too soon. This was almost David's funeral. I can't lose a future with another man I care for."

"I think your mom would say the pain is worth the joy."

Judah let the words soak into her spirit. When her backside began to protest the cold and numbness, Judah glanced at her watch. Only twenty minutes before she was due graveside.

"I am sorry I waited so long to come visit, Dad. Graham has been a wonderful man to fill in for you. He is the reason I am in the Navy. But I am always your girl."

Navy Lieutenant Commander Judah Wakefield rose, walked to the end of Marine Captain James Wakefield's grave and gave him her best salute. "I'd say thank you, sir, for the chat, but I'm not sure if I'm grateful yet." She pursed her lips to the side and bit the inside of her cheek.

At the service, there were about 30 people seated and another dozen or so talking in groups of twos and threes. She was still mulling over the identification of fear in her heart as she picked out the back of David River's head. He'd gotten a haircut. He was in uniform and under cover, and he wore a confidence evidenced even from the set of his shoulders and #2 razor-shaved head that she had never seen duplicated. He had an empty seat next to him, on the outside aisle.

She caught the chaplain's eye, and the senior officer nodded to her before she slipped in next to Rivers.

"How're you feeling?" She whispered and lightly bushed his sleeve.

"I was feeling way too early, since I beat you here." He let a teasing smile touch his lips. His skin was paler than she remembered and he looked tired. More than just a lack of sleep, a weariness that was deeper than his eyes.

"I've been visiting with my dad." She turned to stare ahead and pulled her hands to her lap.

"Admiral Graham got leave to come?" Rivers looked around, stretching to see over people's heads from his seat.

The chaplain cleared his throat and the rustle of clothing filled the air while people tried to find seats. "No. My real dad. He is buried over there." She whispered, gesturing with her head toward section 11.

The service began, but Judah's mind was otherwise occupied. *Can I really do this again for Rivers when it is his turn? Do I have the strength? Probably not, but I know the Source of all strength.* She twisted her fingers in her lap. *Why didn't she see it earlier? God, you have never failed me before, I know I can trust you to hold my heart with David.*

Perfect love casts out fear.

My love is not perfect, Lord. It never will be. David's love, well, it's not so perfect either, though, I'm sure he tries. Judah glanced at Rivers' imposing figure that filled the chair next to her. *But your love is perfect, God. How do I—*

"Lieutenant Commander Wakefield?" Judah startled at the sound of her name over the sound system. The chaplain looked at her expectantly. It was her turn to speak. Dietz had requested it in the instructions he left for his funeral.

All the little anecdotes she had planned flew out of her head with the first step toward the microphone. *Just remember to speak in English*, she prompted herself. The first of three class sessions she had taught at the Naval Academy two years back, she had been so nervous she had begun the teaching the class in French until a pleb in the front row raised a hand and pointed it out.

*****

Rivers heard Wakefield's name and felt her rise from beside him before he realized that Judah was going to participate in the service personally.

She looked different. Not quite gloomy, almost regretful. He identified it in the set of her jaw, the tilt of her head. Was it grief?

He liked the way she scanned the audience before she began speaking.

"I've worked with some unusual men during my time with the Agency." A titter waved through the crowd. "Character qualities that are considered too eccentric on the outside are promoted behind CIA doors.

"People who juggle four or six stressful projects at once are labeled ADHD and given medication. For the excelling man in the CIA, four to six projects is another day at the office." Wakefield included in her address Director Hammond and the two other officials with her on the make-shift stage. "People who get inside someone's head, follow them and anticipate their next move are called stalkers on the streets. At the CIA, it is an imperative skill set to master." Ms. Cravits, Dietz's long-time secretary, and one-time date, squirmed in her seat in the mid left section and for perhaps the first time since they had met, she nodded in agreement.

Wakefield adjusted the microphone gooseneck as it started to slip. "Trusting your life to your partner, if you are lucky enough to be assigned one, and still double-checking his honorability is distrust in the civilian world. Here, it is how you live to tell your story."

An appreciative chuckle rumbled through the crowd.

"It is our job to be paranoid, so the American people can rest easy. The elite can take paranoia and turn it into a calculated energy to expend.

"But occasionally, there is one who stands apart from even the elite handful he is honored to work with." Wakefield's eyes moved left over the crowd and stopped as she caught his eyes. Rivers felt like a specimen under her microscope. She stood with her shoulders tall speaking to the audience and speaking to him.

"One who will throw away a promising career to eliminate a threat against you. One who will sell his soul to make sure you can sleep at night." She was still staring only at him. His neck warmed as he realized the double intent of her speech.

"One who will go head to head with pure evil to see justice prevail. One who," her voice dropped dramatically, "will give up his life for his friends.

"It is that man whom I am here to honor today." Her blue eyes that used to look like ice to him, felt like warm tropical water as they washed over his ache. "He is the one who took an interest in me when I was preoccupied with my own selfish interests."

Thunder rolled over the funeral service, but Judah did not look up as most of the crowd did. Her eyes seemed magnetized to his.

"He honored me, challenged me, taught me, and then introduced me to myself. A better self. One who is capable of great loves, and able to lean on *the* Source of strength during great losses.

"He can never be replaced. The value of the treasure that he is, will never be diminished. Because of his great sacrifice, I will hold him always in my heart.

"It is he who forced the stubborn me to lean on the One who loves me more than life itself. I hope you can hear me when I say, you are greatly loved."

*****

Judah Wakefield took a deep breath of the humid cemetery air and spoke her final words and stepped back from the microphone. A spattering of applause sifted in the crowd. A few women dabbed at their eyes with lace hankies.

As she pried her eyes away from Rivers' magnetism, she noticed that the president had joined their small party of CIA friends and family sometime during her speech. He stood, holding a curved-neck, black umbrella. He had arrived with no fanfare and only two obvious body-guards. He nodded to her in acknowledgement as she rejoined Rivers to stand for the remaining moments of the ceremony.

She whispered up to him, "I did not realize the risk would be worth any days I got to spend loving you, until today." *Please, Lord, let him understand*, she prayed.

There would be no fly-over in the missing man formation, but the honor guard behind her prepared for their 21-gun salute. The weapons clicked and clacked as they flipped and turned in the gloved hands of the Marines. She turned with the others and braced herself for the shots. Seven guns, three jarring shots.

Taps, the saddest notes ever composed, bid Richmond Dietz his final good night. A fine mist began to fall as the notes faded into the heavens. Judah brushed away her tears as the chaplain said, "Thank you all for attending."

Her eyes seized Rivers' eyes again and she found understanding in the new darkness of their blue-green depth. It felt like gliding as she sat back in her seat.

"Why did you come after me, Judah?" Rivers asked. He seemed to be searching her face for a specific answer.

"I love you."

"I thought you couldn't love a SEAL."

She let her eyes wander down over his uniform jacket's brass buttons and she reached out to touch their shiny surface. "I believe I said I could not live with the constant dread of a phone call telling me I was a widow."

Rivers stilled her hand by placing his larger palm over hers. "At least my colleagues are prepared to defend me. Think how I feel about you. Your job is just as dangerous as mine, yet your backup leaves a lot to be desired."

She tilted her head back to look at him. "I sit at a desk all day." She chuckled softly. The rain started to drizzle, but standing closer than she had ever been to the man she wanted to be with for the rest of her life, she decided to ignore it.

"Right," he drew out the word. "That is why you have this scar on your face and," he traced the scar sending chills up her spine, he took her hand and touched the bandage still wrapped around the fingernail imprints that had drawn blood, "and this wound on your palm."

Judah summoned as much control as she could find to insure that her knees did not give away and leave her staring at Rivers from a wet grassy patch of ground.

"I am just as concerned for you," he went on, which was good, because she had spent all her words. "But I would like to give it a try. For as long as we both shall live."

Judah's lips turned up and she shared a slow smile with the Lord. Rivers' grand gesture. Finally. But it still left her wanting. "You live in California, and I can't transfer," she jutted her chin out in appeal. "Not after the Admiral was kind enough not to process my resignation or report me AWOL."

"Actually, I already transferred to Little Creek. What about a house outside the base. We can both commute to work. Besides, I am not sure how much longer I will continue to serve with the Teams."

She remembered now talking with his C.O. before leaving for Greece and talking with Michelle at NFCU. She blew some of the rainwater off her lips.

He looked awfully confident. "I'm scared." She confided.

"Me, too." He whispered and drew her against his chest. "But you can't let fear run your life. Then it wins."

Judah leaned her head back out of his embrace to look him in the eye. "So, I should marry you because I am afraid to marry you?"

"Yes."

"David Rivers, that doesn't make any sense!" She pawed at his chest lightly.

He just grinned. Rivulets of rain ran down his face and dropped from his chin, between them.

She watched his face fall slowly until it was a mirror of what she was feeling.

"What is it Judah?"

She sucked in her breath sharply. "Can I tell you a secret?"

He just nodded, his face unchanging.

"She leaned in feeling silly and soggy all at once. "This doesn't feel anything like the fairy tale I thought it would."

Rivers let out a chuckle. "That's the problem?"

Judah started to withdraw and lash out at his making light of her hesitation. Instead she just nodded, and felt stronger for it.

"But that is not a problem at all, my dear. You see, we are not fairies. We are human beings. It is supposed to feel real and—I"

"Fine," she cut him off as somehow David's sentence brought order to her insides. "One condition." She felt a smile play at her lips.

"Fine, what?" David's eyes narrowed.

"Fine, I'll marry you, if," she paused and huffed.

"If what?"

She leaned into his chest, careful for his injuries. "If you will finally kiss me."

His chest pumped beneath her cheek. He actually cackled with laughter. "Okay." He brought her hand up to his lips, his eyes full of mischief.

Her shoulders fell. "I didn't mean there."

"I will arrange something else," he whispered a promise, "Just wait to be surprised.

"Is this a private conversation?" A tenor voice came from behind her, "Or can anyone join?"

She broke out of Rivers' arms. She would recognize that Texan voice anywhere. "Mr. President." Simultaneously, she and Rivers stiffened to a salute. He saluted back. "Of course, you may join us." Wakefield invited. She felt very wet next to the giant umbrella keeping President Bush dry.

"I wanted to take this opportunity to thank you for bringing Dietz's body home for burial." His square lips formed a sad smile. "I read the report. I know it was a hardship. If there is ever anything I can do..." he offered with a pat of genuine gratitude to Rivers' shoulder.

"Actually there is." Rivers was nodding his head when she turned to look at him. She felt her eyes go wide. When the president offers a favor, you don't take him up on it. Especially not immediately. "We are getting married," Rivers said, "and I was hoping to secure your Rose Garden for the occasion." Rivers confidence had returned full force.

"Of course. Let the office know your date." Bush grinned.

"March eighth." Rivers stated.

"Wait a minute," she could not help interrupting. *I guess his over-confidence is catchy.* "I didn't say yes yet. You have not fulfilled your part of the bargain." She challenged her SEAL.

Bush laughed out loud. "It sounds like you better do whatever she says, Commander."

Rivers straightened, "Aye, aye, sir!" Rivers executed a one-quarter turn toward her. His shoes squeaked in the wet grass. Reaching around her waist her gathered her in his arms.

"I think it is time to claim my prize from the manufacturer." He whispered. Moving ever closer, he dipped his mouth and breezed a kiss to her lips. Intoxicated by speed and aroma, Judah let him support her weight.

Rain fell in soft, tingly waves, soaking through her uniform. Her cover fell to the ground, but she was not going to be interrupted.

He grazed his finger down the scar on her cheek, but still did not release her mouth. Judah reached for the back of his neck to hold him a close captive. She wanted to draw their first kiss on the walls of her memory forever.

Applause started somewhere behind her and grew louder. Rivers broke off the kiss in laughter.

Forehead to forehead, he asked, "So, is that a yes?"

A giggle bubbled up from her belly. She pecked his lips again, eager for another taste, despite the audience. "That's a yes."

"She said 'yes'!" Rivers announced to the crowd that had gathered to watch the spectacle. His goofy grin was apparently as infectious as his arrogance. She found one plastered on her lips as well.

Rivers reached into his front pocket and pulled out a tiny silver phone. It vibrated as he held it. On one glance at the caller ID his brow furrowed and he loosened his grip on her waist. "Sorry," he mouthed. "I've got to take this."

Chapter Thirty-one

The rain chilled her insides now that Rivers had taken his body heat away. He stood several yards from anyone with one hand rested on the trunk of a massive oak that still held some red and brown foliage. The other hand held the small cell phone to his ear.

Wakefield wrapped her arms in front of her body and waited for him to return. The cemetery was emptying out fast because of the rain. Several people she did not know patted her shoulders or touched her hands with their thanks for her words and their warm wishes. She nodded and politely smiled but did not listen.

Rivers snapped his phone closed and dropped his hand to his side. He stood still, so she approached him from behind.

Judah touched his back and ran her finger up his soggy uniform jacket. "What is it?" she asked quietly.

Rivers took her hand and brought her back into his arms. The oak offered little protection against the rain that fell much stronger than a trickle now. "I sure did not plan for today to go like this." He touched her hair. "As many times as I practiced my proposal, even before I knew you, I never considered doing it in a cemetery after a funeral."

"You practiced?" She smiled and then Judah shrugged, more concerned about his reaction to the call. "You're a SEAL. You have to take the opportunity when it is presented, right?"

He leaned in and kissed the top of her head. *I love the way I feel small next to him*, Judah stretched as tall as she could in her heels in the sodden grass, *even now, I am not as tall as Rivers*.

"That was my little brother. Sam never asks me for anything, but his daughter was just admitted to Children's Hospital and he wants me to come."

Judah pulled slightly away from him. His voice sounded tortured. "I just don't want to leave you here, not now," he said.

She managed a smile in her disappointment. "Of course not now. You have to change your clothes first. They won't let a man who is still dripping onto an airplane." She patted his chest. "I will be fine. So will you. I'll be waiting when you finish saving him." Judah winked. Now they had another private joke. She just hoped it was not too close to the truth to hurt him.

"Would you mind terribly dropping me at Dulles? There is a flight to San Diego in two hours, according to Sam. I took a cab out here, hoping you would take me home."

Judah smirked and looped her arm through River's elbow. "A lack of confidence has never been a problem, has it, Sailor?"

They hurried their arm-in-arm steps in the direction of her little red Mustang parked by itself now at the roadside. "Nope," Rivers said and opened her car door for her.

*****

Rivers squished into Judah's passenger seat. The cloth was going to get soaked. She buckled her belt before starting the Mustang's engine. "Can we turn on the heat?" Rivers was already looking for the knob to turn it on high.

At the turn to go out back to Memorial Drive, Judah asked, "What are we going to do about Filasek? He did not die in that storm. I can feel it in my bones."

Rivers held his fingers up to the heat vent as he thought. "Leave it to somebody else. I don't have clear objectivity anymore." He hated to admit. "If he comes to my backyard, then I will deal with him."

Wakefield frowned as she stared through the swishing windshield wipers. *I wish I could leave it at that.* "I will be assigned to find him when I go back to work tomorrow."

"Can't they assign someone else?" Rivers sounded tired. She hoped he did not catch a cold from being too wet and tired.

"I know him better than anyone right now." She signaled her intent to get on the Beltway ramp, eastbound. "I will stay as objective as I can. I just thought you should know."

Rivers thrust out his chin and huffed. "Thanks. I think."

Sunshine Construction Co, Office
1617 Brandenburg Ave, San Francisco
Tuesday 15 October 2002
9:15 AM

Arafeh Filasek looked around the posh construction company office for the first time since it was completed to uphold the image he wanted to project to the San Franciscans in the city council. "Looks good in here. More like an insurance company than a construction company, but I like the modern art touches." He adjusted his tie as the long-legged, frizzy-headed receptionist at the clear fiberglass desk cleared her throat.

"May I help you, sir?" At least she was more business-like than she appeared.

"I would like to see Jack Lambert."

"Do you have an appointment?" She raised one thin light eyebrow and reached for the telephone.

"Yes." He lied. He did not want to give the woman too much information about his role as owner. But he would have to give her his real name if he was going to get Lambert to go along with this unprompted visit. "Tell him Mr. Filasek is here for 9:30."

"You're early."

"I'll wait if he is busy." Filasek stroked his chin. It was bare again, more Western looking, he had decided before catching the flight to the States. He sat down in the left-most triangle-backed leather chairs that lined the wall. He wiggled back, so that only his toes touched the marble floor. *Comfortable. At least my profits were well-spent.*

"Filasek. Good to see you, man." Lambert came around the corner into the high-ceilinged reception area inside 30 seconds. The manager offered his raised hand to him. "Come on back to my office."

Filasek settled into a leather side chair in the medium oak office. "I want you to set me up in an office with a fast, secure computer." Filasek told him before Lambert even had a chance to plop himself on the other side of his desk.

"Sure, sure," Lambert nodded. "We can get you set up on payroll. And a couple of boxes came in for you late last week."

Filasek rolled his eyes. "I don't care about payroll."

"Yeah, but we can't have you working without being paid." Lambert argued politely.

"I will not be working on your job. I need the office space. I will be going out to the project site every couple of days though. Have those boxes set in my office. Don't open them."

Lambert swallowed hard. Filasek watched his Adam's apple bob in the open collar of his shirt. "We'll get you set up within the hour." He reached for the phone.

"Just as I expected." Filasek nodded his approval. "Also, set an appointment for me to see your chief engineer with a current set of the bridge blue prints."

"He is on site this morning. He'll be in his office next door after 11." Lambert gestured with his thumb at the right wall of his office. "Don't touch anything in his office. He is a real neat-nick, a perfectionist. Excellent at his job, but he needs some people skills."

Filasek pursed his lips with humor. "We will get along fine."

Naval Intelligence, Suitland, MD
Thursday 17 October 2002
1600 hours

LCDR Judah Wakefield poured over the black and white documentation that had accumulated in her absence. LT Sampson sat across from her with his plaster-casted leg propped in her third chair. "I don't understand why there was such a problem with Petty Officer Tanner while I was gone." She looked up from her reading.

Sampson cleared his throat and checked behind him on both sides before speaking. Wakefield narrowed her eyes, wondering at his cagey movements. "Huntingdon had a problem because he disappeared the same day you did, and NCIS was never called in."

"Yeah, but I talked to his C.O. at Norfolk. He had put in for a transfer, to get away from an abusive ex-wife whose parental rights were terminated by the courts. She wasn't abiding by the ruling." Wakefield shook her head and twisted the leaf insignia on the collar of her khaki uniform. "He did not leave a forwarding address because he did not want her to follow him to California and end up in prison."

"Why wasn't it in his service record?" Sampson cocked his head.

"Maybe they are behind in the paperwork. I checked and he had already registered the kid for fourth grade in the San Francisco County school system. " Wakefield shrugged. "Call Frisco and see if he showed up."

Sampson made the note on the yellow legal pad on his lap.

A short rap tapped out on the doorframe. Huntingdon stood there with Ensign Drury. Wakefield felt her face flush. She knew it was about Filasek. The pen in her fingers was unyielding to her pressure. She glanced at Sampson as she motioned the pair inside. Red crept up his neck as he removed his leg from the chair.

"As you were," Huntingdon told them as they started out of their seats to stand at attention.

Huntingdon raked his thin hair over his bald spot with wide fingers. "We just intercepted an e-mail from two people on the watch list." He passed a single sheet of copy paper to her.

She tried to read, but the captain kept speaking. "Filasek has been in the States for over a week. He snuck through in San Francisco using a forged American passport under the name of Jacobs."

Wakefield dropped the pen she had been threatening to break in two. *He's here. San Francisco. Too coincidental. Too dangerous to go home. Bold to use a Jewish name. He would have hated that. Tanner just transferred to Frisco.* Thoughts jumbled in her head as fast as the neurons could jump around. She licked her lips pulling her fear under control. She forced her breathing to remain normal.

"Sampson, get on that phone call immediately." She ordered. She shook her head and squinted up at her supervisor. "How did he get in? How did we ID him?" That was an even better question. With a fake passport, who would know who he was?

Sampson hobbled to the door and left.

"Ensign Drury found him. The face recognition software that we have been running on security tapes in airports since last September picked him up as he deplaned. But it is days behind, too many people."

"Obviously." Wakefield leaned back in her chair. "He could be anywhere by now." She stared at the World War II nurse in dungarees poster on her wall.

"I already sent a security detail to sweep your apartment." Huntingdon said.

"Thanks." She met his eyes. A measure of trust that she had not seen since she returned to duty was back. She hated to say it though. He might have been right about Tanner. "Sampson is checking up on Petty

Officer Tanner. He transferred to San Francisco the day I left for Greece. I hope it is just coincidental that Filasek showed up in the same city."

Huntingdon melted into the seat Sampson deserted. "Have a seat, Ensign." Wakefield invited the reservist. "You may be here a while."

"I called NCIS while you were gone." Huntingdon admitted. "I just did not trust this guy."

"Good. They have the file already open then. We can get NCIS to follow Tanner if he did indeed show up at Alameda."

Sampson knocked on the open doorframe. "According to Lieutenant Denson, P.O. Tanner reported for duty three days in a row and then called in sick one day, and then requested two weeks leave to help his son settle into school and arrange their housing."

"Two weeks?" Wakefield gaped. Her stomach dropped. Tanner could be protecting his son, but she had a sick feeling in her throat. Reaching for her phone, she told them, "I'll get NCIS to find him and tail him. If he is involved with Filasek, I will hang him out to dry. I hate to be made a fool of," she hissed.

"Believing the best of someone does not make you a fool, Wakefield." Huntingdon said. He looked her in the eye. "However, believing the worst, in a trying situation, *is* grounds for foolishness. I'm sorry I believed you were involved in this mess."

She understood his plea. "Water under the bridge, sir. Don't give it another thought." She smiled with sealed lips and dialed the west coast.

Sunshine Construction Co., San Francisco
Filasek's Office
12:18 PM

Filasek touched his bare chin as he waited the few seconds for his e-mail to download. "Excellent," he exhaled in Farsi when he read the return addresses on the screen.

He double clicked the correspondence from Amir Barhai in Chechnya. A smile grew on his lips as he scanned. Barhai had finally figured out the ratio for the correct weight and density for the gold blocks of syntax that Fort Knox was expecting in five weeks. The formula was included as an attached document. Filasek restlessly jiggled his shoulders as he forwarded the entire e-mail to the assembly party in Chicago. "It is going to work. By Allah, it is going to work."

The second e-mail was from his Navy contact. Tanner had shipped the final container of weapons from a Virginia base to Tikrit, Iraq. He confirmed the Navy's transfer to San Francisco. "I would be happy to assist you any way possible." Filasek read out loud. "Practically neighbors." It couldn't get better than this. He replied with a list of 16 contacts in code to recruit for the November liftoff date.

He glanced at the stacked brown boxes of perfume bottles that had arrived the day before from Qusay Hussein in the corner of his bare office. "Maybe I can even arrange with Tanner for the Navy to pay for shipping. Now wouldn't that be ironic?" He grinned and leaned back in the cloth-covered office chair at his desk. Especially if we expense it to Wakefield.

He had rented warehouse space near Fisherman's Wharf and was already accumulating the needed equipment to begin processing the chemical weapon that would fill the bottles. One shore-to-ship call had rerouted the boxcar of elemental chemicals through the Panama Canal to San Francisco Bay. ETA: October 21.

"If I have to do the mixing and freezing myself, it will be ready to ship two weeks after that." Filasek ran his tongue over his teeth. He chuckled. Working in America certainly had its advantages. People went out of their way to accommodate him in ways he had never experienced in Afghanistan.

In the last week, hundreds of men, at their own expense, had moved their families to new homes around the nation from four or five major cities where they had been putting down roots, establishing their covers and stirring up sympathy for their plight in the Middle East while at the same time building a foundation from which to demand Sharia Law over the next decade or two. It was a perfect plan. The council of Arab leaders had begun re-crafting the Arab message for the world media when he was just a toddler in 1973 after the great humiliation of the Yom Kippur War with the Zionists when everything changed.

The spread of Islam to cover the whole globe whether by conversion, Islamic population explosion, or by the sword was underway and on schedule. Mostly. There had been a few setbacks, but the small little incursions in the west were working. Freedoms were restricted by fear while tolerance was preached from the Capitol. And the EU citizens and Americans went along with it, even while Israel was telling them exactly what the plan was. So great was the propaganda campaign against the Zionists, no one listened to their voice of warning.

His father had been a young man on that Arab Council in 1973; his mother had told him. While Filasek didn't care whether or not Islam was the world religion, setting up a throne for the Twelfth Imam, he did see the opportunity for power. Power would allow him to regain his good name. Vengeance must be extracted from the American population in particular because they had shamed him; they had destroyed his home, twice, and everything he had worked for.

Filasek stroked his bare chin. After this three-pronged attack was carried off to perfection, and the west was in chaos, his father would finally acknowledge him publically. Perhaps they would even share family holidays around the same table. With or without the kings of the region, he didn't care. But one day, soon after his humbling, his father would beg for his forgiveness for rejecting and abandoning him. Filasek's mouth tugged up on the left. He would refuse, of course, right before he put two bullets in the base of the mighty bin Laden's skull. Then the whole Arab world would beg for his leadership and…

Filasek shook his head back to the present in the art deco office of San Francisco. "One step at a time," he promised himself.

Filasek had physical addresses for 484 sympathizers, since UPS did not deliver to P.O. boxes. The U.S. media called them sleepers, but they did not indulge in sleep. Each man had positioned himself in one of the 500 cities that Filasek had designated, ready to receive a small package from San Francisco. They were imbedded citizens, most of them. All of the names and addresses he had gotten from his last visit to Iraq. Each man had lived in the U.S. for at least 5 years. They were beyond suspicion, should any of the authorities live long enough to conduct an investigation after the attack. "The land will then be purged. And I will have surpassed my father's work." He squinted at the computer screen.

Now, how to implicate the Wakefield woman? He tapped the mouse pad in the center of the laptop.

A knock sounded on the doorframe. "Hello?"

Filasek started in his twirling office chair. How long had Lambert been standing there? Filasek perused the ex-con's face. "What do you want?" Filasek barked at him. The man looked like he was hiding something.

"I came to see if you wanted to go to lunch, that's all." Lambert backed away from the door.

Erase any suspicion, Filasek warned himself. "You startled me. I apologize." He broke eye contact to look at his computer screen for anything incriminating, not that Lambert could see it from the doorway anyway. "Lunch? I think I deserve a good lunch today."

Lambert took a tentative step toward him. "Yes," he nodded, "I understand from the evening clean-up crew that you stayed here working all night."

Filasek felt his mouth twitch. The vices of not telling people who he was. His actions got reported to the acting head of the company. "The early bird catches the worm." Filasek dismissed the man's concerned look. He logged off his program so that anyone trying to peek would need a series of passwords. "I am now ahead of my schedule." He grinned. "Grab my jacket, and we'll get seafood. My treat."

Chapter Thirty-two

Wakefield slammed the receiver into the cradle and gritted her teeth in a growl. "They can spare one man to go look for the petty officer. 'We have a manpower shortage. People shifting to the Gulf.'" She mocked. "Don't these people realize he could be a terrorist?"

"Why don't you go out there yourself?" CAPT Huntingdon shrugged.

Wakefield tapped her pen on the desktop again. "I guess I have to." She sighed long. "I am so sick of airplanes."

Huntingdon's sharp eyes landed on her face. He smoothed his hair over the top of his balding head. "You have been in two plane crashes this year. Isn't that correct?" He leaned back in her chair. With his elbows on the chair arms, he touched his fingertips together. Under his scrutiny, Judah felt like fragile glass in a display case. "Have you seen a counselor?"

She lowered her chin abruptly. That was the last thing she expected. It must have shown on her face, because Huntingdon leaned forward slightly when he softened his voice to speak again. "It should have been required. I have the number in my office for a really good doctor, here in Maryland. I saw her after my divorce."

Judah hesitated. She had attended required counseling after three of her missions. She did not feel like listening to the canned garbage again. It was not her father-issues that drove her. She was not constantly trying to measure up to unreal standards for herself.

"Come on, Commander. Counseling is nothing to be ashamed of either."

254 ~ K.J. Frolander

"I'll take her number, but I am not promising anything." Judah tossed her pen on the desk while huffing a heavy sigh. She flashed to remembering making the same motion several times before. "It will have to wait until I get back from my little field trip, now."

"I'll go talk to the admiral with you." Huntingdon stood and opened the door for her to go first.

San Diego 805 Freeway
Thursday 17 October 2002
1420 PDT

David Rivers sat with his long legs crossed in the opposite well of the back seat of his brother's Honda listening to the phone ring in Washington. "So, when do we get to meet her?" Sam Rivers asked from the driver's seat.

"Soon, little bro, I promise." He moved the speaker to his lips as he heard her pick up the extension 3000 miles away. "Hey hon. Got plans for breakfast?" David caught his brother's incredulous look in the rearview mirror.

"Actually, I do." She chuckled deep. "And you may want to join me."

"That sounds like an interesting proposition." David lowered his voice to tease both his fiancé and Sam. "My brother is running me to the airport as we speak."

"How is Lauren doing?" Judah sounded concerned. He could picture the way her brow drew low and crinkled when she was worried.

"She is making an excellent recovery. The doctor released her this morning."

"Oh, David, I am so glad." Judah's voice lightened. He loved to talk to her on the telephone. He listened to the nuances of her voice. It was an exercise in analyzing her communication without the benefit of body language. She left so many clues in her words and pauses. He took in the information she conveyed about Filasek without a word.

He did not hesitate. "I will change my flight and meet you there."

"Thanks. Do you know that Captain Huntingdon suggested I see a shrink?" Her huff told him that a large eye roll probably accompanied her words.

"It probably would not be a bad idea." He slowed his words to sound as if he were thinking of it for the first time. It was closer to the 10th time. He heard her breath catch. "Maybe we could go together." David added quickly. "It's been a rough few weeks."

"Yeah, maybe. Listen, if you get to Frisco first, go ahead and check on the whereabouts of a Marshall Jacobs. That is the name Filasek used to enter the U.S."

"Yes, ma'am. I'll get right on it." He paused. "We'll catch him, Judah. I know it."

"Yes, but we may have to do it through a U.S. Petty Officer Tanner. I'll explain more when I see you. I am at my gate now."

"Love you." Rivers pressed the phone into his ear.

"You too. Bye." She signed off sounding distracted.

Sunshine Construction Co.
Lambert's Office
Friday 18 October 2002
10:30 AM

Jake Lambert reached for the black phone on his desk. He stopped short and let his left hand fall to the edge of the open telephone book pages. "What if I am wrong?" he asked himself in the largest voice he could muster. He was barely able to hear himself in the silent office.

Yet, he knew he was not wrong. Jack Lambert had served eight years behind bars in Dade County Prison. He recognized a guilty look when he saw one. "But if I *am* wrong, he'll fire me when he finds out."

Lambert shook his coal black hair. He could feel it move on the back of his neck. Time for another accursed haircut. On the inside, they didn't care how long your hair grew. Finding reputable customers with money had forced him to maintain a short cut that he resented having to take the time to maintain.

He pounded a fist into the book, as if he could squash out the letters he had looked up. "Just do it," he quoted the Nike commercial to himself. "If they find out I had information that I did not report, I'll be back to walking the line." Lambert closed his eyes. Sometimes, like now, he could still smell the husky man-odors mixed with strong lye used to clean the concrete floors of the prison.

Before he could change his mind again, he dialed.

"San Francisco County office of the FBI, how may I direct your call?"

Lambert froze. She sounded like a high schooler. He had not considered this part of the call. "Um. I'm not sure. Please. I, uh, need to, that is, I think I need to report—" *What is it exactly that I was going to report?* Filasek had committed no crime. Nor did Lambert know of any crime he was planning. "Can I speak to an agent who might deal with people coming into the country. Illegally." He added quickly.

"Sir, you need ICE. Not the FBI. I'll transfer you to Homeland Security," the girl said.

"Yeah, that will do." Lambert told the on-hold music. When an agent came on four and a half minutes later, Lambert stuttered through his fears. "I went to lunch yesterday with my boss, um, the owner of the company I work for."

"His name." Agent Trinsey interrupted. He had a lazy sounding voice.

"Filasek. I think this first name is Arina, no, Arafeh. While we're eating he reaches into his jacket pocket for his wallet, you know." Lambert thumbed through the pages of the telephone book as he spoke. Every three seconds he glanced at the door. "He pulled out an American passport and then shoved it back in. Then he wouldn't look at me. He just acted real suspicious, you know."

There was a pause on the line. Lambert could hear Trinsey breathing. "That's it?" The man asked dryly. "A man pulls out his passport and you call in."

"Well, yeah." Lambert shook his head in disbelief.

"Mister, what did you say your name is?"

"Lambert. Jake Lambert."

"Mr. Lambert, we do not go around arresting people who take unannounced trips."

"Sir. You are just going to let it go? What if he is a terrorist? At the very least he is a thief or a forger."

Agent Trinsey's sigh sounded much too tired to come before lunch. "What makes you think that, Mr. Lambert?"

Lambert smacked his forehead with an open palm. Where did these agents evolve from? "A non-American who is from the Middle East, is carrying a new American passport and you wonder why I called? What's wrong with you people?" He bobbed his head in an airy circle.

"Hold up. You didn't mention that he was not American."

Lambert stopped moving with his head tilted awkwardly to the left. *I thought I said that first off. Maybe I didn't.* "Well. Uh, sorry. He is not American. That is why I called. There is no reason for him to have that passport."

The lazy cadence in the agent's speech vanished. "Did you get a look at the name on the passport. Filasek is probably not his name, nor the name on the passport."

"No, sir. I told you. I just glanced at the binding."

"All right, I am entering this all in the database. Do you know his current whereabouts?"

Lambert swallowed. "Yeah," his voice dropped. "He is in the office next door." He gestured at the wall and gave his office's address.

"We'll take it from here. Thanks for the tip."

Lambert could not quite form a smile. "Don't mention it." He hung up and grimaced. "Please, don't mention it." If nothing turned up, maybe Filasek wouldn't guess it had been him.

NCIS Office, San Francisco
Officer Zella's Office
1045 hours

LCDR Judah Wakefield grunted under her breath. "This is so maddening." She pushed her rolling office chair back from the computer terminal. "We're never going to find him."

"He seems to have gone to ground." LCDR Rivers paced like a caged tiger in the small cubical. P.O. Tanner and his son were not at the address listed in his transfer papers. The apartment looked practically empty, according to the patrolman who had asked the building manager to let him in to take a quick look. Finding record of the transfer had taken a miracle in itself.

"God, we sure could use some help." Wakefield stretched her long, khaki-clad legs out in front of her under the lap drawer that held the keyboard she had bent over all morning.

Zella, a navy-reservist-gone-civilian, was the NCIS officer assigned to help them. "So, how did Naval Intel manage to snag search-party jurisdiction for a missing petty officer?" Zella looked over the top of the

258 ~ K.J. Frolander

divider between the office spaces. He rested his wide chin on the upholstered barrier.

"Jealous?" Wakefield stared at the computer screen without looking at their pear-shaped liaison.

"A little." He admitted with a chuckle.

Rivers joined him. "For the last couple months, we have been hunting down a terrorist named Arafeh Filasek. I am beginning to wonder if they are correlated."

Zella raised his head and backed away from the divider. "Hold on. What did you say his name was?"

"Filasek." Wakefield turned her shoulders toward the NCIS officer and tore her gaze out of the staring trance she had fallen into. Focusing on the top of his head that was visible above the wall, she asked, "Why?"

Papers rustled under the officer's fingers. He mumbled something she couldn't distinguish. "Ah-ha!" a piece of printer paper appeared high in the air. Zella's exclamation ignited a bubble of excitement that she could not explain in her belly. "Type in this address." Zella shot out a list with four backslashes. A screen popped up on her monitor with headlines. "Scroll down about three times."

"What is this site?" She could hardly believe what she was reading.

"It is a database for real-time notes about leads reported to all the different agencies. It's searchable too."

"Why doesn't Naval Intel know about this?" Her eyes snapped up to study Zella's face peering over the barrier again.

"They do. But it is still experimental. We've been on-line four weeks."

Wakefield moved her eyes back to the screen. She read entries by the CIA, Homeland Security, FBI, ATF, Secret Service. "I assume this is password protected." Her eyebrows rose as she read about open cases. All posted in the last few minutes.

"There. Stop." Zella pointed. "An entry by ICE 19 minutes ago."

Rivers placed a hand on her shoulder and leaned in smelling like a spicy forest.

"Arafeh Filasek," Wakefield spoke the words almost reverently. "He is accused of possessing a stolen passport." She reached up to cover Rivers' hand with hers. "Confirmation of what we already knew." She scrolled down further. "Oh, my—Is this his address?" She tapped her finger on the cold screen.

"Yep." Came the answer she had hoped for but did not quite expect. "Up for a field trip?"

Wakefield grabbed her purse and stood in the same motion. "I'll drive. One of you can navigate." She backed out of the small cubicle.

Sunshine Construction Co
10:50 AM

Filasek paced in the restrictive office. He breathed deeply with closed eyes. "It is time to get out, before the walls close in on me."

He grabbed the key to his rented Miata. "Think I'll check on that bridge foreman again today." He loved to spend time standing over the bay. The wind rushing over the bridge cooled his fiery insides. He liked to fantasize about which end would buckle first.

His men were packing every cable with what they thought was rust deterrent. A gray plaster the consistency of modeling clay, courtesy of the U.S. Navy in Norfolk, was applied to each bolt securing a wire in the suspension bridge. The distinctive orange paint used in the construction of the bridge would boil with the heat generated by that much explosive before the structure crumbled into the bay.

Filasek exited the building. "It will be such fun to watch. I should get a video camera and sell the tape to the media. If any are still alive after I finish with the chemicals." He shivered with excitement as he stepped down into the car. He fastened his seatbelt and breathed the sharp alkali air. "Delightful," he pronounced the air and the video idea.

Sunshine Construction Co
1145 hours

Wakefield skidded to a stop and threw the gear shift into park to leave the blue sedan in the fire zone in front of the construction company beside the bay.

She dug for her ID while Zella climbed out of the front seat and Rivers unfolded himself from the back. A pudgy man in his early 40's in a too-large suit pushed off the wall near the door. "Commander Wakefield?" He approached with an outstretched hand. "Agent Trinsey, ICE."

"Good morning, Agent Trinsey. Thank you for joining us. I am glad we are not going to have a turf war over taking this man down." She gave the man her iciest look. She would not allow this to blow up and Filasek to sneak away in the billowing smoke.

"Commander Rivers." David introduced himself to the agent while nudging her closer to the door. "That is her way of giving orders to people who don't accept orders from the Navy." Wakefield smiled at her reflection in the glass door. *Nice of Rivers to warn the man, even at my expense.*

"I don't order *everyone* around." Wakefield called over her shoulder, allowing a tad of sass to creep into her voice in her eagerness. She breezed into a stately lobby and approached the receptionist's desk.

She felt Rivers step in behind her. "I hate to correct the control queen, but, even the President of the United States had me jumping to comply with your orders."

Wakefield felt her eyebrows rise. *He was teasing, right?* She plastered on a smile that did not break the seam of her lips. "Who better to correct the queen of control than the king of control?"

"May I help you?" the kinky-haired receptionist rose to her feet.

All four of them held out their ID badges at the same time. The woman literally took one step backward. Her chair rolled back until it hit the wall a yard behind her desk.

"Sorry. Nothing for you to worry about, ma'am." Wakefield saw panic begin to rise in the woman's eyes. "We need to see this man." She held out a sketch of Arafeh Filasek.

"Oh, Filasek. But he left." The woman clutched a hand to her chest and did not venture any closer to the four of them.

"When?" Wakefield asked at the same time as Agent Trinsey spoke, "Then we need to see Jake Lambert."

The woman smoothed a hand over her tiny, gelled curls. "I'll ring his office." The woman forced herself to take a step toward them to reach the telephone. "That man tore out of here about 45 minutes to an hour ago. Said something about seeing to the bridge. We're contracted to repair the Golden Gate, you know." Once she got started, jabbering seemed to be the way she released tension. Wakefield could feel the men stiffen in irritation behind her at the reception desk.

"Strangest thing, I thought to myself," the receptionist chattered. "That man came in here out of the blue, and asked Mr.Lambert for a job a couple weeks ago. Mr. Lambert, he's nice, he don't mind taking a chance on people with a past. But," her voice dropped with drama, "that Filasek, he don't draw pay. He sits up in his fancy office, locks his door at lunchtime, but that's only when he leaves, mind you, works sometimes all the way through the night." She gave a jittery laugh. "His car was cold a couple times when I come in and he was already here." The woman shook her head. Wakefield could hear the clipped sound of dress shoes on polished tile. Hopefully, it was Mr. Lambert.

"I always thought that was the strangest thing. You know. No pay, all those hours, his appearing out of nowhere..."

The footsteps rounded the corner. The man looked too casual for the grandeur of this lobby. Wakefield did not care what he looked like when he held out his hand and said, "I'm Jake Lambert. Please come to my office."

Chapter Thirty-three

Petty Officer Darren Tanner locked his front door behind him and set the two brown grocery bags on the table. He noticed the Caller ID blinking the knowledge of new calls.

Tanner pressed the power button on his laptop and sat in the old armchair he had brought with him from the east coast. He glanced at his watch then scrolled through the Caller ID log while he waited for the computer to boot. No calls from the school. "Well, he made it to lunchtime today. Good kid." The excuse he had given his new C.O. of having to ease Tyler into the new situation at school was not entirely made up. The adjustment had been hard on the kid. The benefit of having extra time to prepare for Filasek's November project more than made up for having to leave around 10 or 11 o'clock every day to pick up the boy from his classes.

He was a little nervous about the project, but it was good money. "This is the last time I'm going to have my arm twisted though." He promised himself as he retrieved his e-mail. "I just need enough money to get out of the Navy and, " he shrugged with the barest hint of a smile, "pay that extortionist off for good."

He pulled up his email. "One little mistake," Tanner shook his head, "and he won't let me live it down. So what if a man died? I should have taken my chances with a court martial." But it was too late for that now.

Chief Jackson, his former boss, was stationed in Pensacola now, but that did not stop the man's black and white typed notes from their journey up the coastline to Norfolk.

Tanner clicked on the email from Filasek's address. Tanner had helped recruit Hasrit Jutin for Filasek's November project to cover the city of Pensacola. Filasek had promised that one man in each of 500 cities, unrelated, coming down with a form of dysentery and the authorities would see the vulnerability of the U.S. medical field and put new safe-guards in place. Tanner had seen the vulnerability himself, and while this plan was outside his comfort zone, he wanted more safeguards in place.

After Tanner had told Jutin of the extortion he was under—with some adjusted details—by Chief Jackson, Jutin had slapped Tanner on the back and volunteered to stand on Chief Jackson's lawn when he released the poison.

Filasek told Tanner it would make people throw up and sit in the bathroom for days on end. Tanner smiled. The tables would be turned then. Tanner planned to have his own little black and white letter arrive at Jackson's house within a few hours of the first outbreak of symptoms around the nation. He had worked on the wording in the back of his mind since he found out about this plan three months earlier; it even dominated his dreams. He would promise Jackson that there was more where it had come from, never mind that there wasn't. He would threaten to double-dose Jackson if he ever sent another message or told the authorities about his little mistake.

Yes, getting Jackson off his back was worth a bit more risk.

Sunshine Construction Co
Lambert's Office
1220 hours

LCDR Rivers fell into full hunter mode. "Where are your workers on the bridge today?" He asked Lambert. So far, the man had been very helpful.

Lambert pulled down a spring-driven roll-up schematic drawing of the Golden Gate Bridge from the ceiling in his office. "They are scheduled here." He pointed a finger with a gnawed nail. He read out the marker numbers and Rivers committed them to memory.

"I think it would be most productive if NCIS stayed here and went through Filasek's computer. See if you can find our missing petty officer." He directed the comment at the pear-faced Zella who had been mooning over Judah. "Gunsmoke, you're with me. We'll take ICE, so the arrest will be unchallengeable."

He saw Wakefield's back straighten and he braced himself for the onslaught. "Who put you in charge, Commander?" she asked.

Not so bad, he decided. "Would you like to change anything?"

Her lips poked out in the way they did when she was considering. "No, I suppose that is what I would have done."

Lambert spoke up as the four of them were walking toward the door. "Please. Just in case I was wrong, go easy on him."

All four of them turned together, but it was Wakefield who found her voice first. "You were not wrong." Her voice was gravelly. "Filasek has held me captive twice and he is the one who did this to my face." She reached up and traced the pink scar with practiced fingers. "It is time he met justice."

Rivers was surprised to see a gleam of water in her eyes as she turned back to the door.

"But he owns this company. What will happen to us?"

Agent Trinsey cleared his throat. "I would contact an attorney if I were you."

*****

Judah Wakefield looked over her shoulder at Rivers and Trinsey. "Hurry up. I don't want him to get away."

"He doesn't know we're coming." Trinsey puckered his brow in a way that made her feel overzealous.

"Whatever," she dismissed the agent's disapproval with a wave of her hand and did not change her pace to wait for the slow pokes.

Rivers had reminded her that she would not have any place to park the sedan on the bridge. They had to park and walk the quarter mile to the job site. She had to let go of the daydream of skidding to a stop with sirens blazing. She hoped the handcuffs would still be a reality. *Or I am not riding back with him.*

Her thigh muscles began to heat as she speed-walked the famous orange bridge. Striped barrels cordoned off the two slow lanes of the traffic coming toward them. The steam from the heavy equipment laying tar rose like mist in the diesel air. The sharp asphalt smell stung her nose.

Three men in hardhats sat on the tailgate of an old red pickup truck eating sandwiches and drinking from red thermoses. The man closest to her waved, but none of them spoke. Judah nodded in acknowledgement as she steamed past.

It was hard to distinguish the men because of their matching hats. Until she spotted the shiny white one on a familiar small figure.

She slowed.

It is not like I can just go over and bodily force him to comply. I don't even have the handcuffs.

"I see him, too." Rivers said right behind her. "I've got the cuffs, Agent Trinsey is circling around the back way. Here," he pressed his service pistol into her hand.

Wakefield looked to her right and saw the ICE agent jogging on the white dotted lines between rows of cars with his gun drawn and facing the sky next to his right ear. She felt her eyes go wide. As soon as somebody honked at him, Filasek would turn and see Trinsey's gun.

Filasek bent over at the waist to inspect something at the base of one of the cables. When he turned around to look back out to the bay, she noticed that he was on his cell phone. *Good, a distraction.* She increased her pace. Rivers must have noticed the same, for he sped up too.

They maneuvered out of Filasek's line of vision. Whomever he was talking to seemed to be getting a tongue-lashing. The noise of traffic and wind dampened the specifics of the conversation.

Rivers motioned two of the construction crew back with a small sweep of his hand. They both stared open-mouthed at the guns and badges. They looked like fish, but at least that way they could not warn Filasek.

Rivers looked at her, raised a single eyebrow, and jutted his chin toward the long-sought terrorist. She nodded, glad to be offered the lead in approaching.

Wakefield swallowed and tapped her finger on the chilled trigger guard of her partner's gun, wondering briefly how this day would end.

Reaching forward, she tapped Filasek on the shoulder. He started visibly and snapped his phone shut before turning around.

Filasek's brown eyes bulged like twin hatches with thousands of tons of water pressure trying to force them open from behind.

"Arafeh Filasek, you are under arrest." She told him, unable to keep the corners of her mouth from turning up. Rivers clinked the cuffs together with a metallic sound as he pulled them from his pocket.

"What for?" Filasek's chin rose with indignation. "You can't arrest me for no reason." He spat on the sidewalk grate where he stood. "I have not broken any laws." A touch of his native Farsi accent began to color his English.

"You forgot to—" Rivers began but Trinsey interrupted him with a chuckle.

"Actually, judicial code 4589A dash 78 subsection 3 of the California State Constitution forbids expectorating on public walkways."

Wakefield stared at Trinsey.

"We are pressing charges for every infraction you have committed, Mr.Filasek. Including illegal entry into the country, using a false identity, working without a green card, conspiring to..." Trinsey droned on with his list of offenses, but Judah tuned him out. One handcuff snapped over his olive skinned wrist. Each tightening click sounded like a safety chain on a roller coaster's tension-filled uphill track. There was no going back.

*****

Arafeh Filasek felt white heat flash over his body as his adrenaline surged. He had felt it many times before during narrow escapes when he was driving and when he thought he murdered the wrong man, when his house and then his arsenal exploded, and once just before he fell out of a tree.

Today, it did not go away. The heat ran hotter.

He did not struggle against the cold metal around his wrist. His mind embraced one phrase: "Do not go." It ricocheted in the corners of his consciousness.

He looked down and saw Rivers' folding the scythe of the cuff over the bone of his own thick wrist. *That can't happen*, Filasek instructed himself. There was no avenue of escape if they were handcuffed together.

Filasek bit into the swelling heat. Before metal touched metal on Rivers' arm Filasek yanked his arm toward his stomach with all his strength. In the same moment, he twisted in a circle, jerking the cuff out of the officer's grasp and freeing himself from their custody.

Scurrying to the railing of the bridge, he squeezed between two support wires and scooted out to the secondary railing. Jumping up, he grasped the top rung and walked his feet up the vertical bars.

His shoulders and wrists screamed their disapproval as his full body weight hung mid-air before he dropped to the far side.

The landing stung the soles of his feet. He looked back over his shoulder. The woman had a gun trained on him. Her blue eyes flashed as she looked left and right. She would not pull the trigger.

The wind whipped around him carrying someone's scream. "We have a jumper!"

That is not a bad idea. He had only planned to get away from them, but the probabilities of survival after a jump were better than after being arrested by the Americans.

He peered over the edge. *Have to watch the support structure,* he warned himself. Big rock piles formed tiny islands to relieve some of the bridge's overhead weight.

Filasek glanced back at the officers. Now there were three. Rivers was motioning him back and creeping forward at the same time. After what happened a few weeks earlier in his basement and spare room, Rivers was probably just as likely to push him over the edge as bring him in to custody. *But if I go on my own terms, I still win.*

The cuff dangled, twisting in the air current. Filasek grabbed it. It was too bad he had not had more time to implicate the woman in the November Endeavor. *But she will always have a keepsake of me. And everything is in place to run without me.*

Filasek turned his neck to the left, exposing his right cheek to the woman. He looked her in the eye and then traced with his finger on his own cheek, the line of the scar he had left on her. He gave an exaggerated grin and stepped backward one step.

He could feel the line of the edge under his heel.

Throwing his arms wide, Filasek shifted his weight backward. It was like bungie jumping, without the cord. He watched her face for the moments it took gravity to pull him down.

"Stop!" her words cut through the air. A frail puff of smoke emitted from the barrel of her gun.

His shoulder registered the pain first. A biting sensation reached for his bone. It threw his balance wrenching to the right. Then a sting in his left hip straightened out his fall.

The project can survive without me. More and more of the iconic orange bridge structure came into his line of sight. He didn't struggle to turn over and watch for the water rushing up to meet him face to face. *I wonder if it is time to hold my breath yet.*

Sunshine Construction Co
1:45 PM

Zella's hands flew over the computer. His eyes roamed the screen as fast as he could get it to load. He alternated between curses low under his breath and soft whistles of disbelief.

He reached for his cell phone and dialed his home office. He read the morning's e-mail between Arafeh Filasek and Petty Officer Tanner. "That arrogant son—oh, no, not you, sir."

"Who then?" Agent Thomas Ford, Zella's boss, asked over the connection.

"A Petty Officer Tanner. He has been helping a rising terrorist smuggle weapons that belong to the U.S. Navy and a host of other things that I think you should see."

"This is not like that Smitherman fiasco last month is it Zella?" Ford responded slowly.

"No, sir," Zella dropped his left hand into his lap. Why didn't people just let that go? "It is much bigger than that."

"All right, but you better not be yanking my chain this time, or your next assignment will be in Reykjavik."

Zella ignored the threat. There was no question in his mind as to the validity of these plans. "Bring a charged cell phone. You are probably going to need to coordinate a joint forces team in at least three cities."

"Um-hm." Ford groused. "See you in 45 minutes."

Chapter Thirty-four

"Can you see?" David Rivers heard his partner call over the traffic and wind, neither of which would stop for a fallen sparrow or a suicidal shootout.

Filasek lay in the air like he was lying on a mattress. As he grew smaller, he seemed to draw into himself. Rivers squinted against the mid-day sun reflecting off the tips of the choppy water hundreds of feet below. If he was dropping butt first into the water, curled up as he appeared, he just might survive the impact. His head and lungs would be protected, his arms and legs would not be torn from his body by the force of impact. "If he can swim with those bullet holes they poked in him," Rivers trailed off.

"He just hit the water." He called back to her. The splash would not have been noticeable except that he was waiting for it. The view was too far away to determine if his head came back up or not.

Rivers backed away sighing. The odds were so far removed.

Wakefield's slim smooth arms slid around his waist from behind. He felt the weight of her head collapse against his back. He rubbed his fingers over her arms to soothe her.

"It is finally over, isn't it?" She asked. He could hear her struggle against tears.

He turned around in her embrace and gathered her close to him, cupping one hand over her hair as the other splayed across her back. "You don't have to fear Filasek ever again." David smoothed the wisps of hair that had escaped her French braid back from her face.

"Let's go home." She hiccupped.

"And live happily ever after?" He pried her shoulders away from his chest to look in her eyes. The deep blue reminded him of the summer sky in Kansas.

A small grin began at the corner of her lips and grew wide. "Between the two of us, and the amount of trouble that seems to find us, I don't think that is a possibility. But I sure would like to try."

David chuckled. She was too right. "Okay, but we have to draft an order to drag the bay before we go. Who knows what else we'll find."

Judah groaned. "Don't even suggest—"

"Suggest what?"

"Anything. Don't suggest anything."

Sunshine Construction Co
3:15 PM

Agent Zella scratched the side of his face where the beginnings of a five o'clock shadow bit through his skin. He leaned over his boss's shoulder as Ford read Filasek's e-mail. "Okay, Zella, I think we have a real ball of twine here."

Zella refused to give into the "I told you so," that begged to dive off his tongue. He clamped his lips together until he thought of something constructive to say. "What should we do first?"

"Report up the chain of command." Ford finally looked at him. Of course, the look came down the man's long nose, maybe it was better before, when Ford stared at the computer and ignored him.

"Shouldn't we call NASA? They need to know as early as possible. The launch they were talking about in the last e-mail is only a month away. I can make the call." *I would love to make the call.* He felt his heart rate increase. Zella had dreamed of being an astronaut since he listened to the moon landing when he was 10.

Ford touched a few buttons on his cell phone and held it to his ear with the speaking end rotated down near his neck. "We wait for instruction from H.Q., Zella." Ford twisted the phone back to his mouth. "Yes, I'll hold." His boss glanced back at him, "But I would venture a guess that the first call goes to Fort Knox."

Filasek's office door pushed open and LCDR Rivers poked his head inside. "What have you got?" the large man asked.

Zella motioned him inside and put a finger to his lips to caution him to be quiet for Ford. The door opened wider and Wakefield walked in behind Rivers. Zella did not miss the joined hands as they snuck inside.

Zella pushed aside his disappointment that the blonde was taken, and he joined them in the far corner. Ford was winding down his conversation but it always took a long time to get off the line with Deputy Director Sheldon.

Zella adjusted his tie and noticed a line of mustard from his hotdog lunch decorating the middle of the light blue silk. *Attractive*, he applauded his most recent upset. "You are not going to believe what we've found." He loosened the tie with his free hand.

"What's up?" Wakefield looked a little haggard.

"Your little petty officer is in this up to his ears." Zella felt his mouth split with pride as he smiled. "He is on his way to Leavenworth as soon as we catch him. It is so huge. He'll never see daylight again."

"What is so huge?" Rivers asked in a voice that dampened his excitement a tad.

"I recovered e-mails detailing a plot for a series of attacks on the United States." Zella unthreaded his tie from his shirt collar. "It is highly organized, involving Petty Officer Tanner who wrongfully misappropriated tons of weapons and shipped them to factions in the Middle East for one Arafeh Filasek." He pointed at Wakefield. "There is a three-pronged attack set for the night launch of the Space Shuttle Endeavor at the end of November. Filasek is planning to blow up the shuttle!"

Zella stuffed the stained tie into his pocket but he was unable to stuff his enthusiasm. He felt high on adrenaline as he rocked from the balls of his feet to his heels and back again.

"Not anymore." LCDR Wakefield's low voice cut into his party. "Filasek is dead."

Zella felt his chest deflate. His rocking stilled. The woman's touch grazed her scarred cheek as she brushed some fallen wisps of hair behind her ear. She wore an expression he could not read.

"In the last three hours?" Zella had to make sure. He had read the last set of missives himself.

"He decided to launch himself, instead. Right over the side of the Golden Gate Bridge." Rivers used his left hand to indicate an upward motion and then a falling splat. The SEAL trainer had an amusing quality about him that Zella had never associated with the "killing machines" before.

"The bridge was also mentioned in the material. It was to be the third explosion on that November night. Right after Fort Knox."

Wakefield gasped. "Filasek was going to blow up Fort Knox! How in the world?" Her blue eyes widened.

"There's no way." Rivers shook his head with a skeptical half-smile. "He could not get his hands on that much explosive material without attracting a whole lot of attention."

"He manufactured some explosive gold bars, sir. It is scheduled for delivery from Chicago." Zella shook his head. "I saw the confirmation e-mail from an Agent Kenworth at Fort Knox myself."

The SEAL shook his head again and shrugged. "One deposit could never be enough. Have you seen the security at that place?"

"He doesn't have to destroy the whole place to rock the currency value beyond repair," the woman said. "You saw the market last September after 9-11." Wakefield touched Rivers arm with long lean fingers.

"The entire bridge needs to be searched." Zella heard Ford speak from behind him. Zella turned to look at his boss who was finally free of the telephone. "According to a conversation I had with Jake Lambert," Ford gestured through the wall at the manager's office, "Filasek has spent a lot of time out on the job site. You know Filasek owned this company for years and used it to secure a city contract to repair the bridge, only to destroy it." Ford shook his head and rubbed a palm over his face.

*****

LCDR Wakefield watched the NCIS officer's face. It was obvious that he was floored by the corruption a man's soul was capable of.

She remembered being that naïve once.

Agent Ford's posture was spent. He perked up long enough to gesture to the wheeled office chair beside the desk where he was slumped. "Sorry about my manners. Please, Commander Wakefield, have a seat."

She squeezed Rivers fingers slightly in her left hand. "Why don't you sit? You are the one with the broken ribs."

Ford peeled himself out of Filasek's chair. "Why don't you both sit?" he invited. "I am going to see about some coffee. It is going to be a long evening." The man's long legs bowed backward like an ostrich as he stiffened his stance at the door. "Where's that agent, uh, Trinsey, that went with you?"

"Went back to the Homeland ICE office to file some paperwork that he was not looking forward to." Wakefield told Ford with a chuckle as she remembered how Trinsey had cursed when he saw Filasek jump. "He is going to start the bay dragging for us."

"Great. There are more computer files," Ford pointed to the black and white screen of text with a blue rim framing it, "if anybody is interested."

Wearily, Wakefield spun her chair to face the screen for a more comfortable position as Ford shut the door behind himself. "I can't believe he didn't finish the computer search before he made the calls." She mumbled, reaching for the mouse.

"What was that?" Rivers sat carefully in the second chair.

Wakefield closed five windows and double clicked the C drive. "Oh, nothing. I'm just compl—oh, Lord!" She had clicked on the downloaded file in the history section that was filed in Microsoft Outlook. She was silent while it loaded.

"I bet Ford didn't get a look at this file, yet." It was titled in Farsi: CONTACTS.

"What is it?" Rivers scooted close. One of the wheels on his rolling chair was shorter than the others and it tilted him precariously forward when he shifted his weight.

She did not answer; she couldn't. Judah scrolled down the right side of the chart. It went past 15 and then 25 pages. It stopped on page 31. Her eyes bulged wider as she read, "Five hundred entries in this application."

"What application?" Rivers voice was short. She felt him inch closer to her.

"I think this is a list of the sleepers Filasek, or some organization we have not yet come across, has planted in the U.S. These are all United States addresses. And they look to be from all over." Wakefield paged up trying to control her returning nausea. A lot of the names were Islamic but many were American, too.

274 ~ K.J. FROLANDER

Rivers leaned in closer and rested his chin on her right shoulder. It made it awkward to use the mouse, but the contact was nice.

She traced the file to its original location. "This came from Petty Officer Tanner, but the original writer is some computer registered from Syria." *Why does that IP number look so familiar?* Wakefield searched the crevices of her mind for the information to complete the puzzle. "My word! I remember."

She gasped as more implications began to dawn on her. "This is even bigger than we thought. The original author of these address files is Osama bin Laden. I've studied files sent from his computer to—well, that's classified." She eyed Zella's pear-shaped body standing 10 feet from them. "This is bad. Very bad."

Rivers covered her right hand on the mouse. "Or, it could be the beginning of the biggest take down in history." His voice sounded dreamy, like he was not even aware he was speaking out loud. He scrolled up the list where she left off. "This has names and addresses, current ones, according to this date here." Rivers pointed to the screen.

"Do you suppose that is enough for warrants?" Zella walked over and stood off Wakefield's left shoulder.

"No." She shook her head as she continued to read as Rivers scrolled up, "but we can put a tail on each of them."

"Thirty-one pages worth of people to tail?" Zella sounded incredulous.

Wakefield did not answer. She read and began to notice a pattern or rather no pattern. With two pages to go, she could hear Rivers making little noises of disappointment in his throat.

"So *that's* it." She leaned back in her chair as she remembered a conversation she'd flunked with Filasek in his home in Greece.

"What's it?" Rivers asked when he reached the first entry.

"You don't see the pattern in the addresses?" Judah asked. She looked at Rivers and then Zella. They both shook their heads. "You really don't see it?" It seemed so obvious to her now.

"Ugh, you can be frustrating, Woman. Spit it out." Rivers tapped the back of her hand with his first finger.

"There are about 500 cities represented in this address book. All metropolises. None duplicated. *All* the large cities are here. It is one of the questions Filasek kept after me about." She looked at Rivers' blue-green eyes. "He just kept repeating, 'Just give me the names of twenty cities.'" Judah quoted.

"And so you just gave them to him?" Zella sounded disgusted.

Anger rose within her. Zella had no idea what it had been like over there. How dare he sound so accusing. She could not decide what to say first, and Rivers beat her to the punch.

"It was a very difficult situation, Agent Zella." His voice was soft, almost honey-like in the way it flowed over her roused pain. "You would do well not to judge until you have been in a similar scenario."

"I went through hostage training." Zella's arrogance bled through his tone.

"I have too." Rivers told him. Wakefield felt him tighten his fingers on her hand, as if he was drawing strength from her. "This was nothing like training." His soft words were not the words of a hardened SEAL, but of a man who had seen the betrayal he was capable of, and found himself weak.

Wakefield had studied enough psychological profiles and interviewed enough people to recognize that though Rivers did not give into Filasek, he acknowledged, that if left to himself, he would have. She smiled as the last of her humiliation ebbed. She had never met anyone as courageous as David Rivers. And as soon as they were alone, she determined to tell him so.

She flipped her mouse hand over and fit it into his palm. "These men need to be identified and followed then rounded up if they are up to something with Filasek." She re-read the first page as if they could give her some clue as to their purpose. "Each of these men could have a contingent of others under him who are planning some sort of take over during the other crises Filasek had planned for November. I have never seen this many organized like this."

"We'll have local police forces bring a couple of them in for questioning." Rivers stiffened beside her. "Whatever is going on, it is far too organized for me to feel comfortable."

Chapter Thirty-five

"That was the most delicious fish I have ever tasted. And I didn't think I'd ever look at a fish again after that one-eyed monster Filasek drugged me with." Wakefield closed her eyes banishing the man from her mind. It worked and she wished there was no end to the boardwalk, content to walk in Rivers' embrace for eternity.

"I thought you hated fish." Rivers rubbed his hand down her left arm. His arm fit over her shoulder like the capstone of an archway.

"So did I." Wakefield giggled. She slowed their pace for a moment just to breathe in the air. It was a little fishy, but distinct, all the same. "I want to remember this moment for the rest of my life." She felt a little silly admitting it out loud, but with Rivers, it was okay. "Church was incredible. The meal was amazing and the company even better. I never knew being loved could make me feel so different inside." She shook her long hair, loving the sensation of its movement when it was down.

"Is it being loved or loving that is different?" Rivers asked as they walked again. "You have been loved all your life."

"Perhaps you are too perceptive for your own good." She tapped his chest with her left hand as she turned into him and tightened her right arm around his lean waist. She loved him in civilian attire, even more than in uniform. "I have not allowed myself to love without reserve since my father was killed."

"When you were nine?"

Judah nodded. "But you know what I decided? If God has given me to you, even for a short time, you are never going to wonder if I love you. I want to show you the length and breadth of my heart so that if you don't come back from a mission, even if it is just a week, or a day from now, we will both know I have loved you with everything that is in me. I want no regrets."

"I concur." Rivers brought his right hand up in front of them. In his fingers, a shiny diamond on a gold band sparkled in the October afternoon sun.

Judah gasped.

"Your proposal was just too perfect to let pass." He shrugged. "I have found the one whom my heart longs for. Please, be my wife for the rest of our lives, whether it be a day or a century."

Judah felt water fill her eyes as she held up her left hand. She wiggled her fingers to help him push the gold ring over her knuckle. "I'd love to."

She turned in his arms, dismissing the Sunday crowd on the Wharf, and pulled his head down to hers. His cool lips refreshed her. She tasted salt as her tears spilled over her cheeks. She deepened the kiss with a sigh. Giggling, she finally pulled back for air. "I feel like a teenager. But I think I could stay here," she snuggled closer in his arms, "forever."

Rivers' chin dropped to the top of her head. "After waiting for you for 37 years, I might just let you." His chest expanded under her cheek and she detected the bandage around his torso. "Did you look at your ring?" The vibrations of his voice were new when Judah could feel them as well as hear them.

She held it up.

"It was my grandmother's engagement ring. I had two round amethysts mounted on either side, to remind us that you are my treasure. My bag of purple M&Ms which the Manufacturer has approved and stamped with His seal of approval."

She saw the ring through Rivers' eyes and his long ago explanation of his consideration of worth for his future wife. "It is more perfect than I dreamed it would be. And so are you. I love you, David Rivers."

He kissed her lips again. "I love you, Judah A. Wakefield."

She loved it when he called her that. No one else ever said her name like he did. She leaned up to peck his lips again.

Rivers phone chirped at his waist. He looked at the caller ID before answering.

His smile was weakly apologetic. "Go ahead," she told him with only an ounce of disappointment. "It will probably always be like this with us."

Three minutes later, Rivers snapped the phone closed. "That was Homeland. They have a body and want one of us to come identify it. Also, NASA found and replaced a series of exploding bolts on the *Endeavor* that had been over-packed with TNT. They traced it to a man who is now sitting in a jail cell."

"Excellent." Wakefield clucked her tongue between her cheek and teeth.

"I am told a waterlogged body can look pretty nasty. Do you want to do it? Because I can, if you would prefer."

Wakefield smiled. "You ought to know by now that I am not squeamish. IDing the ugly body of our torturer would only make the day complete."

Rivers squeezed his eyes shut with humor. "You have always had a way with words, my dear."

San Francisco County Morgue
1620 hours

The young coroner accompanied them to the cold concrete block room where bodies lay in chrome drawers. The rollers on the long drawer whirred as the black-haired man in his late twenties pulled the handle.

The white sheet swelled in strange places. The form did not look human. "We've taken some samples of his DNA, and are running them through the lab, in case he is too badly disfigured for you to recognize. Of course, it could be some other lost soul that has not been reported missing yet."

The coroner peeled back the sheet. Wakefield swallowed hard. A stab of pity gouged out her stomach. The shoulder she had put the bullet in was swollen like an over ripe watermelon. His fingers looked like fat carrots. His inflamed face appeared inflated like a three-day old latex balloon. The side closer to her was bulbous and the other was sunken in with missing flesh.

"It's him." Wakefield was sure. "Arafeh Filasek."

Rivers tugged at her waist and she willingly turned away. The long, underground hallway from the hospital was chilly and damp. "Do you think," Judah asked, "If we had an address on Osama bin Laden, they would let us send Filasek's body back?"

Rivers snorted. "Maybe. But we don't."

"Too bad." Judah fingered the back of the engagement ring with her thumb. She savored the new sensation of a ring on that finger. Someday, she knew she would not even feel it any more. But today, she did, and it felt wonderful. "I always thought belonging to someone was a bad thing, a thing of weakness." Judah laced her fingers with his, amazed with the ease she felt with him. "But I see now, that belonging is the very significance I sought with my independence."

As they walked into the remains of the five o'clock sunshine Wakefield's phone buzzed. "My turn," she said, digging it out of her purse.

"Captain Huntingdon." It was 9 PM on the east coast. "I was going to call you on the secure line first thing in the morning." She straightened her shoulders as she walked toward some benches outside the hospital. Only one of the four was unoccupied with visitors or nurses taking a smoke break.

"That is fine. Admiral Tamburillo asked me to check in on you. He has heard the official reports as they keep filing into Intel, but he was concerned about you."

"I am fine. Great really." She could not keep the grin out of her cheeks. "You can tell him I am engaged to Rivers, for real now." She felt Rivers lean close to her. His raised eyebrows spoke of curiosity that he seemed determined to satisfy. "The latest news probably has not made it to D.C. yet. They found Filasek's body in the bay a couple hours ago. Rivers and I just ID'ed him."

"It is really him?" Huntingdon questioned. She was sure it was just habit, so she dismissed the lack of confidence.

"It was him." She squeezed Rivers' hand.

"Oh, we got an idea on that formula Rivers sent us at the lab this morning."

"Yeah?" She held the phone sideways away from her ear for Rivers to hear the news, too.

"It is definitely some kind of new chemical weapon. The curing is a very precise process and the CIA is trying to duplicate it. According to their top chemical biologist, Dr. Joseph Lancine, it is the most deadly recipe he has seen. His computer program predicted catastrophic results. But that is all the information we could squeeze out of them. If there are any stock piles of this stuff anywhere, we are in big trouble."

"I don't think it got out. There were 500 perfume bottles in Filasek's office. We assume he was going to send the compound in those bottles to the same number of addresses in that file we sent you, sir. Any luck with that, by the way?"

"No. None of them have actually committed any crime. What is the count on the bridge construction thing?"

Wakefield shook her head. "Last I heard, the company had removed 18 tons of wiring and C-4 from the Golden Gate. It was a minefield, sir. The FBI is satisfied that Lambert was uninvolved with the process. They told him that he is expected to fulfill his contract with the city. Well, you should have seen his face. I don't know if he was scared or relieved."

Rivers rocked with laughter beside her. But it was true; the poor man's face had gone as white as a sheet, then his eyes looked like they were going to bug out of his head.

"I owe you an apology, sir." Wakefield bit the inside of her cheek. "About Petty Officer Tanner, you were right. He *was* in on Filasek's scheme and has been supplying him with weapons for at least three years. The wife story was a smoke screen, though true to a limited extent. But he really did it. You saw the truth and I missed it and then got annoyed with you. I was distracted by personal problems, and it won't happen again, sir."

Huntingdon's chuckle crackled on the line. "Didn't you just say you are engaged? I can guarantee it will happen again. But that is why we are all here. To cover each other's sixes."

Indignant, Wakefield stiffened her back against the slatted bench. Realizing he was right again, she deflated. "Thank you, sir."

"Tamburillo is offering you leave time, if you want it. Otherwise, he expects you here on Tuesday at 0800."

"I'd like to take a couple days. Rivers does not have to report to Little Creek until Thursday." She looked at him while she spoke so she could gauge his reaction. "I think I'd like to take him home to meet the family."

"Take the time. We'll see you Thursday morning, Commander."

Wakefield pressed the talk button to turn off her Nokia and slipped in into her bag on the ground.

Rivers grin was wide.

"So, what do you think?" she asked.

"I think it is a great idea. We can announce our plans officially."

"Officially? What do you mean?" Wakefield lifted her chin and narrowed her eyes at him. His crinkled grin told her he was keeping a secret.

"Did you think I asked you without talking to your dad first?"

"You called the admiral, at sea?"

Rivers widened his eyes innocently. "You didn't want me to get court-martialed for kissing the admiral's daughter, did you?"

Wakefield's head dropped lower and lower and she looked up at her fiancé through long lashes. "What did he say?"

Rivers chuckled. "He said, 'It is about time.'"

He raised his arm up over the back of the bench and squeezed her shoulder. Judah relaxed into him, resting her head on his shoulder. The sun dropped lower in the sky and a light breeze blew the smoke from their distant bench neighbors away.

"David, this is my favorite day of my whole life. I know what the phrase, 'All's right with the world' feels like now. I didn't believe it existed."

"It only gets better from here, Gunsmoke."

Epilogue

"Agent Markley, we just got a new hit on Filasek's e-mail account." Trinsey called out to his boss, twenty feet away. Markley rushed around the partition to Trinsey's desk. Trinsey pushed up the sleeves on his too-big black suit coat. "It is from an account that, according to the CIA's database, is registered to one Saddam Hussein."

As the decrypter worked at the message, Trinsey read aloud. "Filasek, the new perfume works wonders on unpleasant odors to the north. I would like to buy the formula from you, so that we can mass-produce the product here in-country. Name your price. We will hold on to our supply until I hear from you. Bin Laden seems regretful for his outburst, perhaps we can aid in relationship renewal. Blessed be Allah, then he signs off." Trinsey sighed. "I don't know how we're going to keep this under wraps."

"The American public doesn't need to know the specifics." Markley rubbed the bridge of his nose and wrinkling his nose in a way that Trinsey thought made him look like a rabbit. "We just need to inform the president that Saddam definitely has weapons of mass destruction. After that, it is up to him."

Note from the Author

Dear Reader,

Thank you so much for investing your time in reading Rivers' and Wakefield's story. This book has been more difficult to write than any of the others I've worked on. Both the plot and character development. We've seen David and Judah in some pretty difficult places in the past, but they are both guided through some dark places in their souls during these pages.

I hope you never lost hope.

As an novelist, I'm never supposed to spell out in actual language what I hope my readers learn from the stories I pen, but this is too important to leave just in the experiences of "others" in these pages of Grecian Vendetta. I want to do more than hope you took in Rivers' and Wakefield's responses to horrible circumstances and added it to your own arsenal of "what-to-do-if…"

So I'm breaking the rules!

Here's is what I hope you learned: Even Christians who are strong in the Lord and practicing the gifts of the Spirit have places in our hearts that still need Jesus' redemption. There is always more to learn, more of our souls to give over to the Lord, more places in our heart to let Jesus shine His light of love into our motivations and actions.

I hope your heart learned again how deeply the Father loves you, that He would never leave you or abandon you in a place of mediocrity or even in the midst of the consequences of your own sin or someone else's sin against you.

He promised to walk with you through the Valley of the Shadow of Death, and He always keeps His promises. I hope you learned how important it is to hide God's Word in your heart, so that you have it to fall back on for strength in times of trouble or temptation, or if you ever find yourself in a situation like David Rivers where the Scripture you've memorized is your only resource.

If you are just getting started, Psalm 23 and Psalm 91, in an easy translation like NIV or NKJV, are good ones to pack into your Spirit.

While this bad guy, Arafeh Filasek, is no longer pursuing Judah, this is not the end of David and Judah's story.

Yellow Ribbon

Desert Sailors Series #4

Join Judah Wakefield and David Rivers
in another adventure in set in Iraq.
Coming
Fall of 2017

www.ingramcontent.com/pod-product-compliance
Lightning Source LLC
Chambersburg PA
CBHW070318260626
47160CB00003B/881